BOOK TWO OF THE DREAMER'S CYCLE

HOLLY TAYLOR

Crimson Fire

Medallion Press, Inc.

DEDICATION:

To Donald Edgar Taylor, whose wife has gone on before.
You're the bravest man I know, Dad.

Published 2007 by Medallion Press, Inc.

The **MEDALLION PRESS LOGO**
is a registered tradmark of Medallion Press, Inc.

Printed in the United States of America
Typeset in Baskerville

ISBN#978-1-933836-03-4

10 9 8 7 6 5 4 3 2 1
First Edition

Previous accolades for *Night Birds' Reign*:

GRADE: A

"This is an epic novel — fat in heft, rich on detail. The characters of NIGHT BIRDS' REIGN really grab the reader, and they do not — let me repeat ***do not*** — let go . . . Kudos to Ms. Taylor."

—Fantasy Novel Review

"NIGHT BIRD'S REIGN is an intriguing story; one that will wow many fantasy readers . . . At over 500 pages, there is a lot to take in. Don't expect this to be a quick read, but do expect it to be gripping."

—Round Table Reviews

"NIGHT BIRD'S REIGN is a strong fantasy. The story line is action-packed and filled with adventure. Holly Taylor provides a stirring quest that fans will want to trek alongside of Gwydion to partake."

—H. Klausner, Independent Reviewer

It has broken us,
It has crushed us,
It has drowned us.
O Annwyn of the star-bright kingdom;
The wind has consumed us
As twigs are consumed by
Crimson fire from your hand.

Gwenllient ur Caswallon
Third Master Bard
Circa 203

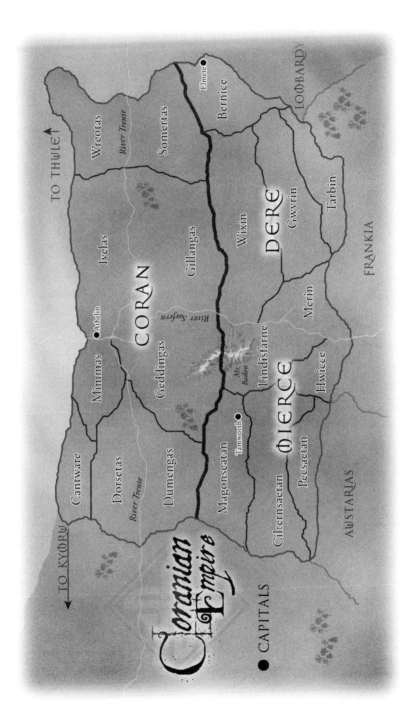

Coranian Empire

● CAPITALS

TO KYÐRU

TO THULE

River Trente

Cantware
Dorsetas
Dumengas
River Trente
Mimmas
● Athelm
Ivelas
CORAN
Geddingas
Gillangas
Wreotas
River Trente
Somertas
Elmere ●
Bernice
LOÐBARDY
Wixin
DERE
Gwyrin
Tarbin
FRANKIA
Merin
River Saefern
Mt. Badon
Lindisfarne
ÐIERCE
Hwicce
Magonseatan
Tamworth ●
Cilternsaetan
Pecsaetan
AUSTARJAS

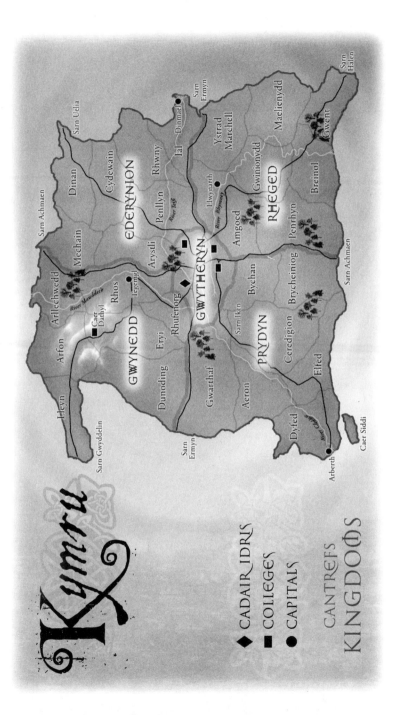

LIST OF CHARACTERS

IN KYMRU
Y Dawnus (The Gifted)

The Dreamers
Gwydion ap Awst var Celemon: Dreamer of Kymru, half brother of King Uthyr, brother of Amatheon

Dinaswyn ur Morvryn var Gwenllian: former Dreamer, Gwydion's aunt, Myrrdin's sister

Cariadas ur Gwydion var Isalyn: Gwydion's daughter and heir

The Dewin
Myrrdin ap Morvryn var Gwenllian: Arthur's guardian, Gwydion's uncle, Dinaswyn's
brother

Rhiannon ur Hefeydd var Indeg: former heir to the Ardewin, mother of Gwenhwyfar

Cynan ap Einon var Darun: Ardewin, uncle to Gwydion, Rhiannon and Arianrod

Elstar ur Anieron var Ethyllt: Myrrdin's heir, daughter of Anieron, wife to Elidyr

Llywelyn ap Elidyr var Elstar: Elstar's oldest son and heir

Arianrod ur Brychan var Arianllyn: cousin to Gwydion and Rhiannon

The Druids

Cathbad ap Goreu var Efa: Archdruid, Myrrdin's cousin

Aergol ap Custennin var Dinaswyn: Cathbad's heir, Dinaswyn's son

Sinend ur Aergol var Eurgain: Aergol's daughter and heir

The Bards

Anieron ap Cyvarnion var Hunydd: Master Bard, Rhiannon's uncle

Elidyr ap Dudod var Llawen: Anieron's nephew and heir, husband to Elstar

Dudod ap Cyvarnion var Hunydd: Anieron's brother, Elidyr's father, Rhiannon's uncle

Cynfar ap Elidyr var Elstar: Elidyr's youngest son and heir

IN GWYNEDD

Uthyr ap Rathtyen var Awst: King of Gwynedd (House of PenHebog), Lord of Rhos, half-brother to Gwydion and Madoc

Ygraine ur Custennin var Elwen: Uthyr's Queen, sister to Queen Olwen of Ederynion

Arthur ap Uthyr var Ygraine: Uthyr's son

Morrigan ur Uthyr var Ygraine: Uthyr's daughter

Madoc ap Rhodri var Rathtyen: Lord of Rhufonoig, half brother to Uthyr

Cai ap Cynyr: Uthyr's Captain; the PenGwernan; his wife Nest and his son Garanwyn

Bedwyr ap Bedrawd: Cai's nephew and Lieutenant

Susanna ur Erim: Uthyr's Bard
Griffi ap Iaen: Uthyr's Druid
Gwrhyr: Bard, son of Griffi and Susanna
Neuad ur Hetwin: Uthyr's Dewin
Arday ur Medyr: Uthyr's steward

IN PRYDYN

Rhoram ap Rhydderch var Eurneid: King of Prydyn (House of PenBlaid), Lord of Dyfed
Geriant ap Rhoram var Christina: Rhoram's son and heir by his first wife
Sanon ur Rhoram var Christina: Rhoram's daughter by his first wife
Gwenhwyfar ur Rhoram var Rhiannon: Rhoram's daughter by Rhiannon
Efa ur Nudd: Rhoram's second wife, sister to Erfin
Achren ur Canhustyr: Rhoram's Captain, the PenCollen
Aidan ap Camber: Achren's Lieutenant
Cian ap Menw: Rhoram's Bard
Ellywen ur Saidi: Rhoram's Druid
Cadell ap Brathach: Rhoram's Dewin
Erfin ap Nudd: Lord of Ceredigion, Queen Efa's brother
Dafydd Penfro: Rhoram's counselor
Tallwch ap Nwyfre: Rhoram's doorkeeper
Tegid ap Trephin: Gward of Mallean

IN RHEGED

Urien ap Ethyllt var Gwaeddan: King of Rheged (House of PenMarch), Lord of Amgoed

Ellirri ur Rhodri var Rathtyen: Urien's Queen, sister to Madoc, half-sister to Uthyr

Elphin ap Urien var Ellirri: Urien's oldest son and heir

Owein ap Urien var Ellirri: Urien's second son

Rhiwallon ap Urien var Ellirri: Urien's youngest son

Enid ur Urien var Ellirri: Urien's daughter

Trystan ap Naf: Urien's Captain, the PenDraenenwen

Teleri ur Brysethach: Trystan's Lieutenant

Esyllt ur Maelwys: Urien's Bard, March's wife

Sabrina ur Dadweir: Urien's Druid

Bledri ap Gwyn: Urien's Dewin

Isgowen Whledig: Urien's steward, sister to Morcant Wheldig

March Y Meirchion: Urien's hunstman, Esyllt's husband

Morcant Whledig: Lord of Penrhyn

Hetwin Silver-Brow: Lord of Gwinionydd

Cadar: Hetwin's Captain

IN EDERYNION

Olwen ur Custennin var Elwen: Queen of Ederynion (House of PenAlarch), Lady of Ial, sister to Queen Ygraine

Elen ur Olwen var Kilwch: Olwen's daughter and heir

Lludd ap Olwen var Kilwch: Olwen's son

Angharad ur Ednyved: Olwen's Captain, the PenAethnen

Emrys ap Naw: Angharad's Lieutenant

Talhearn ap Coleas: Olwen's Bard

Iago ap Cof: Olwen's Druid

Regan ur Corfil: Olwen's Dewin

Llwyd Cilcoed: Dewin of Caerinion, Olwen's lover

IN GWYTHERYN

Rhufon ap Casnar: a descendent of the Stewards of Cadair Idris

Tybion ap Rhufon: Rhufon's son

Lucas ap Tybion: Tybion's son

HISTORICAL FIGURES

Bloudewedd ur Sawyl var Eurolwyn: wife of Lleu Lawrient, lover to Gowrys, imprisoned in Drwys Idris by Bran the Dreamer

Lleu Lawrient (Silver Hand): last High King of Kymru, murdered by Bloudewedd and Gorwys

Gorwys of Penllyn: consort of Queen Siwan of Prydyn, lover of Bloudewedd, murderer of High King Lleu

Bran ap Iweridd var Fabel: Fifth Dreamer, one of the Great Ones of Lleu Silver-Hand

The Shining Ones

Cerridwen: Protectress of Kymru, Mistress of the Wild Hunt, Queen of the Wood, wife of Cerrunnos

Cerrunnos: Protector of Kymru, Master of the Wild Hunt, Lord of the Animals, husband of Cerridwen

Annwyn: god of death, Lord of Chaos and the Otherworld, husband of Aertan

Aertan: goddess of fate, The Weaver, wife of Annwyn

Taran: father god, King of the Winds, god of the Bards, husband of Modron

Modron: mother godess, the Great Mother, mother, goddess of the Druids, wife of Taran

Mabon: King of the Sun, Lord of Fire, god of the Dreamers, husband of Nantsovelta

Nantsovelta: Queen of the Moon, Lady of the Waters, goddess of the Dewin, wife of Mabon

Camulos: god of war, twin to Agrona, Y Rhyfelwr — the

warrior twin

Agrona: goddess of war, twin to Camulos, Y Rhyfelwr — the warrior twin

Sirona of the Stars: goddess of stars, wife to Grannos

Grannos the Header: god of healing, Star of the North

Gwrach Y Rhibyn: The Washer at the Ford, incarnation of Agrona, a harbinger of war

IN CORANIA

The Warband

Havgan: the Golden Man, aspirant to position of Warleader (Bana)

Sigerric: son of the Alder of Apuldre

Baldred: son of the Eorl of Tarbin

Talorcan: son of the Eorl of Bernice

Catha: brother of the Eorl of Pecsaetan

Penda: son of the Eorl of Lindisfarne

The House of Aelle

Athelred: Emperor of Corania

Athelflead: Empress of Corania

Aelfwyn: Athelred's daughter and sole offspring, also called Steorra Heofen

Aesc: Anweal of Coran, brother of Emperor Athelred

Aesthryth: Athelred's sister, the former Queen of the Franks

Aescwine: Anweal of Mierce, the Empress' brother

Aelbald: Aescwine's son, Aelfwyn's cousin, Havgan's rival for war leader

Athelric: Bana, brother of Emperor Athelred

IN CANTWARE

Hengist: fisherman of Dorfas
Hildegyth: his wife
Eosa of Calne: a wyrce-jaga in Cantware
Frithu: a boy from the village of Dorfas
Sigefrith: Alder of Apuldre, Siggeric's father, Havgan's first lord
Elgiva: the Lady of Apuldre, Sigerric's mother
Wiglaf: Eorl of Cantware, Havgan's second lord
Sledda of Cantware: Master-wyrce-jaga of Ivelas
Cenberht: the champion of the Eorl of Ivelas
Athelmar: the Alder of Liminae
Horsa: Hengist's brother, a saltmaker in Angelesford
Whitred: the Byshop of Cantware
Wulf: Captain of the warband for the Alder of Liminae
Anawin: a valla with the fair
Egwina: a valla with the fair
Guthlac: Master-wyrce-jaga of Cantware

IN ATHELIN

Guido Asti: the name Gwydion uses in Corania
Rhea Varins: the name Rhiannon uses in Corania
Whitgar of Mimmas: Archpreost
Ethbrand: Arch-wyrce-jaga of Coran
Sethwald: Archbyshop of Coran
Gytha: a valla in Athelin
Anflaeth: a famous valla in Athelin

Euric Gildmar: an Austarian sea Captain
Theo: his first mate

IN DERE

Ingilda: Talorcan's mother, a descendant of the last King of Dere

Talmund: Talorcan's father, Eorl of Bernice

Torhtmund: Talorcan's younger brother

Hensa of Dorsetas: Arch-wyrce-jaga of Dere

Lingyth: a Godia in Dere; her husband Egild

Berwic: Archbyshop of Dere

Oswy: Byshop of Bernice

IN MIERCE

Peada: Penda's father, the Eorl of Lindisfarne

Readwyth: Penda's son and heir

Oswald: abbot of Hearth Beranburg in Mierce

The New Gods

Lytir: the One God, ruler of Heofon

Sceadu: Lytir's brother, the Shadow, who rules in Hel

The Old Gods

Wuotan: one of the Ostar, god of Magic, with Holda leads the Wild Hunt

Holda: one of the Ercar, goddess of the Waters, with Wuotan leads the Wild Hunt

Donar: one of the Ostar, god of Storms

Narve: chief of the Afliae, god of Death

Nerthus: one of he Ostar, goddess of Earth

Tiw: one of the Ostar, god of War

Fro: one of the Ercar, twin to Freya, god of Peace and Plenty

Freya: one of the Ercar, twin to Fro, goddess of Fertility

The Wyrd: the three goddesses of fate

Part 1
The Night-Bringer

As for what may be, it will not be.
It will not be, because it may not be.

Taliesin
Fifth Master Bard
Circa 270

Prologue

Dorfas, Marc of Cantware
Weal of Coran, Coranian Empire
Natmonath, 458

Sweltan Daeg—night

She was barely alive when her body, battered by the relentless waves, washed up on the sands. Slowly she dragged herself farther up the deserted beach, clutching at the sand with her hands, pulling herself away from the swirling, black water inch by precious inch.

Her breath came and went in harsh gasps as she coughed weakly, expelling water, blood, and bile from her aching lungs. Her sodden gown, its rich materials in tatters, clung to her body, weighing her down unbearably. Blood dripped slowly from her matted hair down her once-beautiful face.

After an eternity she stopped moving and lay on her side, clutching her swollen belly, her face buried in the rough sands. A spasm rippled through her, and she clenched her teeth against the pain. She shuddered as the cold night wind whipped around her and whispered, "No, no, *bachen*. For pity's sake, wait. Not here. Not here."

Slowly she lifted her head to the night sky. The stars were cold and clear and the rays of the waxing moon spilled over her, wrapping her in cold, silvery fire. She wondered vaguely if the Lady of the Moon could see her lying here; wondered if Nantsovelta would take pity on her and send someone, anyone, to help her live through the storm's sullen wake. Another spasm rippled through her pain-wracked body. "No, no, not yet," she whispered. "Wait. Wait."

She had to find help. She closed her eyes. A tiny tug, a feeling of separation, and she was leaving her body behind on the chilled sands. Her soul Rode the Wind as best she could in her weakened state. Knowing she could not go far, she searched for a source of light, of warmth, for someone to help her.

There—to the east—a glimmer of light. Spiraling down, she saw a tiny cottage at the edge of the cliffs and a woman sitting by the hearth fire, humming softly to herself.

She had seen enough. As quickly as she could, she returned her spirit to her body, blinking salt-encrusted lashes and rubbing her eyes. Drawing herself to her knees and clutching her swollen belly, she willed the child not to come now, on this cold beach in this strange land. So intent on this thought was she that she did not even sense the man who was making his way toward the cottage along the cliffs.

Gritting her teeth, she rose to her feet and began to walk.

HENGIST WAS BITTERLY disappointed. The storm had passed, and though pieces of a lost ship had washed up on the beach, no valuable wreckage had been recovered.

He walked slowly up the cliff path, not anxious to return home with empty hands. He had so wanted to bring her some-

2

thing beautiful, something that might make her smile as she had not done since the birthing. Since that terrible day when their tiny, perfect boy had strangled to death as it struggled toward the light, the birthcord wrapped tightly around his innocent neck.

Hengist shivered in his heavy, sheepskin jacket, his rough fisherman's hands thrust inside its deep pockets in a futile bid for warmth. The night was bitterly cold. The waxing moon shone brightly, outlining the harsh rocks, glittering off the now calming sea.

She had not even left the cottage for the festival. He had tried to explain to her how dangerous it was to stay away. People might begin to think that she was one of the Heiden, the followers of the Old Gods. But she had not cared about even that. So he had gone to the Sweltan Daeg festival alone, telling them his wife was ill, doing his best to celebrate the legendary day when Lytir, the One God, had sailed away to Heofen.

Suddenly remembering what tonight was, he quickened his pace. This was no night to be out alone. Tonight those who worshipped the Old Gods would be celebrating their secret rites. And who knew what they would do to a follower of Lytir if they caught him alone? He knew the stories as well as anyone.

When he reached the cottage and opened the door, he saw exactly what he had expected to see. Hildegyth was huddled on a stool by the fire, humming quietly to herself. Her thin, grief-worn face was almost translucent in the fitful light. Her lank blond hair was half undone from its rough braid. Her simple homespun gown was spotted with grease, and bits of straw clung to it here and there.

Hengist said nothing. He made his way to the hearth, holding his chapped, cracked hands out to the warmth. He rubbed them together, looking around the tiny room.

The sleeping pallet was still mussed, the blanket thrown back where he had left it at dawn. The rough plank table jutting from the wall still held his half-eaten bowl of mush from this morning. The room was musty and close—she had not even opened the shutters today. She had done nothing but sit.

A weak scratching on the door startled him. Hildegyth tilted her head a little, and looked toward the door. The scratching sound came again.

"Answer it," he ordered. He didn't think she would do it, but she did. Slowly she stood, moving as if in a dream. She went to the door and opened it. A form was huddled on the ground at her feet. A woman's hand shot out and grasped Hildegyth's skirt. A voice, barely audible, the tone pleading, murmured something Hengist could not hear.

Hildegyth bent down and grasped the woman's hand. For a moment she crouched, frozen, every line of her body stiffened in shock. At last, she turned to Hengist, "Help her. Bring her in and put her on the bed. She has brought me a gift."

Hengist went to the door and picked up the stranger. He laid the woman down on the pallet and then he understood. The woman was pregnant and her time had come.

Hengist looked over at his wife. Hildegyth was smiling. "She brings me a great gift. Our God has provided."

The strange woman moaned, twisting on the bed. And as she did, the bowl on the table rose up, hovered in the air, and flew across the room, crashing into the wall.

"A demon!" Hengist gasped. "O God, what will she do to us?!" He grasped the simple amulet of Lytir that hung around his neck. The tiny carved tree felt cold in his hands as he stared at the woman in horror.

But Hildegyth merely smiled. "She brings me a gift. A gift from the sea." Still smiling, Hildegyth began to loosen the woman's gown, stripping her and putting the blanket over her nakedness. She turned to her husband. "Call no one." Her mad eyes sparkled.

But Hengist knew he could not do that. If anyone ever found out they had given shelter to a witch. . . Thank Lytir that the witch hunter had just been through Dorfas earlier that day. The wyrce-jaga would deal with this demon. The man could have gone no farther than Ottonford and could be fetched in a few hours. He knew it was useless to plead with his wife to change her mind, so without another word, he backed away and was out the door running for the stable.

As he mounted his horse, the locked shutters of the cottage flew open, banging rhythmically in time to the sound of the demon's moans.

HENGIST AND THE wyrce-jaga rode up to the remote cottage, their horses lathered with sweat. It had been more than four hours since Hengist had left, and Lytir alone knew what had happened. But the cottage still stood and the night was quiet.

Eosa hauled himself down from his mount. Hengist, too, dismounted, and the two men stood outside the closed door, listening. A low, wrenching moan reached their ears. "The witch is still alive," whispered Hengist.

Eosa's thin, cruel face turned to Hengist. The witch hunter was dressed in the customary black robe of the wyrce-jaga, his blond hair cut short and tonsured. His amulet of Lytir was made of gold, and it glittered palely on the hunter's chest in the moonlight. "So it would seem. Let us go in, then, and deal with it." Eosa reached for the door. Hengist drew back, afraid.

"Fear not, Hengist. I have killed hundreds of witches for our God and do not fear them. Lytir will protect us."

The stranger on the bed still writhed, bathed in sweat, her honey-blond hair still matted and blood still dripping down her face, soaking the straw. Hildegyth sat on the floor, waiting, smiling her secret smile. Suddenly, the fire flared up; flames leapt and twisted as the stranger caught sight of the two men.

"It is time," Hildegyth said. "See, now she brings forth my gift." The stranger arched her back in agony as Hildegyth reached for her. And suddenly the child was there, squirming on the straw. Hildegyth drew the baby to her, gently blowing into the tiny lungs as it drew breath and began to cry. She laid the body down on the straw and cut the birthcord, paying no attention to the still-suffering woman. She cuddled the tiny form to her breast and turned again to the two men. "See, she brings my child back to me. My beautiful baby boy!"

The woman on the bed was quiet. Her amber eyes, trapped, stared at Eosa.

Eosa pulled a flask from his belt and bent over the woman. "Drink," he commanded. The woman shrank back, turning her face away. A shutter flapped weakly, and the flames in the fireplace writhed. "Drink," the wyrce-jaga said again, grabbing the woman's hair and forcing her to tilt her head back. The woman moaned, and, as she did, Eosa forced the contents of the flask into her mouth. She choked feebly, and swallowed.

"There," Eosa said, standing back. "It's safe now. She can do no more harm. Tomorrow she will be burned. And the child with her."

"No!" Hildegyth cried. "No! Not my baby." She set the child down on the pallet, next to its mother. "You can't. The God has given him to me. He is my gift."

"No. The child is a demon, as is the mother. They will be burned tomorrow."

Hildegyth said nothing, merely turning away and resting her hands on the table, her shoulders slumped. Hengist came to her. "Wife, it must be as he says. The child and the mother must die."

She nodded, and for a moment, Hengist really thought that all would be well. Then Hildegyth sprang from his grasp and launched herself at Eosa, the eating knife in her hand. She plunged the knife into the wyrce-jaga's belly and twisted it. Their faces just inches apart, Eosa gasped in agony, blood pouring from his mouth, the dark liquid covering the glittering amulet on his chest. He crumpled to the floor, staring up at Hildegyth in disbelief. And, still staring, he died.

Hildegyth knelt by the dead man, then nodded her head in satisfaction. She rose and went to the pallet, looking down at the woman and child lying there.

"Hildegyth," Hengist whispered, "what have you done?"

"He was going to kill my baby," Hildegyth said serenely, her hands, her gown, her hair spotted with blood. "I couldn't let him do that."

"But you'll let me be accused of murder? What do you think will happen to us if they find out?"

"But they won't find out," she said absently, picking up the baby and smiling down into its tiny face. "You'll take care of that."

"How—"

"Did anyone see you when you fetched him?"

"No, no, but—"

"Well then." She cooed to the child, dismissing Hengist from her thoughts. She looked down at the mother, lying spent on the pallet. The woman looked up at Hildegyth, hope stealing into her amber eyes.

Hildegyth, still holding the baby, said gently, "The wyrce-jaga was right. You must die. You are a witch. But I will save your child and bring him up as my own. He is my gift. My gift from the sea. The God has sent him to me."

The dying woman reached out a trembling hand toward the baby, and then looked up at Hildegyth.

"I will care for him." Hildegyth smiled. "He will grow up bright and strong. He will be my child. And I will never tell him about you. He will never know the truth."

The woman's face twisted in horror. "Oh, but you must," she gasped. "You don't understand what could happen. Send him home. Please, I beg you, send him back to Kymru."

"To Kymru! The land of witches? Oh, I could never send him there. He stays with me. He will be of Corania, and serve the One God."

"My baby, my child," the woman whispered. "Oh, what will you become?" Again the woman looked up at Hildegyth, pleading one last time. "I am no Dreamer, but I tell you this. He will bring death and destruction to your land unless you send him home. Will you?"

"No. He is mine."

The stranger gave an odd, twisted smile. "Then may the gods help us all," she whispered, as she turned her face to the wall and died.

Chapter 1

Soldaeg, Sol 4—Gewinnan Daeg Eve

The celebration in the mead-hall of the Eorl of Cantware was at its height. The air was hazy as smoke rose from the hearth in the center of the huge hall, whirling and eddying its way under tables, past benches, between boisterous warriors, up to the tall rafters and out the small hole in the timber roof. The coarse laughter of drunken men rebounded off the rough wooden walls, tangling and wrangling in the smoky air until it rose, like the smoke, to the rafters and out, escaping to disturb the night.

Surrounded by merriment, coarse jests, and bawdy songs, Havgan sat self-contained and controlled, as always. He smiled at the jests and joined in the war songs, but his thoughts were elsewhere, facing the truth—that the world of warriors he had longed to be a part of was just another world in which he was out of place, cut off. It was almost as though his very soul spoke a different language than all the rest. He had thought, long

9

ago, when he was just a fisherman's son, that if he could exchange that old world with this new one, his nebulous longings would be satisfied. So he had planned and schemed and drawn himself up out of the world of lowly peasants and into this world of privileged warriors. He had been so sure that this new world would fit him. But it had not.

Havgan glanced up at the high table where his lord, Wiglaf, the Eorl of Cantware, surveyed the warriors packed into his hall. The Eorl's large, meaty hand grabbed his gold-banded drinking horn and, draining it to the dregs, held it out to be instantly filled by an attentive slave. Wiglaf's long, graying braids almost dropped into the cup. His beard was spotted with food, and his dark blue tunic strained to cover his large belly. But his blue eyes were alert and cunning, as always.

Havgan glanced at the others at the high table. Sigefrith, the Alder of Apuldre, the father of Havgan's closest friend, laughed and drank, but something in the man's dark, intelligent eyes showed he wished to be elsewhere. The Alders of Grenewic and Liminae both had glazed looks in their eyes, their movements becoming more and more clumsy.

Last of all, Havgan glanced at Sledda, Wiglaf's nephew, who sat very quietly at the end of the table. He drank his mead sparingly, as a clever man should. He was wearing the black robe and yellow taBard of the wyrce-jaga. His white skull gleamed through his recently tonsured hair, and his pale gray, heavy-lidded eyes glittered, searching the hall restlessly. It was a look that all wyrce-jaga had, even if they were newly come to their posts, as Sledda was.

For a brief moment Sledda's eyes met Havgan's. Havgan forced himself not to stare boldly, or to look away too quickly.

Either gesture would surely alert Sledda that Havgan was afraid. Deep down within, terror stirred, along with something else hidden there.

Havgan's amber eyes, showing nothing of this hidden terror, shot a glance of innocent inquiry at Sledda. But the wyrce-jaga ignored him, his cold, restless gaze continuing to move across the hall. Havgan took a deep breath and relaxed.

"Not long now," Sigerric said in Havgan's ear. Havgan turned to him, his terror stilled. Sigerric, the Captain of the Eorl's warband, was the closest friend Havgan had in this strange, alien world. Sigerric smiled at Havgan, his dark eyes sparkling with amusement. Tall and lean, he ran a hand through his light brown hair, cut short to fit under his war helmet. At that moment the Eorl stood and bellowed for silence—a silence instantly achieved.

"Wulf, Captain of the gesith of Aethelmar, the Alder of Liminae, stand!" Wiglaf commanded. Wulf stood, his mailshirt gleaming in the firelight of the now silent hall. His black hair was short, and his clipped black beard framed thin lips. An old scar ran down from the corner of his left eye and down his face, disappearing into his beard.

"Sigerric, Captain of the gesith of Wiglaf, Eorl of Cantware, stand!" Wiglaf bellowed. Sigerric stood gracefully, smiling his easy smile.

Wiglaf went on. "I declare that today the warbands of the Alder of Liminae and my own warband have defeated all comers and have won the Gewinnan Daeg tournament, which we fight in memory of Lytir, the One God. As winners, these Captains have the honor to choose a champion for tomorrow's battle. These two champions will fight until one either yields or is killed. The winner is to be proclaimed Gewinnan Daeg King and receive a purse of fifty gold pieces. Wulf, who do you choose for the battle?"

Wulf, his voice dripping with arrogance, said swiftly, "I choose myself!"

"Sigerric, who do you choose for the battle?" Wiglaf went on.

"I choose Havgan, son of Hengist." A low murmur of surprise broke out. All eyes turned to Havgan, who was sitting frozen on his wooden bench, staring up at Sigerric in amazement.

Wulf cried furiously, "I refuse to fight the son of a churl!"

"He is a warrior," Sigerric shot back, his dark eyes flashing dangerously. "I have the right to choose any member of my warband that I wish."

At Sigerric's words a subtle shifting in the ranks began. Swiftly, four members of Eorl Wiglaf's warband began making their way through the crowded hall. These men were close friends of both Sigerric and Havgan, as well as being the sons of some of the most important men in the Empire. And they were not of a mind to stand any insult to their war brothers. Baldred and Talorcan, Catha and Penda, proudly came to stand behind Havgan and Sigerric, and stared at Wulf's furious face with silent disdain.

But Wulf, too angry to care, went on in spite of the danger. "I don't fight peasants. I am a thane's son——"

"And I am the son of the Alder of Apuldre," Sigerric broke in coldly, "and the Captain of the warband of the Eorl of Cantware, the gracious lord in whose hall you are taking your ease. And I say that Havgan, son of Hengist, fights the battle tomorrow. Are you afraid of him? Is that why you will not fight?" Sigerric mocked.

"Why you—" Wulf started toward Sigerric, but was held back by his own warriors.

"Enough," Wiglaf roared, as Wulf continued to struggle. "This is my hall. I will be obeyed." The Alder of Liminae hurried from the high table and laid a restraining hand on his Captain's arm, whispering furiously into his ear. Wulf subsided, but there was murder in his eyes.

"It is the right of the Captain to choose a champion," Wiglaf continued. "The champion can be any member of the Captain's warband." Wiglaf's sharp, blue eyes bored into Wulf. "Are you saying that there is a member of my warband who is unworthy to fight you? Are you saying that the men of my gesith are no better than peasants?" He leaned forward, dropping his voice lower. "Are you saying that my warriors are not worthy of sticking a sword into your arrogant guts?"

The crackling fire was the only noise in the hall as Wulf, his face pale, finally realized his mistake. "Your pardon, great lord," he said haltingly.

"Havgan, son of Hengist, do you accept this task that your Captain has given?" Wiglaf asked.

Havgan stood. His honey-blond hair gleamed and his amber eyes glittered. He stood proud and straight and in the uncertain firelight looked almost to be fashioned out of pure gold. "I do."

"So be it," Wiglaf said quietly. "Tomorrow these two champions will battle. To the strongest goes the victory." At this the Eorl abruptly left the hall, followed by his three alders and Sledda. The warriors in the hall began pushing the benches against the wall, preparing to wrap their cloaks around them and lay down on the rush-strewn floor.

Baldred, Talorcan, Catha, and Penda quickly and efficiently claimed a large share of the floor for themselves and their friends. As they did so, Havgan turned to Sigerric. "I can't believe you did that," he said, his voice showing his astonishment.

"Believe it," Sigerric grinned. "And get some sleep. You need to be well rested for tomorrow's fight."

"But why? Why did you choose me?"

"Why not?" Sigerric shrugged. "You're the best warrior we've got."

And though Havgan knew that was true, he also knew that Sigerric had other reasons. His friend saw very, very far with those dark eyes of his.

"You'll win tomorrow," Sigerric said quietly. "You know it. And I know it, too."

"But Wulf was right," Havgan said bitterly. "My father was a peasant."

"You think so?" Sigerric said, so unexpectedly, so quietly, that Havgan was stunned. "Do you really think so?"

Havgan stared at Sigerric, unable to answer the question that had lurked for years, just below his waking thoughts.

"Good night, Havgan. Sleep well." With that, Sigerric wrapped himself in his cloak and lay down on the straw, instantly falling asleep.

But Havgan was not ready for sleep. Too much had happened tonight for that. In a daze he sat down on the rushes amid recumbent, snoring warriors and stared into the glowing embers of the hearth fire, his knees huddled under his chin.

He began to remember how he came to be here; to remember the sea and how it drew him so, even now, even here. To remember how he longed to sail away across the ocean and find whatever waited for him in a land far, far away.

HIS FIRST MEMORIES were of the sea. Before he even knew the sound of his own name, he knew the sounds of the ocean. He knew the rush of the water as it grabbed the shore and the hiss when it slid back again. He knew the sound of the gulls, crying of loss and beauty, stirring something deep inside. He knew the smell of the saltwater as it wafted up the cliffs, reaching for him, inviting him to come down and float forever in its green-blue silences.

He remembered that his mother always insisted on walking down to the beach with him, never letting him go alone. "You are my gift from the sea," she would say in her off-key, high voice. "And it might try to take you back again, unless I am there." Often she would say these strange things he didn't understand—though never in the hearing of his father. When Hengist was around his mother rarely spoke.

His father was a big man, his skin burned dark by the sun. Every day Hengist and the other men of the village would go down to the jetty and sail their tiny boats far away from shore, casting their nets for the fish that swam beneath the waves.

Some days they caught nothing, and there would be only milk and bread for supper in their tiny hut. Some days the catch was good, and they feasted on fresh fish wrapped in herbs. And some days the men caught other things from the sea washed up from wrecked ships. Sometimes there were bolts of cloth and crates of fruit. Sometimes there were jeweled cups and pieces of wood. And, sometimes, there were bodies.

One day, when he was only five years old, he was running down the beach, collecting shell after shell in his tiny hands, leaving his mother far behind. The roar of the waves crashed against his ears, the waves themselves glittered in the morning sun, flashing silver as they arched toward the shore. And as he ran he saw something in the distance. A bolt of cloth, he thought, and hurried toward it.

But when he reached the dark blot on the beach, he saw it wasn't cloth at all. It was a dead man. His sightless gray eyes were open and staring at the sky. He wore a tunic of blue and a strange necklace made of silver and a single sapphire. Cradled against his dead body he held a curiously carved harp, its strings broken and silent. Havgan thought that maybe the man had come from a place very far away. And he thought that he would like to go there, and find a harp just like this one that seemed to call out to him. And he reached out to touch that harp.

But his mother had called out to him and made him come away. She had looked at the man's necklace with loathing and had whipped Havgan for running away from her. "That man was a witch," she screamed. "A demon of Kymru. The God hates witches. You stay away from them. Or the God will hate you, too." And he had sobbed and sobbed, frightened that the God would hate him. If the God hated him, he couldn't go to Heofen, but would have to go to the realm of Sceadu, the Shadow, who ruled in Hel. And there he would have to endure fire and pain forever and ever. His mother had told him so.

After that he had been very careful to be good so that the God wouldn't hate him. And he had been good—until that day when Frithu made him so angry.

Frithu was a great big boy of nine years old, the son of the village blacksmith. On that terrible day Havgan had been sent to the blacksmith to collect the newly mended cooking spit for his mother. While walking back, he had felt a stinging blow on his bare leg. Someone had thrown a rock. Looking around wildly, he had spotted Frithu perched in an oak tree, laughing.

Havgan had shrugged and begun to walk on. But Frithu began to say things. He said that Havgan's mother was crazy. He said that when Havgan grew up, he would be crazy, too. He said that they would have to chain Havgan up, chain him next to his crazy mother. And Frithu laughed as he said those terrible things.

And Havgan, boiling with rage and fear felt—something—happen. Something unleashed inside him and grew and grew and lashed out with a roar, deafening him and dimming his sight. And when he could see again, he saw that the oak tree had cracked, split down the middle, pinning a now silent Frithu under the heavy, broken branches. The people from the village had come running. Frithu's father pulled the boy out from under the tree while the men strained to lift the trunk. As they began to fuss over the injured boy, Havgan's father detached himself from the crowd and walked slowly up to his son.

For a moment Hengist said nothing, staring down at Havgan with an expressionless face. Then he slowly turned and stared back at the broken tree. And when he turned around again to gaze on Havgan's still, white face, Hengist's eyes began to glow with a dangerous light. "What have you done, boy?" he whispered, his anger cutting through Havgan's daze. He grabbed his son's arm in a grip that hurt. "What have you done?" And then he dragged Havgan away from the others, across the streets of the tiny village, and threw him into their hut. His mother, who had been crouched before the fire, slowly straightened as Hengist slammed the door.

"What? What's happened?" she asked, her voice tight with fear.

"What's happened? Just what I always said would happen!" And then Hengist struck Havgan across the mouth, sending the boy crashing into the wall. Hengist grabbed Havgan by both arms and hauled him up, screaming into his face. "Never, never, never do that again. I'll kill you if you do." And then he released the boy's arm and hit him again. "Never. You keep your temper, you understand? Do you understand?"

And Havgan nodded weakly. Yes, yes, he understood. But he hadn't. He hadn't understood then and he didn't understand now. He couldn't have done anything to Frithu. Didn't do anything to the tree. No one could do those things. No one except witches. And he wasn't a witch. The God hated witches. His mother had said so. He wasn't a witch, and he hadn't done anything. And never would. Never again.

THEY LEFT THE little fishing village of Dorfas soon after that, to live with Havgan's uncle, Horsa, in the city of Angelesford, many miles away. And though no one ever said it, Havgan knew that they were moving away from Dorfas because he had done something bad. And he thought how unfair it was. For they had taken him away from the sight and the smell of the sea. They had taken him away from that shining road that led to other places, places that he might have been able to call home.

For six years Havgan worked for his uncle in the tedious, sweat-soaked business of rending salt from the brinepits. For six long years he spent his days winching up bucketfuls of salty brine from the pits and pouring the heavy liquid into huge pans of lead. For six years he built fires to boil and stir the mixture, to evaporate the water and skim the salt. For six years he drew the salt from the boiling water with a long rake, pouring the salt into baskets and setting basket after basket after basket under the hot sun to dry.

After a time his young body grew strong and hard with this heavy labor. He began to outgrow tunic after tunic, his muscles bulging against the material. His skin darkened to bronze, making his amber eyes seem lighter than ever, and his tawny hair shone like spun gold in the relentless heat of the boiling sun.

Ever since he could remember, his dreams had been vivid. Sometimes he would wake up, his mind a jumble of images he could not understand—a throne fashioned in the shape of an eagle; silver dragons and black ravens with opal eyes; pearl-white swans and blue nightingales; black wolves with eyes of emerald and hawks with wing bands of bright blue. But he did not understand these images, though they called to him in a way that puzzled and frightened him.

Sometimes he dreamed of the harp that he had seen on a dead man long, long ago and what it would be like to go to the land where the man had come from. Sometimes he dreamed that the sea called to him, and that he walked her path to come to his true home.

As he grew he watched the warriors of the Alder of Apuldre, the man who ruled the shire. He saw these strong, big men as they rode out to the hunt, to border skirmishes, to tournaments and fairs. He saw their glittering weapons, their armlets of gold, their arrogance and assurance. And his dreams began to change. He dreamt of a time when he, too, would be a warrior. He would receive rich gifts, booty from wars that he himself won singlehandedly against all odds. He would give his life to save his warband, and the walcyries, the women who collected the souls of dead warriors, would fight amongst themselves for the honor of gathering his spirit to take to the One God.

When he was thirteen years old, his parents sent him to work for the Alder as a kitchen boy. It was then that he understood that this was the best he could hope for—that his life would be to serve meal after meal to these great warriors, to clean up after them, and to survive the occasional casual beating when he was not quick enough with the mead. He would never become a warrior. Because he was only a fisherman's son.

Often while wrestling with platter after platter for the evening meal, Havgan would catch sight of the Alder's son, who sat at the high table with his father. The boy, Sigerric, was a few years younger than Havgan. And Havgan envied him bitterly his place in the world. Envied him the love that shone out of the Alder's eyes. Envied him his beautiful mother and her tenderness. Envied him his rich tunic and his easy smile. Envied him his bright future.

And though he was still bitter, he continued to hope that one day something might happen to him, some great thing that would lift him out of the filth in which he lived.

And then, one day, something did. That day the fair came to town. And he had a silver penny to spend. His mother had given it to him when he first went to work in the kitchens. She had said no word, merely pressing the penny into his hand. Havgan had never spent it. He had been saving it for just this day. He had made up his mind that when the fair came to town he would go there and see the valla, the seeress, who traveled with the fair. For the price of a silver penny, she would read his fortune, and then he would know if any of his dreams would ever come true.

Havgan hurried to the valla's tent, easily identifiable by the dark blue cloth marked with silver stars and crescent moons. He sidled up to the entrance where a thin, bearded man sat crosslegged on the ground, paring his nails with a sharp hunting knife.

"I've come to have my future read," Havgan said breathlessly.

The man didn't even bother to look up. "She don't do it for free, boy."

"I have money." Slowly, Havgan handed out the silver penny.

The man grabbed the coin and bit down on it. "One silver penny will buy you one seid with the runes," the man said. "And that's all, understand?" Havgan nodded. "Go in, then," said the man as he drew back the tent flap.

Havgan entered the tent and stood still for a moment, waiting for his eyes to adjust to the dim interior. He smelled the sweet, cloying scent of burning incense. The tent was illuminated by the soft light of two white candles set on a low table that squatted in the middle of the floor. A woman sat crosslegged behind the table on a small, woven carpet. She wore a dark blue robe, embroidered with rune signs in silver thread. Her head was completely covered by a long, gray veil. He could not make out her features behind the veil, but he could see the flash of her eyes in the dimness. She gestured with a bony hand, and he sat down behind the table on the small carpet opposite her.

For a time she said nothing, merely studying him behind her veil. At last she spoke, "My name is Anawin. I am the valla. I am the keeper of secrets. I am the teller of truths. I speak for the Wyrd, the three goddesses of fate. I speak for past, for present, for future. What is it that you wish to know?" Her voice was ageless, neither old nor young, a voice of power and, therefore, a voice to be feared.

But Havgan, undaunted, took another step down the path he was following. "I wish to know if . . . if I will ever be a warrior."

"This question from a kitchen boy?" she asked quietly.

"I'm not. Not just a kitchen boy. I am Havgan. My mother says that I am her gift from the sea. A gift from the God, she says. And once, one time, something strange happened to me." He seemed to be babbling. Why was he doing that?

"Yes, something very strange did happen to you. Do you know what you are?"

"No," he said, leaning forward eagerly. "What? What am I?"

Her hands were clenched together tightly. "You ask two questions, boy. I will read the seid for you. But you may ask only one question at a time. Do you wish to know if you will be a warrior? Or do you wish to know what you are?"

And it was then, in that dim tent of the valla, that he made a decision from which he would never turn back, a decision that would remain unchanged, even to the last moments of his life. He would not ask about this dark thing inside. Not ever.

He licked lips that were suddenly dry. "My question is, will I be a warrior?"

"Very well. We will answer that question. You will choose three runes—one for the past, one for the present, one for the future. Then we shall see."

She picked up a golden bowl from the table, filled with small, flat sticks of wood. On each piece a rune was carved deep into the wood and filled with gold. "Close your eyes and choose one piece," she said. "The first piece is for the past."

Havgan did as he was told, plunging his hand into the bowl and pulling out a piece of wood. "Open your eyes and lay the rune on the table," she ordered. Havgan did so and she stared at the wood. "This rune is for your past. It is called *thorn*," she said quietly. "Your past has been haunted by a dark force. But you have fought this force. And it has been the fight itself that has become the doorway for you. Now choose the next rune, the rune for the present."

Once again, he plunged his hand into the bowl, pulled out a piece of wood, and laid it on the table. She leaned forward, studying the rune. "This is *needan*. It is the rune for constraint, for necessity, for what must be. There has been sorrow for you, but it has been needful to make you what you must be. Choose now, the rune for the future. This will tell us if *needan* has destroyed your dream. Or only delayed it."

Taking a deep breath, Havgan did as he was told, and laid the last rune on the table. The valla was silent; the only sound was Havgan's harsh, uneven breathing. Finally, she looked up. "This last rune is *eho*. It is the rune of change, of progress. Soon there will be a new home for you, a new life." She hesitated, then went on. "You shall have your dream, kitchen boy. You shall be a warrior."

As Havgan leapt to his feet, she grabbed his wrist and yanked him back down. "Listen, boy. Listen to me," she hissed. "You will be a warrior, as you wish. Someday you will be more than that. But I give you a word of warning. Stay away from the sea. Never, never leave this land. If you cross the sea, you will find such sorrow as you have never known. Such sorrow as no one should ever know."

Havgan looked at her uncomprehendingly. What was she

23

talking about? Whatever it was, it didn't matter now. He would be a warrior! His wish would come true. That was all that mattered.

She clung to his wrist for another moment, then slowly released him. From behind her veil he thought he saw a crooked smile. "No, you won't heed me, will you? They never do." She flapped her arm in a shooing motion. "Go," she said harshly. "Go."

He turned and ran from the tent. In a daze of happiness he wandered around the fair. He soon found himself weaving through the laughing, singing, and dancing crowd. But he wasn't really seeing anything. He was thinking only that he would become a warrior. His dream would come true. And he felt that he couldn't contain his building joy—sure that it would burst out of him in a wild leap, a thing of light, not like the dark thing he always kept inside.

Then he heard it. Later he would say, both to himself and to others, that the man had been talking out loud. But that was a lie. The man had been thinking. And Havgan had heard his thoughts. *I'll kill his boy. That will teach him. I'll kill his only son.*

Havgan looked wildly around. A farmer, plainly dressed, leaned against the boards that fenced in the cattle for sale. The man had a thin, scraggly brown beard, and long greasy hair. His face was scarred with the harshness of scratching a living from reluctant soil. His back was bent as if still under the weight of the plow. And his eyes were focused on the figures of a man and a boy, stopped in front of the armourer's stall. *Kill his boy. Like he killed mine.* The man's thoughts swarmed out like angry bees, buzzing and stinging in Havgan's head. And then Havgan recognized the two figures at the stall with their backs to the farmer. It was the Alder and his son, Sigerric.

As Sigerric and his father turned from the stall, the farmer drew his hunting knife in a swift motion, and cocked his hand back to throw. But as fast as the farmer was, Havgan was faster. He leapt at the farmer, crashing into him and spoiling his aim just as the knife was leaving his hand. A woman screamed as the knife arced through the air and plunged into the ground, coming to rest just between Sigerric's feet.

Havgan wrestled with the farmer, pinning him until the Alder's warriors came rushing up and hauled them both to their feet. And then the Alder was there in a towering rage. Havgan glanced at Sigerric, who had been standing pale and silent by his father's side. He saw that Sigerric was looking back at him with his fine, dark eyes. But he was unable to tell what the boy was thinking.

The Alder had turned to the farmer. "You, why did you try to kill my son?" His voice was quiet as death.

The farmer replied, his voice shaking with hate, "You killed mine. You killed my boy. He stole a pig from you. Just a pig. You had his hands cut off. After that, he didn't live long. You killed my boy."

"I killed your boy," the Alder repeated, his face devoid of all expression, and his tone, for all the world, sounded as if he had just heard some marginally interesting news. For a moment, Havgan thought that the Alder would let the man go. But the warriors knew better. They gripped the farmer's arms even tighter. The Alder went on, his quiet voice slicing the still afternoon air into jagged pieces. "Killed your boy," he mused. He held out his hand and a warrior handed him the knife the farmer had thrown. "And so you were going to kill my son. With this?" he asked, holding the knife up in front of the farmer's face. "This is what you were going to use? I have a better use for it, you filth." And with that, the Alder plunged the knife into the man's guts, and twisted.

The warriors dropped the body of the dying farmer as if the man were nothing more than a sack of grain. The Alder turned away, ignoring the man's death moan. "Who are you?" he asked Havgan, his dark eyes intent.

"My name is Havgan, great lord."

"You look familiar."

"I work in your kitchens, lord."

"Ah. And your father?"

"He is called Hengist. He and my uncle, Horsa, make the salt here. Before that, he was a fisherman in Dorfas."

"Yes, of course." The Alder studied Havgan for a moment. "You don't have the look of a fisherman, boy. Or of a salt maker. Or even, I think, of a kitchen boy."

Havgan knew he had to be careful, or he would end the day with a knife in his own guts. "As my lord says," he replied, careful to keep his head down to show respect.

"I have a task for you, boy."

"Yes, great lord?"

The Alder gestured to Sigerric. "This is my son. From now on, you are to go with him everywhere. You will be his personal servant. And you will answer with your life for any harm that comes to him."

Both boys stared at the Alder in astonishment, but he gave them no time to reply. "Off with you both. See the fair. I have business to attend to." The Alder turned on his heel and left, trailed by his warriors. The two boys stared at each other. Havgan couldn't believe what had happened to him. He was a

hero. He had thought the Alder was going to make him a warrior. But, instead, he was to spend the rest of his life fetching
and carrying for this boy whom he envied with all his soul. His
dream of a warrior was crushed, and he hated this boy with all
his heart.

Sigerric studied Havgan, and his dark eyes seemed to be
reading Havgan's thoughts. And then, in a turning that no one
but a valla could have foreseen, Sigerric said, "You saved my
life. What do you want most of all?"

So Havgan told him. And Sigerric, with serenity far beyond his years, said simply, "It will be done."

ELEVEN YEARS AGO now, Havgan mused, since Sigerric had
said that. As usual, Sigerric had been right. It had been done.
Sigerric had begged his father to allow Havgan to train at arms
with him. And the Alder had finally agreed. So well had Havgan learned that when the day came, seven years later, to send
Sigerric to the Eorl of Cantware's warband, Havgan had gone,
too. He had gone to the Eorl knowing he would have to prove
himself, over and over, because he was not the son of a lord. He
was the son of a fisherman, and there were many who would
have to be convinced of Havgan's worth.

But Havgan, whose heart was filled with the joy of at last at-
taining his dreams, didn't really mind the trouble. As necessary
Havgan and Sigerric together had split heads and broken bones
in order to impress upon the other members of the Eorl's warband that Havgan was just as good a warrior as the son of any
lord. And, after a time, when he had shown his prowess on the
field, the other men began to accept Havgan as one of them.

Of the one hundred men in the Eorl's warband, there were

only four others whom Havgan counted as his true friends. There was Baldred, the son of the Eorl of Tarbin, and Talorcan, son of the Eorl of Bernice. There was Catha, the brother of the Eorl of Pecsaetan, and Penda, the son of the Eorl of Lindisfarne.

For a time, Havgan had been happy. But it had been all too brief. For as year followed year, he discovered that being a warrior wasn't enough, after all. He discovered that he was just as out of place in this world as in the old one. And sometimes he felt despair in his soul so heavy that he could not breathe.

That was when the dream began for him—the dream of the woman on the rocks, the dream from which he always awoke weeping though he did not know why, the dream that often made him afraid to sleep.

Trapped in the waking world, trapped in the sleeping one, he sometimes thought he would go mad. As mad as his mother was.

Mad enough, perhaps, to let out the dark thing buried deep inside, damning his soul to Hel.

NOW IN THE near-silent hall fitfully illuminated by the embers of the dying fire, he quietly rose and slipped outside. He breathed in the crisp night air with a sigh of relief, glad for this momentary illusion of freedom.

To the left of the hall the kitchens and storehouses bulked, dark and quiet against the night sky. Across the courtyard the weaving rooms and workshops were also still. The horse pens were quiet, the animals asleep beneath the feeble beams of the waning moon.

Overhead the stars winked and glittered slyly, as though holding a secret. He picked out the constellation of Tiw, the

Warrior, and thought again of what was facing him tomorrow. He knew he needed to be well-rested, but he almost feared to sleep—thinking that the woman on the rocks was waiting for him, and he feared her almost as much as he longed for her.

And as he stood there in the shadows, his cloak wrapped around him, he thought he heard the faint sound of hunting horns and baying hounds. The horses shifted uneasily, some of them lifting their heads to stare toward the north.

He shivered, afraid that tonight the Wild Hunt was riding, afraid that Wuotan One-Eye himself would come to claim his soul. He shook himself, for that was no way to think. He was a true believer in the One God. He was not, would never be one of the Heiden who worshipped the Old Gods in secret, nor one of the Wiccan, those with powers given them by Sceadu, the Great Shadow. He was a man of Lytir, and he would find a way to please the God, in spite of the thing inside him.

Tomorrow he would be champion. He would win the battle, just as Sigerric had said. But for now, he must sleep, dream or no dream. He swiftly returned to the hall, telling himself that he was not running, telling himself that he was not afraid.

He picked his way across the crowded floor and returned to his place by the fire. As he wrapped himself in his cloak and settled on the rush-covered floor, he had one last coherent thought as he gazed at the dying embers. In the name of Lytir, he begged silently, don't let me dream tonight. Don't let me dream.

Chapter 2

Aecesdun, Marc of Cantware Weal of Coran, Coranian Empire
& Caer Dathyl, kingdom of Gwynedd, Kymru,
Ostmonath & Ysgawen Mis, 486

Mondaeg, Sol 4—Gewinnan Daeg

When he woke the next morning there were tears on his cheeks. Sigerric helped him to sit up, handing him a cup of warm, spicy mead. As Havgan gulped the brew down, Sigerric asked quietly, "The dream again?"

Havgan nodded but did not bother to speak. They had said it all before, hundreds of times.

The dream never changed. In the dream he walks by the sea, the damp sand scrunching beneath his boots. His ruby-red cloak flares out behind him in the sturdy breeze. Wave after wave washes onto the shore, and then retreats with angry hisses. The sun is a baleful orange orb, setting the water ablaze as it sinks slowly into the ocean. The sorrowing cry of a seagull splinters the air and is carried away by the stiffening wind.

Then and only then, Havgan raises his eyes and sees a promontory jutting out to sea. The stones are black with sea spray. He sees the woman who stands on the outermost rock.

Her back is turned to him so he cannot see her face, but every rigid line in her slender body shows her need. Her arms are outstretched to the west in unbearable longing. Her long, honey-blond hair tumbles down her back, the outer strands caught and lifted by the steady breeze. The wind begins to moan with a low keening wail.

He calls out to her. It is dreadfully important that he see her face, dreadfully important that she speak to him, dreadfully important that she turn to him, so he can see himself reflected within the eyes he knows are full of tears, so he can know himself to be real.

When he calls out to her, her arms drop to her sides. Her head lifts at the sound of his voice. She begins to turn.

Then, everything stops. There is no sound. The waves still crash on the shore, but they are silent. The gulls wheel overhead without a sound. The wind whips his blood-red cloak, but he can hear nothing. He freezes there, motionless.

And sees only the woman, her back still to him, now frozen on the rock. Forever turning, never turning, her face hidden from him forever and ever.

With tears running down his face, he is crying to her with the voice of the sea for her to turn to him. Crying to her with the voice of the gulls. Crying to her with the voice of the wind. And crying with her, the lost and lonely woman who looks out to sea.

And always, when he jerks himself awake, there are salty tears on his face, as though the sea itself has returned with him from the place where he has been.

"The battle is at noon," Sigerric said quietly, refilling the cup held in Havgan's trembling hands. "Meet us one hour before and we will arm you."

Havgan took a deep breath. "The fair is here today."

"Yes," Sigerric said easily. "Fairs do gather at tournament time."

"I'm going to see the valla." Something inside, perhaps something he brought back with him from his dream of the sea told him he must go back to the valla today. He could feel it. Today was a turning on the path. A crossroads.

Sigerric nodded, his dark eyes serene. "Don't be late."

THE FAIR WAS crowded as Havgan absentmindedly made his way through the throng. He was preoccupied with the feeling that today would mark something momentous. The word had come to him as he woke up that morning—*crossroads*. Crossroads. Today.

He neared the tent of the valla, marked with the traditional stars and half moons. There was a scruffy man sitting on a stool in front of the tent, drinking ale with a contented air. His breeches and tunic were worn but clean, and his long brown hair, sprinkled with gray, was braided in the old-fashioned manner. His small blue eyes looked alertly up at Havgan, as he dragged himself to his feet. Taking in Havgan's well-made boots and rich tunic, the man bowed slightly. "A reading, good lord? One seid for a penny."

Havgan, his face unmoving, dropped a large, silver coin into the man's hands. "The runes. Two readings."

The smaller man nodded. "Yes, good lord. Enter and learn the future." With a showman's gesture, the man opened the tent flap and motioned him inside.

The tent was dim, lit only by a small brazier set to the side of a low table. A woman sat at the table, dressed in a long, black robe. Her face was covered with a filmy black veil. Her smooth hands, with long, tapering fingers, rested quietly on the table-top. Beneath the veil he caught a hint of shining, blond hair. Wordlessly, Havgan sank down on the opposite side of the low table, tucking his feet beneath him.

The woman spoke in a low, musical voice. "I am Egwina. I am the valla. I am the keeper of secrets. I am the teller of truths. I speak for the Wyrd, the three goddesses of fate. I speak for past, for present, for future. What is it you wish to know?"

"Today I woke with a dream I have had for many years. And today I fight a battle. I have two questions."

"Ask your questions, then, warrior, and I will see what we can learn."

"First. Today I stand at the crossroads. What path do I take?"

Slowly the woman reached out a hand and laid it gently on Havgan's arm. After a moment, she gripped his arm convulsively, then snatched her hand away. She rubbed one hand with the other, as though to slough off whatever she had felt.

"Yes," she said in a strained voice. "You stand at the crossroads today. There are those among us who have dreamed of this."

"What do you mean?" Havgan asked coolly. But his heart was beating wildly.

She gazed at him, still rubbing her hand. "You are powerful, warrior. The more so because you know not what you can do."

In a flash, Havgan reached out and grabbed her wrists in a grip of iron. "You will tell me nothing about that. Do you understand? No words of what I can do, or I will kill you." His voice was deathly quiet.

She shrank back, but he did not loose his hold. "Do you understand?" he asked again. She nodded, and he slowly released her. "My reading. Read the runes for me. Answer my question. And only that question. Now."

She swallowed hard, then lifted a golden bowl to the table. "Choose three runes—one for the past, one for the present, one for the future," she said, her voice low and subdued. "Close your eyes and choose one piece. The first piece is for the past."

Havgan plunged his hand into the bowl and picked out a small piece of wood, with a rune marked on it outlined in gold, and laid it gently on the tabletop.

The valla leaned forward and studied the rune. In a trembling voice she said, "This is *chalk*, the dead man's rune. It is a sign of barrenness, of emptiness, of hopes and dreams that have turned to ashes. This has been your life up to now."

As though, he thought bitterly, *I needed runes to tell me that.* But he said nothing.

"Now choose the next rune, the rune for the present," she went on.

Again, Havgan choose a piece of carved wood and laid it on the table. "Ah," the seeress said, with relief. "You have chosen *ansuz*. This is truly a momentous rune. It means that you will soon experience the divine. The God himself will send a message to you, a signal from his Holy Presence."

"A signal to show the way to take at the crossroads?"

"So it would seem, warrior." Her voice sounded more confident now. "Choose the last rune, the rune for the future. We shall see where the signal will take you."

Havgan chose the last rune and laid it down. The valla, glancing at it, took a ragged breath but said nothing.

"What does this one mean?" Havgan demanded, startled out of his calm demeanor.

"This is *gar*. It is a symbol of power." She raised her head, and he knew she was staring at him. "It is a symbol of royalty," she whispered.

Havgan was stunned. Royalty? Power? But how? The Coranian Empire had an emperor, secure on his throne. And yet, the emperor had only one child—a daughter. The idea that came to him seemed farfetched beyond belief. And yet, he felt power here from the seeress. If that is what she saw. . .

He interrupted his own musing. "Now answer my second question. For many years I have had a dream that will not leave me. My question is, who is the woman who stands on the rocks?"

"For such a question we must use the runes of Achtwan, the Great Wheel of Existence. These runes are powerful, and a seid with them can be dangerous." She paused, then tilted her head challengingly. "A seid with these runes could lead again to words of what you can do. Words you have said you will kill me for."

Havgan smiled, without warmth. "Then you must be very careful, mustn't you?"

She swallowed hard, then reached under the table and grasped a bag made of swan's skin. "Reach your hand into the bag of Achtwan, then, and choose a rune. You will choose three runes. They are not for past, present, or future. They will tell you the answer to your question in their own way."

Havgan reached into the bag. These runes felt heavier, and when he pulled one out, he saw that they were made of solid gold. Gently, he laid the rune on the table. The golden symbol glittered in the fitful light. "You have chosen the Wolf's Cross," she said slowly. "This is the rune for unchangeable fate. Choose another."

Havgan chose, and laid the golden rune on the table. "You have chosen the Dragon's Eye. This is a symbol for the dweller on the threshold of the mind—that which is hidden within. Choose the last."

As he chose, he noticed that her hands had begun to tremble. But her voice was steady as she said, "You have chosen Iar, the Magician. It is a symbol for the danger of approaching that which lies hidden."

For a moment she studied the runes with her head bowed. Suddenly, she drew off her veil and looked full into his amber eyes. Her own eyes were dark blue, and they blazed now with both power and fear. Her golden hair vied with the shining runes for brightness. "Warrior, you have chosen runes for a fate that was marked before you were born," she said urgently. "You have chosen runes that say that to fulfill your fate, you must not look too closely inside yourself. You can break this path only by looking at that which is hidden there. And if you do not break the path, thousands will die."

She took a deep breath, her voice shaking. "I cannot answer your question, warrior, because the woman who stands on the rocks in your dreams lives on the threshold of your waking mind. She is that which is inside of you, that which made you. And you know who she is. You know what she is."

She went on, her voice pleading, "Listen to me. I beg you. Face what is hidden. Break the path that leads over the sea. Let me help you do this. Let me help you."

He looked at her, his face expressionless. Yes, he would have to kill her. It was a shame, because she was a beautiful woman, but she knew too much. But he wouldn't have to kill her right away. He could take his pleasure with her first.

"Perhaps you can help me," he said, putting just the right amount of hesitation and doubt in his voice. "I have never spoken to another of that which is inside of me."

"Then it is surely time. I can help you do that," she said eagerly. "Let me help."

He smiled at her then, willing warmth into his amber eyes. "Today I fight a battle. A battle that I know I will win. And later I will need a woman to help me celebrate." He reached out a hand and stroked her cheek gently. "Will you be that woman?"

She hesitated for a moment, her eyes taking in his hard muscles, his handsome face, his honey-blond hair, and his amber eyes.

"Yes," she whispered.

Because even a seeress can make a mistake.

As HAVGAN AND Wulf faced each other on the field, the shouts of the crowd sounded far away. Wulf grinned unpleasantly at Havgan as they waited for the signal to begin the fight.

Eorl Wiglaf and his retainers stood on a wooden platform at the edge of the field. Sigerric stood with the rest of his warband to the right of the platform, while Wulf's warband gathered on the left. The field was ringed with spectators, and the noonday sun beat down mercilessly, making the air heavy and still.

Havgan's byrnie of interwoven metal covered his body down to mid-thigh, and beneath it his tunic and breeches clung to him like a second skin. His plain helm was like any other warrior's—fashioned of metal with the tiny figure of a boar at the top. His shield was painted with a boar's head in the middle, and four rays twisting out from the boar to the edge of the shield. He was wearing the Eorl's colors of red and gold, while

Wulf wore black and green. Havgan gripped his broadsword by the hilt, his elbow bent, letting the sword trail over his right shoulder in the warrior's fighting stance.

Wulf grinned again at Havgan. "Fisherman's son, I hope you have said your prayers to the God. Today you will die, for I will take no pleas for mercy from a churl."

Havgan didn't bother to answer. He would rather save his strength for the fight. And Wulf's taunts meant nothing to him, for he had heard it all before.

At last, the Eorl drew his sword and lifted the huge, scarred blade high. "Now do these two champions meet," he bellowed. "These champions will fight until one is dead. Havgan, son of Hengist, and Wulf, son of Wulfbald, do you understand the terms?"

Both men nodded. "Then," the Eorl declared, "let the battle begin."

Havgan and Wulf began to circle each other, looking for their chance. Both men held their shields close to their bodies, just under their eyes. Quick as a snake, Wulf feinted left, and as Havgan's shield moved a fraction to counter, Wulf's sword slipped under the shield, catching Havgan in the ribs with the flat of the blade. Havgan leapt back, then moved swiftly forward again, grinding his shield against Wulf's. Havgan moved his shield to the left, forcing Wulf's shield to move away and swung his sword in low, catching Wulf in the leg. Immediately, Wulf pulled back, and the two men circled each other again.

Wulf grinned again, though sweat left a sickly sheen on his face and his leg was bleeding. "It will soon be over with you, peasant. No mercy for you. I promise you that."

Again, Havgan said nothing. If Wulf wished to use his

energy in talk, that was all right with him. He felt very strange, abstracted and detached from the business at hand, as though he watched the battle from far away. He knew he must concentrate on the battle, but he could not. In his mind's eye a crossroads loomed before him, a curious picture of two paths coming together under a darkening, stormy sky.

As Wulf opened his mouth for another taunt, Havgan moved in and caught Wulf's shield with the edge of his own. Pulling with all his might, he flipped Wulf's shield up and away from Wulf's body. Even as he did so, his sword came down at an arc, knocking against Wulf's helmet with a ringing sound. Wulf leapt back, shaking his head to clear it.

"Time now for you to die, peasant," Wulf spat and leapt forward, hammering with shield and sword, driving Havgan back with the fury of his onslaught.

Havgan fell, tripped up by Wulf's shield cutting below his knees. And Wulf stood over him, his sword rising, glittering balefully, beginning the deadly arc that would end with the blade buried in his heart.

No! Havgan cried silently in panic. *It must not end like this!* And so he let the dark thing inside him reach up and out. Wulf's blade stayed unmoving, high in the air, stilled for an all too brief moment.

And in that moment, those watching the battle thought only that Wulf was playing with his victim, savoring Havgan's moment of helplessness. They did not know that Wulf's muscles had frozen. They did not know that, for all his striving, Wulf could not make the blade fall. And in those few seconds, Havgan rolled to his feet, grasped his shield and sword, and the dark thing receded, releasing Wulf from his bonds.

Wulf's eyes were wide and shocked. "You! How did you—" but it was too late to ask such questions. Havgan was upon him, pushing Wulf back, back, farther back with shield and sword. For now Havgan was well and truly focused on the battle. And now he showed himself as the great warrior he was.

In the end, it was easy. Just his warrior's training, no dark thing, just his sword and his shield as he beat Wulf to the ground, laid his foot on Wulf's gasping chest, and plunged his sword through this man who now knew him for what he was.

Suddenly, his warband surrounded him. Cheering him, they lifted him onto their shoulders and carried him from the field, through the city streets, and to Eahl Aecesdun, the temple of the city. The crowd followed shouting, singing, and tossing flowers to Havgan as he was carried by.

The inside of the temple was dark to eyes accustomed to the sun. Whitred, the Byshop of Cantware, stood next to the altar as Havgan was carried to the front bench and deposited, none too gently, upon it. Sigerric, Talorcan, Baldred, Penda, and Catha all sat down next to him, as they continued to clap him on the back and congratulate him on his victory.

The crowds filed in, quieting down now, for the atmosphere of the God's temple dampened their enthusiasm. Wiglaf himself stamped in, followed by his three alders and his nephew, Sledda.

The ceiling of the huge temple, held up by eight pillars, hung dark and shadowy overhead; its rich carvings a dizzying array of light and dark wood lost in the twisting shadows and fitful light. The pillars and walls were carved with the shapes of dragons, boars, eagles, and bulls, and some animals that there were no names for. So real were these carved figures that they seemed frozen into the walls themselves, trapped there for eternity at the whim of Lytir, the One God.

The stone altar by which Byshop Whitred stood was draped with a fine, white cloth, on which the golden runes for Lytir gleamed in the light of four white candles set at each corner of the altar. The altar was set with a drinking horn on the left, and the blot bowl, the bowl used to catch the bull's blood, sat mutely on the right. The hwitel, the ritual knife, glowed wickedly. The pit in front of the altar was uncovered, and nothing could be clearly seen in its shadowy depths, though it seemed that deep inside a darker shadow shifted. Two men stood by the pit, both holding burning torches. One man held his torch up; the other held his torch pointing down to the floor.

At last the aisle cleared as the crowd took their seats on the wooden benches. Byshop Whitred had tonsured blond hair and large blue eyes. His robe was green, and his sleeves fell away from his heavily muscled arms as he raised his hands to begin the ritual. "Praise now to the Guardian of Heofen, the power of Lytir and his mind-plans who fashioned the beginning of every wonder."

And the crowd responded, "Eternal Lord."

"He made first heaven as a roof," Whitred intoned.

"Holy Creator," was the response, rushing from hundreds of throats.

"Then made Middle-Earth as a dwelling place for men."

"Master Almighty," the reverent crowd chanted.

Then the Byshop shed his robe, picked up the knife and bowl from the altar, and, clad only in a white loincloth, jumped silently into the pit.

From the pit came a bull's angry bellow, rebounding throughout the temple as the bull and man fought for life. The two torchbearers stood impassively as the battle went on. The crowd was hushed and still. Then the bull gave a final bellow, and all was silent. A preost shuffled to the edge of the pit, lowering a small ladder into that pool of darkness. Triumphantly Whitred emerged, clutching the knife and the bowl, which was full of blood.

Cheers rang out as the Byshop calmly handed the knife and bowl to the preost and put back on his robe. The preost poured the blood into the drinking horn and passed the horn first to Havgan as he sat on the front bench. As Havgan took a sip and passed the cup to Sigerric, he began to think again.

He was still stunned by his good fortune, for his waking mind had already made him forget that the dark thing had brought him escape earlier in the battle. He thought only that he had won. That today he would be Gewinnan Daeg King, and wear the golden helm of victory. That today was the crossroads, the day that the God would send him a message that would set him on the right path and help him to fulfill a glorious destiny.

At that moment he became conscious of a buzzing in his ears that he could not dispel. No, it was more of a murmur, the words too low and indistinct to be understood. Was this it, then? His message from the God? He concentrated harder, and almost he could understand. He strained to make the words clear, but his concentration was broken as, when the crowd had finished drinking the bull's blood, Whitred took the golden helmet and came to stand before him.

"Today is Gewinnin Daeg, the Day of the Conqueror," Whitred said. "This is the day when we honor the great Lytir, the hero who won every tournament, who was victorious in every battle, until he sailed away to Heofen. In his honor, we choose the strongest warrior among us for this day. Today we honor Havgan, son of Hengist, who has won the helm of Lytir." While he said this, Whitred held out the golden helm, fashioned like the head of a boar with large, ruby eyes. The light washed over the helm, as though it was made of pure fire. Slowly, Havgan reached out to it, and then set it on his golden head.

"We have not in life set eyes on a man with more might in his frame than this helmed lord," the Byshop continued, his hands upraised. "Between the seas, south or north, over earth's stretch, no other man beneath sky's shifting excels this warrior."

"All hail to Lytir's heir," the crowd shouted. "All hail to the Gewinnan Daeg King!"

As he heard these words, Havgan's heart felt near to bursting with pride, for the fisherman's son had won a great honor. And it was at that moment, when his joy was at its height, that the muttered words in his mind became clear to him.

Death to all witches, the voice said clearly. *It is not enough to bring death to witches in the Coranian Empire. We must bring death to those in Kymru, that blighted island. We must take Kymru back, we who once held it, and cleanse the land of taint.*

And Havgan closed his eyes with the knowledge. This was it. This was *ansuz,* his message from the God that had been promised him. He could see it all now so clearly. He could see the stepping stones to power. He would become Bana, the Slayer, the war leader to all of the Coranian Empire. He would marry the emperor's daughter, and the might of all Corania would be his for the asking. He would hunt the witches in Kymru and kill them all, every one. And perhaps, if he did that, the black thing inside him would diminish and be gone from him. *The One God will not turn from me,* he thought, *if I come to him with*

43

the blood of witches on my hands.

THE CROWD CARRIED Havgan off then for the feast in his honor, and the temple emptied. One man only remained, sitting on his bench staring at the altar. Sledda, wyrce-jaga, hunter of witches, had not really been paying any attention to the ceremony at all, and did not realize that he was alone in the temple. His thoughts were concentrated on one thing only. That, more than anything, he wished to go to Kymru where witches abounded, to hunt and kill them for his God. His thoughts buzzed and shot out from him like arrows, to be buried in the hearts of those who knew how to listen. *Death to all witches*, he thought. *It is not enough to bring death to witches in the Coranian Empire. We must bring death to those in Kymru, that blighted island. We must take Kymru back, we who once held it, and cleanse the land of taint.*

Gwyntdydd, Lleihau Wythnos—early evening
GWYDION, THE DREAMER of Kymru, was on the floor of his study in the Dreamer's Tower of Caer Dathyl. He was crouched on all fours, growling, baring his teeth at his prey. She shrieked and ran away as quickly as her legs could carry her. But he leapt forward and caught her at the door. She raised her hand and, with an unintelligible sound, called for Druid's Fire. His back arched as the invisible missile hit him and he went down, moaning.

The fire from the hearth flickered over the book-lined walls as she crept to him cautiously, looking down at him as he lay prone on the rich rug of red and black. His close-cropped, black beard shadowed the lower half of his handsome face, and his eyes were closed.

Suddenly, he opened his eyes and smiled, and she crowed with delight. He sat up, and she put her arms around his neck to ensure that he was all right. Her nearly toothless grin was wide and happy.

"So," he said with a laugh, "the great Cariadas, heir to the Dreamer of Kymru, has defeated the terrible monster! You win, my daughter. Savor your victory!"

She laughed again, her one-year-old fresh face delighted. Her red-gold hair clung to her head in riotous curls and her gray eyes, so like his, were sparkling with glee.

They heard footsteps outside the study door and looked at each other, both with mock terror on their faces.

"Oh, no!" Gwydion cried. "She's come to take you! Well, I will not let her, not I!" He leapt up, Cariadas in his arms, and faced the door. "Fear not, fair maiden!" he went on. "For I will protect you!"

The study door opened, and Dinaswyn, Gwydion's aunt, stood there, her arms on her hips, a scowl on her face. Her dark hair, lightly touched by frost, was held back from her face by a red ribbon, and her gray eyes were sparkling with irritation.

"She should have been in bed an hour ago," Dinaswyn accused.

"I wanted to spend more time with her. I haven't been back very long," Gwydion protested. "And I was a long time away."

"Nonetheless, it is past her bedtime," Dinaswyn insisted. "And you've been back for over a week. Not, of course, that I have any idea where you were."

Gwydion sighed to himself. That he had not told Dinaswyn exactly where he had been still rankled. Knowing his aunt, it always would. It wasn't that he didn't trust her as much as it was that he needed to distance himself from her. He had been the Dreamer of Kymru now for four years, and she still seemed to have trouble remembering that.

Besides, where he had been and what he had been doing was far too secret to be bandied about. He had recently taken young Arthur, the Prince of Gwynedd, from Tegeingl and deposited the boy in the care of Myrrdin in the tiny village of Dinas Emrys. And that was something he wanted no one to know who didn't have to. And Dinaswyn didn't have to.

"Where I have been and what I have been doing is surely my business," he said coolly.

"As I well know," Dinaswyn replied as she crossed to him and took Cariadas from his arms. "Now, little one," Dinaswyn said softly to the little girl, "say good-night to your da and go to bed."

Cariadas yawned and leaned forward to put her little arms around Gwydion's neck. She kissed his cheek then nestled against Dinaswyn's chest, her eyelids already drooping. He smiled as he gently stroked her hair, then whispered his good-night.

Dinaswyn turned and went to the study door. She hesitated a moment, then turned around. "I see the signs," she said quietly. "You will dream tonight. If there is need, call me."

"I will," he said, knowing that he wouldn't.

She knew it, too, but did not say it. She left, cradling the already-sleeping Cariadas.

She was right. The signs were there. He had been restless all day, and had been having trouble concentrating. There was a dream awaiting him, and it was an important one, as he had learned to judge these matters.

He climbed the steps leading to Ystafell Yr Arymes, the

Chamber of Prophecy at the top of the Dreamer's Tower. When he entered the room, he lifted his hand and called Druid's Fire. Blue and orange flames immediately flickered from the brazier that stood next to the simple pallet in the middle of the room. Sapphires, pearls, opals, and emeralds glittered around the four round windows that pierced the tower walls. Onyx and blood-stone gleamed from the floor as he crossed over to the pallet.

He discarded his robe and lay down, his hands behind his head, eyeing the constellations that glittered through the glass roof of the chamber. His eyes picked out the constellation of Arderydd, the High Eagle, the sign of the High Kings of Kymru. He thought of young Arthur, safe for the moment, in the tiny mountain village of Dinas Emrys. He wondered again what terrible thing the future had in store that a new High King had been born to combat it. He knew that it would be revealed to him in time, and he hoped with all his heart that he would be able to meet whatever challenge was in store.

Still looking up at the stars, he recited the Dreamer's prayer:
"Annwyn with me laying down, Aertan with me sleeping.
The white flame of Nantsovelta in my soul,
The mantle of Modron about my shoulders,
The protection of Taran over me, taking my hand,
And in my heart, the fire of Mabon.
If malice should threaten my life
Then the Shining Ones between me and evil.
From tonight till a year from tonight,
And this very night,
And forever,
And for eternity.
Awen."

And then he slept, as the waning moon bathed him in its dying, silvery beams.

HE WAS STANDING at the crossroads. On either side of the road, tall grass stretched to the horizon as far as he could see. Wind rippled the grass, creating patterns that lay just beyond the edge of understanding. Around and around the wind played, drawing shapes that constantly flickered and vanished, shifting over and over across the plain.

Storm clouds hovered, piled high in the darkening sky. The threatening black and purple clouds were laced with flashes of lightning. But there was no rain. And no sound other than the wind whipping mercilessly past him as he stood at the crossroads, unable to go on.

It was here that the road parted. The road leading to the right stretched out to the horizon, shining with a warm, steady glow in the flickering light of the gathering storm. Wide and straight, it was a safe path, the one he wanted to take. The one he would have taken, if he could only move. But, somehow, the decision was not his to make.

He glanced at the left-hand road and shuddered. It twisted horribly as it made its sluggish way across the plain, like a dying serpent. It was full of shadows that stretched across the road like greedy fingers. The road led into a tunnel of darkness unimaginable. It frightened him to think of what was waiting in that dark tunnel in the middle of the plain. If only he could move, he would run like the wind up the glowing right road, run far away from this terrible crossroads and from this terrible choice that was not his to make.

Then he became aware that there were others waiting at

the crossroads. People began to emerge from the tall, waving grass and step reluctantly onto the road, pulled there against their will by a force they could not break.

He saw Uthyr and Ygraine with their daughter, young Morrigan, followed closely by Cai, Gwynedd's Captain. He saw Queen Olwen of Ederynion put a protective arm around the slim shoulders of her daughter, Elen, and ignoring her son, Lludd, while Angharad, Ederynion's Captain guarded them all. He saw Urien, the King of Rheged, with his wife and four children clustered around him, followed by Rheged's Captain, Trystan. He saw King Rhoram of Prydyn with his son, Geriant, and daughter, Sanon, shadowed by Achren, Prydyn's Captain.

More and more people were stepping onto the road behind him, all waiting silently to travel the road they were destined to take. Dinaswyn and Arianrod appeared, their hands linked by a silver chain Arianrod was struggling to break. Cathbad, the Archdruid, his expression serious and thoughtful, stepped onto the road, followed by Aergol, his heir, whose face was carefully expressionless.

He saw Anieron, the Master Bard, step from the tall grass and look around him with knowing eyes. He was followed closely by his brother, Dudod. Then Anieron's daughter, Elstar, and her husband, Elidyr, and their two sons stepped onto the path. Gwydion's daughter, Cariadas, was with them. He longed to go to her but somehow knew that he could not.

Myrrdin made his way up the road, his arm around the shoulders of a young man whom Gwydion knew to be Arthur. And Arthur, slim and tall, with his auburn hair and his dark eyes, left Myrrdin to stand next to Gwydion at this terrible crossroads.

And then, most surprising of all, a woman stepped out of the tall grass. Her long dark hair was black as night and her eyes were a startling emerald green. She walked up the road to stand on Gwydion's other side, and he instantly knew her—Rhiannon ur Hefeydd, the woman of the House of Llyr who had disappeared so long ago. She was holding the hand of a young girl with blond hair whom Gwydion somehow knew to be her daughter, Gwenhwyfar. The sunny-haired girl reached out and clasped Arthur's hand tightly.

Thus the four of them—Gwydion, Rhiannon, Arthur, and Gwenhwyfar—stood together, the rest of Kymru fanning out behind them, standing silently at the crossroads beneath the darkening sky, waiting for the one who would make the choice. And at last he came.

Out of the tall wind-swept grass a man rose up, golden and proud. His hair was honey-blond, and his eyes were amber, set above high cheekbones in a handsome, powerful face. As he made his way up to the crossroads, the crowd parted before him like water. And then he stopped, staring at Gwydion. For a moment they looked at each other. And for a moment it seemed to Gwydion that he had always known this man. Face to face they stood silently as the wind grew stronger, whipping around the Golden Man and the Dreamer.

The man looked up the road to the right and took a hesitant step in that direction. Gwydion sighed in relief. But then the golden man looked back to the left road and all was lost. For in the middle of that road a helmet of gold appeared. It was fashioned like the head of a boar, with tusks of ivory and ruby eyes. Transfixed, the Golden Man stepped onto the left road, reaching for the helmet. He raised it high, and the lightning began to flash. Jagged spars reached down from the sky, bathing the left road in fire. The golden man lowered the helmet over his head, and the right road suddenly vanished from the plain. There was only one road now, the road of fire leading into darkness.

One by one the people took the left road, following the Golden Man down, down into the dark. Gwydion was pulled helplessly along with the rest, terror-stricken, his heart pounding. But Rhiannon held tightly to his hand, giving him strength in this horror as the darkness loomed over him and swallowed him whole.

As GWYDION JERKED awake, the thought came clearly. Crossroads—the place where decisions are made. Something had happened, somewhere. The Golden Man, whoever he was, wherever he was, had made a decision to travel the left road down to darkness, taking everyone with him.

And as he thought that, the wind came up, whipping through the mountains, reaching even into the Chamber of Prophecy, stirring the fire in the brazier. The gale shook the tower, scraping over the stone, tumbling leaves with the sound of bones rattling, making the mountains shiver. And bringing with it the faroff sound of a hunting horn as the Wild Hunt rode the night sky.

Chapter 3

Camlan, Marc of Gillingas,
Aecesdun, Marc of Cantware &
Athelin, Marc of Ivelas
Weal of Coran, Coranian Empire
Falmonath & Sifmonath, 488

Wodaeg, Sol 11—early afternoon

Havgan walked through the ruins of the once-white halls of Ealh Galdra, the Temple of Magic. Though the roof was long gone, the stone pillars that had once held it were still standing. Here and there white glimmered from stones stained with dirt, age, and soot—for the fire that had raged through the temple centuries ago had burned fiercely, imprinting its deadly memory onto the stones.

Behind him the others stood in a knot just outside of the ruins. Catha and Baldred appeared to be almost bored, but Havgan had expected that. They and their families had long ago accepted the worship of Lytir, and they gave no credence to, nor had any real understanding of, the power of the Old Gods.

But Talorcan and Penda did, and for that reason, Havgan knew, they both were tense and wary. They had done their best to argue him out of coming here, to this place where the Old Gods had once reigned supreme through the once-revered

Maeder-Godias, the mother-priestesses. Before the new religion of Lytir had come to Corania, women of the royal family had often become Maeder-Godias, leading the country in the worship of the gods. But when the worship of Lytir had become universally accepted, this place had been burned, and the reigning Maeder-Godia, Valeda of Dere, had been taken away to Athelin and burned at the stake.

Before her death Velada had chosen her successor, a princess of Dere named Infleda. But whom Infleda had chosen as successor was unknown, for by that time Dere had been absorbed into the Empire and the Heiden, as those followers of the old religion were now called, had been outlawed, as had the Wiccan, those who had special gifts akin to the witches of Kymru. Rumor had it that the line of Maeder-Godias still continued, in secret. Their capture was the dream of every wyrcejaga in the Empire. But those women who had held the position since Infleda had been far too canny to be caught—if they even really existed at all.

He brushed his hand against a blackened stone and shivered as an unexpected chill ran through his body. The wind moaned softly as it made its lonely way among the stones. Since the time of Velada's execution, the ruins of Ealh Galdra had been deserted and no one willingly came here—even in the daytime. No, Havgan had not been at all surprised that Talorcan and Penda had tried to prevent his coming here.

Talorcan's family came from the marc of Bernice in Dere, the marc that contained Wodnesbeorg, a place most revered by the Heiden. Havgan even had some suspicions that Talorcan was related to the old ruling family of Dere, a family long steeped in magic.

Penda came from the shire of Lindisfarne, in Mierce, and had lived at the foot of Mount Badon, that mountain from where the Wild Hunt itself was said to ride. Though Penda's father professed the new religion, Havgan was not so sure that his worship of Lytir descended beyond lip service. And Penda was promised to the daughter of the Alder of Minting, a man once accused of being one of the Heiden. The Alder had successfully defended himself against the allegation, but there were many who still believed it.

Havgan was aware that Sigerric, too, was uneasy, but for different reasons from the rest. Sigerric knew Havgan best of all. They all knew that something very important had happened to Havgan during the Gewinnan Daeg celebration almost two years ago. They all knew that he had heard the voice of God, telling him to exterminate the witches of Kymru.

But only Sigerric seemed to suspect that Havgan had recently set in motion a train of events that would carry him to the notice of those who ruled the Empire, an essential step in his plan. Not that Sigerric knew details—Havgan had been very careful for, though he trusted Sigerric, he did not want to burden his friend. Some details involved cold-blooded murder, something Sigerric would surely frown upon.

He walked back across the ruins toward his men, eyeing the huge, blackened, T-shaped stone that rested in what had once been the central courtyard. Around the stone, fire-blackened urns rested. Hundreds of runes were incised into the granite rock, their stiff, angular shapes menacing beneath the gray sky.

Havgan nodded toward the rock and turned to Penda, his brows raised.

"It was carved in the shape of Donar's hammer," Penda

said reluctantly. "It was here that the bodies of the Maeder-Godias were laid to rest."

"Then they burned them," Talorcan went on, "and gathered their ashes into urns."

"Why are the urns still here?" Catha asked curiously. "I would think that destroying them would have been paramount when the temple was burned."

"They tried to take them," Penda said softly. "But those who even so much as touched them sickened and died. And so Asbru Hlaew, the Rainbow Mound, stays inviolate."

"Why is it called the Rainbow Mound?" Baldred asked.

"Because it is said that this is the place where the Asbru Bridge, the rainbow of the gods, touches the earth," Talorcan answered. "It is said that on Ragnorak, the Twilight of the Gods, the gods themselves will ride over that bridge and onto Middle-Earth to begin their destruction."

"It is further said that only one will hold them back—and that one is not even a Coranian. One of the Kymri will save the world that day, here at the Battle of Camlan," Penda said solemnly.

"A most unlikely tale," Havgan said. "For why would a Kymri save Corania?"

"Even more unlikely that one of Kymru would be alive to save us," Sigerric said harshly. "For do you not plan to kill them all?"

Havgan whipped around to face his friend. For a moment the two stood there, facing each other, unmoving. Sigerric's brown eyes held both disdain and a hint of sorrow. Havgan's amber eyes flashed, but subsided. Sigerric was his dearest friend, and Havgan knew that, no matter what, Sigerric would not desert him. Not ever.

"These are old tales," Havgan said softly, "from before the

time Lytir came to us and showed us that the Old Gods had no power. Now Lytir reigns supreme. He will send someone to hold back that destruction—if, indeed, the Old Gods are even capable of it."

"You think they are not?" Penda asked.

"Their power is long since faded," Havgan replied.

"Do you truly think so?" Talorcan asked softly. "You do not know, I think, of what you speak."

"I know that Lytir himself commanded me," Havgan said. "I know that his power is within me. I know that I cannot be stopped. Penda, Talorcan," Havgan went on, "tell me of the signs on the wall of the temple itself." He turned and led them to the crumbling inner walls that brooded silently beneath the cloudy sky.

Penda spoke first. "These are the signs of the chief gods, those that are honored in the six festivals." He pointed first to three concentric circles within a triangle, painted in black and silver. "This is for Narve, the father of all, the God of Death. He is also called Yffr, the Terrible One, and the One that Binds."

"The next symbol is for Nerthus," Talorcan said, pointing to a symbol on the wall of two half circles, one brown and one green, joined at their arcs. "She is the Goddess of the Earth, the daughter of Narve and Ostara, the Warrior Goddess. She is said to live on an island in the ocean, and boars are sacred to her."

"The next is for Donar, the God of Thunder. When he throws his hammer, Molnir, lightning plays across the sky. He has red hair, and both the oak and the bull are sacred to him. He is much to be feared." Penda pointed to a T-shaped symbol painted in dark blue and silver.

Talorcan continued. "The next sign is for Tiw, the God of War," he said, pointing at a large arrow painted in red and gold pointing upward. "His sword, called Tyrfing, could only be sheathed if human blood was on it. He is the son of Wuotan and Nerthus."

"The next two symbols are for Fro and Freya, the Lord and the Lady," Penda said, pointing to two intertwined symbols in white and gold. One was two triangles lying on their side, and the other was a line with two jagged perpendicular lines jutting from it. "They are the twin children of Narve and Erce, the Goddess of Peace. They are the givers of peace and plenty. Freya is the goddess of fertility, and Fro is the one who bestows dreams and visions."

Talorcan gestured to the last symbol, a circle cut into quarters, painted in gray and purple. "This is the sign of Wuotan, the God of Magic, the son of Narve. His secrets of magic are called seidr. He hung on Irminsul, the World Tree, for nine days to gain the knowledge and mastery of the seidr. He is called the Wanderer and also One-Eye, for he gave one of his eyes to the Wyrd to drink from the well of knowledge. The eagle is sacred to him. Along with the goddess, Holda, he leads the Wild Hunt."

Havgan lifted his hand to silence the rest as he stared at the symbol for Wuotan, not taking his eyes from the circle. He had felt something, something he could not name, as Talorcan had spoken of Wuotan. It almost seemed to him that the air grew thicker, the wind perhaps a little sharper, even the leaden sky above them seemed to have darkened. He was not afraid, for he knew Lytir would defend him against Wuotan. But he knew, somehow, that the God of Magic had power still. And he knew, for he had felt it many times in his life, that Wuotan had long fought Lytir for the possession of Havgan's soul. But One-Eye had lost, for Havgan belonged wholly to Lytir. He would do Lytir's bidding, for he knew what happened to the Heiden when they died. He knew that they were sent to Hel, where all those who did not worship Lytir were sentenced.

He would not, he would never be, one of them.

Without speaking, he turned away from the painted walls and began to make his way slowly through the ruins, away from the others. He wanted to be alone with his thoughts. He had come here because he had thought that it might be useful, that he might gain some insight into the witches of Kymru by coming to a place once sacred to the witches of Corania. They were different from each other only in that they lived in different parts of the world. They were both evil.

He had been commanded to destroy the witches of Kymru, the Y Dawnus, and he would not be distracted from that purpose. The wyrce-jaga had already made it their life's work to destroy the witches of Corania. While he would not actively aid them, for it would distract him from his purpose, he would not even think to hinder them. Yet it had occurred to him that the Wiccan themselves might be useful to him. It might be that he could tap into some of their power. He would use anyone and everyone to do what was necessary. He would even use Wuotan himself if it came to that.

"That might be a problem, for he is not trustworthy, you know."

Havgan whirled around to face an old man. The man had a patch over his right eye, but his left eye was a bright and sparkling silvery gray. His long, gray hair was tangled and dusty, and he wore a nondescript cloak of gray.

"Who are you?" Havgan asked, his hand going to his dagger.

"I am sorry, lord," the man said, cringing away. "I didn't mean to startle you."

"Who are you? Do not make me ask again."

"I am called Grim, lord," the old man said, making a clumsy bow.

"What are you doing here?"

"I am just passing through, young lord. Just passing through."

"On your way to where?"

"To nowhere, young sir. I am just a wanderer. I seek new places and new things. I tell stories and sing songs. I harm no one."

Havgan hesitated. The man did, indeed, seem harmless, but he was still wary. "What was it you said at first?"

"Why, nothing. Merely a greeting."

"That is not how I remember it," Havgan said softly, his tone dangerous. "You spoke of Wuotan."

"Oh, I would never speak of him in a place such as this. I would be afraid to."

"The Old Gods do not have power anymore," Havgan said sharply.

"As you say sir," the old man said, with a half bow. "As you say." The man turned away, then turned back again. "Oh, by the way, I wouldn't be too sure that the Old Gods are powerless. Why, just look behind you."

Havgan whirled, for he had felt a prickling at the nape of his neck, as though someone—or something—was sneaking up behind him. But there was no one there. The wind picked up and began to howl for a moment, then subsided. He turned around to speak sharply to the old man, but he was gone. Havgan glanced around wildly, but he could see no one except his five friends, who still stood some distance from him.

He called out to them even as he strode toward them. "Where did he go?"

Sigerric looked at him blankly. "Where did who go?"

"The old man!"

"What old man?"

"Didn't you see him? He was right there, talking to me."

"We didn't see anyone," Sigerric said. "Just you, wandering through the ruins."

Havgan opened his mouth to argue, but abruptly shut it. For at that moment an eagle wheeled high overhead, calling with the voice of the wind. And from far, far away, the sound of hunting horns drifted across the plain.

Tiwdaeg, Sol 24—late morning

TWO MONTHS LATER, Sigerric, riding across the grassy plain beside Havgan, was thinking very hard about his friend.

Havgan was up to something, something devious, something possibly very, very dark, something Sigerric was still not certain he even wanted to know. But it had become evident to Sigerric some years ago that his task was to save his friend if he could. The trouble was that Havgan did not want to be saved, did not even seem to see the danger that Sigerric saw so clearly.

Sigerric had not wanted Havgan to go to Ealh Galdra, for it was a dangerous place. He was of the opinion that the Old Gods were not as powerless as some would like to think. And though he had seen nothing, and Havgan had said very little, Sigerric had his suspicions that Havgan had encountered something there. But Havgan had refused to discuss it. Indeed, Havgan always refused to discuss the things that troubled him most.

That was a characteristic of his friend that frightened Sigerric—for he had never known Havgan to have the slightest inclination to face the dark things that lurked inside, to even contemplate a journey toward the truths that surely lay buried there.

And Sigerric had often thought that some very dark things indeed lay hidden deep inside his friend. Sigerric had heard men mutter that they were surprised that Havgan, the son of a fisherman, could have such a hold over his fellow warriors, the scion of lords of the Empire. Sigerric could have told them all that though he had no idea whose son Havgan really was, he certainly was not the son of a fisherman. But even Havgan himself was not ready to believe that, so Sigerric had held his tongue—so far.

Catha, Baldred, Penda, and Talorcan rode behind Sigerric and Havgan, their cloaks fanning out behind them, laughing and calling to each other as they raced across the meadow. Overhead the sun shone bright and warm as the heady scent of a summer morning drifted past them in the gentle breeze.

Havgan laughed with them, his hair vying with the sun for brightness, laughter in his amber eyes. He held up his hand, and they all came to a halt.

"So, Havgan," Catha called, "how in the world did you get Lord Wiglaf to let us go? Blackmail?"

"His winning personality, of course," Talorcan said. His light green eyes danced with laughter in his thin face. "What else?"

"It was easy," Havgan replied with a wicked grin. "I promised him that the five of you would do midnight guard duty for the next three months."

Baldred groaned. "You didn't!"

"Why, Baldred," Havgan said with mock dismay, "I thought you would be pleased to be part of the advanced welcome for the Prince."

"But at what price?" Penda asked theatrically. "We are undone!"

"Truthfully, though, we are very lucky to be chosen," Baldred said, scanning the east horizon.

"And we will be luckier still if he takes any notice of us," Talorcan added.

Havgan ducked his head in an attempt to hide his smile at Talorcan's remark. The others did not notice, though Sigerric did. And that was when he got the barest glimmer that something was going to happen today. He suddenly remembered that twice this week he had gone looking for Havgan, and his friend could not be found.

"Well, old Sigerric here is a good friend of Prince Aesc," Catha said, slapping Sigerric's shoulder. "I am certain he would be glad to see you."

"I will be lucky if the Prince even remembers my name," Sigerric retorted. "The last time I saw him I was only ten years old. He came to Apuldre and stopped by to visit my father."

"They are friends?" Havgan asked.

"I wouldn't go that far, though they seem to like each other well enough. My father says Prince Aesc is a good man."

"And my brother says that God made a mistake," Catha said. "Aesc should be the Emperor, not his weakling of an older brother."

Sigerric frowned at Catha. "To speak so is treason to the Emperor," he said. "Do not ever say that again."

Catha's handsome face hardened dangerously, and his bright, blue eyes narrowed as his hand moved to his dagger. "Do not tell me what I can and cannot say, Sigerric."

"Stop," Havgan said softly, his tone deadly for all its quiet. "I will not tolerate arguments among ourselves." Havgan stared at Catha with his bright, amber eyes, the eyes that held such power, that covered such secrets, that challenged and probed, that caught and held in a fierce, relentless grip. Under their gaze, Catha subsided, his hand dropping away from his dagger.

Sigerric, who happened to be facing the eastern horizon, saw it first. "Look!" he cried, pointing to the plume of dust some miles away. "It must be Aesc and his men."

"That's a lot of dust for the Prince and his warband," Penda said with a frown.

"He must be bringing more men than Wiglaf had thought," Baldred offered uncertainly.

"He wouldn't be so rude," Talorcan said. "He would know that the lords he is visiting would count on knowing the number of men in his escort. And his message to Wiglaf said he would be bringing no more than fifteen."

"Trouble?" Catha asked, turning to Havgan.

"Trouble," Havgan replied, his amber eyes intent on the horizon.

"Then we had best see to it," Baldred said, drawing his ax from his belt.

Havgan grinned, his eyes glinting dangerously. "Yes, we had best see to it."

He spurred his horse forward and the rest followed, drawing their spears and their swords as they rode toward the cloud of dust. As they neared the place, they began to hear cries carried to them on the wind. The clang of weapons alerted them that there was indeed trouble long before they rounded the bend in the road and saw the melee.

The Prince, identifiable by his byrnie of gold and golden helm studded with chunks of amber, was laying about him with his sword, roaring. The men of his warband were fighting valiantly, protecting their Prince as best they could, though they were clearly outnumbered.

The men they were fighting were lean and dangerous. They wore no byrnies and carried blank shields. Their clothing was plain—brown leather tunics and trousers—and their hair was long and braided tightly to their skulls.

The lack of identification alerted Sigerric immediately that these were outlaws. He was surprised that they would attack what was clearly a formidable group, for outlaws did not generally do so, even when numbers were on their side. They must have been lured beyond bearing by the rich weapons and jewelry that the Prince and his men were sporting. Still, Sigerric thought it very odd, indeed.

And odder still was the expression on the outlaw's faces when Havgan and his men leapt into the fray and Havgan began to kill the outlaws—swiftly, efficiently, brutally. The closest Sigerric could come to identifying the expression was downright shock at the sight of Havgan and his men.

There were more than thirty outlaws in the band, outnumbering Aesc and his men by two to one. But with the inclusion of Sigerric and his friends, the scales were tipped. For a few moments the outcome was in doubt. But as Sigerric spitted two more men with his spear, as another man went down beneath Baldred's ax, as Catha thrust his sword into the back of another, as Talorcan speared an outlaw through the heart, as Penda's ax sheared off the head of one more, the balance shifted.

Havgan seemed to be everywhere, using ax and spear and double-edged sword. Outlaw after outlaw went down in a welter of blood as Havgan flew into the fight like an avenging angel. The one who was clearly their leader called out for his men to retreat, but Havgan cried out that no man was to escape, that they were to pay with their lives for the terrible crime of attacking the Prince.

Sigerric and the others, obedient to Havgan's wishes, gave no quarter, cutting down the outlaws left and right. Finally, the only outlaw still standing was the one who appeared to have been the leader. He slowly backed away from Havgan's spear. He turned to run, but tripped and went sprawling. He turned over on his back and lay for a moment, dazed. His eyes lighted on the glittering end of the spear that was aimed straight at his belly. He raised his dark eyes to behold Havgan's bright, amber gaze.

Only Sigerric, who was just at Havgan's elbow, heard what the outlaw said.

"So, fisherman's son, this is how it ends."

"This is how it ends," Havgan said softly as he thrust his spear into the man's belly. The outlaw's back arched in agony. As the light fled from the man's eyes, Havgan jerked his spear from the man's body.

"You there!" someone called from behind them.

Havgan spun around to find himself face to face with Prince Aesc. The Prince was a huge man. His powerful shoulders strained against his sleeveless tunic of supple brown leather. Golden armbands encircled his huge upper arms. His blond hair, cut short to fit under his helm, was sweat-soaked. His blue eyes, startling with their intensity in his tanned face, shrewdly took Havgan's measure.

"You and your men are from Eorl Wiglaf, are you not?"

"We are, great lord," Havgan said, instantly on his knees while the rest of his men followed suit. He bowed his golden head before the Prince.

"I thank you for your timely aid," Aesc went on. "Get up, sir, for you and your men have done me and mine a great service."

Havgan rose and Sigerric, Talorcan, Penda, Catha, and Baldred followed suit.

"I believe I know most of you," Aesc said. "You are Sigerric, the son of the Alder of Apuldre."

Sigerric bowed briefly. "I am. And I am flattered that you recognize me."

"You have the look of your father," Aesc said. "And you are surely Penda, son of the Eorl of Lindisfarne." Penda bowed and nodded. "And you are Catha, brother of the Eorl of Pecsaetan, and you are Baldred, son of the Eorl of Tarbin." The two men bowed as Aesc named them. "And you are Talorcan, the son of the Eorl of Bernice." Talorcan nodded and bowed in his turn.

At last Aesc turned back to Havgan, who stood there quietly, his bloody spear gripped tightly in his hand. "Indeed, the only one of you I do not know is this man who led our rescue."

"This is Havgan, son of Hengist," Sigerric said. "He is my foster-brother."

"Sigerric strains the truth, great Prince," Havgan murmured. "I was made Sigerric's servant when I was a lad."

"And he is now a full member of Eorl Wiglaf's warband," Sigerric said.

"Your father?" Aesc asked Havgan.

"Was a fisherman," Havgan said quietly. "He is now a salt-maker in Angelesford."

"You are in illustrious company, indeed, son of a fisherman," Aesc said, his keen blue eyes glittering.

"I am a lucky man, my Prince," Havgan said humbly, his amber eyes lowered to the ground.

"A man who makes his own luck, I think," Aesc said.

Havgan swiftly raised his eyes to Aesc, but the Prince had already turned away, calling for his horse. "Lead on, men of Cantware," Aesc said to Havgan and his men with a smile. "I must go to Eorl Wiglaf and tell him of the valor of his warriors. And I must further ask him if he would be generous enough to give them to me."

"Prince?" Havgan asked, as he sucked in a startled breath.

"I could not leave such valiant men behind. What, would not all six of you be willing to join my warband?"

Smiles broke across their faces at Aesc's words. Sigerric himself could hardly believe it. To be in the warband of Prince Aesc was an honor beyond his dreams. He never could have believed that such a thing might happen.

Indeed, Havgan did make his own luck. Sigerric just hoped Aesc would never feel moved to inquire about the details, for such an exercise would be fruitless, as Sigerric had learned long ago.

Tiwdaeg, Sol 10—early afternoon
TWENTY-EIGHT DAYS LATER, Sigerric, Havgan, and the rest arrived in Athelin. The streets of the Empire's capital were crowded and seemed strange to Sigerric's country-bred eyes. Merchants and whores, churchmen and beggars streamed down the wide streets, expertly weaving in and out, somehow avoiding

crashing into each other as they hurried about their business.

There were mounted men aplenty, some with the sunburst of four curved, golden bars—the device of the Emperor—on their shields; some with the device of the warlord—a boar's head with ruby eyes. Often Sigerric spotted the tonsured head of a wyrce-jaga and noticed that the people of Athelin gave these men a wide berth.

Though overhead the sun shone brightly in a clear, blue sky, the streets were dim, for much of the light was cut off from the overhanging second stories of the buildings that lined the streets. Brightly colored flowers flowed from boxes set beneath many of the windows.

Sigerric thought back to the night Prince Aesc had asked Eorl Wiglaf for Havgan, Sigerric, Penda, Talorcan, Catha, and Baldred. Aesc had promised Wiglaf that they would be well taken care of as members of his warband. And the Eorl, acutely aware that the Prince was not to be refused, had given his consent and had smiled widely when he did it, slapping the men on the back and congratulating them on their change in fortune. But there had been something in the Eorl's sharp eyes when Aesc had related the story of his rescue. A flicker of suspicion as he had addressed Havgan, a hint that the Eorl was relieved to be rid of the fisherman's son.

He caught glimpses of the River Saefern on their left in the small spaces between the houses. The river, dappled with sunshine, glittered brightly in the golden afternoon. Though Sigerric had heard descriptions of Cynerice Scima, the royal palace, he was unprepared when they rounded the corner and he saw it for the first time.

The white, gleaming building was set on an island in the

middle of the river, making it seem as though it floated gently on the surface of the water itself. Four tall, graceful spires, roofed in gold, reached up to the sky from the four corners of the square palace. A wide bridge, lined with guards, spanned the distance across the water.

Havgan took a sharp breath at the sight of the palace, his amber eyes glittering with avid hunger as he stared at the home of the emperors.

Aesc turned in his saddle and looked at Havgan. "They call it Cynerice Scima, Kingdom Light."

"And I know why," Havgan breathed.

"And you shall know better in a few moments. Come."

They all followed Prince Aesc across the glimmering bridge. The Emperor's soldiers who lined the bridge bowed as Aesc passed by. The guards at the huge, iron gates jumped quickly out of the way and bowed down to the ground as Aesc and his party dismounted. Slaves came to take the horses and led them away, as Aesc turned to the Captain who waited quietly.

"My brother?"

"Holding audience, lord, in Gulden Hul."

"These six men with me are now members of my warband. You will remember them, and give them the deference you give to me."

"Yes, lord," the Captain said, fixing their faces in his memory.

"Come," Aesc said to Havgan and the others. "Come and meet my brother. I sent word on ahead, and he is anxious to meet you all."

They followed Aesc down corridors lined with jeweled tapestries. Richly dressed men hurried through the hallways, bent on important business, but they all stopped and bowed as

Aesc strode by. The Prince often raised his hand in greeting or called out to a few men cheerfully as they made their way to the throne room.

Gulden Hul, the hall of the emperors, gleamed and shone with a soft, golden light. Eight golden pillars, all carved in the form of many-branched trees, held up the towering, golden ceiling. The floor gleamed with golden tiles, and the walls, sheathed in gold, glimmered softly. A huge golden tree stood in the center of the chamber. Jeweled birds nested in its branches, and fruit and flowers of ruby, sapphire, pearl, and amethyst glowed brightly.

Men in fine clothing, with gold armbands and golden rings, with rich, velvet cloaks and fine leather boots, with ornaments braided in their hair and jeweled collars, filled the golden room. Women with fine dresses of silk and velvet in jewel-toned hues, with delicate veils over bright hair held in place with circlets of fine metals, with brooches at their breasts and gems at their ears and throat, laughed lightly as they turned to the newcomers.

Sigerric swallowed hard, for although he was the son of a noble of the Empire, this place awed him. If he was any judge of his companions, they, too, were awed, though they did their best not to show it.

All, of course, except Havgan. The expression in his eyes was not awe at all. It was, instead, a hunger, a lust to possess what he saw before him. Even more importantly, from the spark in his amber eyes, he had seen the way to do so. Sigerric knew from long experience that nothing would stop his friend from gaining that which he was sure he needed to have. For a moment he could almost feel sorry for the royal family who did not yet know what they had let into their palace.

Trumpets sounded then died away, and the jeweled, me-
chanical birds in the tree began to sing as they followed Aesc,
who made his way through the crowded room to stand at the
foot of the dais covered with cloth of gold. On the wall behind the dais was a tapestry with the King's symbol, the Flyflot,
worked in gold and purple amethysts. Guards lined the dais,
their golden byrnies shining, their axes gleaming, gold ornaments braided in their hair, their faces stern.

The Emperor and his Empress sat on the dais upon golden
thrones. The Emperor's mild, blue eyes gazed down at them.
He was pale and slight, and his scant blond hair hung down
his narrow shoulders. It almost seemed as though the jeweled
diadem he wore was too heavy for his thin neck.

The Empress was quite different from her husband. Empress Athelflead sat with her regal head held high, her light
brown hair elaborately braided and encircled with a golden
crown. Jewels sparkled from her fingers, her ears, and her
throat. Her clear, cold emerald-green eyes rested on Aesc and
his companions, but gave no hint of her thoughts.

On a lower step, another golden chair rested upon which
another woman sat. She rose at their approach and kissed
Aesc's tanned cheek. She had blond hair, the same shade as
Aesc's. Her eyes were clear cornflower blue, and she smiled
at the Prince in welcome. Sigerric guessed that this was Aesthryth, the sister of Aesc and the Emperor, so like was she to her
younger brother.

A man dressed all in black and blood-red rubies stepped
forward to greet Aesc. He wore a golden helmet shaped like a
snarling boar with ruby eyes. He smiled at Aesc and hugged
him, pounding him on the back. His cruel, pale face showed

signs of dissipation, but the smile in his cold, blue eyes was genuine. Sigerric knew that this was Prince Athelric, Aesc's next
oldest brother, the Warleader of the Empire.

And then he looked at the young woman who stood on the
dais between the two golden thrones and his heart was lost in
an instant. Princess Aelfwyn, daughter and only child of the
Emperor and Empress, was only thirteen, but her beauty was
already manifest. Her skin was perfect, pearl-like and glowing.
Her hair, which flowed down her slender, graceful back, was
light blond, like a shimmering river of sun-warmed diamonds.
Her eyes were green and as cool and contained as her mother's,
but Sigerric thought they could be warm, though he did not
dare to think they would ever look with warmth upon him.

He glanced over at Havgan, who was staring up at Aelfwyn
with the hunger still in his eyes. But Sigerric knew he was not
seeing—indeed, would probably never see—the girl herself, but
only what she stood for, only the power that would come to the
hands of the man who became her husband.

"Brother," the Emperor said softly.

Aesc mounted the dais and knelt at Athelred's feet, kissing
his brother's ring. "My Emperor," Aesc answered.

"Glad we are to see you with us again," the Emperor went
on. He glanced at his wife, as though for approval.

At that the Empress rose and went to Aesc, bidding him
rise also. "I echo my husband's joy," she said, but her smile did
not reach her cold eyes, "that you are returned to us, safe and
sound. I have been given to understand that this is due to your
companions."

"It is," Aesc replied as he perfunctorily kissed the Empress's
alabaster cheek. He carelessly reached out a hand and flicked

the cheek of his niece. She smiled back at her uncle and almost giggled, but catching her mother's eye, her smile faded and she formally curtsied to him.

"Let me make my companions known to you—though most of them will already be familiar names," Aesc said to his brother and sister-in-law. "This is Sigerric of Corania, son of the Alder of Apuldre. Baldred of Dere, son of the Eorl of Tarbin. Talorcan of Dere, son of the Eorl of Bernice. Catha of Mierce, brother of the Eorl of Pecsaetan, and Penda of Mierce, son of the Eorl of Lindisfarne."

They each bowed low to the royal family when introduced, and the Emperor nodded his head in acknowledgement.

"And this man is the one to whom I owe the most, for he led the others in my rescue. He laid about him with such fury that, when he was done, all of the bandits lay dead. He killed the leader with sword and spear and deadly grace. His name is Havgan, son of Hengist, and to him, most of all, I owe my life."

Havgan, his golden hair and amber eyes glowing in the bright chamber, produced a graceful bow. Sigerric would always remember that quiet, brief moment when Havgan and the royal family with whom he would become inextricably bound first met. The Emperor smiled kindly, but the Empress studied him carefully, sensing, perhaps, that she had met a formidable player in the game of power. Young Aelfwyn's green eyes widened somewhat as she looked at him in all his raw intensity. Prince Athelric's eyes narrowed, as though he, too, sensed a rival.

But it was Princess Aesthryth whose eyes showed the most surprise when she locked gazes with Havgan. Something, some current, some sense of recognition passed between them, and Aesthryth's blue eyes flickered briefly with fear and astonishment. Sigerric could not be sure, but he thought she sensed, somehow, the latent power in Havgan, that dark thing that even Havgan would not openly acknowledge.

And Sigerric wondered when the dark thing would come out next, and at whom it would strike, as he stood quietly in Gulden Hul, knowing that nothing for the royal family would ever be the same again.

Chapter 4

Athelin, Marc of Ivelas &
Angelesford, Marc of Cantware
Weal of Coran, Coranian Empire
Logmonath, 495

Gewinnan Daeg Eve

Sigerric gratefully breathed in the fresh air of the country-side outside of Athelin. He was glad to be outside the city, weary though he was from the day's strenuous events.

Havgan rode next to him, preoccupied and silent. The fading sunlight brightened his hair into a golden nimbus, but his amber eyes were hooded and still. His hair was still sweaty and tangled from wearing his helmet and fighting beneath the glare of the hot sun. He wore a cloak of ruby-red, clasped at his shoulders with massive, golden brooches. He had a golden armband on his muscular, tanned right arm, and a huge, ruby earring dangled from his left ear.

Havgan had done quite well for himself in the last seven years, having gained much wealth and having formed his own warband, the nucleus made up of his five, longtime friends who rode behind him now, following him blindly as they had done from the beginning.

Indeed, Havgan had done well by all of them, Sigerric thought, as he glanced down at his own rich clothing of tawny amber, and at his companions—Penda in blue and Talorcan in green; Baldred in red and Catha in orange. They all had brooches and armbands of gold and silver, and jeweled helms. Their swords were bright and sharp, the hilts intricately carved and chased with gems. Their horses were strong and bright, and their light canter did not reflect the hard work they had done today in the games.

They had all done well today in the tournament—they had always done well throughout the past seven years. In fact, they had tied at the last with the warband of Ethelwald, the Eorl of Ivelas. Tomorrow Havgan would fight Cenberht, the Eorl's champion. And if Havgan won—as he had won all the tournaments in the past seven years—he would again be crowned the Gewinnan Daeg King. And crowned by the hands of Princess Aelfwyn herself, an honor that Sigerric coveted, and one that Havgan coveted himself, though for different reasons. Sigerric had lost his heart long ago to the Princess of Corania, but Havgan had not, for to him Aelfwyn was merely a final stepping stone to the power he craved.

Just how Havgan thought he would ever be able to marry the princess, Sigerric did not know. For all his wealth and prowess, Havgan was still the son of a fisherman, a man who would never be seen as a fit mate for the heir of the Empire. Yet Sigerric was sure that Havgan had a plan. Exactly what that was, was not yet clear. It would not be clear, Sigerric thought wryly, until Havgan was ready to reveal it, for his friend had always kept his own counsel.

For example, none of them knew, even now, why Havgan

was leading them out of the city. He had only said to come, and they had gone. They would, Sigerric thought, always do just that.

They had passed field after field filled with golden wheat glistening in the sun and groves of trees whose shining green leaves bent and waved in the light breeze. At last Havgan turned his horse off the dusty road and they followed him to a grove of oak trees that loomed silently over a tiny clearing. A small brook splashed through the clearing, the water sparkling like tiny diamonds. Sunlight dappled the forest floor, turning it into a carpet of green and gold.

Following Havgan's lead, they tethered their horses just outside the clearing. Havgan reached into his saddlebags and took out a gleaming dagger, a wineskin, and a small, golden cup chased with rubies.

At Havgan's gesture they formed a circle in the center of the clearing. None of them spoke as they waited for Havgan's next words. Sigerric felt his throat close and his heart beat faster. He wasn't sure what was coming next, but it was something important, he could tell. Something that had a touch of doom to it—but for good or for ill, he wasn't sure. Not then.

At last Havgan spoke. "For many years we have been together," he said softly as he looked at each one of them. "We have been through much. And you must know that we will be through much more. For God himself spoke to me years ago, on Gewinnan Daeg. He commanded me to cleanse Kymru. Everything I have done from that moment has been toward that end."

Havgan fell silent, and Sigerric noticed that the forest itself seemed to hold its breath. No birds nested in the branches above them, no small animals rustled in the undergrowth, even the splashing of the brook seemed hushed.

"In everything I have done, you have been with me. You have been faithful to me and to our God. Momentous things are in store for us all. And so, my brothers—for that is how I feel for you in my heart—you shall truly become my brothers today."

They all stirred at Havgan's words, for now his meaning was clear. He had brought them here to take part in the Brotherhood Ritual, one of the most sacred ceremonies in the Empire. Once having taken part in it, it would be impossible to ever break the ties that were forged. A man who broke faith with his blood brother would be outcast, denied even the simplest necessities, denied even the smallest of rights under the law.

Knowing what Havgan was offering him, knowing even at that moment that he would not refuse, though he had a dim understanding of the fate that awaited him, Sigerric did not move. He felt the dry taste of ashes in his throat. He knew the words he would speak would come with difficulty. But he knew he would say them. He knew. With Havgan, somehow he had not had a choice. Not even, he thought confusedly, in the beginning all those years ago.

The others were taking in this news in their own way. Catha's handsome, cruel face lit up at Havgan's words, and Baldred's dark eyes shone with glee at the offer, his heavy face bright. Those two would blithely take the oath and never think twice.

But Penda swallowed hard. His dark eyes were unreadable, but he did not protest or demur. Talorcan paled considerably, and his green eyes in his too thin face held the look of a man suddenly realizing that he had made a bad bargain long ago, a bargain already regretted but too late to walk away from.

But Havgan was going on, and there was no more time for

thought. "Will you, then, my brothers, truly become my brothers today?"

They all nodded—some hesitantly and some eagerly, but they all gave their consent. In that silence the world felt heavy and still, as though the earth itself sagged beneath the weight of their assent.

At Havgan's gesture they all turned east. Havgan lifted his hands, then spoke in a powerful voice, "O place of air, write our words before the wind." At his words a slight breeze did indeed swoop through the clearing and then was gone.

Without comment, Havgan then faced south. "O place of fire, burn our words in the sun." The sunlight that dappled the clearing glowed brighter, burnished gold on the breast of the earth like precious coins.

"O place of water," Havgan continued, facing west, "write our words upon the sea." And the smell of tangy saltwater, the cry of a gull, the rushing of the surf came faintly to them.

Lastly, Havgan turned to the north. "O place of earth, chisel our words in stone." And they heard the faint sound of tools scraping against rock, hollow and huge, but from a long, long way away.

Havgan bent to the brook and filled the cup with water. He poured the water on the ground and sank his foot into the wet earth, forming a footprint. Sigerric stepped forward first and placed his foot within Havgan's print. Then Catha, then Penda, then Baldred, and lastly, Talorcan set their footprints over Havgan's.

Havgan took the gleaming dagger and sliced his thumb. As the rich, red blood welled up from the wound, he held it over the footprint, dribbling blood into the muddy hollow. Each man then pulled his dagger from his belt and cut his thumb, all of them dripping their own blood on the earth to mingle with Havgan's.

Havgan placed his hand above the bloody ground, and Sigerric placed his palm on top of Havgan's bleeding hand. Then Penda laid his hand over Sigerric's. Catha laid his hand over Penda's, and Baldred laid his over Catha's. Lastly, Talorcan laid his hand on top of Baldred's.

They spoke in unison, their voices mingling in the quiet clearing.

"So long as there is breath in my body,
I pledge true friendship.
So long as there is blood in my veins,
I will shed it in your defense.
So long as you call, I shall answer.
So long as you ride, I shall follow."

Havgan then stepped back and picked up the wineskin. He took a hearty draught, then passed it to Sigerric, who drank and passed it to Penda. One by one they each drank the blood-red wine.

At last they faced east and said solemnly together, "Air has written the words we spoke today. We will keep faith with one another." They turned south. "Fire has written the words we spoke today. We will keep faith with one another." They turned west. "Water has written the words we spoke today. We will keep faith with one another." At last they turned north. "Earth has written the words we spoke today. We will keep faith with one another."

When they were finished, Sigerric could clearly feel the heaviness, the finality of what they had done. Then he heard one other thing. Somewhere, far, far in the distance, he heard the sound of a hunting horn and knew it for what it was.

The Wild Hunt had heard this vow today.

And Havgan's doom, whatever it may be, had come still closer, reaching out to encompass them all.

THEY RETURNED TO the city as dusk was falling. The streets were still crowded with revelers celebrating Gewinnan Daeg Eve. When they passed the open doors of public taverns, bright lights and noise spilled out onto the streets; the sounds of people singing, shouting, drinking, and laughing tangled in doorways and passed out into the night.

As they traveled north up Lindstrat toward Havgan's house, they passed Byrnwiga, the black stone fortress belonging to the Warleader of the Empire. The building loomed ominously. Narrow windows with iron shutters pierced the dark walls at irregular intervals. Torches burned in brackets across the blank face of the building, faintly illuminating the roof that glittered with tiny jet-black stones. Carved boars' heads with ruby eyes sat among the eaves, dangerous and challenging.

The windows glowed with light, and the sounds of men celebrating came clearly to their ears. Prince Athelric seemed to be fully engulfed in his own celebrations, having evidently turned down the invitation to attend his brother's festivities at Cynerice Scima this evening. Not that Sigerric blamed the Prince for that—he understood that celebrations at the Emperor's palace were far too tame for a man of Prince Athelric's jaded tastes. Faintly he thought he heard the sound of women screaming through the noise.

"The Bana is celebrating Gewinnan Daeg Eve, I see,"

Sigerric said to Havgan.

Havgan's lip curled in contempt. "He brings shame on the title of Bana. The Warleader ought to at least be one who is skilled at arms."

"Havgan . . ." Sigerric began, startled by a sudden thought, jolted by the contempt in Havgan's tone.

"Yes?"

"You can't possibly think to be made Bana. Prince Athelric holds that title and will do so until the Emperor declares Aelfwyn's husband-to-be. And that man will be Warleader until he takes the throne at the Emperor's death."

"I am aware of that, Sigerric," Havgan said, his tone amused.

"The only way you could become Warleader is if the Emperor declares an open tournament and you win. And that he would only do if something happened to Athelric. If Prince Athelric dies while the Emperor still lives, the position can only be filled by a tournament."

"Again, I am fully aware of all this," Havgan replied smoothly.

"You can't think to—"

"To what?"

"To harm Prince Athelric?"

"Sigerric, even if I wanted to, how could I do this? He is guarded day and night. I would never be able to harm him."

"But you would, if you could."

Havgan halted his horse and turned to Sigerric. "Put your mind at ease, Sigerric, for surely you know that God himself is with me. Should something happen to Athelric, you could be sure that it was the will of Lytir."

Havgan turned away, leaving Sigerric unable to move from the sickening feeling in his stomach. It was not the first time he wondered if Havgan had confused his own will with the will of God. And it would not be the last.

WHEN HAVGAN RETURNED to his house, he was greeted with the news that he had a visitor. His steward informed him that he had put the man—a Master-wyrce-jaga, no less—to wait in Havgan's private chambers and had seen to it that he was well fed.

"His name?" Havgan asked as he dismounted his horse, giving no hint that the presence of a wyrce-jaga filled him with unnamable fear.

"Sledda of Cantware. He says he is known to you—that he is the nephew of your former lord, Eorl Wiglaf."

"Ah," Havgan said. "Yes, I know of him. Very well, take me to him."

Havgan's three-storied house was richly appointed. The sloping timber roof glittered in the light of the torches that lined the central courtyard. Inside the house, the walls were white-washed and covered with fine tapestries. Costly rugs adorned the smooth, wood floors throughout. At last the steward stood before the door to Havgan's chambers and opened it.

Havgan's room was large and airy. Huge windows set into the north wall looked out over the city that now glittered with firelight and moonlight. A large four-poster bed was set against the west wall and was dressed with a fine wool spread. The highly polished floor was covered with soft rugs of dark blue. A large fireplace and hearth took up the east wall. Tapestries of battle scenes depicted in red and amber and fantastic forests of gold and green studded the walls except for the south wall, which was covered with a huge map of Kymru. A wooden table stood in the middle of the room, with two golden goblets and a flagon chased with rubies resting upon it.

At Havgan's entrance, Sledda rose from the table, setting down his goblet carefully. The wyrce-jaga looked much as Havgan had remembered him from years ago. His tonsured blond hair was, perhaps, a little scantier. His features were sharp, giving him the look of a cunning weasel. His pale, gray eyes were heavily lidded, shutters over the windows of a soul most had no desire to explore further. He wore the customary black robe of the wyrce-jaga. He had a green tabard over the robe, proclaiming him to be a Master-wyrce-jaga now. Havgan's brow rose at that.

Sledda, correctly interpreting Havgan's expression, spoke. "I am the Master-wyrce-jaga of Ivelas."

"A very recent promotion, or I would have heard of it."

"Very recent, indeed. Just this afternoon, in fact."

"Which would explain your presence in Athelin."

"Not entirely."

Sledda looked at the steward who waited in the doorway for Havgan's orders. Havgan dismissed the man, saying that he would call if anything were needed.

"I saw you in the tournament today," Sledda said, as he again sat down at the table. "You and your men fought well."

"My men always fight well."

"Indeed. You are to fight the Eorl's champion tomorrow. I have little doubt that you will win."

"Because you are sure of my prowess?" Havgan asked, a touch of sarcasm in his voice.

"Because I am sure of our God," Sledda answered. He gestured to the map of Kymru. "Because I know the task Lytir has given you. To complete that task, how could you not win tomorrow?"

"'There are many things," Havgan said quietly, "that stand between me and my goal."

"But they do not matter, because our God is with you. You have sworn to cleanse Kymru. And I am here to offer you my aid."

"Your aid. The aid of a Master-wyrce-jaga is surely much. But not enough."

"Yet I bring you more than you think. I bring you the support of all the wyrce-jaga of the Empire."

Havgan's breath caught in his throat. Such aid would be invaluable. "How can I be sure you speak the truth?" Havgan asked cautiously.

"The Arch-wyrce-jaga of Corania himself sent me here tonight."

"And I am to believe that?"

"Believe this, then. That Ethbrand could not come himself, for political reasons. Surely you know that the Eorl of Ivelas, whose champion you will fight tomorrow, is his brother. He could not take a public stand for you in such a contest. So he sends me."

Sledda reached into his robe and withdrew a ruby ring. The ring was large and glittered in the candlelight. Gold flashed in Sledda's palm as he held the ring out to Havgan.

"This is the ring that belonged to Custhorn, the first Master-wyrce-jaga of the Empire. It was he who wrote 'The Secrets of the Heiden' and first set down on paper their filthy rites, he who first proved that the Y Dawnus of Kymru and the Wiccan of Corania were demons, he who was surely a mouthpiece of God."

Slowly Havgan reached out and picked up the ring from Sledda's cold hand. The massive golden setting was carved with tiny flames that seemed to flicker in the uncertain light. The ruby glittered like fresh blood as he put the ring on his finger.

"The wryce-jaga are with you, Havgan son of Hengist. To that end I have been sent here. I will be in your inner circle. I will be the conduit for the wyrce-jaga to you. I will inform them of your needs and desires."

"My men will take long and long to accept you, I think," Havgan warned.

"No matter," Sledda said. "I do not live to be liked."

"It is as well, wyrce-jaga," Havgan said with a wolfish grin, "for you would surely be doomed to disappointment."

"Oh, I almost forgot," Sledda said casually, his eyes gleaming with malice at Havgan's remark. "I do have another message for you."

"From whom?" Havgan asked sharply.

"From the Lady of Apuldre."

"Sigerric's mother?"

"She begs that you and Sigerric will return to Angelesford as soon as possible."

"Why?"

"Your mother, Lord Havgan. Your mother is asking to see you. She will not, apparently, be gainsaid. She comes to Lady Elgiva every day, asking if you have come yet. She insists on seeing you. Lady Elgiva says that your mother cannot be put off any longer. She will likely come to Athelin to look for you unless you go to her."

"Then Sigerric and I will go to Angelesford after the tournament. I have some things to do first, you see."

"Yes," Sledda said coolly. "I do, as you say, see."

AFTER SLEDDA LEFT, Havgan sat on the hearth for a long time, gazing into the dancing, golden flames. In his hands he fingered the kranzlein, the prayer wheel that he used in his prayers to Lytir. The string consisted of beads of seven colors—white, red, orange, yellow, green, blue, and violet—grouped together in seven groups. He spoke to the beads silently in his head as he had been taught by the preosts long ago: *Praise to the Guardian of Heofen; praise to Lytir and his Mind-Plans; praise to him who fashioned every wonder; praise to him who made Heofen as a roof; praise to him who made Middle-Earth for man; praise to the Makar; praise to the Emperor of All.*

Over and over and over he said these words as he stared into the crackling, shining fire. He did not chant with these beads often. For some reason he only felt compelled to use them when wrestling with a specific problem. But when he did use the beads, speak the words over and over in his mind, concentrate on the problem—well, then sometimes things happened. He had come to the conclusion long ago that when he used the beads, Lytir heard his prayers better. He sometimes visualized them as arrows arcing into the roof of the sky, piercing Heofen itself, gaining Lytir's approval and answer.

Over and over he spoke to the beads as he stared at the fire, seeing only the flames, feeling only the heat, thinking only that he must be Warleader of Corania, he must, or else how could the witches of Kymru fall beneath his hand?

Gewinnan Daeg

HE ROSE EARLY, as was his custom. For some reason he felt very tired. He glanced outside, noting that it was going to be another fine day. A good day, he thought, to defeat the Eorl's champion, a good day to once again be crowned Gewinnan

Daeg King. A good day to fasten his hungry gaze on Princess Aelfwyn as she crowned him and watch her haughty face flush beneath the lust she would see in his eyes.

He went to the basin and splashed cold water on his face, willing himself to fully wake, still conscious of a lingering sluggish feeling. It would wear off soon, he was sure. He dressed casually, donning only a robe of red velvet, for he would break his fast before arming.

He opened his door, and as he stepped into the hallway, the guards on either side saluted, hand to heart. He nodded at them and made his way to the great hall as they followed.

Though he had risen early, his men had risen earlier still, as was expected of them. The large trestle tables were filled with food—steaming porridge with mounds of butter melting over the top, platters of sausages and thick, smoky bacon, fresh bread and wheels of yellow cheese, and frothy ale. The fifty members of his warband filled the benches, eating hugely, calling out boisterous remarks to one another. At the head table set on the dais, his closest friends were all there: Catha, Baldred, Penda, Talorcan, and Sigerric. They were all dressed and armed, ready to assist him to don his own armor and weapons once he had eaten.

"Havgan," Sigerric asked as he took his seat, "are you well?"

Havgan yawned and reached for a sausage. "I'm fine. Just a little tired."

"You could carry away treasure in the bags under your eyes," Sigerric said.

"So kind of you to point that out," Havgan said with a grin.

Before Havgan even had the chance to begin his meal, his steward came hurrying into the hall, followed closely by a man dressed in gold, the Emperor's device sewn on his tunic. Havgan's men fell silent as the steward and the messenger made their way to the head table. Havgan rose, nodding at the messenger.

"You are welcome here, sir," Havgan said formally, as custom demanded. "May I offer you food and drink?"

The messenger shook his head. "Lord Havgan, I am commanded to summon you to the palace. At once."

"Only me?" Havgan asked, his amber eyes sharp.

"You may bring with you one of your men."

"Lord Havgan can hardly go unattended," the steward began.

"Do not fear for your lord," the messenger said quietly. "All the lords here in Athelin are summoned to the palace. And all are commanded to restrict their retinue to one."

Knowing further questions would be useless, Havgan merely nodded at the messenger. "I will dress and come at once."

"All arms are to be left here, my lord," the messenger said.

"Of course," Havgan replied smoothly.

As HAVGAN AND Sigerric neared Cynerice Scima, they were all but swallowed up by the huge crowd that had converged on the palace at the same time. Havgan recognized all of the lords, a great many of whom had come to the capital to take part in the tournament.

Besides the lords, he also recognized many other important citizens. Ethbrand, the Arch-wyrce-jaga of Coran was there in a black velvet robe and a taBard of deep blue, attended by Sledda. Sledda nodded at Havgan and Sigerric, but Ethbrand did not acknowledge them beyond a sharp glance to ensure that Havgan was wearing the ruby ring Sledda had given him the night before.

They streamed across the bridge that spanned the River Saefern. The spires of the palace soared delicately, shimmering like fine crystal beneath the clear, blue sky.

At last they came to Gulden Hul. As always, the room shimmered with golden light. But the jeweled birds in the Golden Tree were silent. Guards ringed the empty dais with the two golden thrones. Havgan noticed that the Archpreost himself, Whitgar, was standing at the foot of the dais, resplendent in violet robes. A huge amulet of gold and amethysts hung around his massive neck, representing the tree upon which Lytir had died. Whitgar's massive white beard stopped just short of covering the amulet, and his gray hair was braided into hundreds of tiny braids, all tied off with gold beads.

They all waited in the golden chamber, for the most part silent. The few who did speak did so in whispers, and only briefly. At last they heard the sound of trumpets and the Emperor and Empress entered, ascended the dais, then took their places on the two golden thrones. Princess Aelfwyn, in her customary white and with a spray of diamonds in her blond hair, entered next, flanked by her uncle, Prince Aesc, and her aunt, Princess Aesthryth. The three came to stand between the two thrones.

The faces of the five royal family members were carefully expressionless. But Havgan thought he saw traces of grief in the set of Aesc's mouth, in the tightening of Aesthryth's chin, in the pale blue eyes of the Emperor. He saw no traces of emotion at all in either the Empress or Aelfwyn.

At that moment Princess Aesthryth's cornflower blue eyes scanned the room until she saw Havgan. As the Emperor's sister registered his presence, she quickly looked away. But not before

Havgan had seen something in her eyes. The merest whiff of suspicion, the vaguest hint of—could it have been?—fear. *But why?* Havgan thought, completely at a loss. He had done nothing. Nothing at all.

In the now-silent hall the Emperor spoke. "I bring sorrowful news to you all. Let it be known that last night my brother, Prince Athelric, Warleader of our glorious Empire, died."

A shocked murmur ran through the room. Havgan started as though from an electric shock. Athelric was dead? How could that possibly be?

The Emperor went on. "He was burned to death in his bed."

"But who?" the Eorl of Ivelas called out. "Who could have done such a thing?"

"He was sharing his bed with a woman. A woman who, apparently, had much cause to hate him," Prince Aesc answered.

"It is obvious that she herself must have set fire to the bed after he fell asleep," the Emperor said.

"Must have? She did not confess?" Ethbrand, the Archwyrce-jaga asked.

"She said only that she woke to flames surrounding the bed. Of course, that is not a story to be believed. However, it is not possible to question her further for my brother's guards, in a frenzy of anger, killed her."

"They arrived too late," Prince Aesc said flatly, "to save my brother."

"Why did they arrive so late?" Archpreost Whitgar asked. "Where were they?"

"They were outside Athelric's door, as they should have been," the Emperor said. "But they were held up at the door when it refused to open. At last they had to take their axes to it."

"It was locked?" Whitgar asked.

"It was not. It simply would not open."

Havgan, his thoughts awhirl, barely noticed that Princess Aesthryth had once again found him with her cornflower gaze. His prayer. His prayer from the night before had been answered. Oh, surely Lytir was with him. Surely he was God's champion and God himself had proclaimed it by bringing about Athelric's death.

The Emperor rose then and took his daughter's hand. Aelfwyn, her white skin as pale as marble, raised her head proudly and looked out over the assembly. Her expressionless face did not change as her father continued. "The death of my brother means that the post of Bana is vacant. By law, the post must be opened to all those who wish to enter the contest to win it. The victor will be proclaimed Warleader of the Empire and will marry my daughter, she who is known as Steorra Heofen, the Star of Heaven, beautiful and bright." At this the Emperor's voice broke. Aelfwyn's hands trembled for a brief moment, and her mask seemed to slip slightly, showing the fear that lay beneath.

But the Empress, after shooting a venomous look at her husband, rose and spoke coldly and clearly. "Formal challenges will be heard by the Witan four months from now, during Ermonath. One year from now, the winner of the Gewinnan Daeg tournament will marry Princess Aelfwyn."

At her mother's words, Aelfwyn regained control, standing so still that she seemed like a statue—beautiful and cold, never to be warm again.

Nardaeg, Sol 7—early afternoon
OVER FIVE WEEKS later, Sigerric and Havgan at last arrived at

Sigerric's home in Angelesford. As they passed the cow house and the barn, their horses threading their way through the scurrying chickens, slaves and serfs looked up from their work and waved greetings to Sigerric. When they entered the gate into the courtyard, slaves took their horses as the two men dismounted.

To their right, the door of the weaving room opened, and Lady Elgiva descended the steps, her distaff still in her hand. Sigerric shouted his greeting and then, upon reaching his mother, boisterously picked her up, swinging her around. Between her demands to be let down, she laughed, her silvery-blond hair shining beneath the sun, her dark eyes alight with welcome.

At last Sigerric set her down and she turned to Havgan, her face flushed with joy. She gave him her hand and he kissed it gently. "You are both most welcome here," she said in her rich voice.

"My mother?" Havgan asked anxiously.

"Was here again this morning," Elgiva said gently. "I assured her that you would be along soon."

"Right as always," Sigerric said. "Havgan, do you wish to see her alone?"

"No," Havgan said instantly, before he even thought. He flushed.

"Of course, I'll go with you," Sigerric said swiftly.

"Thank you," Havgan said gratefully, all his arrogance gone.

"Then let us go, for the sooner we go, the sooner we will return," Sigerric said, in an effort to be cheerful. "Father?" he asked Elgiva.

"Out surveying the sowing," Elgiva said. "He will be back for dinner."

"Then I will greet him upon our return," Sigerric said.

"The soonest done, the soonest over," Elgiva said, sympathy in her eyes as she gently laid her hand on Havgan's arm.

He tried to smile at her but could not. He swallowed hard, and without another word, turned and left to make his way through the town.

Sigerric followed silently as they passed houses of wattle and thatch, recently harvested kitchen gardens, chickens scratching for food, small children playing and shouting, and denuded apple trees. Men and women hailed Sigerric, and the children stopped and stared in awe as the two warriors passed.

At last they came to the last house on the outskirts of the town. The dwelling had walls that had once been whitewashed but were now a dirty gray. The thatch was bare in some places, giving the hovel a diseased look. The garden was straggly and unkempt. Two dispirited hens and one rooster rooted for food in the muddy yard. The door was closed, and no sound came from the silent house.

Havgan marched to the door and opened it, Sigerric right behind him. The shutters were closed and the room was dim. A pallet lay against the far wall, covered with a dirty sheepskin. His mother's spinning wheel was in the far corner, beneath a layer of dust. A fire burned feebly in the hearth, doing little to illuminate the room. A pile of rags huddled in the corner near the fire.

Havgan saw his father first, sitting at the rough table in the center of the room, a wooden cup of ale in his large, callused hand. Hengist's once-massive shoulders were bowed as though under some unseen weight. His golden hair had whitened with age. He raised his head at Havgan's entrance, and his dark eyes did not register any pleasure at the sight of his son.

"Why are you here?" Hengist demanded quietly. "Why have you come back?"

"Maeder has been asking for me," Havgan replied, just as quietly. "Where is she?"

The pile of what Havgan had taken to be rags suddenly moved. Havgan's mother rose, tottering toward him. She was thin almost to the point of emaciation. Her scant gray hair hung lank around her bony shoulders. Her pale, gray eyes in her strangely unlined face were alight as she reached out to him.

"My gift from the sea," she said in her lilting, singsong voice. "My son."

He gently took her in his arms and hugged her, careful not to squeeze too hard. "Maeder," he said softly. "I have come."

"Why did you send for him?" Hengist asked his wife harshly.

Hildegyth did not answer her husband. She looked up at Havgan and said, very simply, "Come home, my son."

"I cannot do that, Maeder," he said as gently as he could. "God has called me."

"To kill witches," Hengist rasped with a ghastly smile on his face.

"Yes," Havgan said evenly. "To kill the witches of Kymru."

"I know a witch who needs killing," Hengist said, the grin still on his lined face.

Havgan's mother stiffened, but still did not address her husband. "My son, I beg you. Come home. Do not pursue the witches of Kymru. Do not go over the sea."

"Why not?" Havgan asked.

"The sea gave you to me. It may take you back again."

"I don't understand—" Havgan began.

"Really?" Hengist broke in. "Oh, I think you do."

The room fell silent as Havgan and Hengist confronted each other. Hengist rose to his feet to face Havgan, his face set and bitter. Havgan stood silently, his red cloak glowing like blood, his golden armbands shimmering like fire, his amber eyes bright.

"Faeder," Havgan began.

"Do not call me that, boy," Hengist said bitterly. "Never call me that."

Suddenly Havgan could not stand another moment in that house. He turned blindly and Sigerric was there, Sigerric who was always there when Havgan needed him. "Get me away from here," Havgan whispered, pleading.

And Sigerric did. He quietly told Hengist and Hildegyth that they would return the next day, saying that the journey had been long and they were tired. He swept Havgan from the house without waiting for any response.

They did not speak as they made their way back to Sigerric's father's house. But the sky began to darken. A storm was brewing in the west, in the direction of the sea. The merest whiff of tangy salt air reached their nostrils as they at last returned to the courtyard. Overhead, clouds were piling up swiftly, purple and swollen. Lightning laced the western horizon, reaching for the earth with bony fingers.

Soon after they reached Sigerric's family home, his father and his men returned from supervising the sowing of wheat and rye. Havgan watched enviously as the Alder greeted his son, as he had watched enviously earlier when Lady Elgiva had welcomed them. He wished bitterly, as he always had, that Lord Sigefrith and Lady Elgiva had been his own mother and father. But his mother was a madwoman. And his father hated him, though he had never known why. And that would not change, ever.

LATE THAT NIGHT he sat before the hearth in the room he shared with Sigerric. Sigerric was asleep on his pallet, his face serene and peaceful.

How he envied Sigerric that peace. He always would. He stared thoughtfully into the flames, fingering the kranzlein in his hands.

Praise to the Guardian of Heofen; praise to Lytir and his Mind-Plans; praise to him who fashioned every wonder; praise to him who made Heofen as a roof; praise to him who made Middle-Earth for man; praise to the Makar; praise to the Emperor of All.

What had his father meant today? Who was the witch Hengist had been talking about?

Praise to the Guardian of Heofen; praise to Lytir and his Mind-Plans; praise to him who fashioned every wonder; praise to him who made Heofen as a roof; praise to him who made Middle-Earth for man; praise to the Makar; praise to the Emperor of All.

Why had his father never loved him? Why did his father hate him so? Why had he taken his hatred, so bright and hard, formed a blade of it this afternoon, and thrust it deep into Havgan's heart?

Praise to the Guardian of Heofen; praise to Lytir and his Mind-Plans; praise to him who fashioned every wonder; praise to him who made Heofen as a roof; praise to him who made Middle-Earth for man; praise to the Makar; praise to the Emperor of All.

His father would surely be better off dead. What good was a life that was so bitter? And, again, what had his father meant about the witches?

Praise to the Guardian of Heofen; praise to Lytir and his Mind-

Plans; praise to him who fashioned every wonder; praise to him who made
Heofen as a roof; praise to him who made Middle-Earth for man; praise to
the Makar; praise to the Emperor of All.

The flames began to fade before his eyes, the walls of the
room dissolving.

His father would be better off dead.

Much better.

Soldaeg, Sol 8—morning

THE NEXT MORNING dawned bright and clear. The rain had
stopped sometime during the night, and the clouds had dissi-
pated. Havgan woke to find Sigerric gone and the sun shining
through the window. He dressed hurriedly despite his fatigue
and sluggishness.

He entered the hall, threading his way around the full tables to the dais. He bowed to Lord Sigefrith and Lady Elgiva.
With a rueful smile, he told them he had overslept and would
take any punishment they cared to give him.

But neither of them laughed. Sigerric rose and came around
the table to him, his eyes dark and sad.

"What?" Havgan began, knowing now that something was
horribly wrong. "What's the matter?"

Sigerric looked to his mother. Very gently she spoke. "Havgan, I am sorry to say this, but there has been an accident."

"An accident?" he repeated, his throat dry.

"Lightning struck your house last night," she said softly.

"My maeder?" he asked fearfully.

"Is safe."

"Faeder?"

"Was not so lucky. I am sorry, Havgan. He is dead."

Havgan said nothing at first. He stared in front of him, but saw nothing. His father. His father was dead. Again God had answered his prayers. His way was clear again to move forward, unencumbered by old hatreds.

"Maeder needs to be taken care of. I will pay well for her keep," Havgan said to Lady Elgiva.

"She will be well treated."

"And watched closely," Havgan said haltingly, not liking even now to refer to his mother's strangeness, even though he must.

"Of course," Lady Elgiva replied softly.

"Tell her," Havgan rasped, "tell her that I will send for her—soon."

"I will," Lady Elgiva replied, knowing that he would not.

For he would not. It would be impossible. It was better to have her here, well-looked-after and kept in close confinement. What might she do or say if she were let out? She would ruin everything if she could. But she was his mother. And she had survived the fire last night. He would bow to the will of Lytir and leave her alive.

For now.

Chapter 5

Meirgdydd, Lleihau Wythnos—late afternoon

Gwydion returned to Caer Dathyl as the shadows were taking hold, creeping over the lonely mountain of Mynydd Addien like dark talons searching for a fresh grip on its prey. The stones of the Dreamer's fortress glistened in the light of the setting sun, slowly turning from fiery orange to shadowy gray as he made his final ascent.

He dismounted at the bottom of the steps that led to the massive doors. The doors glittered golden in the sudden fire-light as the torches that lined the walls burst into flame. On the left door, the sign for the rowan tree shimmered, outlined in fiery opals. On the right door, the opals that outlined the constellation of Mabon of the Sun flickered slyly, as though they had a secret they refused to tell.

The doors opened, and one of the servants hurried to take his horse. Gwydion nodded at the man and handed him the reins, silently thanking the horse for the smooth journey. He ascended the steps and entered the silent fortress.

His footsteps echoed on the flagstone floor as he made his way down the central hall and out into the courtyard. To his right, the grove of rowan trees blazed in autumnal splendor, with clusters of red berries hanging brightly among the crimson leaves. He crossed the courtyard swiftly, refusing to even glance past the grove to the place where the tomb of the Dreamers rested.

Which was foolish. Because whether or not he could see the tomb, he was always thinking of the one whom they had laid in it not long ago. Indeed, he thought about Amatheon so much that his heart was sick with it. He thought about how much he missed his little brother, he thought about his brother's blue eyes and ready smile, he thought about his brother's laughter, and he thought about how he would never hear that sound again on this earth.

But most of all, he thought about his brother's killer. Not the man who had done the actual deed—for that man was long dead. No, Gwydion thought instead about the unknown person ultimately responsible for Amatheon's death. About how one day he would find out who had ordered this terrible thing, and he would see to it that the person—man or woman—died horribly, in the greatest agony Gwydion could devise. And he could devise a great deal of it. He certainly thought about it enough.

Dinaswyn stood in the archway that led from the courtyard to the Dreamer's Tower. She wore a plain gown of black, and her long, silvery hair was tightly braided away from her hawk-like face. Her keen gray eyes were hooded as she silently handed him a goblet of gold chased with rubies.

Gwydion drank the rich, red wine, then handed the cup back to his aunt and waited for her to say what she wanted to say.

"The celebrations?" she asked.

"Were fine," he replied.

"And who put the arrow through the apple?"

"Uthyr, of course," Gwydion said coolly, but with a hint of satisfaction.

"You are sorry you went," Dinaswyn said.

"I went because Uthyr begged me. I was not sorry to see him."

"Nonetheless."

"You should have come with me," he said quietly. "You shouldn't have spent the festival alone."

"You went. And yet you still felt alone. What does it matter where I go? Better to stay away than to burden others with my grief." Before he could answer, she looked at him closely. "You have the look," she said.

"Yes. It came on me today. I can feel it coming."

"A dream. And an important one, if I read the signs right."

"You do."

"Then go to your chambers. Wash off the dust of your journey, and I will send some hot food up to you. Then, you sleep."

"Yes," he replied. He knew better than to say thank you.

GWYDION FINISHED THE last of his meal and pushed the tray away. It was time to sleep, time to dream. He didn't know exactly what awaited him, but he knew it was important. All day he had felt distracted, and a headache had been settled above his eyes since he had awakened that morning.

It had been there when he rode through Dinas Emrys, the tiny village where Myrrdin guarded young Arthur. He had not seen Arthur; undoubtedly the boy was up on the mountain tending the sheep. But he had seen Myrrdin. He had not dared to speak a word, not even to Wind-Speak. But he had seen Myrrdin's keen glance, and he had turned from it, wishing with all his heart that he could speak to his uncle, wishing suddenly that he could ask for the comfort he so desperately needed.

But he could not, even for a moment, forget that secrecy was paramount to Arthur's safety. He could not, even for an instant, forget that even the smallest contact could lead to disaster. So he had kept going, noting only that Myrrdin seemed hale and hearty and taking what comfort he could from that.

Now in his study, sitting before the shifting firelight on the hearth, he sighed. His thoughts seemed to run in circles these days. If he was not thinking about Amatheon, he was thinking of the task the gods had given him long ago—to guard Arthur's life against the day when a High King would be needed by Kymru. For something was coming, some threat for which a Warleader who could wield the combined strength of the Y Dawnus would be necessary. What that threat was, he still did not know.

If he was not thinking of Amatheon, he was thinking of Arthur. And if he was not thinking about either of them, he was thinking of Rhiannon ur Heyfeydd and of how much he longed to see her. Which was why he did not even dare to seriously think of doing so. Sometimes the desire to go to her, to tell her he was sorry for his accusations, to explain that he had been speaking from his own pain, and that his despair was so great he could barely stand against it.

But he always resisted, for he knew better than to see her again. She was dangerous. Dangerous because he did care for her, much as he wished he did not. Dangerous because she was a woman, and women always stood between a man and his duty. It was their nature. How quickly he could lose himself in her emerald eyes and never find his way out again. And then what would happen to Kymru? What would happen if Gwydion wasn't free to do whatever necessary to ensure that Arthur ascended the throne of the High King?

It was not to be thought of. Not to be seriously contemplated. Not to be. Not ever. He must accept that.

He mounted the stairs to his sleeping chamber. As he entered the round, darkened room, he gestured and tongues of fire sprang up in the brazier. The waning crescent moon had not yet risen, and only pale starlight shone through the clear, glass roof. Starlight and firelight fitfully illuminated the jewels set around the four, round windows: sapphires for Taran of the Winds and emeralds for Modron the Mother; pearls for Nantsovelta of the Waters and opals for Mabon of the Sun. The floor glittered with onyx and bloodstone for Annwyn, Lord of Chaos, and his mate, Aertan the Weaver.

He shed his robe and lay down on the pallet, staring up at the starry sky. He said the Dreamer's Prayer out loud, carefully, sure that tonight a dream was at hand.

"Annwyn with me laying down, Aertan with me sleeping.
The white flame of Nantsovelta in my soul,
The mantle of Modron about my shoulders,
The protection of Taran over me, taking my hand,
And in my heart, the fire of Mabon.
If malice should threaten my life,
Then the Shining Ones between me and evil.
From tonight till a year from tonight,
And this very night,

And forever,
And for eternity.
Awen."

He slept. And, after at time, he dreamed.

IT BEGAN AT sunrise. He was a raven, black as night, with ruby eyes. He stretched his wings and shot up into the sky, leaving Caer Dathyl far behind. He flew over Kymru, the wind rushing beneath his black wings, drinking in the beauty of his beloved land.

He flew over Gwynedd in the north, the air crisp and cool beneath his dark wings. The dusky spires of the jagged mountains rose up, piercing the sky, as dark sapphire gave way to pale rose-gold, night giving way to the dawn. The wind blew fresh and clear, rushing by him as he parted it with his wings, diving and cavorting, twisting and whirling in the rosy morning sky.

HE SAILED ACROSS the sky to the east, to Ederynion. The silvery-blue glitter of the lakes and streams that crisscrossed the land in swirling, tangling ribbons delighted him. Clean, white sand shimmered like tiny pearls, swirling and eddying beneath the rise and fall of the sea.

He soared over Rheged in the south. Here the endless fields of wheat shimmered like flaxen fire in the morning sun. Rubyred roses climbed the hillsides, twining around the beehives that dotted the land like tiny fortresses in whose fastness the bees held their rich, golden treasure.

Then he circled west to Prydyn, the land of dark green forests, of gently rolling hills, of rich, dark soil. Here the vineyards grew in profusion, and the rich, purple grapes glistened, hanging heavily on the emerald vines, swaying as though impatient to be changed into delicate, fine wine.

Then he flew to Gwytheryn, the jewel in the center of the island, the land that housed the Druids, the Bards, and the Dewin of Kymru. The vast meadows were dotted with wildflowers. The cool sapphire-blue of light and airy delphiniums and cornflowers, the glistening pearl-white of alyssum and daisies, the red ruby of twining rockrose and fiery yellow globe flowers, the emerald green of the rich meadow grass, hurled a riot of colors up to his wondering gaze.

The dusky walls of Caer Duir, where the Druids lived, the white gleam of Y Ty Dewin, and the cool blue of Neuadd Gorsedd, where the Bards spun their melodies, all glowed richly in the golden light of day. He rode the wind to Cadair Idris, the mountain fortress of the High King, standing alone and deserted on the plains. The closed, bejeweled doors flashed a medley of colors in the bright morning.

He laughed soundlessly, joyously with the freedom of flight, with the timeless beauty of his home.

And then he saw it.

There, to the east in Ederynion was a dark stain, spreading over the shores just outside of the Queen's city of Dinmael. Swifter than the wind, faster than thought, he flew closer. The stain was a herd of hideous boars. Their wicked tusks gleamed, and their pig-like eyes shone blood red. There were thousands of them, and they swarmed up the cliffs and in through the city gates, making for Caer Dwfr, the shining crystal palace in the heart of Dinmael. Gwydion cried his raven's cry, but there was no answer from the silent city.

Then, suddenly, a flight of white swans descended, arrowing down from the clear sky, viciously attacking the boars. But they were too few. Valiantly hurling themselves to their deaths, the swans were impaled on cruel tusks, their broken bodies trampled into the dirt, and the streets of Dinmael began to fill with a river of blood.

But the largest, the proudest, the most beautiful swan, gleaming in the morning light like the full, silver moon, flew low over the herd, hissing, darting in and out, wounding boar after boar until her head and long, slender neck was covered with dark boar's blood. And with the sudden, earth-shattering terror of a dream, two arms covered with boars' bristles shot out of the herd, up into the air, plucking the swan from the sky and dragging her down to be trampled in the maelstrom of blood and death. A triumphant squeal from the hideous herd informed Gwydion that the swan was no more.

In loathing, Gwydion tore himself from the scene of battle and raced south to Rheged. Perhaps there was time to rouse help for beleaguered Ederynion. But as he neared the King's city of Llwynarth, he saw he was already too late. The cancerous stain of boars had already blotted out the shining wheat fields, the stalks trampled and broken.

Then, streaming out from the city, he saw flame-colored horses, challenging the boars to what Gwydion knew was a hopeless fight. Boars rushed to the proud, desperate animals, knocking them to the ground, tearing them apart, until so much blood flowed it seemed to Gwydion that the land was weeping red fire.

The lead stallion neighed fiercely, rearing up onto his hind legs and plunging into the midst of the enemy, followed closely by a fiery mare. Out of the boar's herd, ropes flew, catching the two horses around their necks and legs until they were bound tightly. Still they continued to struggle defiantly, screaming challenges even as the boars ripped out their throats with their razor-sharp tusks. And with the death of the stallion and the mare, the broken fields burst into flame. Mercifully, the smoke covered the land from Gwydion's horrified gaze.

He turned west to Prydyn, already knowing what he would see. As he came to the capital city of Arberth, he saw more of the filthy beasts crawling over the cliffs and into the beleaguered city. And there the wolves that streamed out from the King's fortress of Caer Tir met the boars with a titanic crash.

Slathering and snarling, the huge gray animals with emerald eyes fell on the boars, almost, for one instant, driving them back. But slowly, as more and more boars crawled up from the shore, the wolves began to fall back. Hemmed in tighter and tighter, they were slaughtered by the hundreds. And then the mightiest wolf, its muzzle covered with blood, threw back his head and gave a howl that shook Arberth to its foundations, then it leapt into the fray with its last strength. When the wolf went down under the boar's hooves, Gwydion could bear to watch no longer.

He raced north to Gwynedd, his heart like lead in his breast, racing to the land he called his home, to the land where his brother was King. And there, he saw the hawks of Gwynedd, arrayed in the crystal-clear sky, screaming defiance as the dark stain of boars spread over the land, crawling around the broken walls of Tegeingl. As the hawks plunged through the sky at the enemy, Gwydion saw their leader fold his wings as he swooped down for the kill. And, tears in his raven eyes, he watched as spears shot from the mass of boars into the sky, catching the leader in the heart and felling the hawks by the hundreds. As the birds plummeted to the earth, dropping like stones from the sky, Gwydion's eyes followed the lead hawk, watching as its body slammed into the earth and the blood burst forth, piercing his heart like shards of glass.

Streaking through the air, he made for Gwytheryn, the center, the heart of Kymru. Surely the boars would not dare to go there. But they had. Already he saw that they had overrun Neuadd Gorsedd, the once-fair home of the Bards. Slender, jeweled harps with gold and silver strings were trampled under the boars' hooves, and the broken bodies of nightingales littered the ground. And then he saw the hideous arms again dart out from the black mass as they grabbed a soaring nightingale with feathers of the darkest blue, the largest and finest bird Gwydion had ever seen. Even as the bird was pulled from the sky, it was singing. Even when the bristled arms pulled off the bird's wings, and the blood streamed from its mangled body, the nightingale still sang, until death silenced its beautiful song.

Gwydion flew over Y Ty Dewin and saw silver dragons impaled on spears. Some were trying to fly, but they were caught and pinned to the blood-soaked ground with gleaming spikes of dark iron. The largest, most beautiful of the proud dragons struggled on the broken steps, his wings outspread, screaming defiance as he was pulled down to the bloody earth and butchered.

He saw the leader of the doomed bulls from Caer Duir, the home of the Druids, trot out to meet the invaders, the herd following behind. A few bulls charged the boars, heads lowered, their deadly horns gleaming like ivory, but they were trampled and gored to death for their pains.

Then, with a suddenness that made him dizzy, the scene changed. He found himself hurling across the sky to Cadair Idris, the deserted mountain palace of the High King. It was the one place he knew the boars could not defile, for the Guardian of the Doors was not human and could not be destroyed. Only for the High King would the doors to the mountain open.

As Gwydion neared Cadair Idris, he saw row after row of boars gathered in front of the doors. And as he flew through their ranks, a silver dragon materialized by his side, its wings beating in time to his own.

They flew over the boars' heads and dropped down in front of the massive doors, confronting the enemy. Yes, Drwys Idris still stood, barring entry into the High King's mountain. The Doors gleamed in the sun with the rich jewel-studded patterns of the gods and goddesses of Kymru. The verdant emeralds of Modron the Mother; the luminous pearls of Nantsovelta of the Moon; the fiery opals of Mabon of the Sun; the cobalt sapphires of Taran, Lord of the Air, all blazed with an inner fire. The onyx of Annwyn, Lord of Chaos, gleamed darkly, and the red rubies of Y Rhelfywr, the Warrior Twins, glistened like blood. The flecked bloodstone of Aertan, Weaver of Fate; the diamonds of Sirona's Net; the dark garnet of Grannos, the Northern Star, all caught the sun and glittered, throwing splinters of light into the red eyes of the herd.

But most of all, the amethyst of Cerridwen, the White Lady, and the topaz of Cerrunnos, the Horned One, blazed with unmatched triumph and grace. The signs of the Protectors glittered, as high in the sky, an eagle screamed defiance. At the sight of the eagle, the boars shrank back, afraid to venture farther.

For a moment, all was still, as though Kymru herself held her breath. Then the ranks of the boars parted, and a pure golden boar with amber eyes, razor-sharp tusks, and hooves polished to a deadly sheen made its way to the shining doors. The eagle plummeted down in front of the doors, landing between the black raven and the silver dragon. For a moment the golden boar and the eagle stood face to face. The boar lowered his massive head to charge. The eagle gave a mighty scream, but Gwydion knew that it could not hope to withstand the force of the boar's charge. But the amethyst of Cerridwen and the topaz of Cerrunnos glowed brighter still as the eagle launched itself over the head of the golden boar and into the herd, plucking out the eye of a huge, black boar. The eye clutched in its sharp talons, the eagle screamed in triumph and took to the air, circling the mountain. As it circled, Gwydion saw that it wore the torque of the High King around its slender neck. The necklace flashed emerald, pearl, opal, and sapphire, and then the young bird was gone, a mere speck in the sky.

The golden boar, cheated of its prey, threw back its hideous head and screamed.

GWYDION AWOKE WITH the sound of his own screams echoing in his ears.

Dinaswyn was bending over him, shaking him awake, her silvery hair streaming down her nightrobe of dark red. When she saw that he was awake, she sat back on her heels, waiting for him to regain control.

He sat up, his body bathed in sweat, his dark hair tangling in his short silver-tinged black beard. Overhead the crescent moon rode the sky, and moonlight streamed through the roof and pooled on the floor next to his pallet.

Silently Dinaswyn handed him a cup of wine and he drank, taking deep breaths, trying to get his shudders under control. At last he looked up.

"It was bad," she said quietly.

"Very."

She crossed the room and sat before the low writing desk. She opened the Book of Dreams that lay on the table, picked up a quill, and, dipping it into the inkwell, signaled that she was ready.

And so Gwydion told it. He told it, suppressing any hint of emotion—even at the part where the hawk that led the armies of Gwynedd met its death. At last he told it all and fell silent.

"Interpretation?" she asked crisply, her pen poised.

He turned to look at her, to scream at her for her business-like tone in the face of this horror, to make her understand what he had seen. But he saw the shock, the terror in her eyes, and knew she understood only too well.

"The boar is the symbol for the Warleader of the Coranian Empire," he began, his voice steady. "They will be coming for us someday. Someday soon. And they will defeat us."

"Yes," Dinaswyn said, writing slowly. "They will. Now, the swans."

"The swans are the armies of Ederynion. Their leader was Queen Olwen. She is killed, and her country is taken." He said it softly, with regret, for, though Olwen was no longer his friend, she had once been his lover, and he had never wished her ill.

"Go on," Dinaswyn said, jarring him from his private thoughts.

"The horses are the armies of Rheged. The stallion and the

mare are King Urien and Queen Ellirri. They, too, are killed." He forced the words out, for he felt as though his throat was lined with ashes. He and Ellirri had played together as children. And she had always made him feel welcome in Rheged. Some of his happiest times were times spent there with her husband and children.

Before Dinaswyn could prompt him again, he went on, swallowing past the tears locked in his throat. "The wolves are the armies of Prydyn, led by King Rhoram. He went down beneath their hooves, but I did not see him die."

"The hawks," Dinaswyn said implacably.

"Don't you know?" he asked bitterly.

"The hawks," she repeated, her voice cool and her face expressionless. But her eyes told him again that she knew.

"The hawks are the armies of Gwynedd, led by Uthyr. He . . . dies." This last was a mere whisper as Gwydion spoke the name of his beloved half-brother. "I saw him fall to the earth." Gwydion dropped his face into his hands in despair. The only brother he had left was to be taken from him. Must he lose everything? And for what purpose? For the amusement of the Shining Ones?

"Now for Gwytheryn," Dinaswyn went on relentlessly.

Gwydion lifted his head, blinking back tears, and forced himself to go on. "The nightingales—the Bards—are overrun. And they killed the Master Bard. They tore off his wings, and they enjoyed doing it. It almost sounded as if they were laughing." Though Gwydion did not completely trust the Master Bard, he was aware of a pang at the thought of Anieron's death in such a manner.

He went on. "The silver dragons are the Dewin. Many are

killed. The largest one, the Ardewin, is murdered." He halted, for the Ardewin, his uncle, Cynan, had always been kind to him.

"The bulls," Dinaswyn prompted, her pen racing across the page.

"I could not see all of it," Gwydion said tightly. "They were just starting to be slaughtered when the scene changed."

"So you don't know what happened to Cathbad?"

"I am not even sure he was still alive—I did not see a bull that was big enough to be the Archdruid." He hated to think of Cathbad dead—either before or during the invasion, but it was a distinct possibility.

"Who was the dragon that flew with you?" Dinaswyn asked abruptly, jarring him from that thought.

"I don't know. A female, I think. And a Dewin, obviously."

"Of the House of Llyr?" she pressed.

"Perhaps."

"Arianrod?"

Gwydion snorted at the thought of his beautiful, selfish cousin. "Unlikely."

"Rhiannon ur Hefeydd?"

That made Gwydion very thoughtful indeed. It could have been Rhiannon. And if so, he would indeed see her again. Was there no end, then, to the cruelty of the Shining Ones?

"Possibly," he said slowly.

She closed the Book of Dreams and put down the quill. She sat quietly for a moment, her eyes on the moon that rode the sky overhead. At last she rose and went to the door. But there she paused and looked back at him.

"The dreams are not easy. They never have been. They never will be. And what is coming is a horror like nothing we have ever known. I remind you, then, of your promise to me. Do you remember it?"

"I do," he said steadily. And he did. She had demanded that when the time came, he was to give her an important task, to stop pushing her aside, to make her life—and her death— mean something. He had promised to give her a task, but he had said he would not let it lead to her death. He loved her as much as he was able to love, she who was his aunt, she who had been his teacher.

"See that you keep it," she said coldly.

"Yes," he said. It was all he could say.

Then she was gone, leaving Gwydion to begin his long grieving for the coming death of another brother and the en- slavement of Kymru.

Gwyntdydd, Lleihau Wythnos—early evening

ALL DAY GWYDION had kept to his tower. When Dinaswyn sent up food, he refused it, not even bothering to answer the knock on his study door.

He took no action, for there was nothing he could do. No matter what he did, no matter what he said or where he went, what he had dreamed would come true. All the twisting and turning and evasion he could muster would change nothing.

Uthyr would die. Kymru would be crushed. Nothing could prevent that.

Only two things gave him the slightest bit of hope. The first was the memory of the eagle, the symbol of the High King. The eagle had flown free in his dream, borne away on the wings of the wind.

The second was the memory of the silver dragon that had

stood with him, confronting the boars. He did not know who that was—or, at any rate, he pretended that he was not sure. But the mere fact that he would not be alone was comforting.

Night once again fell over Caer Dathyl. Again he heard a knock on the door, but he did not even stir from his seat before the crackling fire. The firelight played over the silvery globes hanging from the ceiling, the rich bindings of the books that lined the walls, and the glowing silver symbols of the moon's phases carved on the door.

"Gwydion," Dinaswyn called through the closed door. "Let me in."

He did not bother to answer. He reached out with his mind and ensured that the door would not open. He had no wish to speak to anyone. He wanted to be left alone.

But Dinaswyn would not take silence for an answer. The door crashed open, slamming up against the wall. He jumped to his feet and whirled around to face her.

But the angry words he was going to say died on his lips when he saw what was in her arms and realized what she had come for.

She entered the room, her silvery hair falling around her shoulders, bright against her black gown. Her gray eyes were cold and implacable. And in her arms she held a bundle of green wood.

"You need to know," was all she said.

And she was right, he did.

GWYDION FIRMLY SHUT the door of the Chamber of Dreams behind him. He carefully laid the green wood within the brazier next to his pallet. Overhead the stars were shining through the glass roof, cold and clear and impossibly far away.

Dinaswyn was right. He did need to know. He needed to know all he could about the enemy. He needed to know just who the golden boar was, the man who would lead the armies of Corania. He needed to know what he could do to mitigate the destruction. Surely there must be something. Surely the Shining Ones would give him that much.

To know this thing, he must dream. He must search for a specific dream, a specific message from the gods. And to do so he would have to invite such a message.

Thus, he would have to undergo the mwg-breuddwyd, the smoke-dream. And hope that it would show him that which he needed to know.

He called fire to the wood in the brazier. The green wood began to smolder, and the room began to fill with smoke.

He lay down on the pallet, his hands beneath his head, filling his lungs with the wood-smoke. Usually the Y Dawnus endured the mwg-breuddwyd for as long as three days, but he did not think it would take that long to find out what he needed to know.

He felt the messages waiting for him. He felt the presence of the Shining Ones. He felt that there were things in the billowing smoke that flickered and danced and waited for him.

He felt ready to Walk-Between-the-Worlds.

He closed his eyes.

HE WAS STANDING on the surface of a huge map that floated in some unidentifiable point in space. Stars glittered like diamonds all around him. Comets rushed by, spraying him with fiery drops. Planets spun around him in their measured, uncaring dance.

117

Beneath his feet the country of Kymru stretched out before him. The fine, white sands and clear blue lakes of Ederynion glittered. The golden wheat fields and beehives of Rheged glowed. The green forests and purple vineyards of Prydyn gleamed. The craggy mountains and aeries of Gwynedd shimmered. And from the center rose the deserted hall of the High Kings, Cadair Idris. It was dark and silent, but it stood alert and ready.

The wide, blue ocean sprawled between Kymru and the Empire of Corania to the east. But it was obvious that the expanse of water was not sufficient to protect Kymru.

For a man stood like a beam of shining light, a map of the Coranian Empire beneath his feet. His golden hair glowed, and his cloak of red shone like fresh blood. In his hands he held threads of light, threads that stretched across the Coranian Empire, which he gathered one by one. With these threads he spun shapes that Gwydion was too far away to see. At that moment Gwydion understood he must know exactly what the man was doing if he was to save anything of Kymru, anything at all.

As the man gathered these threads, as he spun them into unknown shapes, he never once took his eyes off of Gwydion, who stood in faroff Kymru, fierce hatred in his amber eyes.

And something else. A longing. A hunger. A terrible, terrible need—all the more terrible for not being fully understood.

With a chill Gywdion realized that he had seen the man before. It was in a dream, a dream of crossroads, a dream from nine years ago. In that dream the Golden Man had, by his choice at the crossroads, led them all down a dark path to destruction and death.

Gwydion knew that he must go to the Coranian Empire, must somehow gain access to this Golden Man, must somehow learn what the shapes were that were being made. But every time he tried to move, he found that he could not. There were fetters of silver around his ankles, chaining him to the land. He was trapped, unable to leave Kymru. He searched around wildly for the key to his chains, but saw nothing. He desperately pulled at his bonds, but he could not get free.

And then the cry of a dragon made him look up to the sky.

She came to him, glittering with silver light as though she carried the beams of the moon in her blood. She had emerald eyes.

And a key in her talons.

And he knew who she was. And he knew that she was the key—indeed, she had always been.

He knew that he must go to her. Together they would journey to Corania and see what kind of victory they would be able to wrest from the Golden Man, who carried the desire for their death in his tawny eyes.

Chapter 6

Coed Aderyn, Kingdom of Prydyn &
Cadair Idris, Gwytheryn, Kymru
Collen Mis, 495

Gwaithdydd, Disglair Wythnos—late morning

She sat on the cold, stone floor before the ash-covered hearth, wrapped in a tattered blanket. She shivered, for in spite of the sunlight that streamed into the mouth of the cave, she was cold. It seemed that she was always cold these days. She knew that she should light a fire to take the chill out of the air, but she was too tired. It didn't seem worth the effort. She would do it later.

There were so many things to do. And she would do them. But not now. Later.

She should be hunting in the forest for deer and rabbits. She should be smoking meat for the winter, to carry her through the days when hunting would be scarce. She should be curing animal skins so she would have something to trade in Dillys for the supplies she needed. She should be harvesting herbs and drying them to use for both cooking and medicine. She should be doing any one of a hundred things to make sure that she would survive the coming winter months in her cave deep in the forest of Coed Aderyn.

And yet she did none of them. But she would. Later.

How long had it been since that horrible day on Afalon? How long since the day that Amatheon had died; the day that she saw something die inside of Gwydion? With an effort she concentrated and realized it had been a little less than a year. Just a year since she, Gwydion, Amatheon, and the four Captains of Kymru had located Caladfwlch, the sword of the High Kings, on the forbidding Isle of Afalon. Just a year since Amatheon had been murdered while saving Gwydion's life. Just a year since Gwydion had turned on her, accusing her of being responsible for his death, turning his back on her and walking away.

Just a year since her life had turned to dust and ashes.

Not that what had happened on Afalon had anything to do with that. It was what happened later that changed everything.

She had grieved deeply for Amatheon, for she had loved him as a dear friend, and the fact that she would not hear his laughter, nor see the light in his blue eyes again, had brought her great pain. And she had grieved for the Captain of Ederynion, for Angharad had been in love with Amatheon. She had shrugged her shoulders over Gwydion's accusations. She would show no one the pain that had caused her, for there had been something between she and Gwydion, although she still could not have fully identified exactly what it had been. Whatever it was, its loss was not enough to hurt her deeply, for she had known from the beginning that he was a dangerous man and had guarded her heart.

So she had turned her back on him to return to Prydyn, to journey to Arberth in the company of Achren, Prydyn's

Captain, her dearest friend. She had ridden to Arberth with a hopeful heart. Her daughter, Gwenhwyfar, was in Arberth, and Rhiannon was desperately eager to see her. She had not seen Gwen for some months, ever since leaving her in Rhoram's care. She and Gwen had parted badly, it was true. But she was sure Gwen would have forgiven her by now, would have come to understand why she had been left behind.

Rhiannon had been anxious to see Rhoram. He still held a great deal of her heart, even though she knew, as she had always known, that he was too careless for such a burden. But there was a part of her that still loved him, even as she told herself over and over that he had a wife now. That Rhoram no longer loved his Queen was not the point. Or, at least, that had seemed to be what Achren had been getting at in the conversations they had had during the weeks of their travel to Arberth.

"So," Achren would say, causally, as they rode through the forests and vineyards that sprawled across Prydyn, "do you think you could learn to get along with Queen Efa?"

"What do you—"

"You know what I mean. Rhoram will not put her aside. Her brother is the Lord of Ceredigion and will not take such an insult."

"I have no thought of staying in Arberth, Achren."

"Of course not," Achren would reply, her generous mouth quirking with amusement. "Not in a million years."

"Of course," Rhiannon would say idly, trying to keep the laughter from her voice, "if something should happen to Efa—"

"You would mourn for precisely three seconds."

"Four."

The day she and Achren had arrived in Arberth dawned

clear and fair. They had ridden past vineyards laden with purple fruit just moments away from the harvest. They had ridden through the gates of the city and been saluted all the way to Caer Tir. The gates of the King's fortress were open, and the wolf's head emblazoned in jet-black onyx and gleaming emerald seemed to stare at her with an intensity that made her shiver for a moment.

The courtyard had been crowded with warriors and townsfolk, merchants and farmers, who had come to see King Rhoram, for it was the day he held open court, hearing cases and giving his judgments.

Tallwch, Rhoram's gatekeeper, had helped Rhiannon from her horse and had smiled his welcome.

"Any news?" Achren asked as she dismounted.

"Only the news of Amatheon's death that Gwydion sent out. No information has yet been forthcoming on what you were all doing on Afalon."

"And none will be," Achren said crisply. "Unless the Dreamer himself gives leave."

"Rhoram will want to know," Tallwch said pointedly.

Achren glanced at Tallwch in surprise. "But, of course, I will tell him. He is my King. That was never a question."

"Of course not," Tallwch had replied solemnly.

"Gwen?" Rhiannon had asked eagerly.

"In the court with Rhoram, Sanon, and Geriant," Tallwch replied, naming Rhoram's son and daughter from a previous marriage.

"I must go to her," Rhiannon had said, intent only on seeing Gwen.

"Rhiannon," Tallwch had started to say.

Oh, if she had only listened to his tone. If she had only waited a few moments to find out what he had wanted to tell her, she would have been spared much humiliation. But she had not waited. She had gone on ahead, and walked into a pain so great that sometimes she still thought she might die of it. She had left Tallwch behind, not heeding what he was urgently saying to Achren.

She had proceeded up the steps and into the Great Hall. The hall had been packed with those who had come to hear Rhoram's judgments. Sunlight had streamed through the huge, open doors and through windows set high around the stone walls, but that had not been enough to illuminate the large chamber, so hundreds of torches burned, set in brackets against the walls. A fire had been burning in the huge fireplace, sending its shifting light to play over the faces of those in the hall.

Rhoram had sat on the dais in a massive chair canopied with green velvet. He was wearing a tunic and breeches of emerald, with black leather boots stitched with emeralds on the turned-down cuffs. He had worn his emerald ring, and a ring of glittering onyx dangled from his right ear. His golden hair was pulled back and secured at the nape of his neck with a clasp of emerald and gold. His blue eyes were intent as he listened to the man speaking, a merchant who had been presenting his case.

Rhiannon had scanned the faces on the dais, barely noting that Queen Efa sat next to her husband; that the Dafydd Penfro, Rhoram's chief counselor, was standing by the King's chair, that golden-haired Geriant and gentle Sanon were standing to one side, listening gravely.

Instead she was looking for Gwen, and she had eyes for no one else now. The glint of familiar golden hair in the firelight caught her eye. Gwen stood to one side at the foot of the dais, looking bored. She wore a tunic and breeches of brown leather and was tapping one booted foot impatiently, her arms crossed, a frown on her exquisite face. Clearly Gwen was anxious to return to her warrior's training and resentful of the delay. Rhiannon determined to speak to her daughter about that at the earliest opportunity.

At that moment Achren joined her at the doorway. Achren did not hesitate, but made her way though the crowd easily, with Rhiannon following in her wake. As they came nearer to the dais, the merchant faltered, aware of a commotion behind him.

Rhoram's eyes had lit up as he had seen Achren make her way through the crowd. He had risen, prepared to welcome his Captain home after her three-month absence. And then his eyes had met Rhiannon's and the spark that leapt into his eyes had almost choked her with its intensity. But she tore her gaze from his to seek Gwen. And that was when she clearly saw the turn her life had taken, clearly saw the price that the Shining Ones had demanded of her.

Gwen, gazing at her mother with contempt, had turned away and left the hall.

Rhiannon had stopped midway through the crowd when she had seen that. Rhoram, seeing it, too, had descended the dais, pity in his eyes and the need to explain written on his face.

But she had needed no explanation. It had been clear in her daughter's blue eyes that she had not been forgiven for leaving. Clear that Gwen would punish Rhiannon for abandoning her, punish her for some time—perhaps forever.

So she had turned away, blinded by her sudden tears, pushing her way through the crowd and back into the courtyard where Tallwch still stood by her horse.

"She will forgive you, Rhiannon," Tallwch had said.

"When?" she had asked through the ache in her throat.

But Tallwch had not had an answer for her. She had ridden away, not looking back. Not bidding Achren good-bye, not giving Rhoram a chance to greet her. She had ridden straight to her cave in Coed Aderyn, to the place she had once lived with Gwen.

She knew Gwen would not come here. And she knew her daughter would tell no one the location of the cave. So she had stayed there, alone, during this last year, forcing herself to get up in the mornings, forcing herself to feed and clothe herself, forcing herself to get through each day.

But now she was tired. More tired than she had ever been. She hadn't been eating well for some time, and she knew her clothes hung awkwardly on her too-thin frame. Her hair had lost its blue-black sheen and lay lank and tangled over her bony shoulders. She had not even bothered to dress today and still wore her cotton, low-cut sleeveless nightshift.

Dirty cups and wooden plates were scattered across the surface of the rough table. Her pallet was still unmade, and the blankets were mussed and dirty. Dust covered the surfaces of the shelves and the intricately carved wooden trunk that held her clothes; the same layer of dust lay heavily on the telyn, her father's harp, and on the books stacked next to it. Even the rough walls of the caves gleamed dully in the fitful light that ended less than a foot from the cave entrance, for there was no other light source. It had seemed too much trouble to light the candles, much less a fire. Water streamed over the mouth of the cave, the sunlight turning the shimmering waterfall into a spray of diamonds, for the one thing she had done this morning was to pull back the heavy curtain that hid the mouth of the cave.

And that was when the light shifted. Someone was standing at the mouth of the cave, having made their way across the rocks of the pool and behind the curtain of water.

Dully she wondered if it was someone sent to kill her, just as the man from a year ago had tried to murder her. But then she realized that she did not care. She was already dead, so what did it matter what happened to her body? She would welcome a murderer.

But it wasn't a murderer at all.

It was something worse. Much, much worse.

"RHIANNON," HE SAID. "Wake up."

He was sitting on the cold, stone floor, holding her in his lap, cradling her head against his chest.

She opened her eyes and looked up into his face. His short, dark beard was shot here and there with silvery-gray. There were, perhaps, more lines on his handsome face, lines of grief and sorrow and loneliness. But his gray eyes were as cool and watchful as ever, giving nothing away as he gazed down at her, his face carefully expressionless.

"What happened?" she asked tiredly.

"You fainted."

"Ridiculous," she snorted. "I never faint."

"Do you ever eat?"

"Since when is that any of your business?"

"Ah," he said, his mouth giving the faintest twitch of humor, "the same old Rhiannon. For a moment there I thought you had changed."

She sat up, removing herself from his embrace. The movement, slight as it was, made her dizzy, and she sat still for a moment, her eyes closed, willing the cave to stop spinning. She made as if to stand, but Gwydion, laying his hands on her shoulders, stopped her.

"No," he said quietly. "Do not move just yet."

She would have ignored his command if she had been able to, but she knew he was right—if she stood she would only fall. And he probably wouldn't bother to catch her.

"Do you have any Penduran's Rose?" he asked as he rose and searched her shelf of medicines.

"Third bottle from the right," she answered wearily. She knew what that was for. The plant was known for, among other things, fighting depression. She wanted to argue with him, to tell him that she was not depressed, but she was too tired.

He picked up a small, dirty pot from the table and went to the waterfall. He washed out the pot, then filled it and brought it back to the hearth. He went to her dwindling stack of firewood and laid a fire in the fireplace. Then he raised his hand and gestured, and the wood burst into flames. The fire crackled cheerfully as he hung the small pot from the spit and settled it to warm over the fire.

He glanced down at her as she sat huddled on the floor, the dirty blanket still around her thin shoulders. He looked around and spotted her small rocking chair and drew it up before the hearth. Without a word he helped her up and into the chair. He took off his black cloak and, dispensing with the tattered blanket, wrapped her in the warm, woolen cloth. Tears sprang to her eyes because of his unwonted gentleness, but she ducked her head so he wouldn't see. She must be weaker than she thought to let such a gesture affect her. And from the Dreamer, of all people.

After a few moments, when the fire had taken the chill off the water, he poured it from the pot into a small, wooden cup—one of the few that were not dirty. He crushed a few leaves of Penduran's Rose into the cup and swirled the liquid around. He then handed it to her and stood over her as she drank it, which she did without protest, for she knew he was determined. And she was tired. So tired. Too tired to argue. Too tired to do anything else but lay her head against the back of the chair and let the drowsiness wash over her.

Too tired to even care—then—that Gwydion had seen her in her weakness. Later that would matter. And it would matter a great deal.

Meirgdydd, Disglair Wythnos—late afternoon
SHE WOKE WITH a start, uncertain, at first, where she was. Sunlight streamed in through the cave mouth, illuminating the rock walls where crystal gleamed in the golden light. A fire crackled, warming a large pot from which came a most wonderful, appetizing smell. The dishes were cleared from the table, washed, and put away neatly on their accustomed shelf. Her harp, the bindings of her books, the small trunk all gleamed, free of dust. The floor had been swept, and candles burned brightly, illuminating the dark corners where neither sunlight nor firelight could reach. Her chair was still drawn up before the hearth, but now Gwydion was sitting in it, occasionally leaning forward to stir whatever wonderful concoction bubbled in the pot.

She was still wearing her shift, but she noticed that her body had been washed and her hair was combed out of its dreadful tangles. She was still wrapped in Gwydion's soft, woolen cloak, and she felt more comfortable than she had been in a long time. Most amazing, her stomach growled at the smell of food, instead of responding with nausea, as she was accustomed to.

She sat up and even the dizziness was gone. He turned to her as he sensed her movement. They looked at each other for a long time, silvery-gray eyes meeting emerald green, but they did not speak. Later she would be unable to say what had really passed between them in that look. There had been too much there to allow her to sort it out into neat answers. She finally made herself to rise, and he hurried over to her.

"Hungry?" he asked as he helped her over to the bench at the table.

"Yes," she replied in surprise. "I really am."

"Supper will be ready in one moment. Drink this." He handed her a cup of watered ale and turned back to the fire. Using a cloth, he opened the door of the small bread oven and pulled out a loaf, the crust done to perfection. He set it down on one of the wooden plates and sliced it. Though she knew it was hot, she took a piece anyway and began to eat, for she could not wait. It burned her mouth slightly, but it was worth it, she reasoned, for it was the best bread she had ever eaten. That alone boded well for the stew he was still stirring.

In the end she ate three bowls of the rich, savory stew. He had caught a rabbit that morning, he said. A search of her larder had yielded a few edibles to put in the stew—some dried peas and beans, some onions, and some parsley. She had no idea he was capable of making such a wonderful meal from so little. Indeed, she would have told him so, but with her returning strength came a keen sense of humiliation.

That he of all people should see her in her weakness! That

was surely something he would hold over her head forever. That he had cleaned her home, that he had washed her body and combed her hair, that he had fed her and wrapped her in his own cloak—it was almost too much to be borne.

She laid down her spoon after eating the last drop in her bowl and looked up at him. He had finished eating some time ago and had been quietly sitting across from her at the table, waiting for her to finish. She studied his face, seeking for some hint of superiority, of pity, of contempt. But she could find nothing. Nothing at all, for his face was as much of a mask as it had always been, and his eyes were shuttered.

But she knew what he was thinking. He was secretly exulting that he had seen her in her weakness. He was turning over strategies to use her vulnerability to his advantage. He was here because he wanted something, and he had helped her because he saw that as a way to get what he wanted. The only question was, what did he want? She scowled at him, her brows rushing together.

"You are feeling better," he said, a smile tugging at his mouth.

"What do you want?" she snapped. "What are you doing here?"

"Well, for the past day I have been doing quite a bit. Don't tell me you didn't notice."

"You want to be thanked? Fine. Consider yourself thanked. Now tell me why you are here."

"I need help."

His simple answer disarmed her for a moment. He needed help? Since when did the mighty Dreamer need anything? "Help from the woman who was responsible for your brother's death?"

He flinched then, and she was surprised at the effect of her words. But he answered steadily. "I said those things in my grief. I did not mean them."

"Now you tell me this," she said bitterly.

He studied her for a moment, then replied. "You were not in this condition from anything I did. I heard about Gwen."

Now it was her turn to flinch. She looked away and gazed into the fire. "She refused to see me. I think she may never forgive me."

"Perhaps she will," he said quietly.

"Not likely."

"So you have been here since you left Arberth? Living in this cave?"

"Where else would I go?" she challenged.

"Why, anywhere. You could have gone to Y Ty Dewin and presented yourself to Cynan, asked for a post. You could have found a way to be of use."

"But instead I have chosen to be useless, is that right?" she asked sharply.

"You tell me," he replied, his voice even.

"No, you tell me something," she answered, furious. "You tell me what you are doing here. I thought that it was perfectly clear we didn't want to see each other again."

"I had a dream," he said quietly.

"A dream?"

"A nightmare. War. The Coranian Empire comes to our island, bringing death and our destruction with them."

"They defeat us?" she asked, shocked.

Gwydion nodded. "And they kill, oh, so many of us."

"Rhoram?" she asked with her heart in her throat.

At her question his gray eyes shone coldly. "He went down,

132

yes, but I am not sure he was killed. But Queen Olwen, King Urien, and Queen Ellirri, they were killed."

"And your brother?"

"Uthyr," he rasped. "Yes, Uthyr dies."

"I am sorry," she said.

"Another brother to be taken from me." He went on as though she had not spoken. "The Shining Ones are cruel."

"Why are you telling me this?" she asked, hoping to jar him from his grief. "What does this have to do with me?"

"I had a further dream. There is a man in Corania. I call him the Golden Man, and it is he who seeks to destroy us, who hates us so. I must go to Corania, to gain whatever knowledge I can of his plans, and return to Kymru with whatever information I can gain, with anything that might help us."

"And?"

"And my dream tells me that you must go with me."

"Me?" she asked, startled. "Why me?"

"Who knows?" Gwydion shrugged.

"Certainly you don't. Why, you can't even imagine how I might be of any use," she accused, stung by his careless answer.

"I didn't say that!"

"You didn't have to!"

"Listen—"

"No, you listen. Before you came into my life last year, I was content. I had my daughter, and we had built a life here. Then you came and everything changed. I left my daughter to do your bidding, and now she will not even see me. I live here alone, because of you."

"You live here alone because of you," he accused, his eyes flashing. "This is your choice. Don't blame me for it."

"My choice?" she cried, springing to her feet. "How dare you say that!"

"And how dare you blame me!" he retorted, also rising to his feet. "I should have known you would. I should have known that you were far too selfish to even think of helping me. I should have known that you were incapable of thinking beyond yourself, of thinking for one moment that Kymru needs you."

"Kymru needed me last year, according to you, and look what that got me! Look, indeed, at what that got you!"

He turned white at her words, rage in his silvery eyes. "You do not need to remind me the price I paid for finding Caladfwlch. No one knows that better than I."

"And if you had known the price was your brother? What then? Would you still have paid it to do your duty?"

"You are cruel, Rhiannon ur Hefeydd," he said quietly, stepping away from the table and to the mouth of the cave. "Would that I had never known how much. Keep the cloak—I'd just as soon not have it back."

And with that he was gone.

SHE STOOD THERE for some time, staring at the water that washed over the cave entrance, not certain he had really gone. After a while she looked out. Yes, his horse was gone. She cast her awareness into the surrounding forest, Wind-Riding to the north. He was riding that way, making, she supposed, for Caer Dathyl. Her spirit hovered briefly, carefully, for she did not want him to know she was looking. She was shocked to see the tracks of tears on his drawn face, tears, she knew, for his dead brother, and for the brother who would soon be dead.

She returned to her body and turned away. She surveyed

the now-tidy room and she felt her face burning, shame at her behavior almost choking her. He had helped her, and she had repaid him by hurting him. Yes, he had come for his own selfish ends. Yes, he had helped her because he wanted something from her. But nonetheless, she owed a debt now, and she knew it. If he hadn't come, who knows what would have happened to her? Would she simply have starved herself to death? Was she that much of a coward?

The evening shadows had begun to gather, and she lit more candles. She did not want to sit in the dark alone ever again. She sliced some bread and ate it with the last of the stew. She drank cupfuls of clear, cold, refreshing water. At last she filled up the small pot and set it over the fire to warm. She added chamomile to the pot and then drank several cups of the soothing tea. Then she took her seat in her chair before the fire and prepared to think things through. But even as she settled in, she heard a sound from outside. She rose, cautiously making her way to the entrance. It was night now, and the full moon had risen in the east. Moonbeams shimmered over the surface of the small pool on the other side of the waterfall. The trees that surrounded the clearing were dark and silent, and she could not even hear the sound of animals rustling in the undergrowth. Instead, she heard something else—the faint sound of a harp. It seemed to come from everywhere and from nowhere at the same time. She stepped from the cave, making her way behind the waterfall and out into the clearing, stepping carefully over the wet rocks to come to stand beside the pool.

She recognized the tune, faint as it was, and found that she was silently singing the song that went with it. It was a song by Amergin, the last King of Lyonesse, written a few days before his execution at the hands of the Drui.

Being a stone, I must crystallize within the womb of Earth.

Being a plant, I must root well in the Earth that I may grow.

Being a fish, I must wash in the waters, swim, and be clean.

Being a land-creature, I must set my feet firmly on Earth and look life in the face.

Being a bird, I must soar to the heights.

Being human, I must live in all worlds for I am of all worlds:

Yet must I lose none of them.

If I do not crystallize, I can give no light.

If I lose my roots, I cannot grow.

If I do not swim, or walk, or soar, I have lost part of my life.

Amergin's message—that one must be what one was born to be, that to run was useless and to hide was meaningless—struck her in its simplicity. She had to do as she was called to do, for if she did not, she could not live, could not fulfill her purpose, and would waste the life she had been given.

She turned at the sound of horse's hooves behind her and was, for some reason, not surprised at what she saw.

The god, Cerrunnos, Lord of the Wild Hunt, sat upon his white horse as motionless as a stone. Antlers sprang from his proud forehead and his owl-like, topaz eyes burned brightly. His bare chest gleamed golden, and his breeches were made of deerskin. His leather boots were studded with gems of topaz. The horse, which had no saddle or bridle, shimmered in the moonlight.

The goddess Cerridwen, the White Lady, sat upon her horse of jet-black, her head held high. She wore a simple white shift that just reached her calves. Her boots were studded with amethysts. Her midnight-black hair flowed down to her slender waist, and her amethyst eyes gazed down at Rhiannon without pity.

"You sent the song," Rhiannon said.

"We did," Cerridwen replied.

"Which we should not have had to do," Cerrunnos said sternly.

"I know," she whispered as she bowed her head.

"Rhiannon ur Hefeydd, why is it so hard to get you to lend your aid?" Cerridwen went on, a note of exasperation in her beautiful voice.

"It isn't hard to get me to help," Rhiannon insisted.

"Just hard to get you to help the Dreamer," Cerrunnos replied.

She swiftly lifted her head to stare up at the god and goddess, for Cerrunnos's tone had held a hint of laughter.

Cerridwen shook her head in what Rhiannon now knew to be mock dismay. "Really, Rhiannon ur Hefeydd, has it not yet occurred to you to ask why?"

"I—no."

"Well, give it some thought one day. I think you will be astonished at the answer," Cerridwen said. "But for now, you have other things to do."

"I know."

"See to it that you do them," Cerrunnos said, his tone now firm.

"I will," she said as she made her final bow. "I will."

Meriwdydd, Disglair Wythnos—night
THREE DAYS LATER she caught up with him as he camped for

the night on the steps of Cadair Idris.

The dark mountain hall of the High Kings rose from the tall grasses of the plain like a dark sentinel, silent, brooding, keeping its own counsel. Gwydion had lit a fire at the top of the stairs, just in front of the closed, jeweled Doors. In the firelight, the jeweled patterns glowed with a soft light. The azure sapphires of Taran of the Winds, the verdant emeralds of Modron the Mother, the fiery opals of Mabon of the Sun, and the soft pearls of Nantsovelta of the Moon gleamed. Diamonds and garnets, for Sirona of the Stars and Grannos the Healer, glittered. The rubies for Agrona and Camulos, the Warrior Twins, shone like drops of fresh blood. Topaz for Cerrunnos and amethysts for Cerridwen, the Protectors, glimmered. Onyx for Annwyn, Lord of Chaos, and bloodstone for his mate, Aertan the Weaver, glowed.

She dismounted her horse at the bottom of the stairs and softly ascended the once white, now broken, and muddied steps. To her astonishment Gwydion did not seem to hear her coming, for he was talking to the Doors, confident, no doubt, that Bloudewedd, the spirit that infused the Doors, would have given him warning if danger threatened.

"Tell me about Gorwys," Gwydion was saying, his voice weary.

"Why do you make me speak of him?" the Guardian asked.

"I need to know. I need to know the nature of his punishment. I need to understand how we can use it."

The Doors were silent for a moment. Rhiannon stood beyond the edge of the firelight, wanting to hear how the Guardian would speak of the man she had loved, the man for whom she had murdered her husband, High King Lleu.

"It was Bran's doing, of course," the Guardian said at last.

"His idea. He said that one day Kymru would again be in danger from the Coranians. He said that a sacrifice was needed to ensure the Kymri had warning of this danger. He said that Gorwys's soul was that sacrifice."

"And then?" Gwydion prompted.

"And then he buried Gorwys alive."

Gwydion froze at the Guardian's words. At last he spoke softly. "I am sorry, Bloudewedd."

"Do not be sorry for us, Dreamer. We did a great evil. It is right that we have paid."

"All this time . . ."

"All this time Gorwys has been conscious, waiting, lying in the dark underground. Waiting for his call to ride."

"How much of a warning will he give us?"

"One day."

"One day! It is not much."

"It is as much as you will get."

"I will see if we can get more," Gwydion said.

"You cannot go alone," the Doors said, the tone suggesting that she had said this many times that night.

"I must," Gwydion insisted.

"Yet your dream tells you that you cannot go without her."

"But she will not go. And so I must."

"Perhaps," the Doors said mildly, "she did not fully understand the need."

"She did not want to. She still does not."

"I wouldn't be too sure of that," Rhiannon said as she stepped out of the shadows and into the firelight.

He leapt to his feet, his silvery eyes lighting up at the sight of her. "You came."

"I came to return your cloak," she said, holding out the bundle of dark cloth.

He took it from her, his face guarded.

"And to say that I have a sudden desire to go to Corania. I have, after all, never been," she went on.

He smiled then, and at that sight her heart skipped a beat. "Care for some company?" he asked.

"Why, yes, I believe I would," she replied.

Part 2
Darkness Falls

Woe that I was ever born
And my mother and father reared me,
That I did not die
With the milk of the breast
Before losing my heart's brother.

 From Bran's Poems of Sorrow
Circa 275

Chapter 7

Sar Daeg, Sol 35—early afternoon

Rhiannon stood on the deck of the gently swaying ship, gazing at the city sprawled on the shore. She could just make out the skyline, pierced by sharp spires of gray stone, by soaring bell towers of pine, by tall, sloping roofs of gold-inlaid timber glittering harshly beneath the sun. Here and there she could see the inky shadows of closely packed hovels, huddled together as if in shame.

She found it hard to believe they were finally here, ready to dock at the great city of Athelin, the capital of the Coranian Empire. It had taken them four and a half months to get here, though a journey by ship straight from Kymru to this city would have taken merely a matter of two weeks. But they had not traveled directly to the capital, for it was imperative that their Kymric background be kept secret. So Rhiannon and Gwydion had left Kymru by ship and traveled to Seville, the chief coastal city of Austarias on the western shores of the continent.

143

From there they had traveled by horse and on foot through Frankia and Lombardy, until finally reaching Ancona, a city on the eastern shores of the continent. There Gwydion judged that they were safe from suspicion and that no one would be able to identify them as Kymri. It was then that they took a ship around the eastern coast of Corania itself and made their final way to Athelin. As they traveled, Rhiannon slowly gained back her strength. It felt good—oh, so good—to be strong again.

They advertised themselves as minstrels from Turin, a land in the south of Lombardy, where the people were dark of hair and light of eyes. He gave their names as Guido Asti and Rhea Varins. He taught her how to speak Coranian, which had not been as difficult as she had feared. He taught her song after song, and she was an apt pupil, singing accompaniment to the ballads in a clear, mellow tone. Gwydion was an accomplished musician and could play any instrument he had a mind to. When they performed, they collected what she considered to be an astonishing amount of money.

He had taught her dancing, too, which, to her amazement, she was quite good at. In her costume of clinging white linen, gold belt, and heavy golden collar, she danced to the sensuous beat of Gwydion's drums in the smoke -filled rooms of inns along the way, catching all eyes. All eyes but Gwydion's, it seemed. Not that she wanted to catch his eye—or any other part of his anatomy, for that matter.

They tolerated each other, and had lapsed into a caustic, sharp way of talking, waging a continuous verbal battle to keep each other at bay. For her part, she was still angry he had seen her in her weakness, sure that he was going to find a way to use that against her.

As for him, she had no idea what he was thinking or feeling beneath his habitual mask. He treated her as someone whose company he had to endure, making it clear that he was trying to make the best of a bad situation.

Once again, she gazed at Athelin. The Kymri and the Coranians had been enemies for time eternal. But never had there been so much hatred as when the new religion of Lytir, the One God, had swept through Coran like wildfire, two hundred years before.

So many had died because of this new religion. One of the first to die had been Branwen, the sister of Bran the Dreamer, who had married a Coranian Prince. When she had refused to embrace the new religion, she had been imprisoned, and though she was rescued from burning by her brother, she had later died of grief. The Kymri had never forgiven the Coranians for that—and never would. The countries of Mierce and Dere, which had refused to convert, had been invaded by the Coranians, their Kings and Queens killed, their cities and fields burned, their people taken as slaves and absorbed into the greedy maw of the Empire. Thule, the country to the north, still clung to the Old Gods—Wuotan and Holda, Fro and Freya, Donar and Tiw. Separated from the continent by a narrow channel, they had been able to maintain their independence from the Empire.

The other three countries to the south of the Coranian Empire—Austarias, Frankia, and Lombardy—had accepted the new religion. They kept their own rulers, but they were subject to the Coranian Emperor and the Archpreost. And the Archpreost had at his disposal the wyrce-jaga, the arm of the church that gleefully rooted out and killed those of the old religion. The wyrce-jaga were feared and hated, both by the common folk and the nobility, but they were obeyed.

Gwydion explained more than once that arousing the suspicions of the wyrce-jaga was to be avoided at all costs. Countless times on their trip across the continent, Gwydion and Rhiannon had attended the Sundaeg services in whatever town they found themselves in order to avoid even a hint of suspicion. And they both wore the amulets of the new religion—a medallion carved in the shape of an oak tree.

Gwydion had also impressed on her the need to use her telepathy and clairvoyance as little as possible. The Kymri did not have a monopoly on the gifts, and there were also Coranians who were born with telepathy, clairvoyance, and the like. They were called Wiccans and their gifts were the same as the Y Dawnus of Kymru. Rhiannon thought she would rather be dead than to be one of those poor wretches, for their choices were cruel. They could deny their birthright and live in fear of discovery. Or they could practice the old religion secretly. Many of them were drawn to it because in the old religion these talents were viewed as gifts by the gods, but they risked death if discovered. Some of them became fortune-tellers and mystics, attaching themselves to traveling carnivals. They paid the wyrce-jaga to leave them be, but sometimes more payment than they could afford would be demanded and then they, too, would die.

No, she hadn't wanted to come to Corania at all. As Athelin, the city from which all the darkness sprang, came closer, she shuddered again.

"Get your cloak if you're cold," Gwydion said harshly from his place to the right of her on the deck.

"I'm not cold. I'm nervous. Can't you feel it? There's

something terribly wrong with this place."

"You could say that about any place in this Empire and be right."

"Oh, yes. But here," she lifted her hands and gestured at the tall buildings, at the crowded, noisome dock, at the closely packed houses, at the ragged sailors and the yoked slaves. "It's worse here."

"Get used to it. We'll be here quite a while."

"We hope," she said.

"We will." He sounded confident as always.

She set her teeth and willed herself not to toss him into the harbor. "You're sure we will find him here?"

"He'll be here. I'll find him."

"You'll find him," she said flatly. "Wonderful. Maybe if I'm very, very good you'll at least let me watch."

"All right," he said in that mild way of his, like an adult soothing a child about to burst into a tantrum. "We'll find him, then. Is that better?"

In their journey they had heard of two men, one of which was surely the man they sought, the Golden Man from Gwydion's dreams. One was Aelbald, the Empress's nephew. The other was Havgan, a fisherman's son from Cantware. Both men were vying for the position of Bana, Warleader of the Empire. The man who would be proclaimed Warleader would one day rule all of Corania through marriage to Princess Aelwyn, heir to the throne. The matter would be decided at the Gewinnan Daeg tournament, some months from now.

"Now that we're here," she said acidly, ignoring his question, "perhaps you would care to tell me just how we are to get inside the Golden Man's household to do our spying?"

She hardly expected a response, for she had asked that question of him many times. But to her surprise, he actually answered her as the ship docked, the plank was let down, and they found themselves on the crowded docks of Athelin.

"We sing for him," he said. "What else?"

THEY MADE THEIR way away from the docks, traveling some distance down Lindstrat. The street was cobbled and houses were crowded narrowly on either side, hanging over the road, cutting out the sun and making it dim even in the bright afternoon. To their right the River Saefern flowed through the center of the city, spanned here and there with wooden bridges, arched high enough to allow passage of ships on their way to the sea.

At last they found an inn, somewhat run-down, but lively enough. Gwydion made a deal with the innkeeper for room and board in exchange for entertainment, and they were led to a small, shabby attic room. There was one bed, a small table with a basin and pitcher, and a brazier of coals.

"How long will we be here?" she asked wearily, depositing her bag and harp on the floor.

"Not long," he answered, in an equally tired voice. "We'll rest for a while, play here tonight, and go looking for him tomorrow."

"I think we had best look today."

He looked at her quickly. "Why?"

"We have to go to their temple. Didn't you notice the marks on people's foreheads? As I recall from your interminable lessons, today is Sar Daeg, when all good Coranians, and those not so good, go to church and get the mark in bull's blood. That means we'd best go, too, unless we want the wyrce-jaga to pay

148

us a visit."

"Ah. Yes. Just what I was going to say." In spite of his airy statement his mouth quirked, acknowledging that she had scored a point. Unaccountably she laughed.

His gray eyes lit up as he looked down at her laughing face. He smiled and her heart skipped a beat. Abruptly she stopped laughing and his smile faded.

Stiffly, she turned toward the door. "Coming?" she asked without turning her head. For a moment she thought he was going to say something, but then he changed his mind and followed her out the door.

THEY CROSSED THE Bogastrat Bridge for Gwydion had decided that the best church to go to was the largest one, Ealh Athelin, on the western side of the city. That was the place where most of the rich and influential people of Athelin gathered, and therefore was the best place to locate the Golden Man.

The water in the River Saefern had a brown, muddy cast to it, though it flowed swiftly out to the sea. The late afternoon sun was waning, as the days were short this time of year. The air was crisp and cool, but Rhiannon was unable to enjoy it, scented as it was with the smells of the huge city—ill-dug privies, carelessly tossed trash, unwashed bodies. Occasionally they passed other people, but the streets were mostly silent and subdued.

"And tomorrow," she said, gesturing at the empty streets, "this will all change?"

"Oh, yes. Tomorrow is Undeadlic Daeg, when they celebrate the day Lytir came back to life. Today is Sar Daeg, when they mourn his death. It's the last day of Modcerau, which lasts for about a month. During that time it's gloomy and quiet.

People give up something they like during Modcerau. Not much merrymaking this time of year."

"What do you mean—give up something?"

"For instance, if someone likes their wine, they don't drink it for all of Modcerau. They think of it as a sacrifice to their God, by giving up what they like best."

"Ah." She cocked a sardonic eyebrow. "And does their God appreciate this?"

"You know," he said thoughtfully, "I don't believe he's ever said."

"As closemouthed as you, apparently."

"Do I detect a note of censure?" He shot her a swift glance, his gray eyes keen.

"Would you care?" she demanded.

"That depends on whether or not you ever grow up."

"I see. So you think I've just been sulking for four months."

"Haven't you?"

"You," she said in a firm but relatively calm tone, "are so arrogant you take my breath away."

"Good. As long as you're breathless, you're not talking."

"I'm not asking you for anything I haven't earned," she hissed.

"You've earned nothing yet," he said crisply.

"Oh, yes, I have. I've learned all you've taught me, as painful as it was for you to drop those crumbs of information. All I'm asking you is to treat me as a partner."

"Then act like one. Stop acting like a child and remember that it wasn't up to me to bring you here."

"I won't forget that. You won't let me. It shows through in your every sneer."

They turned down Byrnestrat and walked on in stiff silence

for some time. The sheer nerve of him made her so angry she couldn't speak. No doubt Gwydion was reveling in that. The city seemed to reflect her mood—silent and withdrawn. Of course, Gwydion would translate that as sulking. So she made an effort and spoke in a neutral tone. "What's that up ahead?" she asked, gesturing to a huge complex of gray stone.

He answered quickly, obviously relieved to be talking again, "That's Cirice Garth, where the Archpreost lives, and where most of the church business is carried out."

She studied the gloomy building. "I wouldn't like to live in there."

"I doubt they would let you in. Women aren't allowed. And if they did let you in, I don't think you'd come out again alive. The dungeons of the wyrce-jaga are there."

"That's a cheerful thought—for you, anyway," she said sourly.

"Believe it or not, it's not a cheerful thought for me at all," he said quietly.

Before she could reply, he pointed off over the river to their left, "Perhaps you'd like to live there."

She followed his gesture and gasped. Before her stood a beautiful building of gleaming white stone with a sloping timber roof inlaid with bands of gold and silver. Four graceful towers as delicate as crystal rose from each corner. The entire shining edifice rested on a island in the middle of the river. A bridge, well-guarded by men in helms of gold, spanned the riverbank to the island.

"Is that the palace?" she asked in an awed tone.

"Yes. That's Cynerice Scima. Just on the other side of the bank is Byrnwiga, the Bana's palace. It's empty at the moment, of course. The tournament to decide the Warleader is five months away. We turn here to get to Ealh Athelin."

Reluctantly she tore her eyes away from the palace as they turned west down Flanstrat and finally came to Ealh Athelin, the largest church in Corania.

To her surprise it was not made of stone. It was made of thousands and thousands of carved and polished interlocking pieces of light and dark wood with a series of sloping roofs of different heights, grouped around a large square tower. The tower rose, up and up, reaching to the sky, until she felt dizzy trying to see the top. A walkway ran around the huge building, enclosed by a low wall and topped by an arcade. Protruding from the gables were animal shapes carved with delicate precision—dragons, boars, horses, serpents, and eagles. Some had tusks and claws of gold; others had scales or manes of silver. Some had eyes of ruby, and others had eyes of sapphire. She found her eyes drawn time and again to one dragon shape that hovered over the main entrance. The dragon was rearing up, gold-inlaid wings outspread, with its sinuous neck stretched out and its ruby eyes glittering fiercely down at her, challenging her to enter.

Stone steps led up to the huge, wooden main doors, which were shut, signaling that a service was in progress. A number of people were milling around the arcade and on the front steps waiting for the next service. At last the doors opened and people came streaming out, all with the rune of Lytir marked on their foreheads, drawn in bull's blood. The church emptied out, and the waiting crowd was let inside.

The church was shadowy, lit only by rows of torches set in brackets at intervals around the large, inner sanctuary. The central square was huge, the roof rising up and up until the ceiling was lost in the shadows. Eight round wooden pillars held up the roof, intricately carved with shapes of bird and beast. Row upon row of wooden benches filled the square, all facing a raised wooden dais on which a large, square stone altar rested. A silken banner of white flowed over the altar, the rune for Lytir, the One God, stitched in gold thread.

On the left of the altar stood a drinking horn set in an ivory holder. To the right an empty golden bowl rested. A gleaming knife lay at the front, and four fat, white candles burned in each corner. Intermittent rustlings came from a deep pit at the foot of the altar.

Gwydion and Rhiannon quietly took a place on a bench near the back of the sanctuary. Suddenly, for no apparent reason, she felt a prickling sensation on the back of her neck, and goose bumps rose swiftly on her arms. She turned, glancing over her shoulder to try to locate the source of her unease, and almost gasped aloud.

The Golden Man was exactly as Gwydion had described him.

He was tall and broad-shouldered. His skin was tanned to a golden brown. His shoulder-length honey-blond hair shone briefly in the light streaming through the doors. He wore a tunic of fine, white cloth, belted at the waist with a golden chain. His form-fitting breeches were also white, and he wore calf-length boots tied with golden laces. His red cloak was lined with white fur and fastened at the neck with a ruby-studded golden brooch. He was clean-shaven and had heavy-lidded amber eyes, the eyes of a hawk, of a bird of prey. His eyes darted over the sanctuary and caught her staring at him. He smiled slowly at her. She flushed and jerked her eyes back to the altar.

Incredibly, Gwydion had not noticed. He was frowning down at the floor, lost in some personal abstraction. She nudged his ribs sharply. He turned to her, his brows raised. Without a word, she cut her eyes to the left and Gwydion caught sight of the Golden Man as he walked down the center aisle and took a seat in the front row.

"It's him, isn't it?" she murmured.

"It is. I can't believe we found him so quickly," Gwydion said, studying the back of the Golden Man's head. He glanced down at her, a smile flickering across his face. "Maybe my luck has changed with you at my side."

"He saw me staring at him."

Gwydion shrugged. "That's all to the good. I want him to notice us."

"He noticed me all right. If he notices me like that again, we're in big trouble."

Gwydion stiffened, looking swiftly over at the Golden Man, his eyes lit with some strong emotion that Rhiannon could not identify. "Well now," he said softly, "that's something I hadn't considered."

"Well, don't," she said sharply. "And don't tell me that's part of your plan or I will leave here this minute, do you understand?"

He looked down at her, searching her wide green eyes and accurately reading her panic. Surprisingly, he reached over and took her cold hand in his. "I didn't bring you to Corania to give you away," he said quietly. "Or to let you be taken from me. That's not going to happen. I promise you."

Before she could reply, a man dressed in a robe of green with a golden medallion around his neck rose and lifted his hands for silence. Remembering her lessons, she knew the green robe meant the man was a Byshop. When the crowd was quiet, the Byshop intoned, "Praise now to the Guardian of Heofen, the power of Lytir and his Mind-Plans, who fashioned the beginning of every wonder."

As one, the crowd responded, "Eternal Lord."

The Byshop continued, "He made first heaven as a roof."

"Holy Creator," the people replied.

"Then made he Middle-Earth, as a dwelling place for men."

"Master Almighty," came the response.

The Byshop stood there for a long moment, head bowed. Two men in robes of bright yellow came up and stood on either side of the pit, both holding lighted torches. One man held his torch upright, the other held his torch pointed down. Then the Byshop stripped off his robe and stood before them, clad in a loincloth, his feet bare. He picked up the knife and the bowl from the altar and jumped into the pit. From the pit came an enormous bellow, as man and bull fought each other. The crowd was silent, straining forward. The bull gave a final, anguished scream, then all was quiet. At a signal from one of the torch-bearers, another man in yellow strode up to the pit, lowered a ladder into it, and the Byshop emerged, the knife clutched in his hand and the bowl full of blood.

The crowd cheered as the man handed the knife and bowl to a waiting preost, then put back on his robe. He took the bowl again, and at his signal, people lined up in the aisle, waiting their turn to be marked with the blood on their foreheads.

The Golden Man rose and unhurriedly made his way to the front of the line. He knelt, waiting impassively for the Byshop to dip his fingers into the bloody bowl and mark the rune of Lytir on his forehead. This done, the Golden Man returned to his seat, closed his eyes, and bowed his head. Gwydion nudged Rhiannon, and she reluctantly rose to her feet and took her place in line, with Gwydion behind her. They did not speak, but waited their turn, slowly moving forward to the front of the altar. Surreptitiously, as they neared the front of the church, she eyed the Golden Man, but his head was still bowed.

When she reached the altar, she knelt and refused to shudder as the Byshop smeared a bloody print on her forehead. She rose and turned to go back to her seat, when she saw that the Golden Man had lifted his head and was looking straight at her. Pretending not to notice, she made her way back to her place, but her legs were trembling from what she had seen in the Golden Man's eyes. Gwydion was a pace or two behind her, and he took her elbow and helped her back up the aisle, standing close.

"Did you see that?" she whispered. "Gwydion, we've got to get out of here."

"No. We stay. And don't worry. Everything's going to work out perfectly."

Up in front of the altar, the Byshop lifted his hands to lead them in the traditional closing melody.

"He hung on a windy tree
with spear wounded.
Offered to Donar,
Lytir, abandoned.
Into the depths he descended
And conquered Sceadu,
The shadow of Death,
Lytir, our God.
He died and lived and wisdom got.

*Our mighty King,
Lytir, our God."*

The service was finally over. The Golden Man rose and stood talking to the Byshop, accompanied by two companions. One of the men had light brown hair, dark eyes, and a pleasant, open expression. The other man, a wyrce-jaga dressed in a black robe with green trim, had sharp features, pale gray eyes, and lanky blond, tonsured hair.

Gwydion did not move from his place and tugged her back as she began to rise. "What?" she demanded shortly. She wanted to get out of there.

"Stay here a minute. I've got to think."

"About what?"

"About a way to bring us to his attention."

"I have his attention. I thought you noticed that."

"I did," he said shortly. "We have to get into his household. I thought you understood that."

She did understand that. And she knew what would happen to her if they did. The thought made bile rise in her throat. It was strange that she should feel so repelled by the Golden Man. He was handsome and sensual and she should have felt desire, but she did not. She felt ill. "I can't. You'll have to go in alone. I can't do it."

"Do you really think I'd sell your body to get into his household?" he asked in an appalled tone. "Is that the kind of man you think I am?"

Well, yes, she did think he was that kind of man. But she knew better than to tell him so. Instead she answered his question with one of her own. "Then what do you plan to do?"

His mouth hardened as he realized what she was thinking. "I'm trying to think of something," he said evenly. "Some way for him to be indebted to us. A reason for him to treat us well—and keep his hands off you."

"That's going to have to be a good reason."

"I know. That's why I have to think about it."

Idly, her eyes roved over the sanctuary and out the open doors. The carving of the dragon above the outside of the doors cast a long shadow across the steps. Suddenly, she had an idea. "How about saving his life? Or at least the life of one of his friends?"

"That would do it," he said dryly. "But how?"

She nodded toward the doors. "That dragon outside. The neck is stretched out so that the head hovers over the doors. It's made of wood, and it's probably very heavy. If that neck broke while someone was standing under it . . ."

He considered her words for a moment. "It's risky. The timing would have to be perfect."

"Then you'd better be as good a Shape-Mover as you say you are," she said.

"I am," he replied absently. "I've already loosened it considerably. Come on."

They rose, casually making their way up the aisle and out the doors. Gwydion's eyes were unfocused as he brought the power of his mind to bear on the wooden figure. She took his arm to steady him. They made their way down the steps, not even glancing up at the poised dragon's head. Then they stopped, pretending to examine the carvings on the posts holding up the arcade.

She waited tensely. The Golden Man and his two companions came out the main doors and stood there for a brief moment, talking among themselves. It was only a moment, but it was long enough. "Now," she hissed at Gwydion, just as the Golden Man and the wyrce-jaga began to move down the steps. There was a tremendous crack as the dragon's head broke free from the carved neck and began to tumble through the air to the ground below, heading straight for the other companion, who had been moving more slowly. The man looked up at the sound but did not move, stunned by the sight of the dragon hurling down at him. With a shout, Gwydion leapt up the steps and pushed the man out of the way. The head crashed down and splintered into hundreds of fragments right on the spot where the man had been standing.

The Golden Man and the wyrce-jaga hurried up the steps to their companion just as Gwydion was helping him up. Rhiannon ran up and threw her arms around Gwydion. "Are you all right?" she asked anxiously scanning his face. "You're hurt!" she exclaimed, wiping at a trickle of blood running down his cheek. "Oh, my love, you scared me so!"

The Golden Man helped up his friend, his face pale and anxious. "Sigerric," he asked, "what happened, man? Are you hurt?"

"Not in the least. Thanks to him," Sigerric said, gesturing at Gwydion. The Golden Man turned to Gwydion and surveyed him, his hawk-like amber eyes looking into Gwydion's quicksilver gray ones. For a moment everything was still as they studied each other.

At last, the Golden Man smiled briefly. "You have my thanks. Sigerric's a good friend of mine, and I wouldn't want anything to happen to him. What is your name?"

Gwydion bowed politely, "I am Guido Asti, a minstrel of Turin. And this is my woman, Rhea Varins."

"Your woman?" the man replied, looking Rhiannon over as he had done earlier. "Not your sister, then?"

"No," Gwydion said firmly. "My woman."

"What a pity," the Golden Man replied absently, still looking Rhiannon over leisurely from head to toe. She flushed and looked down at the ground.

"And you, great lord?" Gwydion asked. "Whom have I the honor of addressing?"

"Down on your knees," the wyrce-jaga said haughtily, "this is the great Havgan of Dorsetas, soon to be the Bana of the Empire."

Gwydion bowed, but declined to get on his knees. "This is true luck to meet a great lord such as yourself, for we have heard of your greatness even as far as Turin."

"And what," Havgan asked, "is a minstrel from Turin doing so far from home?"

"Alas, great lord, the lords of Turin have no ear for fine music, and their purse strings are tight. So we have come to Athelin, looking for a lord who can truly appreciate fine entertainment. Dare I hope that you know of someone with discerning taste?"

"He means do you know of someone with a fat purse," Sigerric said cheerfully, apparently fully recovered from his brush with death.

"Give the man a coin," the black-robed wyrce-jaga said impatiently, "and let's go."

"Nay, Sledda, that would be churlish," Havgan replied softly but firmly. Sledda flushed at the reproof and gave Gwydion a venomous glance.

"Perhaps I do know of someone with discerning taste," Havgan went on, "but he would have to hear you play first."

"My woman and I will be playing at the festival tomorrow. Will you be there?"

"I'll be there. Perhaps our paths will cross again. Good day to you." Havgan turned away with one last bold look at Rhiannon, then marched down the steps.

"Our paths will cross again," Gwydion muttered. "Count on it."

"What happened between you two?" Rhiannon asked. "Something was going on."

"I'm not really sure," Gwydion said in a puzzled tone. He shrugged, then turned to her. "Enough of that. We have work to do."

"Like what?"

"Like practice. As of this time tomorrow, we'll be part of his household."

"How can you be so sure?"

"Trust me," he grinned.

Undeadlic Daeg, Sol 1—late afternoon
THE MARKETPLACE WAS packed with laughing, dancing crowds, and crammed with booth after booth selling food and drink, with wandering performers in search of audiences, with hundreds of finely crafted goods made over the long winter and now offered for sale at the Undeadlic Daeg festival. The festival marked the beginning of spring, commemorating the day that, according to legend, Lytir came back from the dead to begin his prosperous rule over the Coranians.

Gwydion and Rhiannon had arrived early, staking out a small space at the edge of the cobbled square. They had been singing songs and chanting poems for many hours now. They were good, much better than the other performers, and each performance gathered a sizable crowd—and many coins when they passed the bag around.

Whenever they spotted preosts in the crowd—they were easy to identify by their brightly colored robes—they sang the festival song,

> *"Fair and strong, Lytir is his name.*
> *In Heofen he lives.*
> *Dauntless he surveys it.*
> *Death shall not touch him*
> *for as long as the world lasts."*

This song usually earned them an extra coin or two from approving churchmen, but by the late afternoon Rhiannon was sick of singing it.

So far they had seen nothing of Havgan, and Rhiannon was torn between relief and worry. Relief, because he made her so uneasy, and worry, because they still had to get into his household, and his absence showed a lack of interest. They had just finished singing Deor's Song and Rhiannon had decided that Havgan wasn't coming when she saw a glint of golden hair at the edge of the crowd. They began to sing Queen Eanfled's Lament, a song that she sang alone while Gwydion piped in a minor key, producing a haunting counterpoint to the sad melody.

> *"I have wrought these words together out of a fated life,*
> *the heart's tally, telling of*
> *the grief I have undergone.*
> *For I loved my lord, and he I.*

Our lips had smiled to swear hourly
that nothing should split us—save dying—
nothing else. All that has changed:
it is now as if it never had been,
our friendship. I feel in the wind
that the man dearest to me detests me.

Some lovers in this world
live dear to each other, lie warm together
at day's beginning; I go by myself
about this prison.
Here I must sit the summer day through,
here weep out the woes of exile,
the hardships heaped upon me."

After she finished, the crowd applauded loudly, and Havgan made his way to the front of the throng. He was dressed magnificently in red and gold, and he shone in the afternoon light like a fiery sun come to earth. "Very well done, minstrels of Turin," he said. "Very well done, indeed."

Gwydion bowed while Rhiannon curtsied. Sigerric, who was by Havgan's side, also congratulated them. "Excellent. If you're looking for a patron, I believe I could recommend someone."

"But not now, Sigerric," Havgan said casually. "It's getting dark. Time to go down to the river." He nodded coolly at them, then turned away.

Thanks to Gwydion's lessons, Rhiannon knew what Havgan meant. One of the festivities on Undeadlic Daeg was to launch tiny boats into the river. Each boat carried a lit candle, and as each person lowered their boat into the water, they made a wish. If their boat reached the opposite bank with its candle still lit, their wish would come true.

"Come on," Gwydion said to Rhiannon, grabbing up his pipes and drum. She grabbed her harp and the bag of coins, and followed. He set a tremendous pace and when she finally caught up with him, she grabbed his arm. "Where are we going?"

"To the river. We've got to stay close to him."

Most of the crowd was also going down to the river, and they pushed their way through, trying to stay close to Havgan. From up ahead she caught glimpses of his golden hair, but the crowd parted easily for him, and they straggled far behind.

"Are you sure he's interested in hiring us?" she asked breathlessly. "He doesn't act like it."

"Of course, he's interested. But he loses dignity if he shows it directly. Sigerric showed interest, and he's Havgan's mouthpiece. That's how you can tell."

"How do you know that?"

He shrugged. "I just do. Hurry up, or we'll lose him."

"And men say that women are strange," she muttered.

At last they came to the river that ran through the center of the city. On the bank was a pile of tiny wooden boats, hollowed out of small blocks of wood, each with a small candle resting inside it. Gwydion grabbed one of the boats and tore a small strip from the sleeve of his forest green tunic, tying the cloth to the tiny mast to make a sail. All around them people were doing the same, marking the boats as their own.

The shadows were gathering as the sun swiftly descended from the sky. Up and down the river people gathered in groups, lighting torches, making laughing wagers on whose boat would likely capsize and whose would make it across. Then, group by group, they lit the candles and lowered their boats into the water.

Hundreds of tiny candle flames flickered over the surface of the water, bobbing and dodging. Many boats collided or capsized, very few of them making it safely across to the opposite bank.

They edged up close to Havgan so that when Havgan set his boat on the water, Gwydion was right beside him.

Havgan glanced at Gwydion and nodded coolly. Sigerric smiled and gestured to the tiny fleet. "Feel lucky today?" he asked Gwydion.

"Indeed, yes, lord," Gwydion replied. "I'll wager any man here that my boat makes it to the other side."

"And do you care to place a wager on your wish being granted, if your boat gains the bank?" Sigerric inquired.

"When my boat gains the banks, you mean," Gwydion replied.

"Come, Havgan, let's bet with this man," Sigerric proposed. "I like his confidence."

"Very well," Havgan replied smoothly. "What is your wager, minstrel?"

"My wager is that my boat makes it across. If I win, you grant my wish."

"Very steep. How do I know what your wish is?" Havgan said.

"You know," Gwydion replied in a level tone. "And the price is not too steep."

"No? I wonder," Havgan said absently, his eyes searching Gwydion's face. "And if you lose?" he went on, softly. "What then?"

"Why," Gwydion said casually, "if I lose, you may take my woman."

Rhiannon gasped. For a brief moment she considered knocking out every single one of Gwydion's teeth.

Don't, Gwydion spoke in her mind. *Trust me.*

You pig, she raged, her Wind Shout so loud that Gwydion winced slightly.

Havgan cocked his head and looked around. "Did you hear something?" he asked.

"What do you mean?" Sigerric replied. "I hear lots of things. It's a noisy crowd."

Still looking around, Havgan did not answer. Rhiannon was horrified. Havgan was telepathic—and he didn't even know it. Oh, this man was even more dangerous than they had ever suspected.

She did not look at Gwydion, afraid her expression would give them away, so she kept her eyes on the ground, as became a woman in Corania who was being given away like a bundle of bad cloth. Grimly she promised herself that, when this was over and she was alone with Gwydion, she would personally rip out his beard, whisker by whisker. It didn't matter that she knew his boat would make it across—with a little psychokinetic help. She knew that he was in no danger of losing his wager—and her with it. But she was furious nonetheless.

Havgan shrugged, giving up looking for the source of the cry he had heard, and turned his attention back to Gwydion. "Done," he said.

They lowered their boats into the water. Halfway across, Sigerric's boat floundered and capsized. "So much for your wish, Sigerric," Havgan crowed.

Sigerric smiled sadly. "It always was a foolish wish," was all he said.

Gwydion's boat with its strip of green cloth and Havgan's boat with its strip of gold sailed side by side. All around them other boats were capsizing, but these two sailed proudly across, matching each other measure for measure.

If Rhiannon hadn't known better, she could have sworn that Havgan was himself using psychokinesis to help his boat along. Or did she know better? She herself did not have this gift and wouldn't know if Havgan were using it or not. Gwydion would know. She'd ask him later. Just before she killed him.

Both boats had almost reached the opposite bank, the only two left afloat. The light of their candles glimmered in the gathering dusk. At last, the boats reached the opposite shore, both at the same moment.

"You did it. You both did it!" Sigerric exclaimed, slapping both men on their shoulders. "Now for your wishes. You first, minstrel."

"My wish is to find a man like that spoken of in the Makar's Song." Softly, he began to sing.

"The Makar's fate is to be a wanderer:
the poets of mankind go through many countries,
speak their needs, say their thanks.
Always they meet with someone, in the south lands or the north,
who understands their art, an open-handed man
who would not have his fame fail among the guard
nor rest from great deeds before the end cuts off
light and life together.
Lasting honor shall be his,
a name that shall never die beneath Heofen."

"I look for a man who wishes for lasting honor," Gwydion said when his song was done. "Are you that man, Lord Havgan?"

"I am. And I accept your service. You shall be my minstrel."

"And my woman?"

"Shall be safe in my household. More's the pity. Unless, of course, she changes her mind." For the first time since they had met him, Havgan grinned, a genuine grin without even a touch of arrogance.

"Your wish is granted, too, Havgan," Sigerric said. "I don't suppose I have to ask what it was."

"No, my old friend, you don't have to ask, for it never changes."

"May I ask your wish, great lord?" Gwydion asked. His voice was humble, but his eyes were keen and alert.

"It is something I have wished for these many years, since God himself spoke to me at a Gewinnan Daeg tournament long ago," Havgan replied, his voice faraway, walking through the past. "A wish which I have dedicated my life to making a reality."

"And that wish is?" Gwydion prompted.

"To make the command of the God come true. For he said to me that I must bring death to the witches of Kymru—those that they call the Y Dawnus—who rule that dark, unholy place. What say you to that, minstrel?"

"I think," Gwydion said slowly, "that your wish will be granted."

Rhiannon said nothing, for she thought so, too.

Chapter 8

Athelin, Marc of Ivelas
Weal of Coran, Coranian Empire
Ermonath, 496

Mandaeg, Sol 1—early afternoon

Gwydion sat alone on a stone bench in Havgan's garden, idly tuning his harp. It was a fine spring day. The sun was warm on his face and a light breeze rustled the hedges of evergreen privet that lined the garden paths. Purple corydalis dotted the garden here and there, and yellow primroses bravely raised their heads to the sun. A few snapdragons and lemon-yellow globeflowers had also ventured into the early spring air.

The garden was located in the central open courtyard of the house. The house was three stories high and built of interlocking planks of light and dark wood. The sloping timber roof glittered with bits of gold leaf, and the eaves were intricately carved with swirling patterns.

Still strumming his harp, Gwydion thought over what they had learned in the month he and Rhiannon had been in Havgan's household.

Many nights Havgan would have guests over to feast, and entertainment was needed. Rhiannon's dancing was always in demand, a fact that Gwydion secretly did not relish at all. He never bothered to examine why this was so, suspecting, perhaps, that he would not like the answer.

The men who feasted with Havgan were, for the most part, Byshops and Archbyshops, or wyrce-jaga, the witch-hunters. One wyrce-jaga, Sledda of Cantware, was almost always there at Havgan's elbow, much to Sigerric's obvious unease. Clearly the wyrce-jaga and the church supported Havgan's bid for power—a bid that would come to fruition three months from now at the Gewinnan Daeg tournament.

Havgan's main challenger for position of Warleader and husband to the Princess was Aelbald, the Empress's nephew. Aelbald's support came from the Empress herself and her cadre of Eorls and Alders who had learned long ago that Empress Athelflead was the real power in Corania. Emperor Athelred, pale and sickly, was an amiable nobody, given to kneeling for hours at a stretch in his private chapel. His daughter and heir, Princess Aelfwyn, was said to be very pretty and as clever as her mother. Clever enough, perhaps, to realize that a marriage with a man of Havgan's stamp would leave her powerless. She, too, favored a match with her cousin, Aelbald, a man she knew she could control. Rumor had it she declared often (and rather loudly) that she would never submit to a marriage with the son of a common fisherman.

Still strumming, Gwydion reviewed all he had learned about Havgan's past and rise as a contender for the throne. Havgan's father had indeed been a fisherman, and, if rumor was true, his mother was a madwoman. The father had died last year. Havgan's mother was still alive, living quietly in the Shire of Apuldre under the care of Sigerric's mother.

Havgan had been apprenticed as a kitchen boy to the Alder of Apuldre, Sigerric's father. When he had saved the life of Sigerric, the two boys had become fast friends, and Havgan was allowed to follow Sigerric into the service of the Eorl of Cantware.

At the age of twenty-four, Havgan had won the local Gewinnan Daeg tournament in Aecesdun where he had, by his own admission, received his revelation from the One God. Gwydion had long since realized that was the very night he had first dreamed of the Golden Man. It had been the dream of the crossroads, where Havgan's choice was to lead the Kymri into darkness. He struck a discordant note on his harp at that thought.

Two years later Havgan had again rescued another important man—Aesc, the brother of the Emperor. Prince Aesc and his warband had been ambushed by thieves on the way to the home of Eorl Wiglaf. Havgan and his friends, sent to greet the Prince, joined in the fray. All the thieves had been killed.

As a result of this rescue, Aesc, impressed by Havgan's prowess, offered him a place in his warband. Havgan accepted, and over the next seven years, he had gathered wealth and power with Aesc's support, enough wealth to begin his own warband, the nucleus made up of his closest friends. Besides Sigerric, there were Talorcan and Baldred of Dere, and Penda and Catha of Mierce, the sons of Eorls from those tributary countries. Gwydion had not met these other men. They were in their own lands at the moment, using their influence to gather certain lords to Havgan's cause.

Last year, the previous Warleader, Prince Athelric, had been killed. The story was that a woman whom the Prince had been raping had gotten away from him long enough to set the bed on fire. Though she had not confessed, insisting that she had awakened to the sight of the flames surrounding the bed, her story was not believed. She had been killed moments later by the guards, who were convinced in spite of her protests that she had set the fire. *Poor woman*, Gwydion thought, for he was quite certain she had not committed that crime.

After the fire, the Emperor declared that the winner of this year's Gewinnan Daeg games would be proclaimed Bana and wed the princess, thereby becoming the future Emperor of the Coranian Empire. And so the stage was set.

Gwydion inhaled deeply, breathing in the shy scent of the primroses, relishing his moment alone. It was not often that he could relax from the stress of either Havgan's presence or Rhiannon's. Both of them, for different reasons, made him tense and wary.

Of course, it would never do to become relaxed around Havgan. The man was stunningly intelligent, as well as a possessor of the gifts, even though he did not seem to realize it. Since the day they had entered his household, Gwydion and Rhiannon had not so much as whispered telepathically to each other, for fear that Havgan would pick up on it. Gwydion had also been exceedingly careful not to use his psychokinesis for any reason whatsoever. Havgan would be capable of sensing its use, though he would not necessarily understand what he was feeling. Gwydion would take no chances with that.

The first time Gwydion had projected his awareness into Havgan's rooms, he had done so warily, uncertain whether Havgan could sense his Wind-Riding. And Havgan had sensed something, putting his hand to his head, complaining of a sharp pain. So Gwydion and Rhiannon were careful not to Wind-Ride unless they must.

Gwydion plucked a discordant note, wondering again where Havgan had gotten his gifts. The Wiccan popped up from time to time in Corania, of course. Some possessors of the gifts often did not even admit to themselves that they were in any way different from everyone else. Many of them became rabid "witch" haters. No doubt there were quite a few wyrce-jaga and preosts with the gifts themselves. He was sure Havgan had gotten his gifts from his mother, for she was said to be mad. Certainly possessing the gifts and living in a country that feared and hated them would drive any talented man or woman insane.

But it was not just the danger that Havgan might sense the use of the gifts, or their true purpose here, that made Gwydion so tense around Havgan. There was far more to it than that. There were times when Gwydion felt that Havgan was hauntingly familiar, like a brother whom he had never known. Like a man who, in another place and time, might have been a friend.

Sometimes he wondered if Rhiannon had sensed this, and what she thought of it. So far, she had said nothing. But that wouldn't last.

Rhiannon. She was another matter that he didn't choose to examine too closely. There were nights when he lay next to her on the pallet in their little room, wondering what it would be like to feel her smooth skin beneath his hands; wondering what it would be like to kiss her; wondering what it would be like to seek the warmth of the inner recesses of her body and take comfort there.

But in spite of her close proximity night after night, he had never made a move to find out. He told himself it wouldn't be fair to push himself upon her here in Corania where her options, should she wish to decline, were few, and the potential for embarrassment extreme. Or, worse still, she might give in and then try to use that against him, as women will, thinking she had a hold on him simply because he had bodily needs and no other way to satisfy them. The thought of going down to the docks for one of the women there did not appeal to him at all.

That didn't stop Havgan, who was far less fastidious. Once or twice a week, a woman was brought to the house, easily identifiable as a whore from the poorer parts of the city. There was nothing particularly special about these women—except that they all had tawny blond hair. They might be thin or fat, clean or dirty, but their hair was always tawny. A little strange, that was. And the fact that Gwydion would never see them again was also strange. They arrived at the house at sundown, they went to Havgan's room, and Gwydion never saw them leave. Perhaps they left in the middle of the night—he thought it quite conceivable that Havgan would want to use them in the night and never see them in the light of day. He had even dared to ask Sigerric about it, once. Sigerric had muttered something about a dream that Havgan often had, some kind of nightmare. But he refused to say any more.

". . . asking for you."

Startled, he looked up and saw Rhiannon scowling down at him. "What?"

"I said, he's asking for you."

"Havgan?"

"Who else? The Archpreost?"

Gwydion sighed. Conversations with Rhiannon always

seemed to go this way. "Did he say why?"

"Not to me. I'm just a woman," she said bitterly.

"I see. Tell me, just out of curiosity, is there anything that's not my fault?"

"I didn't say it was your fault."

"You didn't have to," he replied shortly. He stood up and stretched. "Well, I'd better go see what he wants. Take the harp, will you?"

She snatched the harp from his hands. "If you're not too busy later, maybe you can tell me about it," she snapped. She turned and walked away, her slender back stiff. Gwydion shrugged. She certainly was touchy these days. She didn't like being in Corania. He smiled sourly. He didn't like it, either, but he didn't blame her for it.

They had done the right thing to come here, dangerous as it was. If they could maintain their charade long enough, they would have a chance to learn what they needed to know.

They needed to find out what kind of military support Havgan could count on should he become Bana. The Empress did not favor Havgan, but if he were Warleader, would she support him or try to hinder his plans? Just how many warriors would he be able to muster?

They also needed to discover when the invasion was to take place, and how the Coranians planned to take the country. There were plans, of that he was sure. There was a map of Kymru stretched on the wall of Havgan's chamber. Occasionally Havgan would sit in a chair before it, staring at the map.

In addition, there were a great many messages from Cantware these days. Why? What was happening there? Whatever it was, it was important. He knew that much.

He knew from his dreams that whatever he learned here would not prevent the coming war. But if he could find answers to these key questions, maybe he could save some lives, salvaging something for the future.

When he reached Havgan's chamber, Sigerric was also there, dressed in a long blue tunic glittering with amethysts at the hem and throat. His light brown hair was braided, as was the fashion for Coranian lords on formal occasions. He wore a cloak of brown wool, lined with fur and clasped at his shoulders with glittering golden brooches.

Havgan, on the other hand, was dressed casually in a brown woolen robe. He was sitting in a chair by the fireplace, with his legs resting on the hearth. He was paring his nails with a knife and whistling.

The chamber was large and airy. A huge four-poster bed rested on the far side of the room, the coverlet of red velvet in disarray. The wood floor was covered with fine rugs of deep blue. Tapestries studded the walls, except for the wall that held the huge map of Kymru. A wooden table stood in the middle of the room, stacked with pieces of parchment, some folded clothes, unwashed dishes, a gold flagon, and two gold cups studded with rubies.

"Ah, minstrel of Turin," Havgan said as Gwydion bowed to him. "How good of you to join us."

"My pardon, lord. I was sitting in the garden," Gwydion said humbly.

"I have an errand for you. You are to accompany Sigerric to Cynerice Scima and invite the Emperor, the Empress, Princess Aelfwyn, Prince Aesc, Princess Aesthryth, and that mangy weasel, Aelbald, to a feast at my house three days hence. You arc to sing my praises in such a way that the invitation is not refused. It is your task to issue the invitation with style and be sure they agree to attend. Is that clear?"

Gwydion bowed again. "Indeed, it is clear. But—"

Havgan's brows raised and his hawk's eyes were keen. "But what?"

"I fear they will turn me away at the palace gate." He spread his hands, indicating his plain, gray attire. "I have no rich clothes for such an occasion."

"No, I didn't think you did." Havgan nodded to the pile of clothing on the table. "Put those on. You have a very few moments, so hurry."

Gwydion bowed and picked up the clothing.

"Oh, and Guido . . ."

"Yes, lord?" Gwydion tensed and stopped with his hand on the latch.

"I expect you to prepare suitable entertainment for our royal guests."

"Yes, lord." Again, Gwydion attempted to leave, but Havgan called him back.

"Do not let them refuse," Havgan said softly. "Or I shall have to find a new minstrel who is more persuasive. You may go." Havgan smiled a wintry smile, and Gwydion left, chilled to the bone. It was times like these when Gwydion remembered that Havgan was his enemy. Remembered very well, indeed.

AS THEIR CAVALCADE left the courtyard and made their way down Landstrat, Gwydion urged his horse up to the front, next to Sigerric. They were followed by an honor guard of ten men, dressed in byrnies trimmed with gold and armed with brightly burnished swords.

They were a colorful group, Sigerric in his dark blue and Gwydion himself in a splendid tunic and trousers of rich scarlet, trimmed with pearls. His cloak was black, lined with fur, and clasped at his shoulders with huge silver, spiral-shaped brooches.

Gwydion grimaced to himself, remembering the few moments when he had hurried to his room to change and found Rhiannon there. She had been angry (which was nothing new) when she learned that she would be unable to accompany him to the palace.

"I can't help that," he had said wearily. "You know you can't come, and I can't make Havgan let you. I'll tell you all about it when I get back."

"Now why do I doubt that?' she had said dryly.

"I tell you everything you need to know."

"Your interpretation of what I need to know is a little too narrow for my taste."

"So, Wind-Ride along with us, if you want to go so badly," he had retorted and left. He knew she would not do such a thing, since Havgan would sense it, though he would not understand his own reaction. Going to the palace was not important enough to risk that.

"Lord Sigerric," Gwydion said quietly, turning his thoughts away from Rhiannon.

Sigerric turned to him with a brief smile. But the man's eyes were worried. He always seemed to have that look these days. But why? Everything seemed to be going according to Havgan's plans. Maybe that's what Sigerric was worried about.

"Yes, Guido?"

"What if they refuse to come? Would . . ." he made himself

sound frightened, not as hard a task as he would like, "would Lord Havgan really get rid of me?"

"Very likely."

"Would he . . . would he hurt us, Rhea and me?"

"Probably."

Gwydion studied Sigerric carefully. "Would you let him?"

Sigerric glanced at Gwydion. "Do you think I could stop him?"

"Well, you have some influence . . ."

"At one time, yes. But that was a long time ago. Things were different then."

They were nearing the palace now, coming up on the bridge that would lead them to the island where Cynerice Scima stood. Sigerric nodded to their left. "Look there."

Gwydion turned and saw a huge, forbidding building made of black stone. The stone gleamed in the afternoon sun, like the obsidian eyes of a snake.

"That is Byrnwiga," Sigerric went on, "the palace of the War-leader, the Bana. And that, dear minstrel, is one thing that has come between Havgan and I. That, and the map on his wall."

"And Sledda," Gwydion said. Surely he could say that much.

"And Sledda, yes."

"The princess is very beautiful, I hear." It was a shot in the dark, and, to Gwydion's surprise, it hit the mark.

"More beautiful than anyone I have ever seen," Sigerric said quietly. "More beautiful than a spring morning, more beautiful than the storm over the sea, more beautiful than the snowcapped mountains of Thule."

"And destined to be the wife of Havgan."

"Yes."

They reached the eastern bridge that stretched from the riverbank to the island where the palace stood. Armed men guarded the bridge. Their iron shields were rimmed with gold, and in the center was the Emperor's device, the Flyflot—a circle from which four golden bars radiated outward, each curving upward to the left.

The Captain of the guard stepped forward. "Who seeks to enter Cynerice Scima, the Light of the Empire?"

"I, Sigerric, Alder of Apuldre, do seek this in the name of the warrior chief Havgan, son of Hengist."

The Captain hesitated for a moment, then barked a command to his soldiers to step aside. "You may enter here. May the light of Lytir brighten your way."

The cavalcade clattered across the wooden bridge and onto the island. The white stone walls of Cynerice Scima glimmered in the sun, its four slender towers rising gracefully from each corner. They brought their horses to a halt and dismounted outside the east gate. Men came to take their horses, as the iron gate slowly opened.

When they came to the end of a long corridor, they stood in front of closed, golden doors. Smoothly, the doors opened inward and Gwydion almost gasped aloud.

This was Gulden Hul, the golden hall of the Rulers of the Coranian Empire, and it had been aptly named. Eight golden pillars, carved in the likeness of trees, held up the high, golden ceiling. The floor was made of golden tiles, and even the walls shimmered with golden light. Candles filled the hall, making it glow brightly. In the center a huge, golden tree, the symbol of the New Religion, spread its branches. Tiny jeweled birds nested there, glimmering rubies, amethysts, sapphires, and pearls.

At the north end, a dais stood, covered with a cloth of gold, upon which sat two thrones. On the golden wall behind the thrones hung a large tapestry, worked in gold and amethysts with the Flyflot, the Emperor's symbol. Four ranks of guards stood on either side of the dais.

Emperor Athelred sat stiffly on the largest golden throne. He was pale and had mild blue eyes. His scant, fine blond hair hung lankly to his shoulders. He wore a cloak of purple and a tunic and trousers of gold. On his head he wore a jeweled diadem and his thin neck seemed bent under the weight. In his hands he held a scepter, carved with the names of the ruling houses throughout Corania's history—the Cynmaegth and Wufmaegth; the Ealmaegth and the Sigmaegth; and the current ruling house, the Aelmaegth; a house that would end when Princess Aelfwyn's husand came to the throne.

Empress Athelflead sat on the smaller throne. Her rich, light brown hair was elaborately curled and braided, piled on top of her head, and held in place by a delicate golden crown. Her green eyes were sharp and cold.

Between the Emperor and the Empress, Princess Aelfwyn stood. She had long, light blond hair that hung freely to her knees—another cascade of light in this golden hall. Her eyes were cool green. She was dressed in white with a girdle of silver and pearls. She wore a single pearl pendant on a fine silver chain around her slender neck, the pearl resting in the deep pool between her breasts. Steorra Heofen they called her, as bright and as cold as the stars themselves. Beautiful, as Sigerric had proclaimed. But so very cold.

Princess Aesthryth, the Emperor's sister, stood to the right of her brother's throne. She wore a dress of blue silk with a girdle of silver and sapphires around her slender waist. A circlet of sapphires bound her long, blond hair back from her delicate face. Her clear, cornflower blue eyes gave Gwydion the feeling that she could see right through him. But what she thought about him remained a mystery.

Sigerric and Gwydion came to stand in front of the dais, then bowed deeply.

"My Emperor," Sigerric said as he went to his knees. Emperor Athelred nodded, then bade Sigerric to rise. "My Empress," Sigerric said, and again bowed. Empress Athelflead said nothing but watched him closely, her green eyes hard as emeralds.

"Princess," Sigerric said as he bowed again, his heart in his eyes. She would have seen it, if she had bothered to look at him. But she did not.

"Princess Aesthryth," Sigerric went on, bowing low. Aesthryth nodded to Sigerric but did not speak.

The silence spun out and Gwydion knew his time had come. He took a deep breath, preparing to do what minstrels did best—spread it on thick. Rhiannon would say that's what Dreamers did best, too. "O great Emperor, mighty ruler of this mighty land, I greet thee humbly in the name of Havgan, son of Hengist, a great warrior whose reverence for you is unbounded."

Quickly, Gwydion turned to the Empress. "O Empress Athelflead, helpmeet and heart's love of our mighty Emperor, I greet thee in the name of Havgan, son of Hengist, whose mighty sword arm is ever at thy service."

"O Princess Aelfwyn," he went on, "Star of Heaven. Fairer than silver, fairer than gold, you outshine the very hall itself, until the eyes of Havgan, son of Hengist, are dimmed by thy heavenly beauty."

"O Princess Aesthryth, one-time Queen of the Franks, how grateful we are that such a jewel was returned to the Empire, for while you were gone from us, the sun itself was dimmed and cold."

It was a fine speech, but the royal family said nothing. The silence was smothering. Gwydion cleared his throat. "Havgan longs to taste the joy of your presence. Many nights has he paced the floor, anxious hours has he spent, hoping against hope that you will grace him. Restless has been his sleep in his longing. Pale has he grown with fears that he is unworthy of the supreme joy your presence would bring to him. Until, lo, as he walked in the deep watches of the night, he resolved to put his fate to the test. A brave man, surely, who knows in truth how humble, how unworthy he is, yet still hopes on that his years of loyal service may count for even a little."

The silence was deafening. "And so he begs the honor, begs from the depths of his heart, that you will come to his house, three days hence, and let him feast his weary soul in your presence and bask in your glory. He begs that you, mighty Emperor and Empress, and you, two beauteous Princesses, and the mighty Princes Aesc and Aelbald come to his house."

Still silence. Then the Emperor spoke, hesitantly, while turning to the Empress, "I think, my dear, that we should——"

"No," Princess Aelfwyn said. Her voice was clear and cold. "I think not."

"No, indeed," a young man to the right of the dais said as he came bounding up to stand next to the Emperor. He was tall and broad shouldered. His light brown hair and green eyes showed a great resemblance to the Empress. So this must be Aelbald, the Empress's nephew, Havgan's chief rival. "We cannot come.

And that," Aelbald said, "is final."

Gwydion opened his mouth, to say he knew not what, but the Empress forestalled him. "Yes," she said crisply. "We will come."

The Princess turned to her mother, her jaw dropping in surprise. "What?" Her voice rose. "What do you——"

The Empress held up her hand and her daughter instantly fell silent. Empress Athelflead turned to her husband. "Havgan is a loyal subject, a great and worthy man. I believe that we should go as he requests." She stressed the last word somewhat. "Do you not agree?"

Athelred nodded. Aesthryth smiled gently, but the smile did not reach her eyes. Aelbald and Aelfwyn were furious, but said nothing, subsiding after a sharp glance from the Empress's cold eyes.

It was then that Gwydion felt a prickling at the nape of his neck. She was here, Rhiannon, watching him. She had chosen to come Wind-Riding after all. He felt her presence like a pressure in the air around him against his skin. Oh, he was angry with her for taking this chance. But there was nothing he could do about it now. In fact, he was so angry that he did not notice Princess Aesthryth's eyes widen, then flicker, searching the hall for something, but saying nothing.

Empress Athelflead turned to Sigerric, ignoring Gwydion. "Tell Havgan that we will honor him. You may go now."

Bowing, Sigerric and Gwydion backed away from the throne, then left the hall, their entourage following.

WHEN HE RETURNED to the house, Gwydion bounded up the stairs and into their room as fast as he could. Rhiannon sat next to the window, calmly plying her needle to one of her gowns.

"Oh, you're back," she said.

Panting, Gwydion growled, "Yes, I'm back. And so, apparently, are you."

"So I am," she agreed pleasantly, still stitching.

Gwydion reached out and grabbed the dress she was sewing on, throwing it to the floor. "Look at me when I'm talking to you," he demanded.

"You seem a little upset," she said mildly.

"Upset? Upset? Just because you risked your life to follow us to the palace? Just because if you had been caught Wind-Riding you would have been killed? Why should that upset me?"

"Why, indeed?" she asked, raising her brows.

"Because it would have gotten me killed, too," he snarled.

"Oh, yes. That explains it. Don't you want to know what happened after you left the palace?"

Gwydion took a deep breath, willing himself to calm down. "What do you mean?"

"After you left, the Empress had a few quiet words with Aelfwyn."

Curiosity got the better of his anger. "What did she say?"

"Maybe you would rather not talk about it. You seem a little upset."

"Tell me, right now, what she said," he replied through gritted teeth.

"She said that Aelfwyn could not marry a dead man. She said that the feast at Havgan's house would prove dangerous for the host."

"She's planning to kill him? How?"

"Unfortunately, she neglected to say. Aelfwyn wanted particulars, but the Empress said that the less she knew, the better."

"I can't believe it. She's really going to kill him?"

"Well, I assume she's actually going to have someone else do it."

Gwydion sat down slowly at the edge of the pallet, stunned. "I can't believe it. Do you realize what this means?"

"Of course, I do. No more invasion. Only Havgan could gather the might of the Empire. Without him it all falls apart."

"Then the Empress had better succeed in her plan," Gwydion said grimly.

Dondaeg, Sol 5—late evening

GWYDION BEAT THE drums in a savage rhythm. THUM, thum, thum. THUM, thum, thum.

Rhiannon's slender body, lightly covered by her gossamer white gown, twisted to the beat of the drums. Gold flashed at her wrists and ankles as she dipped and swayed, her black hair fanning out behind her like a shadow.

THUM, thum, thum. THUM, thum, thum. The hall was smoky from the hearth fire. The light of hundreds of torches flickered fitfully off the golden and silver goblets, the platters of broken meats, the fine robes and tunics of the people who watched Rhiannon's sensual dance.

Havgan's hawk eyes were fastened on Rhiannon's twisting body, and the hunger in them blazed fiercely. It was a blaze that was in Gwydion's own eyes as he, too, watched Rhiannon dance, but he did not know it. The same hunger was also in Sigerric's eyes as he looked at Princess Aelfwyn, sitting so cool and aloof on Havgan's left. It was a hunger she would never bother to see.

THUM, thum, thum. THUM, thum, thum. Gwydion,

tense and wary, darted anxious glances at the crowd, trying to see everyone at once.

The Emperor, seated on Havgan's right, gazed politely but absently at Rhiannon's dance. The Empress's cold, green eyes were fastened on Havgan and her daughter, flickering occasionally to where Aelbald sat, the fury clear on his face. Aelbald had been seated far down the table away from Aelfwyn, and he, too, fastened his gaze on Havgan and the Princess. Aelfwyn herself never looked at Havgan at all but stared down at her platter, her face pale and set.

Prince Aesc watched Rhiannon closely as he drank his wine and joked with his friends. He laughed often and seemed to be enjoying himself. His sister, Princess Aesthryth, was smiling at the jests as she, too, slowly sipped her wine. Her blue eyes did not watch Rhiannon, but rather darted around the hall as though seeking something or someone.

Sledda, his weasel-like face covered with a film of lust, licked his lips and watched Rhiannon's every move. Briefly Gwydion thought how terribly satisfying it would be to shove Sledda into the fire and watch his flesh blacken and peel.

THUM, thum, thum. THUM, thum, thum. Slowing the pace now, the dance nearly done, Rhiannon sank to her knees, her arms outstretched as though eager to caress the warm flesh of every man at the feast. Then she threw her head back, her face and bare arms glistening with a fine layer of sweat, and arched her back, slowly bending backward until her spine touched the cold stone floor. One last beat from Gwydion, and the dance was done.

The guests thundered their applause, beating on the table with knife hilts, calling out ribald comments, cheering heartily.

Rhiannon rose and bowed, then took her place next to Gwydion on the hearth, picking up her harp. Without a pause, they began to play.

Rhiannon, still breathing heavily from her exertions, said, "Well?"

"Very nice," he replied. "I think the Emperor almost actually woke up."

"Are you absolutely sure that a compliment would kill you?"

"I thought Sledda was going to take you right on the floor."

She shuddered. "That's a compliment?"

"Minstrels!" Havgan roared through the laughing crowd, and Gwydion and Rhiannon stood up quickly. "Come here!"

They made their way through the throng and halted before the central table. Havgan, dressed magnificently in red and gold with rubies braided through his tawny hair, smiled down at Princess Aelfwyn. It was a wolfish smile, and Aelfwyn flushed. Gwydion glanced at the Empress who sat calmly in her chair, emeralds dripping from her ears, her neck, and her hands. Her rich, elaborately braided hair was piled on top of her head, baring her long, slender neck and white shoulders. She had a half smile on her face, as though Havgan amused her.

"Minstrels," Havgan went on, "the Princess wishes to hear a song." He grasped Aelfwyn's cold hand and lightly kissed her fingers, one by one. "You need only command me, Princess."

Aelfwyn snatched her hand away. Her golden hair, sprinkled with diamonds, shimmered in the candlelight, and her green eyes were cold. Havgan laughed mockingly. "Any song you wish, it shall be yours."

"Deor's Song," she replied coolly.

Gwydion nodded to Rhiannon, knowing full well that this

must be the signal for Havgan's murder, and they began to sing.

"*Ceanwalh mourned her murdered brothers,*
but her own plight pained her more,
her womb grew great with child.
When she knew that, she could never hold
steady before her wit what was to happen.
That went by; this may, too.

Ine knew the wanderer's fate:
that single-willed Prince suffered agonies,
sorrow and longing the sole companions
of his exile. Anxieties bit
When Yffi threatened his life,
laid wondering doom to the better man.
That went by; this may, too.

All have heard of Cyneburga's ravishing:
while her dead child lay still at her side.
Sigger's lust was ungovernable,
their bitter love banished sleep.
Long she was in the grasp of that grim Emperor.
That went by; this may, too.

When each gladness is gone, gathering sorrow
May cloud the brain; one cannot
See how sorrows may end—"

There. The glitter of a knife, clutched firmly in the hands of a preost in a yellow robe standing just behind Havgan. The knife rose and began its deadly descent.

The moment seemed to go on forever.

And the next thing he knew, Gwydion gave a tremendous shout and leapt across the table, grabbing the wrist of the preost, and the knife clattered to the floor, unblooded.

Pandemonium broke out. Princess Aelfwyn screamed. Havgan's guards wrestled the preost to the floor. The Emperor and Empress leapt up, the Emperor ashen with shock, the Empress ashen with rage. Prince Aesc, too, leapt to his feet, roaring. Princess Aesthryth remained seated, looking at Gwydion with what he thought might be pity in her eyes.

Havgan grabbed Gwydion by the shoulders and spun him around to face him. "Minstrel," Havgan breathed. "Guido. You saved my life."

Rhiannon stared at Gwydion in shock, and her hands tightened on her harp, tightened so strongly that the strings broke, snapping with a moaning sound.

Gwydion stared at Havgan, his face white, his gray eyes dull and shocked.

"You saved my life," Havgan repeated in a stunned voice.

Sigerric, the preost subdued, snarled at the man. "Who are you?"

The preost's mouth tightened. "I'll tell you nothing," the man spat.

Two soldiers grasped the man's arms and Sigerric grabbed the man's hands, examining them closely. They were covered with nicks and scars. "You're no preost. These are the hands of a warrior. Who are you?"

"Who did he come in with?" Havgan asked. But it seemed that no one could remember. Certainly no one owned up to it. "Take him to my chamber," Havgan said. "I will question him later."

"No," the Empress said sharply. "The Emperor will question him."

"My Empress, I think—"

"I am appalled that such a thing could happen, and I intend to get to the bottom of this," she cut in. "Guards," she gestured to two of the Emperor's soldiers, "take him back to the palace. I will come along shortly."

At Havgan's nod, his men released the preost to the care of the Emperor's soldiers, who dragged him roughly out of the hall.

The Empress turned to Havgan, "Thanks be to blessed Lytir that you are unhurt. Your minstrel was very quick." As she said this, she glanced at Gwydion, and he saw his own death in her eyes. "Perhaps I could find a use for such a brave man."

"I think not. It pains me to deny you, but I find this minstrel very useful."

"A pity," she replied absently. "Good night, my dear Havgan. Perhaps you would come to the palace in a few days and let us entertain you."

"I regret to inform you that I will be leaving the city on an extended journey very soon. Perhaps when I return."

"A journey," the Empress said flatly. "Where to?"

"Oh, here and there," Havgan said carelessly.

"And how long will you be gone?"

"Some months. But never fear. I will be back before the tournament." Havgan turned to the Princess and leisurely kissed her hand, holding her eyes with his own. "Until then, Princess. I bid you good-bye. I will count the hours until I return to you."

There was a slight commotion outside, and one of Havgan's soldiers came running back into the hall. "My lord, the assassin is dead! He killed himself. He had a small knife strapped to his arm, and he slit his own throat."

"Did he now?" Havgan said with no surprise whatsoever. He glanced at the Empress. "A pity. Now we will never know who hired him."

"A great pity, indeed," the Empress replied.

And Gwydion, still standing frozen on the spot with the enormity of what he had done pounding in his bewildered brain, felt a touch on his sleeve, and turned then to meet Rhiannon's blazing eyes.

MUCH LATER, WHEN all the guests were gone, they returned to their room. Gwydion slumped onto the bed while Rhiannon, tight-lipped, took a chair by the tiny window. He waited dumbly for her to tear him to shreds for what he had done. He would almost welcome it. He deserved it, and he knew he did.

Why had he done it? Even now he didn't know. It had to do with a bond between him and Havgan—a bond that Gwydion had not known existed until now. Some kind of recognition, perhaps. Some half-understood thought that he and Havgan were one and the same, two sides of the same coin, brothers in some strange way.

All that might be true, but how could he have done what he did tonight? He had saved the life of his greatest enemy. He had saved the life of the man who would bring death and destruction to Kymru. How? How could he have done that?

Still Rhiannon did not speak. She sat still as a statue and looked out the window at the night sky. The silence pooled between them, rising like a wall, slowly thickening, crowded with unsaid words. It went on and on until Gwydion felt he could not stand it another moment. Then, at last, she spoke.

Without turning her head, she said, "If you're interested, I found out earlier today why Havgan is getting so many messages from Cantware."

Gwydion, who had been holding his face in his hands, lifted his head in surprise. This wasn't what he had expected at all. "Why? What is happening there?"

"He's building ships." She stopped, letting this sink in. Then she went on. "He's building great, huge ships. To sail his army to Kymru with, and kill us all."

That was all she said. But it was enough.

Chapter 9

Athelin, Marc of Ivelas & Camlan, Marc of Gillingas
Weal of Coran, Coranian Empire
Ermonath, 496

Fredaeg, Sol 13—late morning

R hiannon was in the garden when the call came. Gwydion, she knew, was in their tiny room, probably staring at the floor as he had been doing for a week now, ever since he had saved Havgan's life.

He had seemed to close up inside of himself since then, stricken with horror at what he had done. And Rhiannon had left him alone. She could not offer comfort because he didn't deserve it. And she could not do anything to bring him out of his dark place because she was too angry, too bitter, to forgive.

Sitting now, with her face lifted to the late morning sun, she thought that the lack of forgiveness was a grim habit of hers. Hadn't she done that to Rhoram for years and years? Well, if it was a habit, then so be it. If hers was not a forgiving nature, didn't she have cause? Viciously she hoped with all her heart that Gwydion's suffering would go on and on. He could not suffer enough for what he had done.

She heard someone making their hurried way down the path and stood quickly. The man, one of Havgan's soldiers, caught sight of her and breathlessly told her that Lord Havgan wanted to see her in his chambers. At once. She nodded and turned to go back into the house, the soldier dogging her steps as though afraid she would run away.

If only she could.

THE DOOR TO Havgan's chamber was open, and she hurried inside. The door shut firmly behind her, and she blinked with eyes still dazzled by the sunlight outside, trying to make out who was there in the sudden shadows.

"Ah, Rhea. Please, sit here," Havgan said as he took her arm and guided her to a chair at the long table in the middle of the room. She didn't like it when he touched her. He loomed over her, looking impossibly handsome, impossibly virile, and hideously alive. O gods, how she wished he was dead. She blinked again and realized that, thank the gods, they were not alone. Sigerric was there, looking slightly uncomfortable, as he always seemed to look these days.

A slight movement by the hearth caught her attention. It was Gwydion. He was haggard, and there were dark circles underneath his eyes. Rhiannon, looking at him fully in the face for the first time in a week—for he had always turned his head away when they were alone—was shocked by his appearance.

Havgan caught her looking hard at Gwydion. Oh, he was always so quick. How much more of this man could she stand?

"I was just saying that Guido seems to be unwell. I see that you feel the same, my dear Rhea. You don't seem to be taking good care of your lover."

The word *lover* was almost a question. Did he think that they had quarreled? Did he hope for that? Or could he possibly suspect that Gwydion was regretting his action that saved Havgan's life?

With a sharp tone in her voice, she replied, "A slight digestive problem. I've been trying to give him some potions to help, but he refuses to take them."

"Yes," Gwydion said with a ghost of a smile. "I keep telling her that the cure is worse than the illness."

"Now, you must take care of yourself, minstrel," Havgan said. "After what you have done for me, I insist."

Rhiannon saw Gwydion's fingers tighten together and knew that Havgan saw it, too. She hurried over and put an arm around his shoulders. "Another cramp, my love?" she asked gently.

Gwydion nodded. "I'll be all right." He straightened then, determined to act as if nothing very much was the matter. She sat down next to him on the hearth, her arm still around his shoulders.

"Perhaps we could get on with this," Sigerric suggested in a mild tone.

"Of course, Sigerric. Rhea, you must perform a task for me."

Rhiannon straightened. "Yes, lord?"

"You are to come with us to the palace where the Witan, the Emperor's council, will be in session. You are to announce my formal challenge at the Gewinnan Daeg tournament for the position of Bana."

"I am to announce that?" she asked in surprise.

"You are a minstrel. Presenting formal challenges are all part of a minstrel's tasks."

"Of course, but—"

"But what?" There was an edge to his tone, but his eyes were laughing at her.

"It is an insult," she said slowly, "for a formal challenge to be spoken by a woman."

"Is it?" Havgan said, his brows raised in mock surprise. "I hadn't realized that."

She sighed. "All right. When do we leave?"

"At noon."

"I have nothing to wear."

Havgan sighed. "That's all you minstrels say to me. You will find a new gown in your chambers. Guido, I expect you to wear the clothes I provided for you last week. That is, if you feel up to going."

"Oh, yes," Gwydion said, as heartily as he could. "I shall go."

"Good." Havgan walked them to the door. "As you know, I will be leaving Athelin in four days. I have decided to take you both with me. I am beginning to find the services of minstrels to be very valuable." He warmly clasped Gwydion's shoulder and smiled. "Very valuable, indeed."

After the door closed behind them, Gwydion winced, his face crumbling into a spasm of pain. Rhiannon saw it clearly, and, for a moment, thought of offering a bit of comfort to him, after all.

But as this thought passed through her mind, the image of Rhoram stopped her. Rhoram who, as King of Prydyn, would surely lead his warriors against the Coranians on that fateful day. And just as surely would die at their hands.

And it occurred to her then, for the first time, that perhaps it was the image of King Uthyr, Gwydion's half-brother, leading his own warriors to their deaths, which brought the haunted look to his pale face.

For a moment she almost felt pity for him.

Almost.

THE CHAMBER WHERE the Witan met was high up within the Emperor's Tower at the north end of the palace. Their party climbed up the stone steps single file, with Rhiannon in the lead. Havgan was just behind her, then Sigerric, with Gwydion following last.

Rhiannon walked with her head high, but she felt a little self-conscious in her new gown. It was of dark, green velvet, and fitted her breasts and hips like a glove. A girdle of gold embroidered cloth was doubled around her waist and then tied in front to lie low on her hips. Her dark hair was worn loose, held back from her face by a matching band of gold. It was a beautiful gown, but it was cut very low in front. She knew that she had Havgan to thank for that. It was times like these when she most wanted to kill him.

Finally, they reached the closed door of the chamber at the top of the tower. Two guards stood outside the door, their swords drawn. One guard said formally, "Why have you come here to the Witan?"

"To present a challenge," Rhiannon answered.

The other guard sneered, after looking her up and down. "You are presenting a challenge?"

"As a minstrel of Turin, I have the right. Should you wish to contest that right, Lord Havgan himself would be happy to discuss it further with you."

The guard, taking in Havgan's silent presence behind her, swallowed nervously. "Uh, never mind. You may enter." He opened the door quickly and stood aside.

Around a large table sat the Emperor, looking vague, as always; the Empress, who looked up coldly, her face tightening; Archpreost Whitgar, dazzling in his purple robe and golden medallion; Aesc, the King's brother, the frown on his face lightening at their entrance; Sethwald, the Archbyshop of Coran in a robe of blue; and Ethbrand, the Arch-wyrce-jaga, his black robe trimmed in blue and his pale eyes like chips of ice.

Havgan bowed low to the Emperor and Empress, drew his sword, then stood stiffly, legs planted slightly apart, hands on his sword hilt, the point resting on the floor.

Rhiannon began, "Mighty Emperor and Empress, great lords, I greet you in the name of Havgan, son of Hengist. He is a warrior of great renown, eager to serve you to the utmost of his ability, a warrior proven as master in death skills. A warrior whose mind is keen and whose sword is sharp. He begs for a moment of your time."

Smoothly, Archpreost Whitgar rose to his feet. He was a broad-shouldered bear of a man, his hands covered with scars from the years when he had been a warrior, before he had received his call from the One God to enter the church. He had a bushy, gray beard that spilled down the front of his rich robe. "You are welcome here, Havgan, son of Hengist. How may we—"

Whitgar broke off as a disheveled, breathless Aelbald sprinted into the council chamber. Aelbald skidded to a halt next to Havgan. It was an unfortunate place to stop, for the juxtaposition of the two men did not show Aelbald to his best advantage. Havgan, dressed magnificently in red and gold, seemed to glow in the small chamber. Aelbald, who was dressed in a casual woolen tunic and trousers of brown, looked insignificant beside his enemy.

"What's going on here?" Aelbald demanded. "I hear Havgan has dared to disturb this council. I insist you tell me the meaning of this."

Aesc replied shortly, "You are not a member of the Witan and, as such, are not owed an explanation of our business."

Aelbald, his mouth opening and closing like a fish out of water, cast a pleading glance at the Empress, who spoke in her firm, clear voice, "We do not yet know Havgan's business, Aelbald. And though you are not a member of the Witan, my husband feels that you should stay, since we suspect his business concerns you also. You may be seated." Aelbald spotted a chair in a corner and swiftly sat.

Now that the council room was quiet, Rhiannon began again. "The mighty Havgan—"

Aelbald jumped to his feet. "What is the meaning of this?"

Rhiannon turned swiftly to him, her green eyes flashing. "That question has been asked already, Aelbald, son of Aescwine. And I will answer it just as soon as you shut up."

Aelbald stiffened. Gwydion and Havgan hid smiles behind their hands. Sigerric coughed lightly. Aesc was openly grinning. Archpreost Whitgar, after a mighty internal battle, managed to keep a straight face. The Emperor did not seem to be paying the slightest attention. And the Empress looked at Rhiannon as though she were a new kind of insect.

"You insult this council by speaking here. You—a woman!" Aelbald continued.

Rhiannon looked at Aelbald, her brows raised. "It is my understanding that in the Coranian Empire, minstrels may pronounce challenges."

"You are a woman! A woman has no right——" At the last moment, Aelbald remembered the Empress and broke off what he had been about to say. Rhiannon let the silence spin out long enough for Aelbald's flush to brighten as much as it would.

"As I was saying," she went on, "the mighty Havgan will test his prowess at the Gewinnan Daeg tournament. If there are any who will gainsay him the right to fight for the hand of Princess Aelfwyn, and for the office of Bana, let that person come forth now."

Complete silence. Aelbald stirred, but the Empress shot him a venomous look that seemed to nail him to his chair.

At last, the Empress spoke. "We, the members of the Witan, acknowledge the right of Havgan, son of Hengist, to battle for the hand of Princess Aelfwyn and the office of Bana," the Queen said formally.

Havgan bowed his head in acknowledgment that his challenge was accepted.

"Are there others in this room who also wish to register their challenge?" the Empress went on.

"Yes." Aelbald stood and brushed past Rhiannon to stand in front of Havgan. It should have been a dramatic moment, but Rhiannon, as she stumbled, swiftly thrust out her foot, and Aelbald promptly went flying into Havgan's arms. Gravely, Havgan hauled Aelbald upright and set the Prince back on his feet, but Havgan's lips were twitching with amusement.

Aelbald turned to Rhiannon in a fury, "You——"

"Your pardon," Rhiannon said, bending down to rub her ankle. "I slipped."

Another choking sound from Sigerric greeted this statement. Gwydion had his head down so no one could see his face, but his shoulders were shaking. The rest maintained sober faces as best they could. The Empress sighed. She prompted Aelbald before he could say anything else. "Do you wish to challenge, nephew?"

"I do." Aelbald turned to Havgan again, standing almost nose to nose. "I, too, will fight in that tournament. I will win the hand of Princess Aelfwyn and the office of Bana for myself. And I will leave your guts scattered across the field."

"Well," Havgan said softly, "you can always try." He smiled, but with such menace that Aelbald actually stepped back a pace.

"Very well," said the Empress. "The challenges are noted. You may all go."

They left the room quickly, Aelbald trailing as far behind as he could. Havgan led the way, with Rhiannon behind him, followed by Gwydion and Sigerric. Halfway down the stairs, Havgan said to her, over his shoulder, "I slipped?"

"Well, I did," she said defensively.

"I can't believe that you told the great and mighty Aelbald to shut up," Havgan grinned. "I don't think anyone's ever done that before."

"Wrong, my lord," Rhiannon grinned in return. "The Empress tells him that all the time."

Havgan laughed. His amber eyes sparkled, his handsome face lit with genuine amusement. And as they all began to laugh, Rhiannon saw what Gwydion had seen all along. As she heard her enemy laugh with her, he seemed to be a friend.

Soldaeg, Sol 15—late evening
TWO NIGHTS LATER, Gwydion and Rhiannon sat with Havgan in his chambers. It was very late, and most of the candles had burned down, tiny flames gleaming through mounds of hot, soft

wax. Each time she or Gwydion finished a song or a story, she expected Havgan to dismiss them. But he did not. Instead, he paced. He paced as they sang, paced as they played their tunes, paced as they told story after story.

What was Havgan waiting for? Every moment tightened and stretched her nerves. They were ready to break, had been ready, would have broken by now, but for Gwydion's calm voice, his steady hands on his harp, and his occasional light touch on her cold arm.

And then they heard the soft tap on the door.

Swiftly, Havgan crossed the room and opened it. Sledda, dressed in a nondescript tunic and trousers of brown wool, stepped into the room, followed by two soldiers who were dragging an old woman between them.

The old woman was clearly terrified. Her scant gray locks hung to her shoulders. She was pale and blinked constantly, as though even the dim light in Havgan's room hurt her eyes. The eyes themselves were dark with fear and hopelessness as the soldiers tossed her into a chair, then left, closing the door.

"You are sure of her?" Havgan asked Sledda, gazing fixedly at the old woman, who huddled in the chair with her head bowed.

"Quite sure," Sledda replied firmly.

"Where did you find her?"

"At Cirice Garth, in the Archpreost's dungeons. She is to die tomorrow."

"What is your name?" Havgan spoke softly to the old woman.

"Gytha," she replied, not raising her head.

"You have been condemned to die, Gytha, as one of the Wiccan, as a witch."

"Yes," the old woman said tonelessly. Then she raised her

head and spoke in a nervous, desperate tone, "But I tell you, it's a lie! I am a good daughter of the church. I believe in Lytir, the One God. I swear it."

"Gytha," Havgan said softly, "I will be so disappointed if what you say is true."

Sledda came to stand by the old woman and cuffed her viciously. "You are insolent to the great Lord Havgan! Learn manners and he may let you live!"

Gytha flinched back, then raised her eyes to Havgan, a desperate light in them. "Is that true, lord? You will let me live?"

"I may," Havgan replied, stressing the second word, "if you can do as I ask."

"Anything, lord." Gytha rose from the chair and sank to her knees. "Anything. Let me live," she cried in a broken, shamed voice, tears streaming down her seamed face.

"Are you a witch?" Havgan pressed. "Can you see the future?"

Gytha tensed, looking up at Havgan as though he were Sceadu, the Great Shadow himself. The room was so silent that when the embers in the hearth shifted, Gytha cringed.

With anguish in her face, misery in every line of her body, Gytha finally replied, "Yes. Yes, sometimes I can see the future." She bowed her old head, tears streaming down her wrinkled face. "I didn't want to. I never wanted to," she sobbed. "I would pray to God to stop it, but he didn't. He wouldn't."

"Do you know how to read the wyrd-galdra?"

"Yes," the old woman whispered, her voice full of terror. "Yes."

Wyrd-galdra, Rhiannon thought. Fate-magic. The word for reading the cards of the Old Gods. Oh, Havgan was treading the brink here, indeed. The wyrd-galdra were pasteboard cards, painted with representations of the Old Gods themselves. And this was looked upon by the church as magic of the blackest kind.

Suddenly it occurred to her that if this Gytha was really a witch, if she was truly gifted, she might sense something from Gwydion or herself. And she might betray them. At that thought Rhiannon hardly dared to breathe.

"You, Gytha, will read the wyrd-galdra for me. Now."

"Lord, I cannot. I have no cards."

"Ah, but I do." Havgan moved to his four-poster bed and reached under the mattress, pulling out a pack of cards bound together with a wisp of red silk. He brought the pack to Gytha, unwrapping them as he did so. "For the past week, I have slept with them under my pillow every night. They are attuned to me. Now, read them."

With trembling hands, Gytha reached up and took the cards. Havgan sat down at the table, clearing an empty space on its surface.

Gytha took a deep breath, "Ask your question, lord."

"Will I defeat the Kymri?"

Gytha fanned out the brightly colored pack of twenty-two cards, her gnarled hands shaking. She presented the blank sides to Havgan. "Choose a card."

Havgan chose and laid the card face up on the table. It was a painting of a man with tawny hair, walking happily on the edge of a cliff. At his heels a little dog nipped and yapped. The golden sun shone brightly. He carried a stick on his shoulders, a leather bag attached to the end of it.

"This Covers Him," Gytha said formally. "This is the card that influences your question. This card is you. It is called The Fool."

"And it means what?"

Gytha licked her lips nervously and hesitated. Havgan reached across the table and yanked Gytha to him, gripping her by her hair. Havgan's eyes shone fiercely as he glared at the old woman. "Make it a true reading, witch. Hold nothing back. Understood?"

Gytha nodded frantically. Slowly Havgan released her, and the old woman sat back, breathing harshly. After a moment, Gytha went on, "The card that you have chosen is a symbol of the mystic who seeks to find his way. A symbol of one who has certain gifts, gifts given to him by the Old Gods."

"What kind of gifts?" Havgan growled.

"The gifts of the Wiccan. Gifts such as Soul-Speech, such as Fire-Bringing, such as Fate-Telling, such as Wandering the Sky." Gytha closed her eyes tightly, waiting for the blow. But it did not come. Gytha cautiously opened her eyes.

Havgan's face seemed to be carved from stone. Only his eyes were alive—alive with knowledge of something dark and dangerous that stalked him, that could not be escaped, twist and turn as he might. The eyes of a trapped man.

"Lord?" Gytha asked nervously. "Should I go on?"

"Yes," Havgan said quietly. "Go on."

Quickly, Gytha laid out nine cards, face down. One she laid crosswise over The Fool. She placed four around the two center cards making a square, and four more in a vertical line to the right of the square. Gytha cleared her throat, and then tapped the back of the card that lay on top of The Fool.

"This Crosses Him," she intoned. "This is the card that represents the force that opposes your will." Gytha turned the card over slowly. It was a painting of a man in a white robe, with a cloak of red fastened to his shoulders. Above his head was a figure eight, the sign for Annwyn, the Kymric Lord of Chaos. A vine of red roses bound the man's brow, a snake curled around his waist. On a table in front of him was a clod of dirt, a flaming torch, a cup of water, and a feather. "This is The Magician. Before him are the elements—earth, fire, water, air. He is the opposing force, the force that seeks to stop you."

"A Magician? You mean one of the Wiccan?"

"No, lord. This is a symbol of the Kymri."

"So," Havgan said slowly, "you are a true witch, after all."

Gytha bowed her head, but said nothing.

"How do the Kymri seek to stop me?"

Rhiannon tensed and she felt Gwydion do the same. "I cannot say, lord," Gytha replied. But did her eyes flicker over to them briefly? Rhiannon thought they did. "The cards will answer one question only, and you have asked it already."

"Very well," Havgan replied. "Go on."

"This Is Beneath Him," Gytha said, pointing to the card just below the crossed Fool and Magician cards. "This card stands for your past, for that which is a part of you." Gytha flipped over the card. "The High Priestess. This is Holda, the Goddess of Water." The Goddess stood on a rocky shore, the sea streaming out behind her, the folds of her gown pooling at her feet. Havgan jumped as though he had been stung. "My dream," he breathed, stunned. "The Woman on the Rocks."

"Lord?"

"Nothing. Go on." With an effort, Havgan got control of himself, but his face was pale. "What does it mean?"

"It is a symbol for the hidden influences at work within you. For that which you feel, but cannot grasp. Holda is the keeper of those truths we hide even from ourselves."

"Go on."

Gytha tapped the card to the left of the Fool and Magician cards. "This Is Behind Him. It is the card for the influences in your life that are just passing away." She turned the card over. A man with a flowing gray beard hung upside down by one foot from the branch of a mighty tree, his hands bound behind him, his face sad and wise. "The Hanged Man. This is Wuotan. It is he who has influenced you, who has gotten you to where you are now."

"Wuotan?" Havgan said sharply.

"Yes. The . . . the God of Magic." The silence was heavy. Sledda gave Havgan a sharp look with his pale, glittering eyes, but did not move.

"And it is he who has influenced me?"

"Oh, decisively. Without him, you would not be here in this place."

"Yes, I understand."

Rhiannon saw from Havgan's face that he probably did, indeed, and wished with all his soul that he did not. She could almost see him push this away from him, push it away far inside and lock the door against it.

"Go on," Havgan said.

Gytha tapped the card at the top of the square. "This Crowns Him," she said. "This card shows your future." Havgan leaned forward, intent. Gytha turned the card slowly. A warrior, with accoutrements of gold stood tall and proud within a wooden chariot. Two golden lions were hitched to the vehicle. In the warrior's strong hand was a sword of silver. "The Chariot," Gytha smiled. "Oh, very auspicious, my lord. The figure is Tiw, the great God of War. The card means victory and success."

"Success? I will defeat the Kymri?"

"Oh, most probably. But remember, this is just one card. The final card, the tenth card, will tell you truly."

"All right. Continue."

Gytha tapped the card to the right of the crossed Fool and Magician cards. "This Is Before Him. This will tell you something important that will happen in the near future, or that is already happening, though you may not know it." Gytha turned it over and frowned. "This is not so good," she muttered. The painting showed a full, silvery moon, shining brightly down on two towers. At the foot of the towers, two wolves howled. "It is Mani, The Moon. And it means peril and deception. Someone close to you will betray you in some way. Sometime soon, if he or she has not done so already."

Gwydion stiffened slightly beside her. Havgan did not even look their way. Even Sledda did not. Havgan stared down at the card, thinking deeply. "Do you know who?"

"I cannot tell," Gytha replied easily. But Rhiannon, who was watching her closely, thought she saw a gleam in her eyes. For one split second, Gythas's eyes met hers, then skittered away.

"Shall I continue?" Gytha asked, breaking Havgan's train of thought.

"Hm? Oh, yes. Go on."

Gytha tapped the back of the seventh card, the lowest on the row to the right of the square. "This Is to Come to Him. It is the card to show of a great happening in your life that awaits you." Gytha turned over the card. A naked man and woman stood before a winged goddess. The goddess's face was kind and gentle, and the rays of the sun shone in her wise eyes. In her hands she held two golden apples. "The Lovers," Gytha said. "They stand before the Goddess Erce, the gentle mother, as she blesses them."

"This is my great happening? A love affair?" Havgan said sarcastically.

"Not at all," Gytha replied promptly. "It is not a love affair. It is a symbol that shows unity, a union of you with you, harmony with both the inner and the outer aspects. Although," Gytha frowned, "there seems to be something more intended."

"What makes you say that?" Havgan said sharply.

"I don't know. A feeling. I think. . ." Gytha paused, not in fear this time, but in deep thought. "I think, my lord, that somewhere. . .in Kymru itself, perhaps. . .there is someone waiting for you. A woman, perhaps. Just a feeling, you understand. Nothing definite."

"Yes," Havgan said absently. "I understand. Go on."

Gytha tapped the eighth card. "This Is What He Fears," she intoned. She turned the card over. It showed a man, cloaked and hooded, carrying a flame in his hand. The man stood on top of a snowy peak, peering down. "Ah, it is Fal, the God of Light. Here he means the guide for one who seeks what is deep inside. You fear him, and you will not look. This is a danger for you—"

Gytha broke off as Havgan raked her with one burning look from his hawk's eyes. "No moralizing, Gytha," Havgan said softly. "Just read the cards."

Gytha swallowed nervously. "Yes. Yes, lord." With a shaking finger she pointed to the ninth card. "This Can Change All," she said in an unsteady voice. "This is the card that symbolizes another path you could take, one that in your deepest self you desire, but do not know it." Gytha turned the card over. A skeletal figure, cloaked in black, rode through the sky on a gray steed. The steed had eight legs and shone with a silvery light.

"Oh," Gytha said, in a small voice. "It is Narve. The God of Death."

Havgan barked bitter laughter. "Yes. I suppose my death would change things greatly. And this is what I seek but do not know it?"

"You do not understand. Death is the ultimate change. It is renewal, becoming something else entirely, transformation into something wholly different than you are now."

"Transformation? Into what?"

"I cannot say," Gytha spoke slowly, her eyes studying the cards. All but the last card had been turned up, and the brightly colored figures seemed to dance before their eyes. She opened her mouth to speak, then shook her head. "I cannot say."

"Witch," Havgan said, gesturing to the last card, "finish this."

Gytha nodded and pointed to the card. "This shows the final outcome, the ultimate answer to your question. We saw with Tiw, the God of War, that you will defeat them. The last card will show what will happen after."

"Then show me. I am weary of this game."

Gytha again pointed to the last card. "The Final Outcome," she said, and flipped it over. It was a picture of a mighty, silver tower, jutting up from a mountain peak. In the upper right corner of the card, a huge hand wielded a hammer. The hammer was shooting a bolt of lightning at the tower. The tower was in flames, and a man and woman were falling to their deaths from the crumbling tower. Gytha swallowed hard, then spoke with resignation. "The Tower. This is the card for Donar, wielder of the mighty hammer, Molnir, which destroys evil, burning it away."

"The Tower is evil?"

"The Tower is the tower of ambition built on false grounds. The card means catastrophe for you. An overthrow of all your notions of life. A disruption that may bring true knowledge of yourself in its place. . .if you live long enough."

"What do you mean?"

Gytha took a deep breath, then said quietly and with dignity, "I mean that it will all come to nothing. You will defeat them, yes. But later you will be destroyed by what you find there. You will be destroyed because you will not understand. You will not see the truth. Not until it is too late."

Sledda jumped up and grabbed Gytha by her thin shoulders, hauling her to her feet, then spoke in a deadly quiet tone, "You are a dead woman, Gytha."

Quietly, the old woman said, "I was dead the moment I took the cards. Did you really think I didn't know that?"

Sledda turned desperately to Havgan. "This woman is a fake. I'm sure of it. Don't pay any attention—"

Havgan raised his hand and Sledda fell silent. He stared at the cards laid out before him. Then, without even looking up, he said, "Kill her."

Sledda smiled cruelly and pushed Gytha toward the door, calling for the guards. Just before she was hauled from the room, Gytha turned around one last time. Havgan did not look up, but the old woman was not looking at Havgan. Instead, she was looking directly at Gwydion and Rhiannon. Her eyes flickered to the card of The Moon, the card of deception, then back to them again. She smiled.

Nardaeg, Sol 21—early afternoon

RHIANNON STOOD WITH Gwydion and Sigerric at the rail of the gently swaying ship, gazing at the eastern shore as it slowly floated by. The day was warm, with a hint of summer coming. Fields of growing wheat dotted the countryside. Occasionally they passed by tiny villages, nestled on the banks of the river.

They had embarked on this ship two days after the doomed Gytha had read the wyrd-galdra. If Sigerric knew anything about that night, he had given no sign. He stood now at the railing, his tanned face joyful in the warm sun.

They had been five days now on the River Saefern, making their way down to Mierce, one of the tributary countries of the Empire. The ship was over sixty feet long. The deck and the huge mast were made of pine, giving off a sharp aroma. The sail was rectangular, made of strips of red and white cloth. It filled now with the breeze, billowing out as the ship caught the wind, pushing them swiftly down the river.

"Where are we now?" Gwydion asked Sigerric as they passed a town on the bank. Gwydion was still pale and hollow-eyed. The night after Gytha had been killed, he had woken up screaming from a nightmare, jabbering that the cards were soaked in blood.

"That's Camlan," Sigerric replied, "in the shire of Liodis, which is one of the three shires that make up the marc of Gillingas. Never been down this way, eh?"

Gwydion shook his head. "No, I'm afraid not."

"You haven't missed much. To tell the truth, it's a good place to stay away from."

"Why?" Rhiannon asked curiously.

"The folk of Gillingas never really took to the religion of Lytir. There are many, many Heiden in this marc. And you know what that means."

"No," Gwydion answered. "What?"

"Don't you know what they do? Why, they take the babies of the True Believers, and they sacrifice them and drink their blood. They put the curse of Sceadu, the Great Shadow, on those they hate. They do unspeakable acts. Unspeakable."

She heard footsteps behind them and turned quickly. Havgan and Sledda walked up to them. Havgan put his arms on the rail, while Sledda stood stiffly next to him.

Down the river, far off but steadily drawing closer, a dark smudge on the bank caught her eye. She could not yet make out the details, but the patch of land was bare and black as though a great fire had burned it, a fire that had been so deadly that no living thing could grow in its wake.

"What's that?" she asked, pointing south.

Sledda hissed between his teeth, and Sigerric answered quietly, "It is Ealh Galdra, the place where the Maeder-Godias, the High Priestesses of the Old Religion, used to live. Here, at the outskirts of Camlan."

"Really? Why here?"

"Legend has it that it is the place where the Asbrubridge touches the earth. That is the bridge between Middle-Earth and the realm of the Old Gods. The ground there is—or was—sacred. It hasn't been used now for hundreds of years."

"Since the last Maeder-Godia of Coran died?" she asked.

"Yes, though she did not die there. She was burned at the stake in Athelin," Sledda said, obvious satisfaction in his cold voice.

"Yes," Havgan mused. "She did not die there. But she left us something to remember her by, just the same."

"What was that?" Gwydion asked.

"A prophecy. As she was burning, she spoke of Ragnorak, the day of doom. And this is what she said:

"Brothers shall fight and fell each other,
And sisters' sons shall kinship stain;
Hard is it on earth, with mighty whoredom;
Ax-time, sword-time, shields are sundered,
Wind-time, wolf-time, ere the world falls;
Nor ever shall men each other spare.

"The stars turn black, earth sinks in the sea,
The hot stars down from heaven are whirled;
Fierce flows the steam and the life-feeding flame,
Till fire leaps high about heaven itself."

At his words a shiver ran down Rhiannon's spine. A cloud passed over the sun, leaving them all in its cold shadow. Havgan's hands gripped the rail tighter. When the shadow passed, bathing them in the sun once more, Havgan's hands did not relax. He fixed his gaze on the black shadow that rushed toward them.

They were close enough now to make out some of the details. Crumbling pillars stood exposed to the blue sky. Blackened stones were scattered about in the long grasses. Portions of the walls still stood here and there. A huge, blackened, T-shaped stone squatted malignantly on the bare ground. All around the stone were fire-blackened urns. Runes were carved in the stone by the score.

"What is it?" she asked.

"It is Asbru Hlaew, the Rainbow Mound, where the Maeder-Godias were burned after they died. It is fashioned in the shape of Donar's hammer. Their ashes were placed in the urns," Sigerric replied.

"But . . . but all the urns are still there! Surely someone must have tried to——"

"Yes, they did try," Havgan broke in. "They did try to take them and destroy the place. But they could not."

"The place is haunted," Sigerric said, not taking his eyes from the stone as they sailed slowly by. "They couldn't even set foot on the ground without being stricken by sickness. So the urns stay where they are."

As they passed directly opposite the mute, blackened stone, Rhiannon reached out and gripped Gwydion's hand. There was something about this place. She could feel it in every bone of her body. An anger. Heavy, oppressive, not yet honed to a killing force.

She glanced at Gwydion. His hand was cold, and he was surely feeling that anger, too. Sigerric apparently felt nothing, nor did Sledda. But Havgan did. He shuddered briefly and closed his amber eyes against the sight of the black stone.

As they sailed by, the color seemed to seep out of the day, like life's blood from a mortal wound, leaving the afternoon dry and lifeless, as the harsh cry of an eagle sounded out overhead. But then the stone flowed away from them as they rounded a bend in the river, shutting out the sight. The colors returned, and so did the warmth of the sun.

Havgan took a deep breath of pine-scented air and turned to Sigerric. "Come, my friend, how about a throw or two of the dice?"

216

Sigerric laughed. "I don't know, Havgan. Your dice aren't too lucky for others. That's what the sailors say."

"Oh, they're just sore losers," Havgan said, laughing in his turn. But the laughter seemed forced and his face was a little pale.

Sigerric and Havgan went off, with Sledda trailing behind. Rhiannon and Gwydion were alone at the rail. She spoke in a low tone. "Did you feel it?"

"Oh, yes," he whispered.

"It feels ready to explode."

"It will. Soon, I think. I give it another twenty years or so. Then . . ."

"Then what?"

"Ragnorak. The day of doom. The day when the gods return in anger and battle to their deaths."

She said nothing for a time as they stood at the rail. She looked at Gwydion and did not like what she saw. She saw the face of a man who had poison eating at his vitals.

And the pity that she had refused to feel flooded into her.

What was she? What was she that she could for one moment have stood unmoved before such sorrow and pain as Gwydion's? If she were a stunted, twisted, barren thing, that was something she had done to herself. That was her handiwork and none other. No one else had done that. Only she.

But if that were true, if she were responsible for what she had become, there was a certain freedom and power in that, wasn't there? Enough power to turn herself around, perhaps. A struggle, yes. But wasn't everything?

And what of what Gwydion had done for her, the time he had come to her cave and found her suffering? Why, he had fed her, washed her, stayed with her, enduring even her anger. And what had she done for him in return? Nothing.

Was there really time to change? Could she do it?

She didn't know, but she could at least try.

So she reached over and gripped Gwydion's hand on the rail, closing her own hand over his clenched one. And she began to speak the words she should have said weeks ago.

"Gwydion, you must stop. You must stop doing this to yourself."

Gwydion looked at her, then up at the towering mast, his eyes unfocused. "It's ships like this that he's building, isn't it? That's what you said."

"Forget about what I said before! Listen to me now." She reached out and turned his face to hers, her hands gently resting on his hollow, sunken cheeks. "You did what you had to do. Maybe even what you were born to do. You saved his life."

Gwydion winced and tried to turn away.

"No!" she said urgently, drawing his face back to hers. "Listen to me. I believe that you had to do it, that you were meant to do it. It's one of the reasons we're here in the first place—maybe the only reason. You can't see to the end. No one can. You don't know that what you did was wrong. It may have been right."

"Uthyr . . . so many others," Gwydion rasped.

"Yes. But who is going to kill them? Not you. It is their fate for this turn of the Wheel. You did not begin this. And you can't end it that easily. The death that is coming for them is not on your head."

"It is," he whispered.

"No and no and no." Then, she had an inspiration. "You told me once that you had a dream, a dream of the Protectors, of the Wild Hunt. And Cerridwen and Cerrunnos came to you. Remember?"

"I remember," he said tonelessly.

"And in that dream they told you your tasks. Your task was to keep Arthur safe, to find the sword of the High Kings. At no time did they say to you, 'Oh, and by the way, kill the Golden Man.' Isn't that so?"

"Yes." His tone was stronger, but still tentative.

"So, he wasn't meant to die now, and you weren't meant to let it happen."

"But you have been angry at what I did. And you were right to be."

"I was wrong," she said evenly. "The invasion cannot be turned aside. I was wrong to blame you. I'm sorry."

"You're sorry?" he asked in baffled astonishment. "I saved the life of our most bitter enemy, and you're sorry that you were angry? You had every right—"

"No," she cut in. "I didn't. It happened. And I think that was how it was meant to be. You just remember something, Gwydion. And I can assure you that if you forget, I'll be right at your shoulder nagging you to remember."

"Nagging?" Gwydion asked, with the ghost of a smile.

"Yes, nagging. It's what I do best, after all."

"And what will you be nagging me to remember?"

"That it's not your fault. It was not your task. There was nothing—is nothing—you can do to turn the dream aside. The dream is and cannot be unmade."

"Rhiannon," he said hoarsely, a gleam of hope in his tired eyes, "do you really believe that?"

She looked into his tortured face and answered firmly. "I

do. And you must. Kymru needs you. She needs you to come back to her and work to save her from her coming captivity. And you will."

"You think so? Truly?"

"I know so. Truly."

He straightened up a little, his defeated posture gone. He gazed out at the countryside, his eyes firm with purpose again. And Rhiannon felt that at last, for once in her life, she had done the right thing. She had reached out and comforted a suffering soul, forgetting herself for a few moments. And who could say what might come of the effort? Who could say what rich, beautiful thing might grow from such a seed? Gwydion was back among the living again. Ready to do what he could to make the Golden Man's coming victory short-lived and bitter.

And she was ready, too.

Chapter 10

Nardaeg, Sol 7—evening

Gwydion sat at the edge of the bed in his room at the inn, trying to follow the advice Uthyr had given him years ago. Uthyr had said that, in a situation like this, it was best not to think too much. You could plan, but you had to be flexible—because plans had a way of changing. You could never tell for certain what unpremeditated action a man might take when he knew himself to be at the edge of death.

Gwydion wasn't afraid for himself. He was afraid of what would happen to Rhiannon if he failed. So he tried to follow Uthyr's advice, because his brother had much more experience in this kind of thing.

Gwydion would certainly do his best, but he had never been a proficient murderer.

The room Gwydion shared with Rhiannon was comfortable and cheery. A fire burned merrily on the hearth, casting a warm glow over the oak-beamed room. A coverlet of blue and white covered the soft feather bed where Gwydion now brooded.

He was alone, Rhiannon having gone to the baths. He had declined the luxury, saying he would bathe later. If successful tonight, he would surely need it. Unless he was careful, he would be covered with blood.

He replayed in his memory the conversation from yesterday that had begun this horror, a horror that would end, one way or another, before the sun rose in the morning.

SEVENTEEN DAYS AGO they had disembarked at Windlesora, a small town in northeastern Mierce, then hired horses and ridden to Tamworth, arriving yesterday. Once there, Havgan had been greeted coldly by Aescwine, the Empress's brother—and the father of Havgan's chief rival, Aelbald. Aescwine had tried to insist that they all stay at his palace, but Havgan had graciously declined. Instead, they had taken rooms at the best inn in Tamworth.

Gwydion had been in Havgan's room, playing the harp for him, when Sigerric had burst in, agitated.

"Why do we stay here?" Sigerric had demanded. "Do you want to die so badly?"

Havgan had given Sigerric a bland look, "What in the world do you mean?"

"You know what I mean! I mean that Aescwine will have your head if he can."

"Well, he can't have it," Havgan replied, "I need it."

"Havgan," Sigerric had said, shaking his head sorrowfully. "You are too reckless. There was no need for us to come here in the first place, and there is no need to stay."

"There was a reason to come here. I explained it to you. I wanted to know if I had the full support of the Miercean Archwyrce-jaga and the Archbyshop."

"You didn't have to come here for that!" Sigerric had accused. "You came here just to irritate Aescwine. And you have. I tell you, your life is in danger."

"I think not," Havgan had said in silken tones, looking at Gwydion. "I have my minstrel to protect me."

"Your minstrel! What's he supposed to do—sing someone to death?"

"My minstrel, Sigerric, was very quick that night of the feast. So quick that anyone would think he had known something was going to happen."

At this, Gwydion's blood had run cold, his fingers frozen on his harp.

"You see, Sigerric," Havgan had gone on, "a good minstrel always has his ear to the ground. A good minstrel can find out anything."

"Guido, forgive me," Sigerric had said, "but I must point out something to Havgan here. Havgan, minstrels can be bought. Anyone can."

"So they can," Havgan agreed. "Why, I myself have recently been warned to watch for treachery. But I believe that it is in this minstrel's best interests to keep me in good health."

"Why? Because he'd be out of a job?" Sigerric had inquired sarcastically.

"Because, my dear Sigerric," Havgan had said, watching Gwydion closely, "if something happened to me, you can be sure that Rhea would not enjoy good health and a happy life for long. Sledda might very well decide that he has a place for her in his household. And I couldn't very well gainsay him if I were dead, now could I?"

Sigerric had looked at Havgan, looked at Gwydion's white face, then back to Havgan. "Well," he had said after a long, long silence, his mouth twisted and bitter. "You do know how to get people to do their best, don't you?"

Yes, Gwydion thought now as he waited, Havgan did know how to do that.

Gwydion had carefully "watched" Aescwine whenever he could for the rest of yesterday and all of this morning. He had been careful not to be near Havgan when he did so, knowing that Havgan could sense Wind-Riding if he was in the vicinity. Rhiannon had been curious so he had picked a fight with her—never very difficult—and she had left him alone.

He had not felt right about that. In fact, if he had room in his heart for anything but fear for her, it would have grieved him to be so cruel. After what she had done on the ship to help him, he had pushed her away. But he couldn't, he couldn't tell her of Sledda's plans for her should Havgan die. And, in spite of what she had said on the boat, he could never tell her that he was planning on saving Havgan's life—again.

For this morning, as he was Wind-Riding, he had seen Aescwine in conversation with two of his soldiers. These men were to wear plain, shabby clothes and station themselves in the narrow alleyway between the inn and the stables. Havgan and his party were due to leave Tamworth early the next morning. In the confusion of the preparations for departure, the two men were to shoot Havgan full of arrows and run.

So, tonight, Gwydion was waiting for the men to arrive and take up their stations. Waiting to kill them, if he could.

Rhiannon entered the room, her hair wet from her bath. She wore her emerald cloak over a shift of cream-colored linen. She glanced at Gwydion, gauging his mood, then looked away. Tight-lipped, she sat down on a stool by the fire and began to comb out her hair.

"I thought you'd be asleep by now," she said after a long silence.

"No, I'm not sleepy."

Another long pause. She stopped combing her hair and looked at him. "Gwydion, what is the matter?"

"Nothing."

"You mean nothing you're willing to tell me about."

"Yes," he said shortly, "that's what I mean."

She looked away and gazed into the fire. But not before Gwydion saw the hurt in her eyes. He stretched out his hand to touch her, but slowly drew it back. "Rhiannon," he said hesitantly.

"Yes?" she answered, without turning around.

"I . . ." He what? What was he to say? "Go to bed." It came out harshly, because it wasn't what he had meant to say at all. "I'll sleep on the floor."

At that she did turn around, her face cold and hard. "Fine," she said in a clipped tone. "Get off the bed."

Soldaeg, Sol 8—morning

THE NEXT MORNING Havgan was in a hurry to be off. The bustle and confusion in the courtyard was tremendous. Gwydion saddled his horse, and Rhiannon's, also. She was barely civil, but he did not blame her and did not take offense.

It was Sigerric who saw the blood spilling from the alley. He gave a shout and Havgan came running. Rhiannon was immediately behind him, while Gwydion followed much more slowly.

Two men lay dead, their throats cut. Sigerric knelt down beside one man to examine the wound. "Look," he said, "do you see this? Blood coming out of their ears, too, in addition to the throat wound." He frowned. "I wonder why."

Sledda said impatiently, "Perhaps whoever did this knocked them out first, and then cut their throats."

"But their skulls are not broken, not even cracked. Just blood coming from the ears."

Rhiannon swiftly looked at Gwydion, and then just as swiftly looked away. He had known she would understand as soon as she saw the bodies.

"Any identification?" Havgan asked. "Badges, marks, anything?"

"No," Sigerric replied. "Do you think you need it to know who sent them?"

"Innkeeper!" Havgan bellowed, and the poor man came running.

"Lord?" the little man inquired breathlessly. His eyes widened as he took in the two dead bodies.

"There is some filth in the alley that must be cleaned," Havgan said, casually kicking one dead man with his foot. "Send a messenger to Lord Aescwine. Tell him to clean up his mess."

With that, Havgan swung himself into the saddle, and the rest of the company followed suit. He fixed Gwydion with a sharp eye. "You see, Sigerric," he said, not taking his eyes off Gwydion, "the minstrel is a good-luck charm. I told you as much." And then he turned his horse and made for the gates of the city, riding away as though he hadn't a care in the world.

Rhiannon raked Gwydion with her hot gaze. But she said nothing and followed Havgan.

Gwydion, following more slowly as their horses made their way through the winding streets of the city, wondered if she would forgive him for the manner of the deaths that he had caused. For Gwydion had killed them in a way that, in Kymru, was forbidden. A mighty shout to the unsuspecting, unshielded mind, directed to a single bright thrust with all the force of one who was supremely gifted in telepathy, could rupture the brain itself, leaving blood leaking from the ears of stunned, unconscious men. Leaving them vulnerable to further attack.

A forbidden act in Kymru, punishable by permanent exile.

Perhaps when this was done and they returned to Kymru, he would be exiled for this act. Perhaps Rhiannon would see to it. But at least she would be alive to do so. And that was all that really mattered.

Wynlic Daeg—mid-morning

TWO WEEKS LATER they reached the town of Beranburg at the foot of Mount Badon. Gwydion was intrigued by the mountain and the many tales he had heard of it.

Before the Coranians had taken the country of Mierce in battle, the land had been devoted to the Old Religion. The King of Coran, using the Miercean refusal to embrace the New Religion, began a holy war, invading Mierce and putting thousands of Old Believers to the sword. Mierce was destroyed as a separate country and became an appendage to Coran, creating the Coranian Empire.

In the old days, before that invasion, Mount Badon was a holy place. It was from this mountain, so legend said, that

227

Wuotan, the God of Magic, and Holda, the Goddess of Water, led the Wild Hunt.

Havgan had come here to meet up with Penda, the son of the Eorl of Lindisfarne, who ruled this marc. Penda was a prominent member of Havgan's warband and had been a close friend of Havgan for many years. Gwydion understood that Penda's young wife had died in childbirth six years ago and their son lived here with Penda's father. Penda and Catha, the brother of the Eorl of Pecsaetan, had come to Mierce some months ago to gather support in Havgan's bid for power. They were to meet both men here at Beranburg. Then Catha and Penda would join their party and they would all go on to Dere, the other tributary country of the Empire.

Gwydion glanced up at Mount Badon, which seemed to loom over Beranburg. The mountain was heavily forested with tall pine growing almost all the way up to its jagged tip.

He rode behind Rhiannon's horse, trailing behind as he had been doing now for the last two weeks. For two weeks they had not exchanged a single word. Not one. Rhiannon's silence had hung over Gwydion like a pall.

The dirt-packed streets of the town were deserted. It was Wynlic Daeg, the day the New Believers celebrated in remembrance of the beginning of Lytir's rule over Coran, many, many hundreds of years ago. No doubt the town's inhabitants were in the church now, celebrating. Gwydion idly wondered how many of those in church this moment would steal up to the mountain later in the dark of the night and secretly celebrate Deore Necht, the festival of the Old Believers, the outlawed Heiden.

They made their way to the church, which stood in the center of the town. It was a tall, wooden structure, square in design with a series of roofs of varying heights, all grouped around the central square. The walkway that ran the length of the building was deserted, but a pile of weapons near the closed outer doors indicated that a service was in progress. From the closed doors drifted the sound of singing.

"Blessed Lytir, One God,
Smote his enemies with terror.
He grew strong under the clouds
And grew in honor great.

"Till each and every peoples,
Each and every tribe,
Were forced to obey him
And pay him tribute.

"Blessed Lytir, One God,
Was rich beyond compare.
Golden plate and jeweled rings,
Generous with gold was he.

"He was a goodly King.
Blessed Lytir, One God,
He was a goodly King."

"The service is almost over, Havgan," Sledda said in a gloomy tone. "I knew we were going to miss it."

"You'll just have to stand it," Sigerric said sharply.

Sledda turned his pale, venomous gaze to Sigerric. "I wasn't talking to you!"

Havgan held up his hand. "Stop your squabbling. Now!"

229

So, Havgan had also lost his habitual calm detachment. No doubt he was feeling the same thing that Gwydion and Rhiannon were feeling—the tension in the air that emanated from that pine-studded, jagged mountain, like a brooding storm just before it breaks.

They all fell silent and dismounted, hitching their horses to the rail of the wooden arcade. Gwydion looked at Rhiannon and saw that she was pale. Knowing it was useless, that she would just shrug him off as she had done for the last two weeks, he nonetheless held out his arm for her to lean on. And, for a wonder, she did. Her green eyes fastened on the mountain and did not look at him at all, but still she took his arm. He walked her up the wooden steps of the church and sat down with her on a hard, wooden bench resting against the wall of the arcade.

"Are you all right?" he asked softly.

"That mountain . . ." she trailed off. "How can people live here? Don't they feel it?"

"Perhaps. Less, I think, than you and I—or Havgan. But I'm sure they feel something. I suspect there are more than a few Wiccan here in Beranburg."

Havgan, Sigerric, and Sledda had not followed them to the arcade, but stood with the horses, waiting for the service to finish. Sigerric and Sledda watched the doors, but Havgan never took his amber eyes from the mountain.

Gwydion's eyes caught a faint plume of smoke, about halfway up the slope, rising into the air from some sort of wooden structure. That would be Hearth Beranburg, the monastery. "Rhiannon," Gwydion began, then stopped.

"Yes?" she answered in an absent tone, which would have fooled him if he had not seen the sharp glint in her eyes as her gaze flickered to him then back to the mountain.

"I must . . . I must explain what happened in Tamworth. Those men who died."

"Explain? And break the habit of a lifetime? The mountain must have turned your head," she said bitterly.

"I'm sorry."

She tore her gaze from the mountain and looked him full in the face for the first time in weeks. Gwydion almost wished that she hadn't. Her green eyes shone in the morning light like emeralds.

"The habits of a lifetime," he continued, "are hard to break."

"Yes, they are."

"But you did, on the ship. And so I suppose I must, too, or at least I must try."

She said nothing, only waited.

"Havgan . . . Havgan caught me in a trap. Caught us, I should say." And then he told her what had happened, and why he had done what he had done. "So, you see," he finished lamely, "I didn't want you to have a part in it. I never wanted you to have to say to yourself, 'I saved his life.' Can you understand?"

"Oh, yes," she said harshly. "I understand. And Gwydion, if you ever try to protect me like that again, I'll slice off your ears and feed them to the fish. Do you understand?"

He gaped at her. This was the thanks he got for trying to spare her. Women were so disgustingly unfair. So monstrously selfish. He could have throttled her.

"You listen to me," she went on in a low, passionate tone. "I've had enough of your pigheaded, selfish ways. You dragged me here, and we're stuck with each other for a least a few months longer. Now you get this through your head. We're partners.

You try to protect me again, and we're through. I'll go back to Kymru without you."

"Don't try to threaten me, Rhiannon. Don't even think about it. I said I was sorry, and I am. I will try not to do it again. But don't ever try emotional blackmail with me. I had enough of that with my mother—and others. Do you understand?"

She looked at him for a long time. Then she said, "You understand nothing. The moment we get back home, the instant, I wash my hands of you."

"I may not be so lucky," he said, between tightly clenched teeth. "I said I was sorry. What more do you want?"

"You wouldn't understand."

Oh, gods, they all said that. How could he have thought for one moment that Rhiannon was any different from other women? What a fool he was.

"You idiot!" she went on, her green eyes blazing. "You could have been killed! All because you couldn't bring yourself to trust anyone. You've got to be more careful! Can't you understand that? You—" she broke off, as the doors of the church opened and the brightly clad townsfolk began to spill out of the building.

A man with dark blond hair and brown eyes came out of the church. There was an older man with braided gray hair on one side of him and a young boy on the other. The man spotted Havgan standing at the bottom of the steps, and gave a shout. "Havgan, you made it!"

Havgan grinned as the man bounded down the steps and caught him in a bear hug. "Penda, you dog!" Havgan said, still grinning.

"Oh, ho. Dog, is it? And after all I've done for you?" Penda turned and raced back up the steps to help the older man down.

He led the man to Havgan, then said, "Havgan, this is my father, Peada, Eorl of Lindisfarne." The pride in Penda's voice was unmistakable. The older man's brown eyes, so like his son's, were wary, but he smiled and clasped Havgan's hand.

"Welcome, Havgan, son of Hengist, generous and worthy lord of my son. You are welcome in Beranburg."

"The pleasure is mine, Lord Peada. Your son has been invaluable to me these many years."

"And this," Penda went on, his hand resting on the shoulders of the boy, "is my son, Readwyth."

Havgan squatted down in front of the boy. "We met once, Readwyth, many years ago. You were just a baby, so I am sure you don't remember me."

"But Faeder has told me all about you," the boy said eagerly, his brown eyes shining.

Havgan laughed. "Not everything, I hope."

"I wouldn't be so foolish," Penda said mildly. He turned away to greet Sigerric, then presented Sigerric to his son and his father. This time the old man's smile was genuine, finally reaching his eyes.

"Oh," Penda said, "uh, this is Sledda. Wyrce-jaga of Ivelas."

Eorl Peada inclined his head a fraction, but did not offer his hand. His voice was slightly chill. "Welcome, Sledda, to Beranburg." The boy stood silently, eyes wide, tightly grasping his grandfather's hand.

Sledda bowed as slightly as courtesy would allow when another man came down the steps. He was tall and broad-shouldered, with blond hair and light blue eyes. He was extremely handsome and obviously aware of it. "Havgan," the man said as they embraced. "So glad you made it! And right on time, too. Sigerric—it's good to see you again."

"We've been here for a while, Catha," Sigerric said, smiling. "Where were you?"

"Catha was inside chatting with the ladies," Penda said. "You know how he is."

"It's a difficult job, but someone has to keep them happy!" Catha replied airily.

"And who better?" Sigerric quipped.

Havgan gestured to Gwydion and Rhiannon. "My minstrels," Havgan said. "Guido Asti and Rhea Varins of Turin."

Gwydion bowed and Rhiannon curtsied. Catha instantly extended a hand to help Rhiannon up. "Why, Havgan, you never told me you had such a beautiful songbird."

"She is unavailable to you, Catha," Havgan replied easily. "Unfortunately, it is part of the terms of their employment."

"A pity," Catha said, still smiling and looking Rhiannon up and down.

"Isn't it?" Gwydion replied insolently.

Catha's smile faded. Havgan put a hand on his arm. "No," he said quietly. "My minstrel is too important."

"But—"

"I won't tell you twice."

Penda stepped into the breach. "Come, Havgan, let's all go to my father's house. We have a feast prepared."

"Yes," Sigerric said instantly. "By all means, let us go."

Havgan walked with the Eorl, while Penda and Sigerric, obviously close friends, walked behind them. Readwyth walked next to his father, holding his hand. Catha and Sledda came next, and Gwydion and Rhiannon followed at a respectful distance.

"I suggest that, in public, from now on, we pretend that we like each other a great deal," Gwydion said quietly.

"Indeed," Rhiannon agreed.

SOME HOURS LATER Gwydion and Rhiannon sat on the hearth in the Eorl's great hall, playing their harps softly. The hall was bright and cheerful, with many colorful hangings adorning the walls and large windows to let in the light of the afternoon sun.

The hall was almost empty now that the Eorl had dismissed his warriors from the tables. Penda's son had been taken away to the care of his nurse. The Eorl sat in a high-backed intricately carved chair at the middle of the table on the dais, with Havgan on his right and Penda on his left. Across from them sat Sledda, Catha, and Sigerric. A few platters of crumbled meats and crusts of bread were left on the table. Each man drank from goblets of gold studded with sapphires.

Penda and Catha were telling Havgan that his support in Mierce was all but total, the thanes, alders, and eorls having all professed a deep interest in conquering Kymru. "Of course," Penda was saying, "we need to be careful. No more than one hundred warriors from each Eorl, no more than fifty from each Alder. We don't want to find ourselves in a power struggle against our own people over there."

"And when we position them to invade, we must be sure to have Penda and myself lead the Mierceans. They won't follow Coranian leaders," Catha added.

"Talorcan and Baldred can lead the Dereans," Penda said. "They're both from Dere and can handle them." The Eorl said nothing, but his gnarled hands were clenched tightly around his goblet.

"What time do we leave tomorrow, Havgan?" Penda asked.

"About mid-morning, I should say. That will give us time to get back here."

Penda looked at him blankly. "Get back here? Get back here from where?"

"I intend to go to the monastery on the mountain. To Hearth Beranburg. We will spend the night there and return here in the morning."

Penda and his father exchanged a quick glance. Penda cleared his throat. "I don't recommend it. Not tonight."

"Why not?" Havgan asked sharply.

Again the quick look between father and son. The Eorl said, "We have entertainment planned for tonight. You must stay here or my folk will be grievously disappointed. Tomorrow will be time enough to visit the monastery, if that is your wish."

"It is not my wish," Havgan said softly. "My wish is to go there today."

"Lord Havgan," the Eorl said earnestly, "tonight the Heiden will celebrate Deore Necht, their festival. They will celebrate secretly on the slopes of Mount Badon. And they might very well raise something that—"

"What my father means to say, Havgan, is that tonight there will be much activity on the mountain. The Heiden will be celebrating, and the wyrce-jaga will be looking for them. There will be too much confusion. It is best to wait until tomorrow if you are so determined to go to the mountain."

"Tell me, Eorl," Havgan said in a friendly, confidential tone, "is it true that the Wild Hunt really rises from Mount Badon on festival nights?"

"It is," the Eorl said. "And so I really think—"

"The Old Gods are powerless," Sledda broke in confidently. "Powerless over those who believe in the One God. There is no danger for us on the mountain from the demons of Hel."

"I tell you, Havgan," Penda pressed, "there is danger in the Hunt. Danger that you cannot count on Lytir to protect you from. Why do you wish to see it? For what purpose?"

"Why, Penda, you know that new experiences always enrich the mind."

Penda's brown eyes bored into Havgan's amber ones. "You cannot think to speak to them."

"What harm can there be in that? The One God himself has given me the task to defeat Kymru. I am His Chosen. He will protect me."

"Lord Havgan," the Eorl said, his face flushed. "You do not know what you are asking for. The Hunt stops for no man."

"They will stop for me," Havgan said.

THE SUN WAS almost setting by the time they reached Hearth Beranburg. A tonsured monk in a robe of deep red opened the gate for them and they rode through.

Of the original party there were only Havgan, Gwydion, Rhiannon, and Sledda. The Eorl and Catha had refused to go, and Penda had insisted that Sigerric, too, should be left behind.

The monk silently led them to the stable, and two novices in white robes took the horses. The monk bowed. "The Lord Abbot is in the refectory with the brothers. Who may I say has come to Hearth Beranburg?"

"I am Havgan, son of Hengist. This is Sledda, Master-wyrce-jaga of Ivelas. These other two are my servants."

Again the monk bowed. "We have heard of you, Lord Hav-gan. You are most welcome here. Follow me, please."

The monastery, though small and clearly not rich, was neat and well-kept. A large, well-constructed barn stood to the left of the gate. The pigs, sheep, and cows, already in their pens for the night, looked well-fed and cared for. Beyond the sanctuary, Gwydion caught a glimpse of a small apple orchard, as well as neatly tended vegetable and herb gardens.

The monk led them to a small, wooden building and opened the door. Inside were rough tables and benches filled now with red-robed monks, white-robed novices, and a sprin-kling of traveling friars in orange robes. Plain fare was laid on the tables—bread, a few meats, apples, and nuts. The monks were observing the ritual mealtime silence, with one man read-ing aloud from the Book of Lytir.

At the head of the far table, a middle-aged man with a com-manding presence sat in a large, high-backed chair. He wore a yellow robe with green piping around the sleeves and hem. His gray eyes were alert in his deeply tanned face. At his signal the reader fell silent. The monk who had escorted them bowed. "Lord Havgan and Master-wyrce-jaga Sledda."

The Abbot rose and bowed slightly. "Have you eaten, my lords?"

Havgan bowed in return. "We have, Faeder."

"Then come with me to my house. We shall talk a while."

They followed the Abbot out the door and across a court-yard to a small two-storied house. The Abbot led them inside then closed the door. "I am Abbot Oswald," he said. "And I am at your service. Please, be seated."

Havgan and Sledda took seats in two chairs set before the

fire that was burning cheerfully on the hearth. Gwydion and Rhiannon sat on a bench pushed next to one wall. The floor was covered with fresh, sweet-smelling rushes. A small table and chair stood against the other wall. There were no windows to let in the light, and the Abbot lit wax candles with a taper kindled from the crackling fire.

The Abbot seated himself in the chair behind the table, then asked, "How may I serve you, lord?"

"We ask only for shelter for the night," Havgan replied.

The Abbot hesitated. "Perhaps, lord, you would be more comfortable in town. I am sure that the Eorl—"

"You do have guest quarters, I trust?"

"We do. But tonight the Hunt rides," the Abbot said bluntly. "This night we spend in the church. All of us. Praying to Lytir to protect us. Everyone must be there."

Havgan nodded. "I understand, Lord Abbot. Sledda and my servants shall be there. But I have business on the mountain."

"That is not permitted, Lord Havgan. I must insist."

"You cannot prevent me."

The Abbot said nothing for a long time, then bowed his head. "It is the will of Lytir, then. I will pray for you."

THE CHURCH WAS crowded. Monks and novices lined the front benches, all of them on their knees. Hundreds of candles had been lit, chasing the shadows into the corners and up to the high ceiling. The stone altar was covered with a banner of white and gold, marked with the runes of Lytir. Four white candles burned in golden holders at each corner of the large stone. Whispered prayers caught in the still air and echoed off the walls.

"Praise now to the Guardian of Heofen . . ."

"Eternal Lord . . ."

"Lytir, protect us . . ."

Havgan and Sledda had taken places in the middle of the sanctuary. Sledda was on his knees, his pale head bowed. Havgan sat upright, gazing at the gleaming banners.

Gwydion and Rhiannon sat at the rear of the church, with no one around them. Gwydion leaned forward and whispered to Rhiannon, "It's dark out. The Deore Necht celebration must begin soon."

"And?" she asked, her brows raised.

"I wish to see it. Guard me while I Wind-Ride."

"What about Havgan?"

"He's far too preoccupied to sense much of anything. And if he does, he will chalk it up to the Hunt."

"What do you hope to learn?"

Gwydion shook his head. "I don't know. But I have a feeling I should see it just the same."

"All right," she said. "I'll call you if someone comes by and looks too closely. Kneel down so it looks like you're praying."

Gwydion sank to his knees and bowed his head. After a moment he could feel a part of him separating from his physical body. That part of him rose and hovered for a moment, looking down at those gathered in the church. He saw his own body, limp and unobtrusively braced by Rhiannon, who knelt beside him.

He flew out of the monastery and over the mountain, looking for a spark of light to guide him to the Heiden. The star-strewn sky was clear. The full moon rode the night, its silvery beams turning the tall pine trees spread below into inky shadows.

There, to his left. A pinpoint of flame. He spiraled down

closer and closer to the clearing, at last coming to rest at the very edge. He hovered, looking down at the crowd of people gathered there.

A stone altar was decorated with candles of gold and white. A gold banner with a rune of white and a white banner with a rune of gold were spread across the stone. He looked closely at the runes. They were for Fro and Freya, the Lord and Lady. These were brother and sister, the Ercar, the peaceful gods, the children of Narve, the Lord of Death, and Erce, the gentle Goddess of Peace.

A drinking horn of silver rested on the left of the altar. On the right was a bowl of gold. In the front a long knife glinted. Tiny bells strung on a peace of leather rested at the back. The trees that surrounded the clearing were hung with long ribbons of white and gold. Torches were placed in a ring around the clearing.

Gwydion studied the crowd and thought he recognized many of the people he had seen coming from the church that morning. A rough count showed there to be over a hundred people gathered here. Up front, near the altar, he saw the Eorl of Lindisfarne, surrounded by ten of his warriors. Gwydion wondered if Penda knew and thought he probably did.

The crowd, which was whispering softly, fell silent at the sound of clear, tinkling bells. A woman dressed in a robe of pure white was standing behind the altar, shaking the bells. This was the Godia, the priestess for this secret group. A man in a hooded robe of black stood next to her. He was called was the Hod, the Sacrificer. In his hands he held a falcon, tied to his wrist with leather thongs. The falcon hissed and spread his wings, but was tethered too tightly to fly.

The Godia said formally, "The Dis are with us, the gods have come. Wuotan and Donar; Fal and Fro and Logi; Dag and Mani; Saxnot and Tiw."

The crowd responded, "Hail to the Dis."

"The Disir are with us, the goddesses have come. Nerthus and Freya; Holda and Nehalennia; Sunna and Sif; Natt and the Wyrd."

"Hail to the Disir."

The Godia continued, "The Afliae are with us, the powerful ones have come. Hail to Narve, The One that Binds. Hail to Ostara, The Warrior Goddess. Hail to Erce, Gentle Mother. Hail to these, the Afliae."

"Hail to the Afliae."

"This is the night of Fro and Freya," she continued. "Freya, bringer of fertility; Fro, bringer of dreams."

"Blessed be the Lord and Lady," the crowd said reverently.

The Godia picked up the drinking horn. Her long, blond hair sparkled in the light of the torches. Her fine, blue eyes kindled. "Drink now, ye followers of the old ways. Drink now, ye hidden, ye faithful ones." She took a sip and passed the horn to the Eorl. He drank briefly, then passed the horn to his warriors. Slowly the horn made its way through the crowd until all had drunk.

Then the Hod, his face still hidden by his black veil, lifted the falcon in his hands.

"All hail to Lady Freya, all hail to Lord Fro.

To she who gives life, to he who gives dreams.

Accept our sacrifice."

THE HOD GRASPED the falcon with both hands and snapped its neck. He then took the knife from the altar and cut the bird's throat, catching the blood in a bowl. Taking up a bundle of leaves, he dipped them into the blood and sprinkled tiny drops of blood on each worshipper, making his way through the crowd. Last, he sprinkled the head of the Godia, and the blood made dark, sinuous lines in her long, blond hair. Finally, the Hod drank the remaining blood, then set the bowl down on the altar.

The Godia lifted her hands.

"A dream came to me
at deep midnight.
When humankind
kept to their beds—
the dream of dreams!
I shall declare it."

The crowd hushed and drew closer to hear the dream given to her by Lord Fro.

"A golden boar with eyes of blood and tusks of ivory was vomited up by the sea. And the boar grew and grew until he was a giant. He crushed the Heiden under his hooves, slaughtering us until the land ran red with blood. There were many who eagerly helped him."

The Eorl bowed his gray head, his fists clenched.

"Hatred for those Across the Water grew and grew in the golden boar's breast, though he did not know why. Then came a raven from Across the Water, black as night with eyes of opal, a harp in his talons. He followed the golden boar, seeking a way to keep him from crossing the water. But the raven could not stop the boar." The Godia lifted her flawless face to the night sky. Her blue eyes seemed to look right at Gwydion, though he knew it was not possible that she could see him.

The crowd was silent. Somewhere in the night, the wind began to rise. "And the boar came to the Hunt," she continued. The crowd gasped as the wind began to blow harder. "And the raven followed." Far off, Gwydion thought he heard muffled cries. The crowd shifted uneasily as the wind began to tug at them.

"The golden boar goes to meet the Hunt!" she cried, and then tore her robe to show an amulet of amber in the shape of a hammer. She plucked the necklace from around her throat and held it high. Just then Gwydion felt a tug, something urging him to return to his body. He resisted for a moment, wanting to hear more.

"He comes!" the Godia shouted over the keening of the wind. "He comes! Fly, raven! Fly to him now. The Hunt rides. And the Old Ones laugh!"

Thunder crashed upon the clearing, and the trees shook. Gwydion fled over the trees, through a night sky that had suddenly filled with dark clouds. The face of the moon was shrouded as thunder rumbled.

He slammed back into his body. Rhiannon was shaking him. He opened his eyes. Thunder rolled over the church, and the monks began to pray louder.

"Havgan," Gwydion gasped. "Where is he?"

"Gone," she hissed back. "Just this moment."

Gwydion leapt to his feet. He grabbed her hand, and they slipped out of the church, thunder crashing in their ears. Up ahead they saw Havgan making his way out the monastery gate and up the mountain.

Lightning flared, almost blinding them as they followed Havgan through the trees. If Havgan heard them over the wind and thunder, he gave no sign. He walked swiftly, almost running. Gwydion and Rhiannon followed as quickly as they could. Still it did not rain, but the wind howled like a mad thing and flash after flash of lightning split the sky.

The trees began to thin as they neared the top of the mountain. Gwydion grabbed Rhiannon's arm and held her back at the edge of the forest. Havgan stood now almost at the peak. Wind whipped his cloak, but he stood firm and lifted his tawny head, staring at the sky as something moved across it.

The Wild Hunt had come.

The dogs were white with blood-red eyes. They tore across the sky on the wings of lightning, baying hungry cries. Behind them rode a dark, hooded shape on a pale horse. The shape held a spear in his hand, and each time he raised the spear, lightning flickered across the sky. Next to him rode another figure in the shape of a woman with a gown of green. Seaweed hung from her tawny hair. A girdle of pearls encircled her slim waist. Her eyes were many-colored—now sea green, now the blue of a calm lake, now the gray of angry waves. She raised a horn to her lips and blew, and as she did, thunder rumbled. The wind had the smell of the sea as it tore across the sky and swooped down the mountain. Behind these two figures, skeletal horses with fiery eyes fanned out across the sky. Hooded riders with hands of white bone screamed of despair and madness.

The Hunt swooped, and the dogs scrambled down the mountain peak. They crouched and growled, crawling on their bellies close to where Havgan stood. The hooded figure on his gray horse swooped down and landed in front of Havgan, who did not flinch. The women's horse landed next, while the skeletal horses and their riders remained in the sky.

The cloaked figure threw back his hood. His hair and beard were long and gray. A scar twisted up one cheek, disappearing into an empty eye socket. The other eye was filled with lightning. "Mortal," the figure said, his voice like the rushing wind. "I claim you for my own!"

"Wuotan One-Eye!" Havgan shouted, "you cannot. I belong to the One God!"

Wuotan, the God of Magic, laughed and thunder pealed. "The One God is not enough to protect you, mortal. Not here!"

"I am Havgan, son of Hengist. I have been called by Lytir himself. And you may not touch me."

Wuotan laughed again. Thunder rolled. "Son of Hengist? Think you so? Then you know nothing. Nothing."

The hounds bayed, and the skeletons laughed their mad laughter. "Nothing," they chanted and the wind hissed. "Nothing."

Then Holda, the Goddess of Water, spoke, and her voice was like that of the waves that crash on the shore. "You were warned, Havgan, son of—" then she laughed and lightning flashed. "Well, no matter that now. You were warned by the wyrd-galdra. But you have not taken heed. I am Holda, who claims your past. And this is Wuotan, the Hanged Man, who made you what you are. You were warned. And still you do not turn from your path."

"I come . . . I come now to bargain."

The hounds bayed again. And Wuotan, with his eye of lightning said, "You have nothing to give us that we want."

"I offer you a chance to hunt," Havgan replied.

"We hunt now," Holda said coldly.

"A chance to hunt in a new land. To hunt the witches of Kymru."

Rhiannon gasped and clutched Gwydion's arm. "Oh, Gwydion," she said in his ear. "What if they accept?"

"Then may the Protectors help us," Gwydion breathed.

Wuotan laughed, and the skeletons laughed with him. "Hunt the Kymri? What care we for them? We do not hate them."

"I offer you—"

Holda cut in, "We know what you offer us. We know you as you do not. Go to those Across the Sea, Havgan. Your destiny awaits you there. And so do I. You cannot run from me."

"I am protected by Lytir. You cannot hurt me."

Wuotan laughed again. "You are wrong, mortal. But that is no matter. You are wrong about so many things. We know you. Go to meet your fate. The Hunt remains here. We have no quarrel with those Across the Sea." Wuotan turned his horse.

"Wait!" Havgan shouted. "Wait!"

"Wait?" Wuotan laughed again, and thunder rolled. "There is another Hunt Across the Sea that waits for you. Go to them!"

Wuotan's pale horse shot back up into the sky. The dogs followed, their white bodies glistening. The skeletal horses neighed fiercely, and their riders howled.

"We shall meet again, Havgan," Holda said, then raised her horn to her lips. Her eyes turned a startling shade of amber, her hair to honey-blond. Lightning shot down and played across the jagged peak of the mountain. "Until then!" And she was gone, shooting up into the stormy sky.

Chapter 11

Mandaeg, Sol 37—late afternoon

Rhiannon sighed in weariness as they made their way through the winding streets of Elmete. They were here at last after six weeks on the road. She shivered, for the city had a pall of hopelessness over it. Elmete was still in general disrepair, even two generations after their defeat at the hands of Aelle, the present Emperor's grandfather.

They occasionally passed shells of burned-out houses that seemed to look at them with empty eyes. They passed heaps of rubble from fallen buildings, cairns for the countless warriors who had died defending their homes. The streets were cobbled in some places, leaving other patches bare, filled now with mud that splattered freely on their cloaks and coated the legs of their horses.

As they rode by, people stopped their work and stared sullenly, resigned to the task of digging a life out of the grave of their once-beautiful city. Sorrow hung over the place like a pall over a corpse. Laughter, warmth, pride—all gone. And Rhiannon's heart felt cold, for she wondered if this was the fate in store for Kymru.

Up ahead Havgan was slowing his horse before a large, rambling wooden house. It was three stories high, built with interlocking pieces of light and dark wood. The shutters on the windows were open, and bright flowers of red and yellow grew in boxes beneath them. The roof was made of wood shingles, and there were gables carved in the shapes of eagles, dragons, and falcons.

The large front door was open, and when they dismounted, a man came down the steps to greet them. Sigerric gave a shout and vaulted from his horse, greeting the man with an exuberant hug.

"Talorcan!" Sigerric exclaimed. "Good to see you, man."

Talorcan grinned. "Here at last. I have been watching for you for over a week now." Talorcan looked to be in his mid-thirties. His hair was dark blond, pulled back now in a leather thong. His eyes were a startling green in a deeply tanned, somewhat thin face. His high cheekbones stood out like spars. Something about his eyes, Rhiannon thought, made him look haunted. But by what, she could not tell.

Talorcan's face brightened even more as Penda came up to greet him, and again as he gripped forearms with Catha. Then he turned to Havgan, and it seemed to Rhiannon that some of the light fled from his face, to be replaced by a tense wariness. "My Lord Havgan," he said formally.

"Where's Baldred?" Havgan asked.

"He's coming," Talorcan said, gesturing them inside the house. "We got word that you were at the gates, so he left to let the Archbyshop and the Arch-wyrce-jaga know that you had arrived. He'll be back shortly."

Rhiannon noticed that Talorcan had not greeted Sledda, and judging by Sledda's face, the wyrce-jaga had noticed it, too.

"These are my minstrels," Havgan said. "Guido Asti and Rhea Varins, from Turin."

Gwydion bowed and Rhiannon curtsied. Talorcan smiled. "You are welcome, minstrels, to Elmete, and to the house of my father. Come, everyone. My father and mother are waiting to greet you."

"Where is your brother" Sigerric asked.

"Not here," Talrocan replied carefully.

"Where, then?" Havgan asked, his eyes swiftly going to Talorcan's face.

"Faeder sent him to my grandsire in Gefrin," Talorcan replied, not quite meeting Havgan's gaze.

"To get him out of my way?" Havgan asked softly.

"He doesn't want Tohrtmund to join your warband, Havgan. You know that. He needs my brother here, particularly when I am away."

"I am anxious to see your father again," Penda said, breaking into the palpable tension. "Is he well?"

"He is," Talorcan said swiftly. "And my mother, too."

"Then let us greet them," Havgan said with a genial smile that did not quite reach his amber eyes, "for I know they are anxious to greet me."

Without reply Talorcan led them through a large hall, and then through a host of smaller rooms, until they reached the inner courtyard. A garden took up much of the space. Bright flowers and well-trimmed hedges lined the paths. Stone benches were grouped in the middle of the garden. On one bench sat a man and woman.

The man was old but hale. His broad shoulders were unbent, but his face was heavily lined. His hair was lightening from dark blond to white, and it was braided in the old-fashioned manner. He wore a tunic and trousers of dark green.

Traces of beauty still lingered in the woman's face, her fine, high cheekbones and her brilliant green eyes, which matched her emerald dress. She was thin, perhaps too thin. Her once-blond hair was nearly white.

"Havgan, son of Hengist," Talorcan was saying, pride in his voice, "you remember my father, Talmund, Eorl of Bernice. And my mother, Lady Ingilda."

The Eorl and his lady stood, and Havgan bowed to them, then introduced the members of his party. Ingilda gestured for them to sit and then signaled a servant to bring them refreshment.

"Welcome, Havgan, to the marc of Bernice," the Eorl said, though his blue eyes were wary.

"This evening," Ingilda said warmly, "we shall have a feast in your honor. The lord of my son is most welcome here."

"Lady Ingilda, I am honored. With your permission, my minstrels will play for us."

Ingilda's eyes went to Gwydion and Rhiannon, who, as befitted servants, were standing off to one side. "Do you know any songs of Dere?" she asked, her eyes lighting up, her voice hungry.

"My Lady, we know many," Gwydion replied. "We know 'The Words of Ine' and 'The Battle of Elmete.' We know 'The Wise Man.' And we know 'The Lament.'"

"'The Lament,'" Ingilda repeated, her eyes taking on the look of one who sees things far away and long ago. "Yes. You must play it tonight."

Talorcan opened his mouth to speak, but the Eorl forestalled him. "I think, my dear," he said quietly, "it would be best if—"

"I wish to hear it," Ingilda said firmly.

The Eorl nodded and managed a strained smile, shooting a sharp look at his son. "Very well."

Just then a man in a tunic and trousers of rich blue wool bounded into the garden. The man had light brown hair and brown eyes. He was stocky and heavily muscled. His heavy face lit up as he saw Havgan. Havgan stood, and the two men embraced.

"Baldred!" Havgan exclaimed. "I heard you were too busy to be here when we arrived. No doubt you were trying on the latest fashions?"

"Ha," Baldred replied. "You're just jealous of my new clothes. I was busy looking after your business. As usual." He grinned and then quickly greeted the other members of the party, clapping Catha on the back, sharing a joke with Sigerric and Penda, even properly greeting Sledda with what seemed to be genuine goodwill.

"Tell me," Havgan said, "how you and Talorcan have been doing here in Dere."

Things were going well. Baldred and Talorcan had managed to gather a great deal of support for Havgan's plans. Names were mentioned, along with their military strength and political connections.

Rhiannon paid little attention to the details since Gwydion would be listening carefully for that. Instead she studied the Eorl and his wife. The Eorl did not, apparently, completely approve of Talorcan's lord, though he never even came close to saying so. He spoke little and did not even appear to listen closely.

Ingilda's expression was uncomfortable at the talk of conquering another country and Rhiannon knew why, for Ingilda was clearly Derean, a woman who had married a man of Corania, a man who was the enemy. A man she had come to love, apparently. What battles had taken place, were taking place still, in that woman's heart? What battles had she passed on to her son? For the talk of subjugating another country struck at Ingilda's heart and, from the look in her son's eyes, struck at his, too.

"Talorcan," Ingilda said, breaking in on the conversation. "Havgan has never seen our city. Perhaps a short tour would be in order."

Talorcan looked at his mother in surprise. Catching his father's gaze, he flushed. "Of course," he said quickly.

"When you return," Ingilda said, forcing a smile, "the feast will be ready and the guests will have arrived."

Havgan rose and bowed. "My thanks, lady, for your hospitality."

AT THE END of their tour, Talorcan led them to a pile of rubble of considerable size. Moss had lined the stones, and tangled briars reached greedy fingers throughout. Here and there wildflowers grew and daisies bobbed gently in the light, mournful breeze.

"This," Talorcan said, clearing his throat, "was the watch tower. It was here that Queen Hildelinda threw herself off to her death when she saw that King Ingild and her son, Prince Indere, were dead."

The wind mourned again, and Rhiannon shivered. Queen Hildelinda's despair laced these stones, surrounding them with misery and sorrow. Gently, she plucked a daisy and twirled it in her fingers. She remembered one of the tunes Gwydion had taught her, a song of the words Queen Hildelinda had spoken to her husband as he went to battle that day. Moved by she knew not what, she opened her mouth and sang softly.

"Let not your royal strength
droop now, nor your daring—
now that the day has come
when, son of Ida,
you shall surely either
give over living or a long doom
have among after-men, one or other.

"Know that whether you fall or triumph
will I hold in my heart always
days that my lord clasped and kissed me,
times when on my breast he laid his
hand and head and heart.

"The covenants of companionship
shall never be broken.
Death cannot touch us.
I am yours forever."

And as the song died away, Rhiannon saw the sheen of tears in Talorcan's fine, green eyes.

THE HALL WAS bright, lit by hundreds of candles and by the glow of the roaring fire in the huge hearth. Gwydion and Rhiannon played their harps softly as the servants brought in nuts and cheeses, signaling an end to the feast.

At the high table the Eorl sat in the center, with Havgan on his right and Ingilda on his left. Sledda, Sigerric, Catha, Penda, and Baldred sat to Havgan's right, while Talorcan sat to the left of his mother. Also present were Berwic, the aged Archbyshop of Dere, in his robe of blue, and Oswy, the Byshop of Bernice in green. Next to them sat Hensa the Arch-wyrce-jaga in a robe of black with blue piping around the hem and sleeves.

The hall was warm, and Rhiannon, who had earlier danced for them, was still flushed. Her white gossamer gown glowed in the light of the fire.

"Sledda and Catha are still drooling," Gwydion said softly. "Are you sure you don't want to take advantage of it?"

"Very funny," she replied. "If you don't like my dancing, why did you teach me?"

"Because that's the way things are here," he said irritably. "I can't help that."

At that moment the Arch-wyrce-jaga stood, and the hall fell silent. He raised his cup. "Let us drink now in honor of our guest, Havgan, son of Hengist, who will soon lead us to victory. Death to all witches!"

Rhiannon was grateful that she and Gwydion, as servants, were not required to drink to such a toast.

"I have a gift for our guest," Hensa went on. He was a thin, cadaverous-looking man, with sharp features and dark eyes. "I have arranged a hunt for you, Lord Havgan."

Havgan bowed slightly. "I am grateful for the honor."

"It is not just any hunt. This one is special. Tomorrow we hunt the Heiden!"

"The Heiden?" Sigerric asked blankly. "What do you mean?"

The Eorl's face was white and still. "Yes, Hensa. What do you mean?" he asked.

"Know that yesterday my wyrce-jaga sniffed out a nest of Old Believers engaging in their filthy rites in Wodnesbeorg. I have arranged for them to be brought here. We will then turn them loose and hunt them down."

"We are honored to take part in such a hunt," Havgan said, his hawk's eyes shining with enthusiasm.

"Our people?" Talorcan said sharply. "You bring our people here to be hunted?"

"They are not your people," Hensa said firmly. "They are the Heiden. The people of Sceadu. Enemies of the One God. They are animals. And, as such, they will be hunted by those faithful to Lytir."

Talorcan, his face white and his green eyes blazing, stood. "My father should have been consulted. He is the Eorl."

"And I, Talorcan, am the Arch-wyrce-jaga of Dere," Hensa said, his own eyes lit with fire. "The right is mine. Do you tell me that your father objects to the killing of these evil ones? On what grounds?"

Ingilda put a hand on Talorcan's arm before he could reply. Then the Eorl said, "We were merely surprised. I am sure that the Lord Havgan and our guests are gratified by your care for their entertainment." The Eorl nearly hissed the last word.

Calmly, Havgan said, "Indeed, we are gratified, Arch-wyrce-jaga. We look forward to it." Havgan obviously meant it, but Sigerric and Penda looked ill. Sledda licked his thin lips in anticipation.

"How many?" Ingilda whispered.

"Fifty men, women, and children. And we captured their

Godia, their priestess, too," Hensa smiled.

"Women and children?" Ingilda asked, appalled.

"Indeed, yes," Hensa replied. "May I remind you, lady, that they are all filth. Even the young ones. Do not distress yourself."

"You have the Godia?" Havgan asked.

"Indeed, we do," Hensa said proudly.

"I wish to speak to her alone, tomorrow. Keep her out of the hunt."

"As you wish, Lord Havgan," Hensa said, obviously curious, but too wary of Havgan's reputation to press for the reason.

The Archbyshop, an elderly man with a kind face, turned to Ingilda. "Do not distress yourself, my child. The Heiden are those who have willfully refused Lytir. We do but send them on to the One God's judgment." He gently patted Ingilda's thin hand, and she forced herself to smile.

"As you say, Archbyshop. But, women and children . . ."

"You must stay with me tomorrow, during the hunt," he went on kindly. "I am too old to take part. We will read the Book of Lytir together and be comforted."

She smiled again, in true gratitude this time. Then Ingilda shook herself, and once again became the proper hostess. "Well now," she said brightly, "with such an important day ahead of you all tomorrow, you will wish to retire. Havgan, if you would have your minstrels play me one last song, I should be most grateful."

"It shall be as you wish, my lady." Havgan signaled to Rhiannon and Gwydion, and they came to stand before the high table.

"The Lady Ingilda requests one last song."

"Yes," Ingilda said. "I wish you to play 'The Lament.'"

Havgan nodded at Gwydion and Rhiannon, and they began to play. The melody was simple but haunting, and they sang together, a mournful harmony, singing of the past glory of Elmete.

"Well-wrought these walls
Yet the stronghold burst
Rooftrees snapped and towers fell
On the day of the Coranian hordes.
The work of stonesmiths moulders.

"Walls stood, then the King fell,
The high arch crashed
Hacked by bright weapons
On the day of the Coranian hordes.
Halls now sunk in loam-crust.

"Oh, Elmete!
Bright were the buildings
High, horn-gabled, much throng-noise
With bright cheerfulness
Many mead halls filled.

"Oh, Elmete!
Here once many a man, mood-glad,
goldbright, of gleams garnished,
flushed with wine-pride, flashing war-gear,
gazed on bright gemstones, on gold, on silver,
On wealth held and hoarded, on light-filled amber,
On the bright city of broad dominion.

"Came the day of fate,
On all sides men fell dead
Death fetched off the flower of the people
On the day of the Coranian hordes.
Broken blocks, rime on mortar.

"Oh, Elmete!
We remember you.
Bright city of our father's fathers.
We remember you."

The hall was hushed as they sang. Ingilda's eyes were wet, her hands clasped tightly together, and Talorcan's head was bowed.

Rhiannon's own eyes filled with tears. Never in all of her life did she wish to hear a song like this about her own beloved Kymru. She would do anything to prevent that. Anything at all.

Tiwdaeg, Sol 38—late morning

THE DAY WAS bright and clear, unfortunately. Rhiannon had hoped for rain, floods, maybe a tornado or two—anything to prevent this awful hunt from taking place. But summer days in Dere were habitually fine, and today was no exception.

She stood now next to Gwydion, outside the city gates. To the north a small forest stood some distance away. Before it was a large field dotted with long grasses and wildflowers. Birds were singing gently.

Her heart beat fast, and her mouth was dry. Her hands were clammy. If fate had been cruel enough to make her a woman of the Coranian Empire, she might very well be one of the hunted today.

Not that the crowd of fifty shivering, frightened people who stood before her now, ringed by mounted warriors, were all Wiccans. Most of them, no doubt, had no powers at all. They were just plain folk who cleaved to the religion of their ancestors. Yet some of the Heiden were gifted. The Godias, the priestesses, always were. And there was always a sprinkling of those with true powers in any coven.

A hand, as clammy as hers, slipped into her own and held it tightly. Gwydion. She squeezed his hand, holding on to it for dear life. And as she did, a little strength seemed to creep back into her spirit.

She glanced at him. He was pale, as pale as she must be herself, but his face was set in stern lines. The agony that she knew he felt did not show, unless one looked closely at his gray, stormy eyes; eyes that looked at this scene and would not forget; eyes that promised retribution, one day, to those who took part in it.

At least, thank the gods, they were merely servants here in this land, and as such, were not expected to take part in the slaughter. To her right, just beyond the doomed crowd, Talorcan, Sigerric, and Penda huddled together, a tight knot of distaste. But they would take part in the hunt, like it or not. They had no choice.

Havgan, eagerly looking forward to the kill, sat tall and proud on his horse. He was dressed in red and gold, and rubies flashed off the shaft of his spear and the gauntlets covering his strong hands. The sun turned his tawny hair to gold.

Behold, Rhiannon thought bitterly, the Golden Man. She felt a fierce contempt for him, anticipating the day when Havgan would meet them again in Kymru, realizing that he had been betrayed.

She felt someone watching her closely. Startled, she looked around and met the eyes of a woman in the crowd of Heiden. The women's gray eyes pierced through Rhiannon, and she knew that her thoughts had been read. The woman smiled, unpleasantly, as though she, too, was looking forward to the day when Havgan would suffer. The woman looked away before anyone else could notice her stare.

"Gwydion," she whispered.

"I saw. It's the Godia, I think."

"Gwydion," she said again, urgently. "I think she knows . . ."

"I think so, too. But we can't help that. We'll just have to wait and hope she says nothing." He squeezed her hand again and she fell silent.

Hensa, mounted on a jet-black horse, his golden amulet of Lytir sparkling in the sun, gestured to one of the huntsmen, who sounded the horn. Then Hensa rose in his stirrups. "Know all that you folk of the Heiden are condemned to die this day for your crimes."

Men put their arms about their wives and children. Women lifted their little ones and held them, crooning softly. Then the crowd hushed.

"I call for the Godia!" Hensa cried.

The woman with the gray eyes turned to the man beside her and gently kissed him. As she drew away, he grasped her hand to stop her. She shook her head, and he let her go, agony in every line of his taut body. As she made her way through the crowd, she stopped occasionally to speak an encouraging word, to dry the tears of a crying child, to gently touch the arm of a shaking man or woman.

Then she stood before Hensa, contempt in her eyes. A slight breeze gusted her gray homespun gown and kicked up dirt before Hensa's horse. The horse tossed his head, and Hensa had to pause to settle him down. The Godia's smile mocked him.

Havgan's amber hawk's eyes fastened on her, and he gestured her over. She raised her brows, then moved over to stand unflinchingly before him.

He folded his arms across the bow of his saddle and leaned forward to look closely down at her. He said nothing, nor did she speak. But something passed between them at that moment. At last Havgan asked, "You are a Wiccan?"

She grimaced. "They say that I am."

"And so do I. Do you think I cannot tell?"

"Oh, I think you see very well, my lord. Very well, indeed," she sneered. He flinched ever so slightly.

"What is your name?" he asked.

"I am called Lingyth."

"We will not hunt you today, Lingyth. We have a task for you."

"No!" she cried, as Havgan gestured for two warriors to take her back to the city. "No! Let me die now, with him. Egild, Egild!" She tried to reach her husband, but the guards held her fast. He tried to run to her, but a warrior knocked him over the head, and he fell, senseless, to the ground.

"Egild, my love! Egild!" she screamed. Suddenly a wind swept the field, flattening the grasses. Wild patterns appeared, disappeared, and reappeared again as the wild wind blew. Dust choked the air.

"Gwydion," Rhiannon said urgently. "Can't we help her? Can't you do something? You are a Shape-Mover, as she is.

Can't you—"

Gwydion turned to her, anguish in every movement. "I can't. Havgan will know. I can't." He turned from her, his shoulders slumped in misery and shame.

She reached for him, placing one hand on his shoulder. "I'm sorry," she whispered. "I know we can't. I just . . . I'm sorry."

He turned back to her urgently, grasping both her hands like a drowning man who clutches at something that will save him.

Suddenly the wind stopped, as abruptly as it had begun. Lingyth stared at Havgan in shock. But Havgan returned her stare with disdain.

"Take her away," Havgan said firmly. "Now." The two warriors guarding her swallowed hard, their faces tight with fear. "Now!" Havgan commanded. "She will do you no harm. I have asked the One God to protect us from her tricks. Have no fear."

The two warriors dragged the sobbing Lingyth away, back through the city gates. Friends helped Egild up from the ground as he recovered consciousness. Blood streamed down his face, and Rhiannon had to turn away from the look in his eyes when he saw his wife dragged away.

"Truly, great lord," Hensa said, his manner servile, "you are blessed by Lytir."

"Yes, Arch-wyrce-jaga, I am," Havgan agreed. "He has given me a mighty task. And I shall not fail him. Enough of this. Now we hunt!"

Hensa nodded, his thin face shining. "Now we hunt! People of the Heiden," he shouted, "All-mighty Lytir is merciful, even to those who hate him. You have a chance for life. Those who make it as far as the trees will live. Run! Run!"

For a moment the crowd remained frozen. Then one man grabbed his wife's hand and scooped up a toddler with the other. The family ran into the field, making for the distant trees. Men and women picked up the littlest children and ran for their lives.

Hensa nodded again, and a warrior lifted his horn and sounded the call to hunt. Instantly, Havgan and Hensa were after the running mob, followed closely by Catha, Baldred, and dozens of other warriors.

Talorcan, Sigerric, and Penda held back their horses for a few moments. "You do not hunt," Talorcan said to Gwydion, pain in his green eyes.

Gwydion bowed. "We are merely minstrels, lord."

"Yes," Talorcan said bitterly. "Would that we were all minstrels," he went on, gesturing to Sigerric and Penda beside him. "Come, my friends, let us do what we must do. The quicker we start, the quicker it is over."

Sigerric nodded. "Havgan leads us. And we must follow where he leads. We swore it long ago."

"Yes we swore," Penda replied heavily. "Swore by blood."

Talorcan gathered the reins, looking out over the field. Already there were fallen bodies littering it, some of them very, very small. "Would that I had known what I was swearing to that day," he said. "I would have kept my blood in my veins." Then they were gone, harrying the Heiden across the field.

Rhiannon watched the hunt, though she did not want to. She watched so that she would remember what happened that day. Watched so that, in the years to come, if she grew weary of fighting the Golden Man, she could close her eyes and summon up what had happened that day. Watched so that she would never forget.

Twisted, bleeding bodies were strewn across the field. Sledda lifted his spear and gutted a running woman and her child. The spear passed right through the woman's back and into the baby at her breast. "Two in one!" Sledda shouted in delight.

A man ran across the field, pushing his wife and daughter before him. A warrior rode closely behind them, his spear leveled. With a despairing cry, the running man turned and yanked at the spear that was aimed at his wife's back, tipping the warrior off his horse. Instantly, three spears thudded into the man. He jerked and cried out for his family to run and sank to his knees. The last sight the man had, before he closed his dying eyes, was that of a spear through his daughter's belly. And the last sound he heard in his dying ears was that of his wife's screams.

Catha rode down a fleeing man who was clutching a little girl to his chest. The man stumbled, and the child flew into the air, to be spitted on Catha's spear. Catha's handsome face lit up, thrilled at the accuracy of this aim, and he grinned madly.

Rhiannon turned away. She could bear no more. Tears blinded her, scalding her skin as they ran helplessly down her face. *O gods, O gods,* she thought, over and over. *Please, please, make them stop. Make them stop.*

Then Gwydion was there, holding her tightly in his arms, crooning to her. "Shh, shh. It's all right. It will be all right. We'll get them all, one day. You and I. You and I, together. One day."

RHIANNON FOLLOWED GWYDION down the dark, slimy steps. The stone walls were unpleasantly greasy to the touch, and she shied away from them. Torchlight glowed fitfully as Hensa led them down to the dungeons of the wyrce-jaga. At last they stopped in front of a closed door of solid oak. Hensa turned to Havgan, who was just behind him.

"She is in here, lord. I beg you, be careful."

"The witch cannot harm me, Hensa. I have told you this before."

"Then let me stay and be sure of it," Hensa begged.

Havgan shook his head. "No. Sledda will be here with me, and my minstrels. We will come to no harm. Now, open that door."

Hensa hesitated, then did as he was bid. He unbarred the door and slowly pushed it open. He held the torch up high as they all crowded in after him.

The floor of the cell was covered with straw, slimy and rank. Lingyth, huddled on the floor in a corner, blinked her eyes in the sudden light. Slowly, she stood, staring at Havgan. Her eyes flickered to Rhiannon, then skittered away.

"Has she eaten?" Rhiannon asked sharply.

Hensa turned to her with a frown. "That is not your business. Who are you to question—"

Havgan turned to Hensa, cutting him off. "She is my trusted servant, Hensa. And when she asks you a question, I expect you to answer it."

Hensa swallowed. "The witch was given bread—"

"With maggots in it," Lingyth spat.

"Feed her," Rhiannon said, her eyes blazing.

"Do as she says, Hensa. Now." Havgan did not take his eyes off Lingyth. "And bring more torches."

Again, Hensa hesitated. Havgan slowly turned to the wyrce-jaga. Hensa was no match for Havgan's stare. Muttering, he handed the torch to Gwydion, then left.

No one spoke. Havgan studied Lingyth again, and she returned his gaze, stare for stare. Sledda moved back toward the door, wrinkling his nose in distaste at the squalor. Gwydion held the torch steadily, his expression set and stern. And Rhiannon looked down at the straw and wished that every last wyrce-jaga was lying dead at her feet.

Finally, Hensa returned, followed by two black-robed wyrce-jaga, one carrying two extra torches, the other a wooden tray on which a hunk of bread and a honeycomb rested on a clean, white cloth. The wyrce-jaga bowed, set the tray down, and backed away. Havgan nodded to Lingyth, and she grabbed the bread, tearing off chunks and stuffing them in her mouth.

The other wyrce-jaga placed the additional torches within the wall brackets. Havgan gestured for Hensa and his men to leave. They left reluctantly, shutting the door behind them.

"Stand by the door, Sledda," Havgan ordered.

They waited in silence as Lingyth ate. When she was done, Havgan gestured to Gwydion. Gwydion put the torch in another wall bracket and reached into a leather bag at his waist. He pulled out something wrapped in a red scrap of cloth. As he unwrapped it, the brightly colored cards of the wyrd-galdra caught the light, glittering balefully.

Lingyth gasped in shock and looked quickly at Havgan.

"You will read the cards for me," Havgan commanded.

"And if I do not?" she asked.

"Then you will die at the stake. The flames will eat your flesh."

"And if I do?"

"Then I cut your throat. Quietly. Painlessly."

Lingyth looked at Rhiannon. "My husband. Is he dead?"

Rhiannon nodded. She had seen a warrior cut Egild down. The poor man had barely started across the field when he was killed.

Lindgyth fell silent for a moment, looking down at the straw. Then she raised her head tiredly. "Very well. I will read them."

"Make it a true reading," Havgan warned. "Hold nothing back."

She nodded, holding her hand out for the cards. "Ask your question," Lingyth commanded, looking at Havgan.

"Will I defeat the Kymri?"

She fanned out the cards, her hands steady, presenting the blank sides to Havgan. "Choose a card."

Havgan chose and laid the card face up on the empty platter.

"The Fool. A good choice for you," she smiled maliciously.

Havgan stared at the card, the same card that had appeared at the last reading that doomed Gytha had given in Athelin.

"The card that you have chosen is a symbol of the mystic who seeks to find his way. A symbol of one who has certain gifts—" Lingyth began.

"I know what it means," Havgan grated.

She cocked her head at him. "Do you? This is not your first reading, then."

"No, it is not."

"Then you know what you are."

"I am the tool of the One God. That is what I am."

Lingyth laughed, the sound shocking in the dank cell. "You carry the gifts from the Old Gods."

He reached out and grabbed her long, tangled brown hair, pulling her to him, her face inches from his own. "I am the champion of Lytir, and that is all," he hissed. "You had best remember

268

it." He shoved her back, knocking her head against the stone wall. Gwydion started forward, then halted. Sledda smiled.

Lingyth shook her head to clear it. She looked at Havgan for a long time, then slowly laid out nine cards facedown on the platter. One she laid crosswise over The Fool. She placed four around the two center cards making a square, and four more in a vertical line to the right of the square. Then she tapped the back of the card that lay on top of The Fool. "This Crosses Him," she murmured. "This is the card that represents the force that opposes your will." She turned the card over slowly.

And just as before, it was The Magician. "This is the opposing force. The one who seeks to stop you," she said.

"A symbol of the Kymri," Havgan said tonelessly.

"Yes. And this you have seen before, also."

"I have. How do the Kymri seek to stop me?"

Lingyth's eyes flickered to Rhiannon. "I do not know. It is enough for me that they try," she hissed.

"But they will fail."

"We shall see," Lingyth replied, her voice cool. "This Is Beneath Him," she said, pointing to the card just below the crossed Fool and Magician cards. "This card stands for your past, for that which is a part of you." She flipped over the card. "The High Priestess. This is Holda, the Goddess of Water."

Again, just the same as it had been before in Athelin. Rhiannon felt a cold tingling at the base of her spine. The Goddess's painted smile seemed to mock Havgan as he stared down at the card.

"She is a symbol for the hidden influences at work within you," Lingyth went on. "She is the keeper of hidden truths. And we know what those are, don't we?" she mocked.

"Continue," Havgan said firmly, his face pale and set.

She tapped the card to the left of the Fool and Magician cards. "This Is Behind Him. It is the card for the influences in your life that are just passing away." She turned the card over. Wuotan. Again.

"The God of Magic. It is he who has made you a great lord. Without him you would be nothing more than a fisherman. Like the man you call your father."

Havgan started. "What do you know of my father?"

Lingyth smiled maliciously. "Did the Wild Hunt not tell you?"

"What do you know of the Hunt?"

"Holda and Wuotan have marked you. They may have let you go for now, but no one escapes them. No one."

Sledda rasped, "You will confine your remarks to the reading before you, witch."

Lingyth smiled again, then tapped the card at the top of the square. "This Crowns Him," she said. "This card shows your future." She turned it over. "The Chariot," she said, disappointed. "Tiw, the great God of War. Victory and success for you, then, in Kymru. But remember," she went on, "this is just one card. The final card, the tenth card, will tell you truly."

She tapped the card to the right of the crossed Fool and Magician cards. "This Is Before Him. This card will tell you something important that will happen in the near future, or that is already happening, though you may not be aware of it."

She turned the card over and laughed. It was the Moon card, the card of deception, glowing silver in the torchlight. "Peril and deception. Someone close to you will betray you in some way. Sometime soon, very soon."

"Do you know who?" Havgan asked urgently.

"I do not," she replied swiftly. But Rhiannon saw a gleam in her gray eyes. "Shall I continue? Or have you seen enough?"

"Go on."

She tapped the back of the seventh card, the lowest on the row to the right of the square. "This Is to Come to Him. It is the card to show of a great happening in your life that awaits you." She turned over the card. "The Lovers. A symbol for unity and harmony of the inner and outer aspects."

"Someone once told me that this is what I would find in Kymru."

"Oh, yes. So you will. Someone waits for you in Kymru, indeed."

Rhiannon frowned, remembering that Holda herself had intimated that she would be there, waiting for him. Who was it who waited in Kymru to join with Havgan?

"Go on."

Lingyth tapped the eighth card. "This Is What He Fears," she intoned. She turned the card over. "Fal, the God of Light. Here he means the guide for one who seeks what is deep inside. Yet you fear him, and you will not look. But we all know why, don't we?"

Havgan said softly, "Just read the cards, Lingyth, if you wish to die quickly."

She bent her head back to the cards, then pointed to the ninth card. "This Can Change All. This is the card that symbolizes another path you could take, one that in your deepest self you desire, but do not know it." She turned the card over. "Narve. The God of Death."

Havgan laughed bitterly. "Again! Again, the card of Death

271

for me. As something I truly desire."

"Yes," Lingyth said quietly. "Deep inside, you desire trans-formation into something new. Into something you despise."

"I think not, witch."

"You understand nothing."

That was exactly what the Wild Hunt had said. And they had laughed while they said it.

"Finish it," Havgan said, his teeth clenched.

Lingyth shrugged and pointed to the last card. "This shows the final outcome, the ultimate answer to your question. You will defeat the Kymru. Now we see what happens after. If you are ready to learn."

In answer, Havgan flipped the last card over himself.

"The Final Outcome," she said. "The Tower. The card for Donar, wielder of the mighty hammer that destroys evil." She smiled. "This card means catastrophe for you. An overthrow of all your notions of life." She laughed again, and sat back. "Everything you built will crumble. You will go to Kymru and defeat them, as you wish. Then they will, in turn, destroy you. The only pity is that I will not be alive to see it."

Havgan pulled out his knife and grabbed her, spinning her around so that the knife was at her throat. He stood behind her, holding her against him with arms of iron.

"The card of deception," he whispered in her ear. "You know. You know who seeks to deceive me. And you will tell me."

"I know nothing," she spat.

"You do."

"I tell you that I do not." She swallowed hard, eyeing the knife at her throat. "Kill me now. I am longing to die."

"You will tell me first. Or you will burn."

"Kill me, you promised!" she screamed.

"I need keep no promise that I make to a witch."

"I tell you again, I do not know!"

"Sledda," Havgan said between clenched teeth, "go call Hensa. Tell him that the witch wishes to burn."

Sledda turned, pushing at the door. But it held fast. He turned back to Havgan, his face a sickly white. "It will not open."

"Stop it, witch. Stop it now," Havgan cried, his arms tightening around Lingyth. Lingyth screamed, but the door held fast. Rhiannon looked at Gwydion, who was standing stock still, his eyes narrowed in concentration. She nearly screamed herself. It was Gwydion who was holding the door fast shut with his mind. And he must stop. He must stop now, or Havgan would discover his mistake and kill them all.

But before she could do anything, a new sound wafted through the air. The sound of a hunting horn. Far off, thunder rumbled.

"The Hunt!" Lingyth gasped. "I will not die at your hand! They come for me!" She wrenched herself away out of Havgan's stunned grasp and huddled against the wall. She lifted her hands high. "Wuotan! Holda! I am here! Take me. Take me now!"

A wild wind began to blow in the underground cell. Straw lifted and swirled in the air. "I am here!" Lingyth shrieked again. A corner of the cell began to glow, and the figure of a man appeared, a figure very much like Egild, Lingyth's husband, who had died that day. Behind the man stood two other figures. One was an old man, with one eye. The other was a woman, with eyes like a stormy sea.

Lingyth reached out her hands to the glow, and the rushing of the wind pounded into the cell. Thunder cracked again, and the cell shook. Egild reached for Lingyth, and as their hands touched, her body fell. Something sprang up from her then, something that glowed too brightly to be truly seen. Wild laughter rebounded off the walls.

And then they were gone. The cell was quiet. Lingyth's lifeless body lay facedown on the floor. Slowly, Havgan stooped and turned her over.

Her dead face was smiling.

Chapter 12

Mandaeg, Sol 30—early afternoon

Gwydion rode alone at the rear of the party as they made their way down the crowded streets of Athelin to Cynerice Scima. Havgan lead the party, flanked by Sigerric and Sledda. Behind them rode Talorcan, Penda, Baldred, and Catha, all dressed magnificently in Havgan's customary red and gold.

Rhiannon had remained back at Havgan's house, claiming she was unwell. She had been pale and listless ever since the hunt of the Heiden in Elmete, and far, far too quiet these days. Gwydion had given her strict instructions to remain in her room. For a wonder, she might even obey. Which worried him. It wasn't like her at all. He had never thought that he would be glad to have her fighting with him. But he wished she would. It would mean that she was herself again, which would relieve him more than he cared to admit.

It had taken them little more than a month to return to the

chief city of the Coranian Empire, and the trip back had not been a merry one. Talorcan, Sigerric, and Penda had been subdued. Havgan had been somewhat subdued himself, ever since his second meeting with the Wild Hunt that had cheated him of Lingyth's death.

They halted their horses at the eastern bridge to Cynerice Scima. The towers gleamed, impossibly beautiful in the afternoon sun. The guards at the bridge let their party through, and they reached the outer courtyard, dismounted, and made their way to Gulden Hul, where the Emperor and Empress sat in state.

As before, the hall seemed suffused with soft golden light. Gold gleamed from the tapestry-covered walls, the pillars, and the cloth on the floor. The spreading branches of the golden tree in the center of the hall shimmered.

The Emperor, still insignificant in spite of his rich trappings, sat stiffly on his throne, dressed in black trimmed with gold. The jeweled diadem that he wore, the famous Cyst Ercanstan, only served to make him look more insignificant. The jewels in the golden crown glowed softly—the large center chunk of amber, for Coran; the emerald, for Mierce; and the sapphire, for Dere. At the top of the helm was a huge amethyst, symbolizing the church.

Next to the Emperor sat the Empress, cold and stern, radiating the power her husband so signally lacked. She wore a robe of gold with delicate chains of amber and gold woven though her rich, light brown hair.

Between them, Princess Aelfwyn stood, dressed in a gown of flowing white, brilliant diamonds threaded through her long, golden hair. Gwydion glanced now at Sigerric, hearing the man's quick intake of breath as he drank in the sight.

Behind Havgan, Catha murmured, "There she waits for you, my lord. Warm, willing, eager. What a lucky man. It's not everyone who gets the chance to bed a viper."

"Viper or not," Havgan murmured, "I mean to have her. And there are ways, Catha, of controlling venomous snakes."

"You cut off their heads," Baldred suggested.

"No," Havgan said serenely, "you charm them."

"Good luck," Baldred said dubiously. "You'll need it."

Havgan marched up to the dais, Sledda and Sigerric on either side of him, with Penda, Baldred, Catha, and Talorcan following behind. Gwydion stayed where he was, blending with the crowd. Havgan and his men bowed to the royal family.

"I come to make my greetings upon my return to fair Athelin," Havgan said. "And to feast my eyes on the even fairer Aelfwyn." He smiled up at the Princess, who colored, but remained silent.

"And how did you find the state of the country, Lord Havgan?" the Empress asked smoothly. "Was all to your liking?"

"You are kind to ask, fair Empress," Havgan replied easily. "I regret to say that the city of Tamworth was not as clean as I would like. But I left word with your brother about the trash littering the streets."

"And was all satisfactory in Dere?" the Emperor inquired innocently.

Havgan smiled genuinely. "Indeed. The Arch-wyrce-jaga Hensa put on a splendid hunt for us. Not one single Heiden was left alive."

The crowd clapped enthusiastically. "Well done, Lord Havgan. It was our hope that your journey was all that you could have wished for," the Empress said with manifest insincerity. She must still be irritated over her brother's failure to kill Havgan, Gwydion thought, or she would have kept her sarcasm under tighter wraps.

Havgan bowed. "Thank you. It was, indeed, all that I could have wished for." He bowed, then started to move away. He turned back abruptly, as though just struck by a new thought. "Oh, one other thing. I have never seen the gardens of Cynerice Scima. They are reputed to be magnificent. Might I take a stroll there?"

"You wish to walk in the gardens?" the Empress repeated in a puzzled tone.

"Indeed. They are very fine, as I understand."

"Oh. Well, perhaps you wish for some company on your walk," she said.

"I think not. You are kind to offer."

The Empress smiled and took her daughter's hand, turning to Havgan. "Aelfwyn knows every inch of the gardens. Allow her to show them to you."

Aelfwyn gasped and tried to snatch her hand back. But her mother held tight.

"I do not wish to trouble her," Havgan said doubtfully. "I really would prefer—"

"No trouble at all, is it, Aelfwyn dear? You must keep Havgan company." She stressed the last word ever so slightly.

After a pause, Aelfwyn nodded. "If you wish for my company, Lord Havgan," she said coolly, "it is yours."

Havgan smothered a grin, and reached out to take Aelfwyn's cold hand in his own. He bowed, then the two of them left the hall. Havgan signaled for Gwydion to follow them, as

he and the Princess walked out arm in arm. Gwydion smothered a grin himself, for this was what Havgan had been after
all along.

THE GARDENS WERE nice, Gwydion admitted, though that was
scarcely the point. Delphiniums and snapdragons blossomed in
spiky profusion against the low, rocky walls lining the graveled
paths. Blue cornflowers and white chamomile set off the red
and yellow rockrose that sprawled across the shining stones.

Irises surrounded a pool in the center of the garden, and
water lilies floated on its calm surface. Havgan guided Aelfwyn
to a bench beside the pool. He plucked a delicate sprig of lily of
the valley and gravely presented it to her. Hesitantly, she took
it in her hands.

"Accept a poor adornment from a man who longs to please
you. Diamonds you have. And this is but a poor flower. Yet
it is only the first of many gifts I will give you." Smiling, he
plucked it from her fingers and tucked the sprig behind her delicate ear.

"The first of many gifts you will give me?" she said sweetly.
"I think the first one of us to give gifts shall be me. After all, it
is only by becoming my husband that you can be Emperor."

"So, Princess. Truly do they call you Steorra Heofen. For
you shine as brightly as the stars," Havgan said. "And as cold."

"To some, perhaps," she said, idly plucking the flower from
her hair and twirling it in her slender fingers.

"Aelfwyn, we are to be wed—"

"That," she said sharply, "remains to be seen."

"Ah. Do you truly believe that Aelbald can defeat me?"

"No," she said, not looking at him. "But I hope for it."

"You prefer that weak fool to me?"

"At least he is not the son of a fisherman. I do prefer him to you. Immensely."

"Of course, you do. Because you will not find a fisherman's son as easy to control. I will not be an Emperor like your beloved father, my dear. And you will not hold the same place as your mother. And it galls you, doesn't it?"

Well, so much for charming the viper, Gwydion thought sourly. Apparently Havgan had given up on that tactic.

Aelfwyn rose, but Havgan yanked her back down. "Now, Aelfwyn," he said in a pleasant tone, his amber eyes glittering, "we can do this the easy way or we can do this the hard way. But we will do this. You and I are to be married. I will win the tournament. And you can be my partner or my enemy. Whichever you please."

"You're hurting me," Aelfwyn said stiffly.

"I mean to. And it can get worse, Aelfwyn. Much, much worse. Now choose."

Again she tried to pull away, but he held her fast.

"I can call the guards," she threatened.

"Yes. Today you can. But later, when we are wed, you won't be so lucky."

She abruptly stopped struggling and stared at Havgan, her green eyes finally showing fear.

"Now, Aelfwyn, let's try this again. Partner or enemy? Answer."

"I'll never feel anything for you but hatred," Aelfwyn burst out. "Never."

"Hate me all you want, Aelfwyn. It means nothing to me. But don't work against me. Don't even think of it. Or, princess and heir that you are, your life will be short."

"You dare to threaten me?"

"Yes. I, the son of a fisherman, do indeed dare. And why not? We all know that peasants have no manners." He smiled wolfishly. "I will leave you to think about it." He ran his finger gently around her ear, down her long neck, and lightly touched the shadow between her breasts. "In the meantime, think of our wedding night. As I will."

Fear washed over her pale features as he stood abruptly and marched out of the garden, not even bothering to look back.

"What do you think?" Havgan asked Gwydion as they made their way to the outer courtyard where the others were waiting.

"I believe you made your point," Gwydion said dryly.

Havgan laughed. "Yes, I believe I did."

THE MOMENT THEY returned to the house, Gwydion hurried up to the room he shared with Rhiannon. As he burst through the door, she started. She had been sitting in a chair, looking out the window at the city, just as she had been when he left.

"You've just been sitting here?" he asked. "You didn't try to go anywhere?"

She looked at him in surprise. "You told me not to."

He studied her for a moment. "What's wrong, Rhiannon?" he asked gently. "What's the matter? Ever since we left Dere, you've been so . . . so biddable."

"Isn't that what you wanted?" she asked tiredly.

"I thought it was," he muttered. "Now I'm not so sure. Talk to me. Please."

She turned and looked out the window. Gwydion waited quietly. At last, without turning around, she spoke. "I hate it here, Gwydion. Truly hate it. There is a sickness in the Empire, and the stench of it makes me ill."

"I want to go home, too, Rhiannon. Don't you think I do?"

She turned and looked at him. "Oh. For a moment I thought we were talking about me. I should have known better."

Gwydion almost smiled. She sounded more like her old self. "We are. Sorry."

She looked out the window again. "It's more than hating it here. It's Lingyth. I couldn't . . . I couldn't save her. Worse than that, I killed her."

"You killed her?" Gwydion was shocked. "Havgan killed her. Or, rather, the Wild Hunt did."

"She died because she knew about us. And she refused to tell."

"She died because she read the wyrd-galdra. Havgan would never have let her live. You must know that." Gwydion took her hand. "You know that," he repeated. "If you must blame someone, blame me. I saved his life." He laughed harshly. "Twice."

She sighed. "You had no choice, Gwydion."

"Neither did you. Have a choice, I mean. You couldn't have saved her. No matter what you did. Rhiannon, look at me." She turned to him, her face expressionless. "Rhiannon, I need you to be in this with me. Completely. I can't do this alone."

She looked at him in astonishment. "Well, that's new."

He nodded, his eyes glued to her face. "Yes, it is. But that's the truth."

Some color returned to her pale face then, and she straightened a little in her chair, never taking her eyes off him. The gods knew that it cost him to say what he had said. And perhaps she knew it, too.

At last she said, "I am going to bring them down, bring

them all down, for what they have done. Somehow, someday."

"Yes," Gwydion said. "We are. You and I, remember?"

"Is that a promise?"

"It is," he said steadily.

"All right. I'll hold you to that. How much longer do you think we will be here?"

"Until the tournament. And until I can find those plans."

"I think I know where they are," she said mildly.

"What?"

"I said—"

"I know what you said. But how did you—" Gwydion broke off, staring at her. "Wait a minute. You said you hadn't gone anywhere today. You lied!"

"I said I stayed here. Which is true. But I did Wind-Ride."

"Where to?" he asked between gritted teeth.

"I Rode to Havgan's room while the rest of you were waiting in the courtyard to go to the palace. He was there alone. He had just let the corner of that tapestry by the fireplace drop down. Then he left."

"You know he senses something when we Ride."

"But he doesn't know what. And it was only for a moment."

Gwydion frowned, thinking of what Rhiannon had seen. "Something behind the tapestry? A cupboard?"

"I would guess so. And he must keep the plans there."

"Why is he so secretive about the plans in his own house?"

"Why do you think? He's been warned about deception from those around him twice now."

Gwydion nodded. "Makes sense. All right, then. That's where I'll look on the day of the tournament."

"Unless we have a chance before then."

"We can hope, but I doubt it. Whenever he leaves, he takes us with him."

"I stayed here today. He thought I was really ill. Maybe you should get sick, too. And soon."

There was a clatter in the courtyard. A man rode up, leading someone on another horse. The man's black robe proclaimed him for a wyrce-jaga. His companion was not so easily placed. Man or woman, they couldn't tell, the figure was so heavily cloaked. And on such a hot day, too. Gwydion looked closely at the figure. "A woman, I think, from the way she moves," Gwydion said. "One of Havgan's whores, probably."

"In broad daylight? That's not like him." She studied the woman as the wyrce-jaga spoke to a guard. "And only if he likes them old now. Look at her hands."

She was right. The woman's hands were gnarled and worn. Sledda came out of the house, and the wyrce-jaga lead the woman to him, talking quietly. Sledda looked shocked for a moment, then his face became bland. He nodded and signaled for the woman to follow him. The other wyrce-jaga mounted his horse and rode off.

Rhiannon looked at Gwydion blankly. "Another reading, do you think?"

"I don't know." He stood still for a moment. "Quickly, bar the door."

Rhiannon did so as Gwydion settled himself down on the bed. "Watch over me. I'm Riding to Havgan's room."

"But what about Havgan?"

"If he senses me too strongly, I'll come right back."

"You don't know that they have taken her to Havgan's rooms."

"Where else would they take her?"

"He might send for us."

"If he does, nudge me and I'll come back. Gods, I can't believe that I wanted you to be the way you were. You'd argue with me all the way down if we both fell off a cliff."

"No one's perfect," she said with a grin. "Go on. I'll keep watch."

GWYDION'S AWARENESS FLOATED down into Havgan's chambers, unseen. Havgan was seated at the large table, surrounded by Sigerric, Penda, Catha, Baldred, and Talorcan. He was regaling them with portions of his conversation with Aelfwyn. Sigerric sat silent and white-faced. Talorcan, too, kept silent. But the rest were laughing.

"And then I said 'choose—enemy or friend,'" Havgan was saying.

"And she chose enemy, of course," Baldred said.

"So she did."

Penda laughed. "You really know how to turn on the charm, don't you?"

"Women just throw themselves at his feet when he does that," Catha said.

The door opened and Sledda entered, alone. "Lord Havgan, you have a visitor."

"Who?" Havgan asked in surprise, as he absently rubbed his forehead.

"The headache again?" Sigerric asked quietly.

Havgan nodded. "It is of no matter. It will stop soon. It always does. Show the visitor in, Sledda."

"I think, my lord, that it would be best for you to see this visitor alone."

"Except for you, eh, Sledda?" Talorcan asked, as he, too, rubbed his forehead.

"It will be as Lord Havgan commands," Sledda said smoothly.

"You have a headache, too?" Penda asked Talorcan.

"Caught from Havgan, no doubt," Baldred said with a grin.

"No doubt," Talorcan said softly.

Havgan frowned, studying Sledda's impassive face, obviously not listening to their banter. "Very well, I'll see this visitor alone." He turned to his friends. "I'll finish the story another time."

"Do," Catha urged. "I'm interested in learning your technique!"

One by one, they filed out past Sledda. When they were gone, Havgan asked quietly, "Who is it?"

"Your mother."

Havgan froze, staring at Sledda. "My mother? How did she get here?"

"Guthlac, Master-wyrce-jaga of Cantware, brought her here at her urging. It seems that some days ago she slipped out of Sigerric's mother's house and made her way secretly to him. She insisted that he bring her here."

"So no one but Guthlac knows where she is," Havgan said slowly. "Well, as long as she is here, I will see her. But after that, she goes right back to Apuldre. And I want her watched more closely."

Sledda bowed and left. His brows knit, Havgan began to pace the room slowly, absently rubbing the back of his neck. Gwydion was intrigued, too intrigued to leave just yet, though he knew Havgan was sensing something. Gwydion had heard hints before that Hildegyth, Havgan's mother, was a madwoman. It was no wonder that Havgan would wish to keep that quiet, particularly now, at the very threshold of his final bid for power.

The door opened, and Sledda escorted Havgan's mother into the room. She threw off her hood and stood still, gazing at Havgan. Neither one moved. Sledda, stationed by the door, said nothing, but his pale gaze glittered as he looked from mother to son.

Hildegyth was thin almost to the point of emaciation. Her cheekbones stood out sharply beneath pale gray eyes. Her hair was white and hung over her bony shoulders. Her face was strangely unlined, as though nothing that had ever happened to her had the power to truly mark her. She stepped forward, holding out her arms.

"My son. My gift from the sea." Her voice was off-key, with a strange lilt to it.

Slowly, Havgan took her thin hands in his. "Maeder. Why have you come?"

"Are you not pleased to see me, my son? It's been a long time. Or so they tell me. But it doesn't really feel that way. Time bends strangely, doesn't it?"

"Does it?" he asked evenly. "I ask you again, why have you come?"

"Why have I escaped my jailers, you mean?"

"The Lady of Apuldre is not your jailer. She is Sigerric's mother. A kind and worthy woman. She took you in when I begged her to."

"Took me in when your father was murdered and I had no one to look after me."

He sighed. "Faeder was not murdered. It was an accident."

"Was it?" Her strange eyes glittered.

"Yes. You remember. It was lightning. Lightning that

struck the house. It was an accident."

"Yes. Accidents do happen, don't they? Particularly when you want them to," Hildegyth mocked. Havgan paled but did not answer, and Hildegyth went on. "There, there, my son," she said, putting a wasted hand on his arm. "It doesn't matter. We never needed him, anyway."

"I don't know what you are trying to say—"

"Yes, you do." Her gray eyes, no longer vague, looked at him sharply. "As to why I have come—I come to warn you."

He sighed. "Of what, Maeder?"

"Of the sea. Of your plan to defeat the Kymri. To tell you that you are a fool."

Sledda jumped as though he had been stung. "Be careful what you say, woman," he said harshly. "You speak to—"

"I know to whom I speak. Do you?" Hildegyth asked, a strange smile on her face.

"I believe that I do," Sledda said, his voice steady.

Hildegyth studied him for a moment. "Yes, I believe that you do." She turned back to Havgan. "I have come to warn you, my son. You must not go to Kymru. I have told you again and again, you must stay away from the sea. Become Warleader, if that is your wish. Send men to take Kymru, if you need to. But do not go yourself!"

"Come, Maeder," Havgan said, his eyes glittering. "You can't tell me that and not tell me why."

"I cannot tell you why. I cannot! You mustn't ask me. No one must ever ask me!" She was becoming agitated. Havgan took her hands to calm her down, but she began to wail. "No, no! You mustn't ask me. I mustn't tell! You can't make me!"

"Maeder . . ." Havgan said. "Maeder, don't . . ."

Instantly she stopped. Her face became blank and she immediately began to gaze off into space. Slowly, she pulled her hands away and sat down on a chair at the table, her back to the door. She huddled there, hugging herself. "Oh," she said softly. "I must. I must tell." She rocked back and forth. "Oh, he'll never believe me otherwise. Must tell. Must."

"Maeder?" Havgan said, kneeling beside her. She raised her head and opened her mouth to speak.

And that was when Sledda sprang forward, grasped Hildegyth by the hair, and broke her neck. Gwydion heard it snap cleanly.

Havgan was frozen in shock, still kneeling on the floor. Sledda let Hildegyth's limp body sink back down into the chair. Havgan looked up at Sledda. And Sledda looked down at Havgan, his face impassive. "You did not want to hear what she was going to say, did you?" Sledda said.

Slowly Havgan shook his head.

"Now you don't have to," Sledda said simply. "Now no one will ever hear it." Effortlessly, Sledda picked up Hildegyth's body. "I'll take care of this. No one will ever even know she was here."

"Guthlac . . ." Havgan said, his amber eyes still wide with shock.

"Will say nothing. Believe me, Lord Havgan, this is the best way. She's out of her misery now." Sledda nodded down at Hildegyth's still face. Havgan reached out, touched her face gently, and then turned away.

Nardaeg, Sol 35—morning
FIVE DAYS LATER, Havgan summoned Gwydion as soon as it

was light, and the two men rode out of the city. Havgan had offered no explanation, and Gwydion had not pressed, but his thoughts were in turmoil. Perhaps Havgan had found out the truth and he was taking Gwydion out of the city to kill him in private. After what he had seen last week, nothing would surprise him about Havgan anymore.

They passed fields and trees by the score. It was a beautiful morning, with just a touch of crispness to the air. Autumn was coming. And soon, very, very soon, Gwydion would be on his way back home. Unless he died today.

At last they reached a grove of trees, set back a little from the road. Havgan turned off and dismounted, tethering his horse at the edge of the grove. Gwydion did the same. Without a word, Havgan plucked his saddlebag from the horse's back and walked through the trees. Gwydion followed, more apprehensive than ever.

There was a tiny clearing inside the grove, and a brook babbled through it. Birds sang, and the sunlight beamed shafts of gold through the trees and onto the forest floor. Havgan dumped the saddlebag on the ground, then turned to face Gwydion. He was smiling. Uncertainly, Gwydion smiled back.

"You have been very patient, minstrel. You ask no questions."

"My lord will tell me in his own time," Gwydion replied humbly.

"The time is now. Twice you have saved my life. You have proven yourself to be a true friend to me. Tomorrow my fate hangs in the balance. And I feel a need to be bound with my friends. Therefore, today we will become brothers."

Gwydion swallowed hard. "My . .my lord," he stuttered. "I am only a servant . . ."

"No, you are more than a servant. You are a true and loyal man. You have saved my life. And now you shall be my brother."

Oh, gods. This was worse than he had expected. His mind raced, but he knew it was useless. Havgan was determined. This was almost more than he could stand. He had no choice—and he would not be able to keep the solemn oath he gave today. His word would be broken. He felt sick. And deep inside, he was ashamed at the level of deception he was being compelled to practice. "My lord—"

"No more protests, brother."

Havgan opened the saddlebag and took out a sharp knife, a wineskin, and a small cup. Then he faced the east and chanted, "O place of air, write our words before the wind." He turned south. "O place of fire, burn our words in the sun." Then west. "O place of water, write our words upon the sea." Finally, he turned to the north. "O place of earth, chisel our words in stone."

He filled the cup with water from the brook and poured it over the ground. Then he placed his foot over the soaked earth, making a footprint. He gestured and Gwydion placed his own footprint on top of it.

Then Havgan cut his thumb and handed the knife to Gwydion, who did the same. They held their hands over the footprints, letting the blood drop into the ground. Then they grasped each other's right wrists with their bleeding hands. Havgan spoke:

"So long as there is breath in my body,
I pledge true friendship.
So long as there is blood in my veins,
I will shed it in your defense.

So long as you call, I shall answer.
So long as you ride, I shall follow."

Gwydion took a deep breath. Then he, in his turn, chanted the same formula. He kept his voice steady, but inside he was screaming. His mind was chaos. Contempt for himself, contempt for Havgan, sorrow, pain, genuine love, genuine hate, all boiled inside, creating a maelstrom of hopeless misery.

Havgan poured wine in the cup and drank. Then he handed the cup to Gwydion, who drank in his turn. Havgan placed his arm around Gwydion's shoulders, and turned until they faced east. "Air has written the words we spoke today. We will keep faith with one another."

They turned to the south. And Gwydion said, "Fire has written the words we spoke today. We will keep faith with one another."

Turning west, Havgan said, "Water has written the words we spoke today. We will keep faith with one another."

They turned north. "Earth has written the words we spoke today. We will keep faith with one another," Gwydion said.

Havgan embraced Gwydion, his amber eyes shining. "Tomorrow I fight Aelbald. And I will win. You shall have a great place in my household, brother."

Gwydion nodded with a tight smile on his face. But beneath his contempt for the part he played today, he felt a stirring of anger. Since the death of Amatheon, only Uthyr had the right to call him brother—only Uthyr, who would die because of this man standing before him now. Gwydion bowed his head, afraid that Havgan would see something in his eyes, something he should not see—not yet. *The day will come, "brother,"* Gwydion thought savagely, *when you shall truly know me. And I hope it destroys you.*

AFTER THEY RETURNED to the house, Gwydion went straight up to his room without speaking to anyone.

"Are you all right?" Rhiannon asked sympathetically, taking in his white face and clenched hands.

"No," he said carefully. "Not at all." She helped him over to the chair and poured him a cup of wine. She handed it to him, closing both his hands around the goblet. She gave the cup a little push toward his lips to get him going, and Gwydion downed a healthy swallow. He waited a moment to see whether his stomach was going to accept or reject it. The issue was in doubt for several moments, but, at last, the queasiness subsided. He drank again, draining the goblet to the dregs.

"Do you know what happened?" Gwydion asked.

"I heard Sigerric and the others talking about it. He made you his brother, didn't he?"

Gwydion turned to her, his eyes glittering. "I feel sick."

"I'm sure you do. Tell me, is it because you hated it or because you liked it?"

"Both," he shuddered. "Both."

She nodded. "Yes, that does make it worse, doesn't it?" Again she fell silent.

He cocked a brow at her. "That's it? No lectures? No reminders that Havgan is a cold-blooded killer? No comments about how I saved the bastard's life? I, his greatest enemy? Nothing about divided loyalties?"

"If you can think of something I should say that you haven't already thought of yourself, by all means let me know," she said steadily. Her green eyes seemed to look through and beyond him. "We should have seen this coming. Isn't this what he did with the inner circle of his warband? Bound them to him through this oath? Bound them so strongly that they would do anything he tells them to do?"

"That's them," Gwydion growled. "Not me."

"I didn't think it was," she said mildly.

"Didn't you?" he shot back.

"For the gods' sake, Gwydion, what are you trying to get me to say? That I don't trust you anymore?"

"Do you?"

"More than you do, apparently. Stop worrying about it. You're not betraying your brother. Havgan is your enemy. And he always will be."

Before he could reply, there was a knock on the door. Gwydion stiffened. Rhiannon went to the door and opened it. A servant stood there. "Lord Havgan requests the presence of his minstrels in his chambers," he said.

Rhiannon nodded, then shut the door. "He wants us," she said.

"What, now? It's getting dark, so he can't want to go anywhere."

"Don't bet on it. Come on, the master calls."

"Don't call him that!"

She looked at him steadily. "Gwydion, don't be angry at me because of what happened."

He ran his hands through his dark hair. "I'm sorry. I guess I'm a little edgy."

"Well, that's new, isn't it?" She was still angry. "Come on."

He shrugged and followed her. She was going to be angry as long as she wanted to be. Women. They were so difficult to get along with.

When they came to Havgan's rooms, Sledda was also there. Without preamble, Havgan said, "Sledda and I are going to run an errand. I want you both to come."

"What's the errand?" Rhiannon asked.

"There is no need for you to know that," Sledda snapped. "It is enough that Lord Havgan wishes you to go."

Rhiannon turned to Havgan, her brows raised. "Touchy, isn't he?"

Havgan's stern face softened into an unwilling smile. "It's his calling in life."

"So, you're not going to satisfy my curiosity, either?" she asked flippantly.

Havgan sighed. "I never could resist the blandishments of a beautiful woman. We go to seek a valla, a fate-teller."

"A fate-teller," she repeated slowly.

"Yes. A very famous one right here in the city. She is reputed to be excellent."

"Then why isn't she in a dungeon somewhere?" Rhiannon asked. Sledda frowned.

"Some of her customers are very important people. And so she is free, for now," Havgan answered. "Come, both of you, it is getting dark."

"Oh," Rhiannon said, looking sharply at Gwydion. "That's too bad. Never mind. If you stay up all night, maybe you can finish it."

"Finish what?" Havgan asked sharply.

"His song," Rhiannon said. "The song for the tournament tomorrow."

Havgan turned to Gwydion with interest. "A song for the tournament?"

Gwydion ground his teeth. He wished that Rhiannon would discuss these clever ideas with him before she put them into action. "A special song that I was working on," he said. "Praising your exceptional warrior's skills. Singing of how you won the battle between you and Aelbald."

"I haven't fought yet," Havgan said, his mouth quirking.

"But you are sure to win," Gwydion said earnestly. Then he sighed. "But Rhea is right. Perhaps I can get it finished if I work all night after we return."

"Hold on a moment," Havgan said. "The song is more important. Rhea can come with me, and you can stay here. But I expect an excellent song tomorrow."

"Your honor is mine. The song will be all you could wish for. Trust me."

"I do," Havgan said softly. "And I am sure that you won't disappoint me." He looked down at Rhiannon. "Come, my dear. Let us pay a visit to the fate-teller."

Rhiannon swallowed hard. Gwydion knew what she was thinking. They had been lucky so far, when Havgan had the wyrd-galdra read to him. Neither reader had betrayed them to Havgan. But they couldn't be lucky forever. Gwydion hoped with all his heart that this fate-teller was a fake. If not, Rhiannon might not return.

But she put a smile on her face and laid her hand on Havgan's arm. "Yes, let's pay her a visit, shall we?" She glanced at Gwydion. "See you when we return, my love."

He leaned over and kissed her gently on the lips. Partly for the benefit of Havgan and Sledda. Partly in tribute to her resource and courage. And partly just because he wanted to.

"I'll return her safe and sound, brother," Havgan smiled.

Safe and sound. Yes. Havgan had better do just that.

AFTER THEY WERE gone, Gwydion went to the tapestry, lifting a corner and peering behind it. There was nothing but the whitewashed wall. He frowned and looked closer. There, a tiny crack, halfway up the wall. The door to a cupboard, obviously. But how to open it? He could not see anything that would do that. He grabbed a candle from the table and held it up, looking closer. Nothing. He pushed and pulled, but nothing moved.

Wonderful. A great hiding place. One that no one but Havgan could get into. No one but Havgan . . . ah. Of course. He closed his eyes and pushed against the tiny door in the wall with his mind. He heard a click as the cupboard swung open. Carefully, he reached in and pulled out the packet. He hurried over to the table, the packet in one hand and the candle in the other. Before he unwrapped the papers, he pushed the cupboard shut with his mind.

Taking a deep breath, he unwrapped the packet, noting the exact folds of the cloth as he did so, in order to wrap them up again properly. He unfolded a paper and found himself gazing at a detailed map of Kymru. Chief cities were marked with red ink—Tegeingl in Gwynedd, Arberth in Prydyn, Llwynarth in Rheged, and Dinmael in Ederynion. In the center of the map, the colleges were marked with green ink—Neuadd Gorsedd, where the Bards dwelled; Y Ty Dewin, where the Dewin lived; and Caer Duir, where the Druids were housed. A splash of gold ink in the center indicated the location of Cadair Idris, the abandoned hall of the High King. Within each country, the individual cantrefs and commotes were marked, as well as the roads and rivers, mountain ranges, and forests.

Lines of blue, green, and amber marked the planned path of Havgan's armies. Blue probably meant Derean forces, and green was probably for Miercean. Amber would be for Coranian warriors. If he were reading this right, a Miercean force under Penda and a Derean force under Talorcan would take Arberth in Prydyn and Dinmael in Ederynion, respectively. Both cities were right on the sea and easily accessible by ship. A second Derean force under Baldred would take Llwynarth in Rheged by using Sarn Ermyn, the great east/west road that cut through Kymru. Another Miercean force, under Catha, would make for Tegeingl in Gwynedd via the River Mawddoch. And the Coranians under Havgan's leadership would head straight for Gwytheryn, via Sarn Ermyn, where Cadair Idris and the colleges lay.

The door rattled. Gwydion looked up and swiftly shoved the plans beneath the table. Talorcan strode into the room. "Havgan, I want to—" He stopped abruptly, seeing Gwydion alone in the room.

"What are you doing here?" he asked. "Where is Havgan?"

"He and Sledda had to go out," Gwydion said. His heart was in his throat, and his racing pulse pounded in his ears, but his voice did not shake. "But they will be back, soon, I think."

Talorcan frowned. "What are you doing here by yourself?"

"Writing a song."

"How? I see no parchment."

"Are you a composer?"

Talorcan frowned. "No."

"Well, then, you don't really know how it's done. You see, you must imagine first how the song will come. You reach out," he went on, warming to his theme, "into the void of pure thought, pure music, pure poetry, and try to pull the song back out with you into the world. Only then, when it is fixed in your mind, do you write it down."

"I see," Talorcan said. For a moment, Gwydion was afraid that Talorcan truly did. His eyes were suspicious. "And why are you composing here?"

"It is a song about the prowess of Lord Havgan. What better place from which to get inspiration than here, where he spends so much of his time?"

"Mm. Indeed. I understand from Havgan that I must congratulate you."

"Congratulate me?"

"As a new brother." Talorcan smiled bitterly.

"Oh, yes. So I am," Gwydion said, uncertain if Talorcan was truly offering him congratulations or condolences. Perhaps both. The two men looked at each other in silence. He thought he saw pity in Talorcan's eyes.

"Well," Talorcan said, clearing his throat. "When Havgan returns, tell him I want to see him, will you?"

Gwydion nodded, not trusting himself to speak. After Talorcan left, he reached under the table with shaking hands and grabbed the parchment. He rolled it up quickly, careful to return it to its exact condition. He folded the cloth over it, and, lifting the tapestry, willed the cupboard to open. He placed the plans back inside, then shut the cupboard with his mind. Then he returned to the table, forcing his heartbeat to slow to normal. He took a deep breath. There was a song to compose by tomorrow. He'd best get to it.

His SONG WAS almost done when Rhiannon returned. He had

left a note for Havgan, giving him Talorcan's message, then returned to his room. When she came in, he sighed in relief.

"Back safe but not very sound," she said, her face pale.

He gestured her to take the chair. "What happened?"

"Oh, just the usual."

"You mean—?

"Oh, yes. The same thing. All of it. The Fool, The Magician. Holda and Wuotan. The Tower. Everything."

"Even the card of the Moon? The deception card?"

She nodded wearily. "Even that."

"And the valla? Did she know who you were?"

"If she did, she gave no sign at all. And I'm not sure that she did. She didn't look at me once the whole time."

"Did he . . . did he kill her?"

"Amazingly enough, no. He thanked her and left."

"I would have thought—"

"I would have, too. But, apparently, she is very famous. The Empress herself has been to see her. Secretly, of course. Did you find what you were looking for?"

"I did. Just where you said it would be. There's a cupboard behind the tapestry. But it can only by opened by Shape-Moving."

She whistled. "So he thinks they must be very, very safe."

Gwydion nodded. "Believe me, he won't have any idea that they have been seen. I was very careful. But Talorcan came in before I was finished."

"Oh, gods! What did you do?"

"Threw the plans under the table and waited until he left."

"Do you think he knew?"

Gwydion shook his head. "I'm not sure. All I can say is, be ready to run."

Chapter 13

Athelin, Marc of Ivelas
Weal of Coran, Coranian Empire
Ostmonath, 496

Gewinnan Daeg, Sol 1—late afternoon

R hiannon sat next to Gwydion as they waited for the final battle of the tournament to begin. She was tired, for they had been watching the fighting since early that morning and the day had been hot and close. She sighed longingly, thinking of home. If all went as planned, they would leave Athelin tomorrow—assuming that Gwydion came to his senses and agreed they could indeed leave. Though he had seen the invasion plans, he was still anxious to discover when the invasion was due to take place.

Rhiannon had argued with Gwydion most of the night about that. It was far more important to get out of Corania alive and return with the information they had. "Just think a moment, if it won't hurt too much," she had said. "How do you plan to find that out? We could stay here for months and never discover it in time."

"Maybe, maybe not. If I had time, I could perhaps get the

date. It's worth a try."

"No, it's not. And if you were thinking straight, you'd know that."

"Look," he had said pointedly, "I have a song to write here, thanks to you. Can we continue this discussion another time?" Gwydion had then suggested she was a coward, and the conversation had gone downhill after that. Since then, they had been icily polite to each other, but they were both still furious. The usual state of affairs.

One of the first battles of the day had been between Havgan and his men—Sigerric, Penda, Catha, Baldred, and Talorcan—against Aescwine, the Empress's brother, and five of his warriors. Havgan's band had won that battle and killed two of Aescwine's men in the process. For the rest of the day, the fighting between warbands had gone on —with the winners of one battle fighting the winners of the next. Havgan's band had now fought over seven battles, and won every time. Baldred had received one cut to his sword arm, but it was shallow. And Penda had a slight cut on his leg. The rest of them had been relatively unscathed. Aelbald's men, too, had won every battle. And now the chieftains of those unbeaten bands—Havgan and Aelbald—would fight for mastery, for the position of Warleader, and for the hand of Princess Aelfwyn.

The crowd was hushed as Havgan and Aelbald took their places in the center of the huge outer courtyard of Byrnwiga, the Warleader's fortress. The building, carved of black stone, loomed ominously over them. The winner of today's final battle would live here from now on. And the loser would be dead.

A tremendous crowd of people ringed the outer courtyard, packed in tightly to view the coming spectacle. A pavilion of white had been erected on one side of the yard for the royal family to view the proceedings in comfort. The Emperor and Empress were sitting there now, both sipping from goblets of wine. The Empress managed to look as though the outcome of the battle was of no concern to her. But the Emperor showed his agitation in his quick, nervous movements and occasional shrill laughter. Between them sat the Princess. Like her mother, she maintained a calm facade, and only if one looked closely could one see that her hands were clasped tightly together—so tight that the knuckles were white.

The Emperor's sister, Princess Aesthryth, sat very still. Though her face was impassive, her cornflower blue eyes kept Havgan in her sight, even when he was not fighting. What she was looking for, Rhiannon did not know. But she was surely watching for something.

Next to the Emperor's pavilion stood Havgan's pavilion of red and gold. Gwydion and Rhiannon sat there now, with Sigerric, Penda, Baldred, Talorcan, and Catha. Sledda stood stiffly, his eyes narrowed as he waited for the contest to begin.

"You worry too much, Master-wyrce-jaga," said Catha breezily. "Nothing can stop him now." He gestured to the two men as they waited to do battle. Each man gripped his broadsword by the hilt, his elbow bent, letting the sword trail over his right shoulder in the warrior's fighting stance, waiting for the signal to begin.

Havgan's byrnie of interwoven metal was chased with gold, and covered his body down to mid-thigh. Beneath it he wore a tunic of gold and trousers of bright red. His plain helm was like any other warrior's—fashioned of metal with the tiny figure of a boar at the top. His shield had no device, but the outer rim was edged with gold.

Aelbald's byrnie was chased with silver, and he wore a tunic and trousers beneath it of pure white. Around his arm was Aelfwyn's token, a silver scarf. His shield contained the Emperor's device of the Flyflot, four bars radiating outward.

Aelbald grinned unpleasantly at Havgan as they waited. "So, fisherman's son," he said loudly, "we have our final meeting."

Havgan nodded, smiling in his turn. "Our last meeting on this earth, Aelbald."

At last, at a signal from the Emperor, Prince Aesc stepped forward and drew his sword, lifting it high. "Now do these two champions meet," he bellowed. "These champions will fight until one is dead. Havgan, son of Hengist, and Aelbald, son of Aescwine, you fight today for the position of Bana of the Empire and for the hand of the Princess Aelfwyn. Do either of you wish to yield?"

"I will not yield to this fisherman's son!" Aelbald shouted.

"I do not yield," Havgan replied calmly.

"Then," Aesc declared, "let the battle begin."

Havgan and Aelbald began to circle each other, looking for their chance. Suddenly, Havgan feinted left, and as Aelbald's shield moved a fraction to counter, Havgan's sword slipped under the shield, catching Aelbald in the ribs with the flat of the blade.

Aelbald leapt back, knocking the blade away with the edge of his shield, then swiftly leapt forward, swinging his sword low, whistling just an inch away from Havgan's leg. Immediately, Havgan pulled back, and the two men circled each other again.

"I will remember you, Aelbald, on my wedding night. And I am sure that Aelfwyn will be remembering you, too," Havgan taunted.

Aelbald's face went white, his eyes flat with rage. He leapt forward, hammering with shield and sword, driving Havgan back with the fury of his onslaught.

Which was just what Havgan wanted. As Aelbald over-reached his sword blow, Havgan moved even closer into the swing and caught Aelbald's shield with the edge of his own. Pulling with all his might, he flipped the shield up and away from Aelbald's body. Even as he did so, his sword was coming down at an arc, again grazing Aelbald's ribs.

Aelbald stepped back, but Havgan was upon him, shields clashing and swords ringing as Aelbald sought desperately to parry Havgan's blows. Back, back, he drove Aelbald, until they stood just in front of the pavilion. A blow from Havgan knocked Aelbald's sword from his hand, sending it spinning. Aelbald stood swaying, gazing in horror at his weapon, which now lay far beyond his reach.

"Aelbald!" Aelfwyn screamed from the pavilion. A flash of silver arced through the air as a dagger left Aelfwyn's hand, speeding directly toward Havgan.

But then inexplicably the knife turned from its course toward Havgan's heart and flew to Havgan's hand instead. He dropped his sword to catch it. He turned swiftly to the Princess and grinned. "Why, thank you, sweetheart," he said. Then, quick as lightning, he turned to Aelbald and buried the blade in his throat.

Havgan's men leapt to their feet, running from the pavilion to surround their leader. Gwydion and Rhiannon followed more slowly. Aescwine, Aelbald's father, leapt onto the field to cradle the body of his dead son. Aelfwyn was right behind him, and she fell to the ground, stroking Aelbald's bloody face, tears running down her cheeks.

Princess Aesthryth was on her feet, staring at Havgan with what Rhiannon thought might be recognition—recognition of what Havgan had done; recognition of what Havgan truly was. Rhiannon noted that the Princess did not seem surprised.

The crowd cheered wildly, and Sigerric and the rest lifted Havgan to their shoulders, carrying him before the Emperor and Empress, who had remained frozen in their chairs. The men set Havgan on his feet and waited expectantly.

But the Emperor did not move, and the crowd began to mutter, pressing closer to the pavilion. Aesc plucked at the Emperor's sleeve, speaking urgently. But the Emperor could not take his eyes from his daughter as she mourned the death of Aelbald. The muttering grew louder, and Aesc abandoned the Emperor to speak to the Empress. He muttered in her ear, then she nodded. Rising, she stepped onto the field and walked stiffly to Aelbald's body. She stooped down and whispered into Aelfwyn's ear. But Aelfwyn shook her head. Fury spread over the Empress's cold face, and she grasped Aelfwyn's arm and hauled her up roughly. Aelfwyn cried out, but the Empress grimly pulled her toward the pavilion, almost flinging the Princess back into her chair.

Aelfwyn tried to rise, but the Empress gripped her arm tightly, holding her to the chair. At last, the Empress raised her stern face, and Aesc signaled the crowd to be silent.

Trembling, the Emperor came to stand before Havgan. Before he could speak, Havgan said, in ringing tones, "I thank your daughter for her timely aid. May we thus stand together against all our enemies, until death does part us!"

Aelfwyn raised her pale, tear-streaked face in astonishment. Yet, heartbroken as she was, she was not the kind of woman to ignore a way out. She stood up slowly and walked, as though in a dream, to stand beside her father in front of Havgan.

The Emperor cleared his throat. "People of the Empire, I present to you now the Bana, he who will command the warriors of the Empire! He who will wed my daughter, the fair Princess Aelfwyn, and become your next Emperor!"

The crowd cheered, and Havgan grinned. He smiled mockingly at Aelfwyn and she averted her eyes.

"To you, Lord Havgan, I give the Warleader's helm." The Emperor gestured, and Aesc came forward, holding a large box of intricately carved wood chased with gold and amber. The Emperor opened the box and took out a helm made of gold, fashioned like a boar's head. The tusks were of ivory, and the ruby eyes glittered balefully.

Beside her, Rhiannon heard Gwydion's swift intake of breath. "What?" she hissed.

"Something I saw in a dream," he muttered, "about crossroads, long ago."

The Emperor placed the helm in Havgan's waiting hands. Havgan raised the helm above his head, then proudly put it on. The crowd went wild, screaming and cheering.

The Emperor gestured again, and Aesc placed a huge sword in his brother's hands. As the Emperor held it up, the sun flashed on the figures of three boars etched into its blade. Rubies glimmered on the golden hilt like fresh blood. "I give to you now Gram, the Bana's sword," the Emperor proclaimed. "Draw it in defense of the Empire."

Havgan took the blade and raised it high. He bowed to the

Emperor and held out his empty hand to Aelfwyn. Trembling, she put her hand in his—a hand still covered with Aelbald's blood. Aelfwyn closed her eyes briefly in despair.

"One of my brothers, O great lords—and ladies—has prepared a song for this day. Let us hear it now," Havgan said.

Gwydion grabbed his harp and stepped forward. Without further preamble, he began to sing.

"By sun and moon   *I journeyed long*
To bring this tune   *For Havgan's song.*
Your praise my task,   *My song his fame,*
If you but ask   *I'll sound his name.*

"My praises ring   *Of a lord so dear*
And I shall sing   *If you will hear:*
Of one who blazed   *A trail of blood*
Till Lytir gazed   *Upon the flood.*

"The Bana weaves   *His web of fear,*
Each man receives   *His fated share.*

"As edges swing,   *Blades cut men down.*
Havgan next King   *Earns his renown.*
Break not the spell   *But silent be:*
To you I'll tell   *His bravery.*

"Scream of swords   *The clash of shields,*
These are true words   *On battlefield:*
A blood-red sun's   *The warriors shield,*
The Bana scans   *The battlefield.*

"The air is torn By flying spears,
His sword is drawn Wolves prick their ears.
The harsh blade shrills The edges bite,
The Bana wills His men to fight.

"On his gold arm The bright shield brings
To his foes, harm; To his friends, rings;
His fame's a feast Of glorious war,
His name sounds best From shore to shore.

"And now, my lords, You've listened long
As word on word I built this song:
From poet's breast These words took wing
Which all the rest Must learn to sing."

Then Gwydion was done. He bowed and stepped back to stand next to Rhiannon. She turned to him. "Think they'll learn to sing his tune?"

He grimaced. "Aelfwyn will, at any rate."

RHIANNON PACED BACK and forth in her new chamber at Byrnwiga, the Bana's palace. She was nervous, irritable, and could not sit still.

After the church celebrations in the late afternoon, all of Havgan's household had removed to this grim, dark fortress. Rhiannon was awed by the sheer magnificence of the dwelling. It was four stories high and built completely of black stone. Narrow windows with iron shutters pierced the walls at intervals. The roof glittered with tiny stones of jet. The eaves were carved with boar's heads, each one bearing eyes of ruby red.

The room that had been assigned to Gwydion and Rhiannon was on the second story and was a great improvement over their last one. A huge feather bed stood against one wall, with a coverlet of emerald green fringed with gold. Tapestries of forest scenes covered the black walls. Rugs woven with strips of green and black fabric dotted the floor. There were two chairs with green cushions resting before the hearth, where a fire blazed.

Poor Sigerric had been pale and withdrawn all evening. Just now, she knew, Talorcan and Penda were with him, helping him to get drunk. That was for the best right now, although the resultant hangover would make tomorrow a double agony for the poor man. Catha and Baldred were also in the process of getting roaring drunk, roistering with the rest of Havgan's warriors in the banquet hall.

As for Havgan, Sledda, and Gwydion, they had left a few hours ago to spend the night on the island of Waelraest Hlaew, the Dead Mounds. It was here on this island, just downriver from the Emperor's palace, where the dead rulers of Corania were laid to rest in ships with their prized possessions. The ships were buried in groups, forming mounds that belonged to each successive royal house. Five mounds stood there now.

Rhiannon continued to pace. She felt uneasy, and she wasn't sure why. Part of it was that she wanted to leave so badly. And something could go very wrong this night. But that wasn't all of it. A part of her felt that something already had gone wrong, and she was at a loss to know what it was.

She bit her lip, casting her eyes to the closed door. She wondered if she dared go look for herself, to assure herself that Gwydion was unharmed. It was foolish and dangerous. Havgan always sensed something amiss. And if anyone came in . . . On the other hand, she could bar the door. And no one was likely to come look for her.

Swiftly she bolted the door, then settled herself into the empty chair before the fire. She closed her eyes, willing her pulse to slow, willing her breath to shallowness, willing her awareness to spring free from her physical body, willing the Wind-Ride.

SHE HOVERED OVER Byrnwiga. The building was alight with torches, filled with the shouts of drunken warriors. It was after midnight and the waning moon had risen, cold and lonely as it rode the night sky. Her awareness sped over the rooftops and streets of the city, making for the river. Ahead she saw the white towers of Cynerice Scima. She rushed over the palace and saw the tiny island downstream. Here and there torches burned in the night, guiding her to where Gwydion must be.

She spiraled down carefully and came to rest on the flat top of a mound next to where Havgan and Gwydion sat. Havgan's legs were drawn up, and he was resting his chin on his knees. Gwydion sat crosslegged next to him, his arms crossed over his chest. Havgan was speaking seriously. "And then, when all is finally ready, I sail to Kymru, as the One God has commanded me."

"Oh, that it might be soon! Then I could write song after song of your glory," Gwydion said enthusiastically.

"It will be soon. And that is all I will say, even to you."

Gwydion bowed his head. "I am sorry, lord," he said humbly. "I did not mean to offend."

"You did not offend, my brother," Havgan said.

At that moment, Gwydion sensed her presence. His silvery eyes flickered to the place where her spirit hovered. Gwydion's mouth tightened in anger as Havgan rubbed his forehead.

The next moment, she heard the splash of a boat being moored on the shore of the island. Soon Sledda was climbing the mound, and a woman was following him.

She was gray-haired, and her dress was a garish blend of purple and red. Around her head she wore a scarf of gold cloth. She was fairly dripping with jewelry—her hands were loaded with rings, and numerous strings of amber, garnet, and jet hung around her wrinkled throat. Rhiannon had seen her before. This was the famous valla that she, Havgan, and Sledda had visited the night before. Rhiannon had sensed some talent in the woman last night, but she did not think it was enough to enable the valla to sense her presence. Nonetheless, she was prepared for instant flight, should it become necessary.

"Ah," Havgan said, and he stood. When the woman reached the top of the mound, he took her hand in his and bent over it. "Anflaeth, you are welcome here."

"Why do you bring me here among the dead?" Her voice was rich and melodious.

"Surely Sledda explained what I wished, Anflaeth."

She shrugged. "He told me that you wish to read the runes, and I have brought them. But he did not tell me why it must be now, in the middle of the night. And he did not tell me why it must be here, at the Mounds of the Dead."

"Anflaeth, I have been warned by your reading and by the readings of others to beware of treachery. I wish you to name the traitor for me now by the runes you cast."

The set of Gwydion's shoulders stiffened slightly. No wonder Rhiannon had felt that sense of danger. This could be very, very bad.

She shrugged. "I will try, Lord Havgan. But as I told you

before, the deceiver is veiled. I may not be able to find the answer for you. He, or she, has mighty protective spells woven about them."

Rhiannon wished that this were true. She'd feel a lot better right now.

The woman reached into her voluminous skirts and produced a bag made of swan's skin. "These are the Runes of Achtwan. This bag contains the most powerful runes of all. They will tell you the answer to your question in their own way."

Without further ado, she sat down on the stone and intoned solemnly, "I am Anflaeth. I am the valla. I am the keeper of secrets. I am the teller of truths. I speak for the Wyrd, the three goddess of fate. I speak for past, for present, for future. What is it you wish to know?"

Havgan answered, "Who seeks to betray me?"

She held out the bag, and Havgan slipped his hand into it, pulling out a rune of pure gold. He laid it on the stone.

"Fire Eye," Anflaeth said. "The rune of second sight. Choose another."

Again, Havgan chose a rune and set it on the stone. "Seid. The rune for a magician, or a sorceress. Choose another."

For the third time, Havgan reached into the bag and deposited his chosen rune on the stone. "Mundilfari. Power and magnetism."

She leaned forward, studying the three runes, a frown on her face. At last, she looked up. "The one who seeks to deceive you has special powers to see into the future. He is a powerful magician. Or, it could be a woman, a powerful sorceress. And—mark you—he or she has had the power to make you trust them."

Havgan's eyes went flat with rage, and his face became as stone. Softly, too softly, he said, "You tell me nothing."

She swallowed hard. "Lord, I tell you what I can. The answer is veiled from me by a powerful force. I can do nothing else with these runes."

"I ask you for a name, and you give me excuses! I want that name!" Enraged, Havgan leapt up, grabbing for his dagger. The valla stepped back in terror and would have fallen but for Gwydion's support.

"My lord, it is not my fault! I'll find out—but I must use the dyrne-hwata to answer this question!"

"Very well," Havgan said between gritted teeth. "Go, consult your dyrne-hwata. And return to me with the answer."

"It may take some time, lord. I tell you that powerful forces are keeping me from seeing the answer."

"Sledda, take Anflaeth back to her house, then return here. I expect an answer from you before noon, seeress. That is when I set out from my house to be married. Do not fail me."

"I will not," she said, her voice shaking.

Sledda took her arm and led her back to the boat. As the boat pushed away from the island, Rhiannon followed.

ANFLAETH LIVED NEAR the corner of Lindstrat and Bogastrat, very near to the docks. This was truly a stroke of luck, for Rhiannon had already decided that the docks were to be one of the places she must visit tonight. After Sledda left the valla's house, Rhiannon hovered outside the woman's window, peering through the gaps in the slats of the wooden shutters. Anflaeth's rooms were on the first floor—another stroke of luck. The valla had gone straight to a cabinet and removed the dyrne-hwata, setting the board on a table in the middle of the room. Then she closed her eyes and began what looked to be a very complicated preparation ritual. That was all to the good. If Rhiannon hurried, she could be back at Anflaeth's house before it was too late.

She rushed back to Byrnwiga and returned to her body. The door was still barred, and when she opened it and looked out, the corridor was empty. Sounds of drunken revelry drifted up to her room from the hall below.

She hurried to their baggage and pulled out her fine, new dress for the wedding tomorrow, along with the matching hair ornaments and shoes. Burrowing through Gwydion's bag, she took out his new tunic, trousers, and boots and laid them on the bed next to her dress. Then she searched his bag for the oldest, most worn tunic and trousers she could find. She located a set of dark gray wool and quickly put them on. She hoped that Anflaeth wouldn't have to be killed. But in case it was necessary, she had to wear something that could be burned afterward. And her own dresses were not made for that kind of work. It was too bad that the tunic and trousers were Gwydion's favorites.

She donned a pair of boots, then slipped her knife into the top of the right boot. She braided her long, black hair tightly, then wrapped it around her head. She slung their bags over her shoulder and wrapped her own cloak of black wool tightly around her, pulling up the hood. The two harp cases were harder to carry, but she wouldn't dream of leaving either of them behind. Quietly and cautiously she stepped into the empty corridor, closing the chamber door behind her. She made her way down the back staircase, the one that led to the kitchens at the back of the fortress. The kitchens were also deserted, and she silently slipped out the back door—straight into Sigerric's surprised embrace.

"What are you doing here?" he demanded in a drunken slur.

Rhiannon looked closely at him in the flickering torchlight. His eyes were unfocused, his hair disheveled, his tunic stained and spotted with wine. "I'm not."

He blinked. "Not what?"

"Not here. You're drunk and imagining things."

"Oh." He digested this for a moment. "And why shouldn't I be drunk?" he demanded belligerently. "Don't you know what's going to happen tomorrow?"

"Yes, such a shame. Well, I must disappear now. You go back inside and get another jug of wine. And don't mention seeing me. They will think you have gone mad and lock you up. And if you're locked up, you can't help Aelfwyn, can you?"

Sigerric looked at her owlishly, trying to comprehend what she was saying. "Oh. Yes," he whispered conspiratorially. "I understand."

Rhiannon only wished she did.

She shook her head as Sigerric went back inside, then she left the fortress, running softly up Lindstrat. The streets were mostly deserted. Occasionally she heard one of the Emperor's patrols ride by and she hid in the shadows until they were gone.

Rhiannon reached the docks at last. The moon shone feebly over the waters on the inlet. Ships loomed dark and strange in the night air. She made her way to where *Fleet Foot* was anchored, the ship on which she and Gwydion would be leaving tomorrow. Or, rather, today. In just a matter of hours. She hoped.

The gangplank was lowered, and torches flamed briefly on the deck of the ship. She made her way up the gangplank, stepping carefully.

"Here, now, just what do you think you're doing?" She spun around. A man dressed in a tunic and trousers stained with salt-water and tar grabbed her arm. He was unshaven and, if the smell was any indicator, had gone unbathed for quite some time.

"What have you got there, Theo?" Another man, dressed in a tunic and trousers of fine blue cloth, stood on the deck.

"A stowaway, Captain. Or a thief," the sailor answered, dragging her up the plank in front of the Captain.

"I am neither," she said with as much dignity as possible. "I have booked passage on this boat."

"Ship, please, my dear," the Captain said in a pained voice.

"Oh. Sorry. Ship. And you are?"

"Captain Euric Gildmar. Of Austarias. And you?"

"I am Rhea of Turin. My partner and I have booked passage, and I wish to stow our belongings here now."

"In a hurry to leave, are you?" the Captain asked, his dark eyes shrewd. "In a bit of trouble?"

Rhiannon hesitated, then smiled slightly. "Only if your boat—I mean ship—does not sail at noon."

The Captain nodded, eyeing her sharply, then grinned. "She will. Go on with Theo. He'll show you to your cabin. And if you're not here tomorrow at noon, we sail with your belongings and without you."

"Captain, if I am not here tomorrow at noon, you can keep my belongings. I won't need them anymore."

AFTER SHE LEFT the ship, she hurried back to Anflaeth's house. Cautiously, she peered through the shutters. She noted it was latched from the inside, but the shutter was ill-made, and there was a gap between the two halves. The latch could easily be flipped open with her knife, if it came to that. She put her eye to the gap and surveyed the room.

The room was small, lit by the light of the fire and one feeble candle on the table. In the corner was a rolled sleeping pallet. A small table held a basin and pitcher. There were a few braided rugs on the floor and a tall cabinet next to the table. A small trunk rested next to the fireplace.

Anflaeth was muttering to herself as she laid her fingertips onto a thin, carved piece of wood. The wood block rested on the wooden board, which was painted with the letters of the Coranian alphabet in bright colors. Rhiannon watched as the block of wood moved over the letters. At last, the block then came to a stop. Anflaeth sighed. "Dreamer," she muttered. "That's all it will spell for me. All night. Just Dreamer. Dreamer. Now what does that mean?"

Rhiannon hesitated. If that was all the dyrne-hwata was going to tell her, there was no need to interfere. But best to wait for a while, since she still had some hours before dawn, when Gwydion and Havgan would return to the fortress.

Once again, Anflaeth rested her fingertips on the wood, and the block touched the letters, one by one. "Dreamer," the valla sighed. "Lord Havgan will kill me for this. I need a name. A name." She clasped her hands in her lap and bowed her head. "O Wyrd, goddesses of past, present, future. Hear me. O Urth, goddess of what has become, hear me. O Verthad, goddess of becoming, hear me. O Skuld, goddess of what shall be, hear me. I seek a name. Give me a name."

Slowly, ever so slowly, the block of wood began to move. Anflaeth leaned forward to see the letters. "G—U—I—D—"

Rhiannon whipped out her knife and slid the blade between

the two halves of the shutter, flipping the latch. Then she leapt over the sill and into the room, pushing the shutters aside. Like a cat, she landed quietly on her feet, and sprang at the valla, putting her hand over the woman's mouth to stifle her scream.

Anflaeth struggled at first, but gave up quickly. When her struggles lessened, Rhiannon said softly in her ear. "Scream and you shall die. Remain silent, and you might live. Choose." Anflaeth stopped struggling. Slowly, Rhiannon took her hand away from Anflaeth's mouth. The valla gasped for air, but did not scream. Swiftly Rhiannon went to the shutter and closed it again. She noted that the door was barred. Then she returned to Anflaeth, who was just recovering from her shock.

"D—O," Rhiannon said. "Those were to be the last two letters that would have come up if you had not been so rudely interrupted."

Anflaeth said nothing. She remained frozen in her chair, staring up at Rhiannon with wide, frightened eyes.

"I am sorry that your prayer was answered, seeress. That was a mistake. But there is no mistake that can't be mended, don't you agree?"

Anflaeth nodded, her face brightening. "I have money. Much money. How much do you want?"

"Sorry, Anflaeth. Not interested in that at the moment. Now, here is what you will do. You will not send word to Havgan. If he sends to you, you tell him that the dyrne-hwata is not cooperating with you."

"I can't," Anflaeth gasped. "I can't. He'll kill me."

"Well, so will I, Anflaeth." She slipped the knife back into her boot top. "Now. You can tell him the name that you have learned, but only after noon has come and gone. That is the deal. Take it or leave it."

Anflaeth's eyes narrowed. "Who are you, really? I recognize you from when you were in here with Lord Havgan. What is your name?"

"That's not important right now, Anflaeth. The important thing is to come up with a way for me to let you live. You are one of the Wiccan, I suppose."

Anflaeth laughed. "Those fools. No. I am not one of them. I am Anflaeth. That is enough. People come to me from all over the Empire," she said haughtily.

"I can't imagine why. You barely have a glimmer of fate-telling. And nothing else. What a showman you must be!"

Anflaeth shrugged. "I make money."

"And live in a dump."

Anflacth shrugged again. "Do you know what would happen to one such as I if I lived in a better place? I would be envied for my wealth. Eventually, someone would kill me. They would say I was a witch and burn me. And take my money. It is well for witches to live quietly. If not—they die."

"Yes, I have seen a lot of that kind of death here. Do you know what Lord Havgan did in Dere for entertainment? He hunted and killed men, women, and children of the Heiden. He rode them down, then sank a blade in their guts. And he laughed when he did it. He thought it the best sport in the world."

Anflaeth shrugged. "They were fools to be caught. It is nothing to me."

"He had the wyrd-galdra read for him by two witches, and he killed them both."

"He did not kill me."

"They were your people!"

"I have no people. They were fools to be caught."

Suddenly, Anflaeth grabbed the edges of the painted board and flung it at Rhiannon. As she ducked, the seeress swiftly leapt up from the table and grabbed the knife from Rhiannon's boot top, slashing upward as she did so. Rhiannon grabbed Anflaeth's wrist, just before the knife would have plunged into her breast. Rhiannon turned the valla's wrist so the knife was pointing at Anflaeth's own heart, then grabbed the back of the woman's neck and pulled, thrusting her forward, impaling her on the knife. Anflaeth gasped. Her eyes were wide with shock. Slowly, she sank to the floor. Rhiannon sprang back, trying to keep the blood off of her tunic.

"I would have let you live, Anflaeth," Rhiannon said sadly to the dying woman, "if you had only given me a reason." She jerked the knife from Anflaeth's body, wiped it on the valla's dress, then stuck it back into her boot top. She looked around the room, and her eyes rested thoughtfully on the trunk next to the fireplace. Good enough.

Mandaeg, Sol 2—dawn

RHIANNON HAD JUST finished burning Gwydion's old tunic when he returned to the fortress. He opened the door to their chambers, a scowl on his face. Carefully, he closed the door and barred it.

"Just what did you think you were doing last night?" he snarled. He glanced at the fireplace. "And what are you burning?"

"Your old tunic. There's blood on it."

"Whose blood?" he asked sharply.

"The valla's."

Slowly, Gwydion sank down onto one of the chairs, never

taking his eyes off her. "The dyrne-hwata? She came up with a name?"

Rhiannon nodded. "She did. Your name. I tried to persuade her to keep it to herself, but she was stubborn."

"Are you hurt?" he asked quickly.

Rhiannon shrugged. "She was an unpleasant woman, but I didn't want to kill her just the same. It doesn't matter, I suppose."

"It does, but not now. What did you do with her?"

"I put her in a trunk. I locked it and threw the key away on my way back here. Oh, and I took all our things to the ship. When the wedding party forms out on the street, we can slip away. The ship leaves at noon. And we'd best be on it."

THE GREAT HALL at Byrnwiga was crowded when Gwydion and Rhiannon joined the forming wedding procession. Havgan would be attended by his inner circle of friends and by fifty warriors. Men filled the hall, talking, laughing, and drinking.

Havgan was resplendent in a tunic and trousers of pure white. Gold glittered from his belts, from the cuffs of his doeskin boots, from the hem and neck of his tunic. The shoulder clasps of his red cloak were made of gold in the shape of two boar's heads. His tawny hair spilled over a golden circlet that bound his brow. The Bana's sword hung from his golden belt.

Sigerric, Penda, Baldred, Catha, and Talorcan all wore Havgan's customary red and gold. They, too, had fillets bound about their brows, but the circlets were thinner, less ornate. Sigerric looked a great deal worse for the wear this morning. He was pale and trembled visibly. Talorcan silently handed him a brimming cup of ale. Sigerric took it without a word and drained the entire contents in three swallows.

Gwydion was dressed in a tunic and trousers of dark blue, sapphires glittering from the neck and sleeves. His cloak, fastened with silver clasps, was white. Rhiannon was dressed in a gown of emerald green, cut—as always—embarrassingly low. Her cloak was black, clasped at the shoulders with emerald brooches. Around her unbound hair she wore a band of emeralds stitched into a narrow strip of gold cloth.

Havgan paced impatiently. He was frowning, and did not respond to the jests that his friends were throwing back and forth. Sledda was nowhere in sight.

"The nervous groom," Catha said, gesturing to the pacing Havgan. "Probably hoping she'll be gentle with him tonight."

"Probably hoping she won't have a knife," Baldred snorted.

There was a slight commotion at the door, and Sledda burst into the hall, making straight for Havgan.

Havgan stooped pacing. "Well?" he growled.

Sledda's face was white. "She's not there!" he gasped out. "Gone."

"Gone! What do you mean?"

"The door was barred, and there was no answer to my knock. Finally, I had my escort break the door down. Everything appeared to be in order, but she was not there. It didn't seem as if any belongings were missing, and there were no signs of violence. So I waited for her to return. But she has not."

"Then go back and wait some more! Search the place. Look around, for Lytir's sake! How could she have gotten out when the door was barred from the inside! Were the shutters closed?"

"No, they were open."

"Do you think she decided to run an errand and slipped out the window?" Havgan asked sarcastically. "Or that she turned herself into a mouse and scurried away?"

"Who knows what these witches can do?" Sledda asked darkly. "The dyrne-hwata is still sitting on the table. It looks to me as though she ran off. Maybe she did go out the window, to throw off pursuit."

Havgan pushed his face just inches away from Sledda's own. In a very steady voice, he said, "Search for her. If she's not at her house, search the city. Find her."

"But, Lord Havgan, the wedding! How can I miss—"

Havgan's hand shot out, grabbing the front of Sledda's black robe. "Find her. Or don't bother to come back. Have you got that?"

Sledda nodded curtly. Havgan let him go, and the wyrce-jaga turned and left without another word. Havgan went back to pacing.

"What was that all about?" Penda asked curiously.

Baldred shook his head. "No idea."

"Oh!" Gwydion said. "The gift!"

Rhiannon turned to him. "You forgot it, didn't you? After I reminded you twice!"

"I didn't forget!" Gwydion said indignantly.

"Then why didn't you bring it?" she demanded.

"Answer that one, brother!" Catha laughed. "And to think, I almost took Rhea for myself. You can keep her!"

The men laughed and Rhiannon flushed. "You—"

Talorcan laid a hand on her arm. "Ignore him, Rhea. That's what I do."

"I'll just run upstairs and get it," Gwydion said hastily.

"You remember where it is?" Rhiannon said sharply.

"Um . . . yes, right where I left it."

"Which would be?" she prompted. When Gwydion did not answer immediately, she sighed. "Never mind. I'll come help you look."

"I can find it myself," he protested.

"To be sure. And the wedding will be over by then." She took his arm, dragging him from the hall toward the stairs. "Oh, Talorcan," she called over her shoulder, "if you have to, start without us. We'll catch up."

"Good luck, Guido," Penda called. "You'll need it!"

"You're telling me," Gwydion replied. A wave of good-natured laughter followed them up the stairs and as they turned down the corridor. When the hall was out of sight below, they ran.

"What a bitch you are," Gwydion said cheerfully.

"Ha, ha," she replied flatly. "Save your breath for running."

Swiftly they descended the back stairs and ran through the kitchens, crowded with servants preparing the wedding feast, but none of them had the authority to challenge their hurried exit, and they passed smoothly out the back door.

As quickly as they could, they made their way up Flanstrat, which ran north of the fortress, then turned north again up Lindstrat, heading toward the docks.

"This is the way to Anflaeth's house," Rhiannon panted. "Is there another way to the docks?"

"I'm sure there is," Gwydion said breathlessly, "but I don't know it, and we can't miss that ship. It would be just our luck to run into Sledda."

Rhiannon nodded, but saved her breath for running. The streets were crowded with people streaming to the palace to watch the wedding. They wove in and out of the colorfully clad crowds, Gwydion in front, dragging her behind him by the hand.

Finally, they neared Anflaeth's house. The front door was open, and they saw movement inside from across the street.

"Hurry," Rhiannon hissed.

"We can't run right now. That would attract too much attention. Just go slowly."

They passed the house, then picked up the pace. Gwydion turned to look over his shoulder, and ran—literally—right into Sledda. The force of the impact threw Gwydion into Rhiannon, and they both almost fell. Sledda did fall, knocking his head against the pavement. Gwydion recovered, and they almost sprinted off, but he saw a contingent of Havgan's warriors standing right behind Sledda, and abruptly changed his mind. He reached down, and helped Sledda to his feet, dusting him off.

"Sorry about that, old fellow," he said genially.

"You . . . you . . ." Sledda seemed at a loss for words. "What are you doing here?"

"Coming to relieve you. Havgan sent us to wait for Anflaeth. And look for clues," Rhiannon said.

Sledda's eyes narrowed. "Why?"

"Probably because you whined so much about missing the wedding. Possibly because he has a greater faith in my abilities than in yours." Gwydion shrugged. "He didn't tell me why, and I didn't ask. It didn't seem like a wise thing to do."

Sledda stood there, chewing his lip. Finally, Rhiannon said, "If you don't want us to do this, just say so. We'll go back and tell Havgan you didn't want to see the wedding after all. That would be fine with me—I happen to hate missing it."

Sledda made up his mind. "All right. Take the warriors and—"

"Havgan said he didn't want a bunch of people under my feet

in that house," Gwydion replied. "Take them back with you."

Again, Sledda hesitated. The sound of merriment to the south apparently helped him to decide. He nodded, then hurried away, the warriors following.

After he was out of sight, they ran as though Sceadu himself was chasing them. They burst onto the docks, jammed with men loading and unloading the huge ships. Then she saw the ship.

They hurried up the gangplank and spotted Captain Euric on the deck. "Captain," Rhiannon called. "We're here! Ready to go?"

"Alas, not yet," the Captain said, shaking his head.

"But it's noon. Right on the dot," she protested.

"So it is, but we still have one last load to take on. Just stay out of the way, and we sail when it's done."

SLEDDA HURRIED DOWN Lindstrat. It was thoughtful of Havgan to be sure that he didn't miss the wedding. After all he had done to get Havgan where he was today, too. All those years of scheming come to fruition at last. His dream was soon to come true.

He arrived at Byrnwiga, just as Havgan was starting out. With a friendly smile, he took his place just behind Sigerric—and almost ran into the man when the procession abruptly halted. Sledda looked up to see Havgan standing in front of him, his face contorted with rage. "What are you doing here? I sent you to find Anflaeth!"

"Guido and Rhea found me. They said that you . . ." Sledda's breath caught in his throat. "You didn't . . . you didn't send them?"

"Send them? They're upstairs, getting my gift. They . . ." Havgan's face turned white. "Guido," he whispered. "It was Guido all the time."

"And Rhea," Sledda said grimly.

"But he saved my life. Twice. Why would he . . .?"

"Not why would he—who is he? That's the question," Sledda said.

"Find them," Havgan barked. "At the docks. They must be leaving the city! Hurry, you fool. Hurry!"

RHIANNON STOOD AT the railing of the ship, scanning the docks. She did not even turn around when Gwydion came up behind her. "Nothing yet," she said.

Gwydion nodded. "The Captain says we will be on our way in a few moments."

"The sooner the better. I—" she broke off, looking intently at the place where Lindstrat emptied onto the docks. The sun glinted off mailed shirts of armed warriors. "It's Sledda!" she gasped. Instantly, Gwydion pulled her away from the railing, behind a convenient barrel. They peered around it.

It was Sledda, all right. Two burly warriors pushed through the crowd, knocking people out of Sledda's path. Behind him were at least twenty more warriors. Sledda's weasel-like eyes searched the crowd. He stopped, grabbing the arm of a man who was hurrying by. He asked the man a question, and then looked toward the *Fleet Foot*.

"Who was that man?" Rhiannon asked.

"The dockmaster," Captain Euric said behind them. They jumped, whirling around to face him. "Probably asked him which ship is leaving dock next. That's us."

"Now?"

"Now. We're pulling up anchor. Just thought you'd like to know."

Rhiannon smiled. "Thank you," she said.

"Just thought I'd mention it." The Captain strolled off as though he hadn't a care in the world.

"There they are!" Sledda shouted. "It's them. Stop them!"

The gangplank was just being pulled up, and two warriors grabbed for it. Unaccountably, they overbalanced and ended up in the dirty water. The rest of the warriors ran toward the ship, but by some coincidence, a pile of barrels tottered and fell, blocking their way.

"Captain! Captain!" Sledda screamed as the ship moved away.

Captain Euric came to the rail, cupping his hand around his ear.

"Stop! I demand in the name of Lord Havgan of Corania that you stop!"

The Captain shook his head, pointing to his ear. "Can't hear you," he bellowed. "What did you say?"

"Stop!"

The Captain shrugged, indicating that he couldn't understand, then turned away. "Best get below," he said to Gwydion and Rhiannon. "Could be a rough trip."

They stumbled to the cabin and slammed the door behind them. Gwydion barred it, then they took their places on the narrow bunks.

"Hurry up," Rhiannon said. "After all this, you don't want to miss the wedding, do you?" They closed their eyes.

THE WEDDING PARTY was assembled at the eastern bridge leading to the palace. The Archpreost raised his hands high, the sunlight flashing off his purple robes and his ornate golden pendant of the Tree of Lytir.

Havgan and Aelfwyn stood beneath a canopy of gold cloth. Talorcan, Catha, Baldred, and Penda each held one corner over the couple. Sigerric stood, pale and silent, on Havgan's right.

Aelfwyn, to Havgan's left, looked deathly pale. Her splendid dress of bright red trimmed with gold only emphasized the whiteness of her face. Havgan was holding her left hand, saying, "With this ring, I thee wed. And this gold and silver I give thee. And with my body I thee worship." He stopped a moment and grinned unpleasantly down at her, then went on. "And with all my worldly chattels, I thee honor."

Aelfwyn answered in a voice that was little better than a whisper. "I take thee to be my wedded husband. To have and to hold. For fairer for fouler, for better for worse. For richer for poorer, in sickness and in health. To be bonny and buxom in bed and at board, till death," she closed her eyes briefly, "do us part."

"You may kiss the bride," the Archpreost said, a benign smile on his face. Slowly Havgan reached out and took Aelfwyn's chin in his hands, forcing her to look up at him. Then he bent his head and kissed her passionately. She struggled, and he abruptly let her go, so quickly that she almost fell. He turned away to receive the congratulations of his friends. Sigerric stumbled away without looking back.

Havgan was laughing with Baldred and Catha when he saw Sledda running up, and his smile faded.

"They got away," Sledda panted. "The ship sailed and would not stop."

"Who are they? By the One God, who are they?" Havgan shouted in rage.

I am Gwydion ap Awst, the Dreamer of Kymru.

And I am Rhiannon ur Hefeydd, a Dewin of the House of Llyr.

Havgan froze at hearing their voices in his mind, and lifted his face to the bright sky, as though seeking them there. At his gesture, the talking and laughing abruptly stilled. People stared at him in bewilderment and backed away from him in fear, until the Golden Man stood alone on the palace bridge, glowing with hatred and writhing with rage.

"You—my brother, you betrayed me!" he shouted, his cry shooting up into the sky like a deadly, shining spear.

I was never your brother. I am your enemy. I always will be.

"I will come to Kymru and kill you!" he screamed, drawing the Bana's sword. As the sword whistled from its sheath, he held it up. The sun glinted off the boar's heads engraved on the killing blade. "I will kill you! I will kill you all!"

Come to Kymru, then, Rhiannon's voice rang softly but implacably in his raging, twisted mind. *We will be waiting for you. Come.*

Part 3
The Nightmare

The whole land, every dale and glen,
Weeps its long sorrow
After the graceful summer;
No tree-top can do more,
Nor weep leaves after that.
Since the earth has covered them,
There is no hope of increase among herds,
The woods are barren-crested,
And fruits do not bend down the branching boughs.

 Feldema ur Gwen Alarch
Ninth Master Bard of Kymru
Circa 420

Chapter 14

Ruthin, Northern Ederynion

Dinaswyn was waiting at the docks when Gwydion and Rhiannon stepped onto shore. Gwydion looked strained and weary, and there were tired lines bracketing Rhiannon's mouth. Dinaswyn gazed at Gwydion in silence, aware of an odd lurch in her heart. For an all-too-brief moment, it was as though Gwydion's father had returned from the grave.

"You're late," was all she said, and deep inside she cursed herself for her coldness.

"We had to wait three weeks in Seville for a ship to Kymru," Gwydion sighed.

"We're lucky," Rhiannon said sharply, "to be back at all."

"Come," Dinaswyn said coolly. "We must be on our way." They mounted the two extra horses she had brought, then followed her out of the town and into the heavily wooded countryside of northern Ederynion. The early evening shadows were lengthening, and when they reached a small clearing by the river, they halted.

Without a word they dismounted and set about making camp. Dinaswyn wondered if Gwydion and Rhiannon even noticed that they worked together so smoothly, not even needing to exchange words in order to parcel out their tasks. Using his Shape-Moving abilities, Gwydion swiftly scraped out a shallow pit for the fire. Rhiannon unloaded the packs and, locating a small pot, she filled it with water from the river. Before long a savory stew was bubbling over a golden fire.

Dinaswyn huddled closer to the flames, as the autumn chill had a way of creeping into her bones. The waning moon rode overhead, her silvery beams vying with the flames.

"Tell us the news," Gwydion said finally. "We've been away for so long."

So she began. The grape harvest had been especially good this year. The winter was expected to be relatively mild. In Ederynion, Queen Olwen was still infatuated with that Dewin, Llwyd Cilcoed. Sanon of Prydyn and Elphin of Rheged were betrothed. Gwydion's daughter, Cariadas, had completed her education at Y Ty Dewin and was now at Neuadd Gorsedd, with the Bards. In Prydyn, Rhiannon's daughter, Gwenhwyfar, was learning swordplay and twisting her father around her little finger.

"Gwen's still in Arberth?" Rhiannon asked, puzzled. "She should be in training at Caer Duir by now."

"She refuses to go," Dinaswyn said crisply. "Like mother, like daughter."

In Tegeingl, Uthyr was well, but quieter than he used to be. Queen Ygraine had miscarried earlier in the year but was now recovering. The child would have been a boy.

In the sudden silence following this pronouncement, she said, "I brought some other things that you might want, besides clothes, food, and horses." She reached into her saddlebag and pulled out two torques. One was of silver, with a single pearl dangling from a pentagon. "Your Dewin's torque," she said, handing it to Rhiannon, "which you left at Caer Dathyl." The other torque was of gold. Opals flashed fire from within the circle dangling from the necklace. "Your Dreamer's torque, Gwydion."

As he reached to take it, her hand tightened involuntarily on the necklace. But at his tug she let it go. Her mouth twisted as she watched Gwydion settle the torque around his neck. With an effort, Dinaswyn tore her eyes away from the torque and stared at the fire. "And now for your news. Did you get what you went for?"

"Yes," Gwydion anwered. "The Coranians plan to invade us, and we have seen those plans. Rhiannon and I go on from here to see Queen Olwen. Then to Rheged to see Urien and Ellirri and then to Rhoram in Prydyn. We will meet with the Master Bard, the Ardewin, and the Archdruid at Neuadd Gorsedd two and a half months from now. Arrange that for me. After that we will see Uthyr in Gwynedd. Oh, and where's Arianrod?"

"I don't know for sure," Dinaswyn replied. "You know how she is."

"So I do," Gwydion mused, glancing at Rhiannon. "Find her and take her back with you to Caer Dathyl. We'll be there three months from now, and stay the winter."

"Then," Rhiannon said, "we go to my old home in Coed Aderyn—to the cave."

"To do what?" Dinaswyn asked curiously.

"To wait," she replied.

Caer Dwfr, Dinmael, Ederynion

QUEEN OLWEN SAT in her canopied chair, sipping wine from a pearl-encrusted goblet. There were pearls scattered throughout her rich, auburn hair. Her amber eyes surveyed the occupants of the room coldly. Her children and her lover were fighting again.

Her daughter, Elen, was flushed, and her blue eyes flashed angrily. Next to Olwen's chair stood Llwyd Cilcoed. His handsome face, too, was flushed, and his dark eyes smoldered. Her son, Lludd, stood stiffly behind Elen's chair, as if to underline his side in the debate. She looked at him in distaste. The boy was growing up to look more and more like his father every day.

With no warning, the door swung open and Angharad, her Captain, stalked in. "Angharad," Olwen said in a bored tone. "I believe I said we were not to be disturbed."

Then, from behind Angharad, the voice of the man she despised most in the world rang out. "Queen Olwen, Princess Elen, Prince Lludd," Gwydion bowed. He was dressed in a tunic and trousers of black with red trim. Around his neck the Dreamer's torque gleamed. "I am delighted to see you all again. May I present Rhiannon ur Hefeydd, Dewin of Coed Aderyn?"

He gestured to the woman standing beside him. She wore riding leathers of dark green. Olwen inclined her head briefly, and Rhiannon inclined hers a fraction in return.

"And what business do you have with the Queen?" Llwyd asked haughtily.

"Ah, Llwyd Cilcoed," Gwydion said enthusiastically. "So

very, very good to see you looking so well." Llwyd opened his mouth, but Gwydion kept going. "No, no. Don't protest. The extra weight looks good on you."

Behind Gwydion, Angharad muttered something derogatory. It sounded like "smart-ass." Olwen couldn't agree more.

"What are you doing here?" Llwyd asked again, his face flushed with anger.

"We're here to see the Queen, of course. Olwen, we beg a moment of your time."

"Here I am, Gwydion ap Awst. Make the most of your moment," she said coolly.

"A moment of your time, alone," Gwydion elaborated.

"Elen, you and Lludd run along now," Llwyd Cilcoed said smugly. "The Queen and I will hear what Gwydion has to say."

"No," Gwydion said gently. "Just the Queen."

Llwyd flushed again. He opened his mouth to speak but stopped abruptly when Olwen lifted her hand. In the sudden silence she studied Gwydion intently.

"Well, Olwen?" Gwydion inquired. "Will you speak with us? Alone?"

She gestured sharply for everyone to leave. Elen stood up with alacrity, took her brother's arm, and left without a word. Llwyd left more reluctantly, followed closely by Angharad, who closed the door quietly behind her.

"Well?" Olwen asked.

"The Coranians will invade Kymru," Gwydion said softly.

She drew in her breath sharply. "When?"

"I do not know. Soon, I think. A matter of months."

"We must set watchers on the coast, then."

Gwydion shook his head. "That will be a waste of man

power. We have a much more efficient warning system."

"What? Your dreams?" she asked contemptuously.

"No. Gorwys."

"Gorwys? Gorwys of Penllyn? He died over two hundred years ago! How can—" she broke off, understanding now. "How much of a warning will he give?"

"One day only. Now, Dinmael is one of their primary targets. It is imperative that you make plans now for getting as many of your people to safety as possible."

"You mean run away? Are you mad?"

"Olwen," he said wearily, "we will lose this battle. I have seen the battle plans. They will land all over your coasts, two thousand men for each of your cantrefs. The largest force, over three thousand men, will come here to Dinmael. I have here a copy of the detailed plans that I will leave with you. But in spite of that information, Ederynion will be overrun. The most important thing is to try to save lives."

"I won't run away," she said flatly. "I will stay and fight, and so will my people."

"Olwen," Rhiannon said urgently, "your son and daughter, at least—"

"Won't run away. And that is that. Tell me, Gwydion ap Awst, by chance, have you seen my death in your dreams?"

Gwydion hesitated. "I have."

"Well, that should please you."

"Not especially."

Her lip curled in disbelief. "I hope you saw that I died fighting."

"I did."

"Good," she said.

Caer Erias, Llwynarth, Rheged

KING URIEN WAS helping his oldest son, Elphin, and his youngest son, Rhiwallon, fletch arrows under his expert direction. His wife, Ellirri, was bending over young Enid, helping her memorize basic herbal remedies. His second son, Owein, was off in a corner by himself, carving a block of polished wood into the figure of a hawk. Urien smiled with contentment to have his family around him. He was a lucky man, and he knew it.

Then the door opened abruptly and the Dreamer walked in, followed by a woman he didn't recognize. "Gwydion!" Urien shouted, enveloping his half-brother-in-law in his customary bear hug. "Where in the name of the gods have you been?"

"Oh, out and about," Gwydion said vaguely, while Ellirri hugged him tight. "Ellirri, Urien, this is Rhiannon ur Hefeydd."

Urien whistled. "So, you're the one who led Gwydion on such a wild chase! But he caught you in the end, eh?"

"And got more than he bargained for," Rhiannon said dryly.

Urien grinned. "I can see that. Sit down, sit down." He introduced Rhiannon to the children, then settled her by the fire. Ellirri was smiling as she handed around Rheged ale.

"Tell us where you've been," Urien said heartily. "You dropped right off the face of the earth. Couldn't get a word out of old Dinaswyn. You know how she is."

"I do," Gwydion said, then hesitated. "Urien, I must speak with you."

"Here I am," he said, grinning.

But Ellirri, apparently seeing something in Gwydion's face that Urien himself did not, said, "Rhiwallon, go to Sabrina for your astronomy lesson. Enid, it is time for your harp lessons."

Enid and Rhiwallon left instantly without even bothering to argue, sensing something ominous in their mother's tone. "Owein, return these arrows to Trystan," Ellirri continued.

But Owein was not so easily cowed. "You're going to let Elphin stay, aren't you?" he flared. "Then why can't I?"

"You heard your mam," Urien said sharply. Without another word, Owein left.

"Ellirri," Gwydion said, "I think Elphin—"

"Should stay," Ellirri finished firmly.

"Very well." Taking Ellirri's hand, Gwydion said, very gently, "Soon, very soon, the Coranians will invade Kymru."

Ellirri paled, but made no sound. Elphin stiffened. "You have dreamed this? Are you sure?" Urien asked slowly.

"We have been in Corania. I have seen the plans myself."

"Tell me," Urien said.

For a moment, Gwydion was silent, his hands still cradling Ellirri's gently. "They will make landfall all across your coasts, sending over two thousand men to each cantref. I will leave the detailed plans with you. The main force will land on the coast just off Ystrad Marchell and come down Sarn Ermyn, then cut across country to the city. It should take them five days to reach Llwynarth. Do you know the story of Gorwys of Penllyn?"

"I do."

"He will rise from his grave and give us warning. One day only."

"Very well. Then we march out to meet them when we hear the call."

"No. Don't do that," Gwydion said sharply. "This is a battle that we cannot win. It is imperative that you begin making plans now to get your people to safety. You and your family most of all."

"Ah, Gwydion," he said, shaking his head, "you are an excellent Dreamer. But you know nothing of ruling the Kymri. I am the King of Rheged. I cannot run away."

"Your wife and children, at least——" Gwydion began.

"No," Ellirri broke in, her voice low and even. "I stay with my husband."

"And I," Elphin said strongly, "will stay with them."

"We will make provision for the other three," Urien said. "Owein will be the hardest to get rid of. But Ellirri will think of something."

"Urien, you don't understand——" Gwydion said.

"Oh, I think I do." He looked down at his wife, sitting so quietly by Gwydion's side. Her blue eyes looked up at him, full of the love he had seen there for the past twenty-three years. No, she would not leave him. And he would not be able to make her. And he saw by her eyes that she, too, knew what Gwydion could not bring himself to say.

Coed Addien, Rheged

THEY STOPPED FOR the night near a tiny stream some leagues out of the city. He had followed them all afternoon, and was relieved they weren't going any farther. He didn't want to cause his mam and da more worry by being away any longer than he had to.

He watched from a distance, safely concealed behind some bushes, as the Dreamer and the Dewin set up camp. Rhiannon gathered wood for a fire, and Gwydion set it alight, conjuring fire in the shape of a huge battle sword. The fiery sword hovered above the pile of wood for a moment, then slashed down, igniting the logs. Owein swallowed hard. The Dreamer would be a bad man to cross. He hoped Gwydion wouldn't lose his temper.

Meanwhile, Rhiannon, who apparently had no such fear, was saying, "Do you always have to start a fire this elaborately?"

"I do," Gwydion replied shortly, as he slipped a hunk of bread onto the end of a stick and held it over the fire.

"That's dinner?" Rhiannon asked incredulously.

"Why not? You said it was my turn to cook. So I'm cooking."

"Maybe we should get Owein to cook for us."

Still hidden in the bushes—or so he thought—Owein jumped.

"Come on out, Owein," Gwydion called. "Rhiannon wants you to cook."

Trembling, but trying to hide it, he stepped out from his place of concealment.

"Can you cook?" Rhiannon asked. "How about making a nice stew?"

Without a word, he took the pot she handed him and began to prepare a stew. It was a good thing he did know how to cook. As the stew simmered, he stole glances at Gwydion and Rhiannon, but whenever he looked at them, they seemed to be looking elsewhere. No one spoke. Rhiannon sewed stitches on a length of green cloth. With a defiant look at Rhiannon, Gwydion made tiny flames dance above the fire. They twinkled in the night like bursts of sunlight.

"That's distracting Owein, Gwydion," Rhiannon said quietly after a while. "He's trying to cook. And I believe you've proven your point."

With a sigh, Gwydion stopped conjuring fire, then went for his own sewing kit and began to mend a tear in his cloak.

When the stew was done, Gwydion and Rhiannon ate

heartily. Owein was nervous. He had come all this way to speak to them, and now he couldn't seem to speak.

"What's on your mind, Owein?" Gwydion asked finally.

"I—I want to know what you said to them—to Mam and Da."

"Ask them," Rhiannon said gently.

"They won't tell me."

"Then neither will we," Gwydion said firmly.

"You must trust them, Owein," Rhiannon said, "to know what is best."

"You don't understand."

"Oh, I think we do," Gwydion said easily. "You are galled that Elphin is a part of their magic inner circle. You want to be first in their hearts, and you think Elphin holds that place. Elphin, who will have everything that you want. Everything. And what makes it worse is that you love Elphin—almost as much as you hate him."

"No," Owein said, looking at the ground. "No, I just—"

"Yes," Rhiannon said firmly. "Now, you go back home, and quickly. Ellirri must be worried sick about you. Besides, who in their right mind would spend the night sleeping outside if they could help it?"

"What's the matter, Rhiannon?" Gwydion said with a grin. "Getting too old to camp out? Getting soft? The brisk night air, a crackling fire—"

"The howl of hungry wolves, the frost—" she snapped back.

"A pile of sweet bracken—"

"Stones digging into my back—"

"What's that?" Owein said suddenly.

"What's what?" Gwydion asked.

"I don't hear—" Rhiannon stopped abruptly as the hunting

345

horn rang out again.

"Owein, stand next to me," Gwydion said sharply, reaching for Rhiannon's hand. They stood together by the glowing fire, straining their eyes into the darkness. The horn sounded again, nearer this time. And with it came the baying of dogs and the sound of horses' hooves, pounding through the distant fields.

Suddenly the hounds were there, surrounding them, panting, baying, circling endlessly. Their ghostly white coats glowed in the flickering campfire, and the flames ignited their hungry red eyes.

A white horse burst out of the night. The rider's chest was bare, and his breeches were made of deerskin. His leather boots were studded with topaz gems. He had the face of a man but the eyes of an owl. Antlers grew from his forehead. The rider grinned with an inhuman grin, a grin to turn the blood cold.

"Cerrunnos," Gwydion said. "Lord of the Wild Hunt. Protector of Kymru."

"Well met, Dreamer," Cerrunnos answered, his voice like the rushing of the wind through tall pines, like the sound of the chase as it closes in, like the heartbeat of a hunter bringing his quarry to bay.

Another horse, black as midnight, leapt into the clearing. The woman who rode it was slender and lithe. Her black hair cascaded down her back. Her shift was glowing white, the length of the skirt barely reaching her calves. Her boots were leather, studded with amethysts, and she looked down at them with pitiless eyes.

"Cerridwen. Queen of the Wood. Protectress of Kymru," Gwydion bowed.

"Well met to all of you," Cerridwen replied, her voice

shimmering like the sound of a string of silvery bells. "To you, Dreamer. To you, Rhiannon ur Hefeydd, and to you, Owein ap Urien var Ellirri, I give greetings."

"Why have you come?" Gwydion asked.

"The time is short. Death will soon stalk our land," Cerunnos said. "We come to tell you, Gwydion ap Awst, of your next task."

"The sword of the High Kings waits in Cadair Idris. And he whose hand will grasp it is safe, for now," Cerridwen said. "And now you prepare Kymru to bear her wounds. All this is as it must be. I charge you now, that when you see us again you will begin the next task. The task to gather the others you have dreamed of, so that the four of you can seek the Treasures, that the High King may take his place and regain what will soon be lost. Be ready, Rhiannon ur Hefeydd, for you are one of these four."

"I will be ready," Rhiannon said steadily.

"And to you, Owein ap Urien, we give warning," Cerunnos said, his topaz eyes shining. "Be careful of what you wish for, boy. For you shall surely get it."

And with that, they were gone.

Caer Tir, Arberth, Prydyn

KING RHORAM WAS sweating profusely. His muscles cramped, aching with the strain. Even his face hurt, so hard was he trying to hold his nonchalant smile. He looked as though he was preparing to savor a coming victory. But really, he wondered if he was going to have a stroke instead.

Parry. Raise his shield. Move his feet. Keep moving. Keep away from the stinging, shining net of steel she was steadily weaving around him. Parry. Attack. Move, move, move. *Gods,* he thought, *if I'm ever fool enough to challenge her again, just kill me then and there.* "Do you yield?" he called.

Achren laughed mockingly. Her black hair braided tightly to her scalp shone in the bright sunlight. Her dark eyes flashed. "You're out of shape," she mocked. "You drink too much. Stay up all hours. Wench too much."

"Can a man ever wench too much?" he asked, trying not to sound out of breath. She was right, but she was wrong. He did do all of those things. But he was in better shape than he had been in for years. And she knew it. It seemed to him that her breath was rasping a little, too. Or maybe that was wishful thinking.

His folk laughed, calling out wagers—and other suggestions. He grinned at their jests, but kept a close eye on her feet. If she would just move one more inch to the left—

She did. And then Rhoram's blade flashed, far to the right, distracting her for one brief moment. Grinding her shield against his own, he hooked his foot around her ankles and yanked. She went down. His blade launched itself at her unprotected throat, and stopped.

"Do you yield?" he inquired politely.

Her dark eyes laughed up at him. "The Captain of a teulu never yields."

"The Captain yields to her King. That's in the law books, Achren."

"Very well, then. I yield."

Grinning, he held out his hand to help her up. She took his hand and suddenly yanked hard, throwing him off balance, and he stumbled to the ground. Quick as a flash, she grabbed the knife tucked in her boot and held it against his throat.

"The Captain, my King, never, ever yields," she said solemnly.

"A draw!" his son, Geriant, called.

"Ha!" Gwenhwyfar called. "Achren wins!"

"How can you say that!" his daughter, Sanon, said hotly. "He—"

"She let him win," Gwen answered.

Rhoram grinned from where he lay prone. "Maybe she did, my sweetling. But have you no pity for your da?"

Gwen laughed. She ran across the courtyard, helping him to his feet, flinging her arms around his neck. "Of course, I pity you, Da."

"Thank you, dear heart. You are the joy of my old age."

Movement at the fringes of the crowd caught his eye. The courtyard was packed with people who had come to watch the challenge, and the gates of the fortress were open. Someone had apparently joined the crowd, someone who was causing quite a stir. He began to catch a few muttered words from those on the fringes of the crowd.

"Dream . . . the Dreamer . . . what dream does he bring to us now?"

Ah. Gwydion had returned from the gods knew where. And Rhiannon? Where was she? And then he heard it.

"The Dewin . . . Rhiannon . . . she has returned to us."

He craned his neck to see them coming. Beside him, Gwen tensed and began to pull away. "No, no, sweetheart," he pleaded. "Don't run away." He tried to hold her, but she slipped away and disappeared into the crowd.

Then he saw her. She wore riding leathers of dark green. A green headband held her dark hair from her face. She was thinner than he remembered, and her skin was stretched too tightly over her high cheekbones. She had changed—in more ways than he expected—in more ways than she, perhaps, even knew.

"King Rhoram," Gwydion said, as the crowd parted to let them through.

"Gwydion," Rhoram clasped his hand, but he had eyes only for Rhiannon. He gave her his most charming smile, but she did not seem to really see him at all. "Rhiannon," Rhoram said, reaching for her hand and kissing it.

"Rhoram," she said absently, looking around. "Is . . . is Gwen here?"

"She'll be right back," Rhoram temporized.

"Rhoram, we must speak to you. Alone," Gwydion said.

His brows raised in surprise. "We will be undisturbed in my chambers."

"Achren, please join us," Rhiannon said.

Rhoram led the way through the crowd to his chambers. As they filed in after him, Geriant and Sanon stopped Rhiannon at the door. "Rhiannon? Won't you even greet us?" Geriant asked.

Rhiannon hugged them both fiercely. "I've missed you two," she said, tears standing in her eyes. "Is Gwen—"

"She is well," Geriant said hastily. "And in her room, I think. Upstairs. Why don't I just go fetch her?"

"Oh, would you? Thank you. Bring her here as soon as you can. Please."

Geriant nodded, exchanging a look with his father. Rhoram nodded back, giving his son permission to try. Well, maybe Geriant could do it. Gwen adored him.

He ushered them into the audience chamber and they sat down. Without preamble, he asked, "Where have you been?"

"In Corania," Gwydion answered. "Very soon they will invade Kymru."

Rhoram's breath caught in his throat. This was worse, much, much worse than he had expected. Achren, suddenly attentive, went still.

"I have seen the plans and will leave a copy of the details with you. They will land off your shores, bringing with them over two thousand men for each cantref. The largest force will land here at Arberth. Gorwys of Penllyn will rise and give warning one day before."

Achren shot him a sharp glance. "Not much time."

"As much as we need, though," Rhoram answered absently. "We take up positions on the cliffs. Have Aidan take command of the defense of the city. Or maybe Geriant."

"No!" Rhiannon said harshly. "You must not be here."

"You will not—you cannot—win," Gwydion said evenly. "You must not try."

Rhoram smiled sadly. It was a shame, really. He did so much enjoy living. "Ah, Gwydion. I have no choice."

"At least," Rhiannon pleaded, "send the children away. All of them."

"I can't send Geriant away. But the Queen, the girls. . .what do you think, Achren?"

"The caves," Achren said succinctly. "Ogaf Greu. Send them there."

A clatter on the stairs halted the conversation. Geriant entered the room slowly. "I'm sorry. She . . . she won't come down."

Rhiannon drew in a sharp breath and turned deathly pale. Before Rhoram had even taken a step toward her, Gwydion had grasped her hands tightly in his.

"Rhiannon . . ." Gwydion said. "I'm sorry. I'm so sorry."

She turned toward him, her face tight with pain. "She still hasn't forgiven me for deserting her."

"You didn't desert her," Rhoram said sharply.

Rhiannon laughed harshly. "Tell that to Gwen. Oh, the Wheel turns round. My father. My turn to pay." She stood up, turning away from them.

"Rhiannon," Geriant whispered. "If there's anything I can do—"

"There is. Look after her. See that she comes to no harm. Promise me."

Rhoram looked at Gwydion, sitting so quietly now, his face a calm mask. But there were things behind that mask. Maybe Gwydion ap Awst wouldn't be brokenhearted if something happened to the King of Prydyn. Ah, what a fool he had been all those years ago, when he had let her go. He supposed that Gwydion owed him thanks for that. But maybe the man didn't know that yet. And maybe he did, but wouldn't admit it.

Poor Rhiannon. She always did have a way of attracting fools.

Llyn Mwyngil, Gwytheryn

RHUFON, DESCENDENT OF the Stewards of Cadair Idris, smiled briefly as he sighted the two figures on horseback. He knew them instantly, though they were still over a league away, for he had expected them. He knew something was coming, had known of something for over a year now. Exactly what it was, he was unsure, but now there was someone come to tell him, and he waited patiently for his answer.

At last they neared him enough for him to read their faces.

The news, then, was bad, indeed, from the look in the silvery eyes of the Dreamer, from the tightness in the beautiful countenance of the Dewin of Coed Aderyn.

He lifted his arm in greeting and hailed them as they halted their horses. "Gwydion ap Awst and Rhiannon ur Hefeyedd," he said quietly as he gently grasped the bridles of their mounts. "You and the news you bring are welcome."

"Welcome news?" Gwydion asked, his brow raised sardonically. "And how is my news welcome?"

"It is always best to know the truth of what must be faced. Turning away from it will surely gain us nothing."

"The Coranians will invade Kymru and defeat us," Gwydion said bluntly. "Is that the truth you wished to hear?"

Rhufon looked up at the Dreamer. "It is not the truth I wished. But it is the truth I needed. The Stewards will be ready."

"Ready to what? You cannot fight them."

"Ready to greet you when we see you again. Ready to fulfill our task of caring for Cadair Idris and the High King who will once again live there."

"Be warned, Rhufon. For the Coranian leader, Havgan, will try to enter Cadair Idris," Rhiannon said quietly.

"And gain nothing for his pains," Rhufon said serenely. "The Doors will open for no one who does not possess the Treasures. And the Doors cannot be forced."

"Yet you and yours can enter Cadair Idris," Gwydion pointed out. "Can you be so sure that Havgan will not find the way in?"

"We can be so sure, Dreamer," Rhufon said. "Fear not, for that way cannot take any but those guided by the Stewards. Cadair Idris will remain inviolate. Caladfwlch awaits inside, resting in the golden fountain that stands in the center of Brenin Llys. No one's hand but the High King's will take hold of that hilt."

"You are sure?" Gwydion pressed.

"I am sure, Dreamer. Very sure."

Neuadd Gorsedd, Gwytheryn

CARIADAS UR GWYDION var Isalyn waited impatiently for the meeting to be over. She had known from the first that the news her father brought was terrible. She had caught just a glimpse of his face as he had come striding up the stairs, and she had seen the tortured lines beneath the surface of his stern countenance. He had not stopped for a moment to even look for her, but had swept into the Master Bard's chambers accompanied by a woman with dark hair and glittering, emerald eyes.

Now, after almost an hour, he was still in there talking to the Master Bard, the Ardewin, the Archdruid, and their heirs.

She sighed. It seemed as though she had been waiting to talk to him for so very long. She remembered when she was just a little girl—a long time ago, for she was all of twelve years old now—when her father had nothing but time for her. From dawn to dusk he had played with her, taken her for walks, carried her when she was tired, helped her to make daisy chains with which she crowned them both.

But then she had been tested and had gone away to school to begin the long, arduous task of learning to be the Thirteenth Dreamer of Kymru. After she completed her studies here at Neuadd Gorsedd, she would go to Caer Duir to learn from the Druids. She could hardly wait, for now she had met Sinend, who, in the space of the last three days, had become her very best friend in all the world. Sinend lived at Caer Duir. Her father was Dinaswyn's son, Aergol, the Archdruid's heir.

She turned to look at her friend, waiting so patiently with her. Sinend was thirteen years old. She had her grandmother Dinaswyn's gray eyes, and the reddish brown hair of her mother, a princess of Rheged. Like Cariadas, Sinend had never known her mother, for the Princess had died in childbirth.

"How much longer?" Cariadas asked, twirling her red-gold hair around her finger.

"Stop that," Sinend chided. "Your hair looks like a rat's nest."

Cariadas laughed. "If it was smooth, my father wouldn't recognize me!" She thought for a moment, then said in a small voice, "Maybe he won't recognize me anyway."

"He will," Sinend said firmly, taking her hand. "You know he will."

They sat together huddled in a corner, just down the hall from Anieron's chambers. They weren't supposed to be there, of course. But there was no one to disturb them, for Elidyr, Anieron's heir; his wife, Elstar, the Ardewin's heir; and Aergol, Sinend's father, were all in Anieron's chambers with the rest of them.

They could just make out the murmur of voices from behind the door. Anieron's mellow tones predominated for a moment. Once she heard the Ardewin's startled exclamation. Great-Uncle Cynan was a good man, she knew, but not a very good Ardewin. At least, that's what Elidyr had said one time when he didn't know Cariadas was listening. Cathbad's rich voice murmured something. Then Cariadas heard her father's anguished tone.

And though she had known the news her father brought was bad, the sound of his sorrow chilled her heart. At last the door opened and her father came out, his eyes searching for her. Finally.

"Daughter!" Gwydion called to her and held out his arms, crouching down to hold her.

In a flash, Cariadas hurled herself at her father. "Da. Oh, Da. I missed you."

"And I missed you, dear heart. You know I did."

She studied his face and was startled to see the tracks of tears. "Da," she began in a small voice.

"Don't be afraid, little one," he said, his voice soft.

"But, Da, you've been crying."

The others spilled out into the corridor. Anieron Master Bard's face was impassive. Cynan Ardewin's face was white and drawn. Cathbad Archdruid's dark eyes were awash with pity. Elstar and Elidyr stood closely together, clasping each other's hands tightly. Aergol held out his arms and Sinend came running to him. The woman with dark hair who had come with her father stood alone, her back to the wall, her green eyes sorrowful.

At last Gwydion released Cariadas and rose to his feet. He laid a hand on her head. "I charge you, all of you, to care for my daughter. When the Coranians come, I will be far away from her. Promise me." His voice broke.

"We promise, Gwydion," Elstar said softly. "We will see that she comes to no harm."

"No harm," Gwydion murmured, stroking Cariadas's hair. "Can any of us come out of this unharmed?"

But to this, they had no answer.

Coed Dulas, Tegeingl, Gwynedd

UTHYR STALKED THROUGH the undergrowth. Closer and closer he crept to the clearing. So silently did he move that not even the slightest stir marked his progress.

The stag had just dipped its head to drink and straightened up, unalarmed. It was a magnificent animal, its hide light brown with a massive chest of pure white. Uthyr lifted his bow and took aim. If he released the arrow, it would bury itself deep into the snow-white breast. Blood would spill, staining the pure, shining hide, making a mockery of such proud beauty.

He shook his head. This would not do. He was the King, and he was expected to bring back a trophy from the hunt. Sometimes—many times, kings had to do things they did not want to do. Like give up their sons and never see them again. Like watch their wives miscarry and draw farther and farther into themselves. Like carry on each day as though nothing was wrong, while feeling such soul-killing loneliness with no one to talk to of his misery. No one.

He sighed silently. Then he slowly released the tension in the bow string, letting the arrow fall to the ground, unused. The stag bolted at the noise. He smiled sadly to himself. Because, sometimes, kings could do what they wanted to do.

"I almost frightened him off myself, until I realized you weren't going to shoot him after all," a familiar voice said from the other side of the clearing.

"Gwydion!" He bounded across the clearing, enveloping his half-brother in a massive bear hug. "Gwydion, oh, thank the gods, you're still alive!"

Gwydion grinned up at him. "Well, I was before you broke all my ribs! Oh, I must introduce you to Rhiannon ur Hefeydd."

A woman stepped out into the clearing. She wore a tunic and trousers of forest green. Her black hair was tightly braided to form a crown at the top of her head, and she wore a Dewin's torque around her long, slender neck. Her green eyes smiled at him.

"So, you are Rhiannon ur Hefeydd. My brother looked long and long for you."

"And found me, much to his dismay," she smiled.

"Ah, so you take him down a peg or two. A woman after my own heart."

"Thanks, Uthyr. As always, your support and unstinting loyalty mean a great deal to me," Gwydion said dryly.

"Come, you must return to Caer Gwynt with me. We will feast tonight, and celebrate your return!"

"Uthyr . . ." Gwydion began, then fell silent.

Uthyr let the silence lengthen. So it had come at last. "It's all right, Gwydion. Say what you need to say."

But it was Rhiannon who answered. "The Coranians will invade. Soon, though we do not know exactly when. The spirit of Gorwys of Penllyn will rise to give warning one day before they land. They will land off your coasts, two thousand to each cantref. The details are in this document, which we leave with you. The main contingent will put to shore off the coast of Arllechwedd and come straight to Tegeingl by river. It will take them eight days to get there. We suggest small contingents to harass them on their way, but no pitched battle."

"No pitched battle?" Uthyr asked quietly. "Why not?"

"Because we will lose. The Coranians will defeat us—for a time."

"I see. And when will the time end?"

"When the Treasures are found and your son gains entry with them into Cadair Idris. Then he will become High King and take back the land from our enemy."

"Ah. You know about my son? Have you seen him?" he asked hungrily. He couldn't help himself.

"I saw him before I left for Corania. A fine boy. You would be proud."

"I am proud." Uthyr walked apart a little way and stood with his back to them, leaning for support against a tree. For some reason his legs felt a little weak. Over his shoulder, he said quietly, "I will prepare a place in the mountains for my people to retreat to. I will try to persuade as many people as possible to go. But I cannot lose Gwynedd without a fight. I cannot."

"Uthyr, O gods, Uthyr, don't," Gwydion said hoarsely. "Please, if you have any regard for me at all, I beg you——"

"Regard for you?" Uthyr turned to his brother. "Gwydion, I gave my son to you because I trusted you. I believed in your dreams and asked no questions, because I loved you. I ask no questions now. But I am King of this land. I must fight for her. Say no more, brother. Believe me, I understand."

Tears spilled down Gwydion's face. "No, no, you don't understand. You can't possibly——"

"Gwydion, Gwydion," Uthyr said sorrowfully, "do you really think that I don't see my death in your eyes? And did you really think I would run?"

"No," Gwydion whispered.

"When you see my son, tell him that I love him. Tell him I know he will make the choice he needs to make to save his people. Will you tell him that?"

Gwydion could not seem to speak. Rhiannon nodded.

"Tell him that my last thoughts will be of him."

"Yes," Rhiannon replied steadily, though tears stood in her eyes. "I will tell him."

"You will keep him safe." It was not a question.

"We will," she replied firmly.

"Thank you," he said quietly. "It is enough."

Dinas Emrys, Gwynedd

HE DIPPED THE ladle into the simmering pot of stew and took a cautious sip. Ah, almost perfect. A little dash of rosemary and it would be a meal fit for a king. Or, in this case, a former Ardewin and a High King in the making. Or so he kept hoping.

"Chaos is not to be feared," Myrrdin said, continuing the evening lesson. "It is to be welcomed, as a necessary part of the turning of the Wheel. The soul that does not face challenges is one that is unfulfilled. Cut the bread, will you?"

Arthur took the knife and began to hack at the loaf. "So, chaos is good?"

"Chaos is neither good nor bad. Just as order is neither good nor bad. They are just parts of the Wheel, and the Wheel turns. Pour the ale, please."

"So we are just at the mercy of the Wheel?"

"Not at all," he said equably. "The Wheel offers choices to us. We take or leave those choices." He took a hunk of cheese from the larder and set it on the table. "And we do this knowing that there is a price both for grasping those choices and for walking away from them. There is always a price."

"What's the price for walking away?" Arthur asked eagerly.

"The price is death. Death of a part of you that was meant to be. But some people pay that, and think it a bargain. These are the people who try to stop the Turning Wheel. They kill something inside. It happens sometimes."

He ladled the stew into trenchers of bread, and they sat

down to eat in silence, Myrrdin unwilling to intrude on Arthur's thoughts. Why bother? He knew what they were.

There was a rattle at the door. Myrrdin looked up in surprise. "Who in the world? Oh. Oh, gods. They're back." He leapt up and flung the door open. "Gwydion! Gwydion, my boy, come in, come in!" He embraced his nephew, noting as he did so that Gwydion's perpetual mask had slipped. The Dreamer now wore the face of a man living with soul-shattering pain.

Behind Gwydion, Rhiannon stood, looking tired and care-worn. There were dark circles under her eyes. "Rhiannon, my dear," he said gently, taking her cold hands in his. "Come in. Sit by the fire."

She embraced him, and he felt her body quiver, as though a sob was working its way up from her wounded heart. But with a mighty effort, she stilled and pulled away, smiling wanly. He settled them both before the fire. Without a word, Arthur poured ale for them, then pulled the sheepskin off his bed, tucking it carefully around Rhiannon.

Myrrdin let them sip their ale and take the chill off their bones. Finally he said, "When do they come?"

Taking a deep breath, Gwydion answered, "Soon. We do not know exactly when. But Gorwys will ride and give us warning. You are to stay here in the village and do nothing."

"All right," he agreed equably. "We do nothing." He knew there was more, and he waited quietly for it to come.

"Uthyr . . ." Gwydion's voice cracked. He swallowed and began again. "Uthyr is planning to create a refuge for his people in these mountains. But you must not go there."

"Why?" Arthur's eyes flashed. "Would it be so terrible for you if I saw my father? Would that ruin all your plans?"

Gwydion ignored him, speaking to Myrrdin. "The gods only know who might find their way into that secret haven. We can't risk anyone knowing that Arthur is alive. Not yet."

"I asked you a question, Gwydion ap Awst," Arthur said belligerently. "I want an answer. Why won't you let me go there and see my father?"

"Oh," Gwydion said wearily, his head drooping. "Your father won't be there."

Myrrdin understood and said nothing. He closed his eyes briefly with the pain.

"Then where . . ." The color drained from Arthur's face. "He's going to die? And you are going to let that happen?"

Gwydion's head shot up, his eyes glittering. He rose to his feet, shaking with rage as he grasped the front of Arthur's tunic. "Let him die?" he shouted into the boy's startled face. "Don't you think I'd do anything to stop it?"

"Gwydion!" Rhiannon grasped his hands, pulling him away from the shaken boy. "Gwydion," she repeated quietly. "Sit down."

Gwydion sat down heavily, covering his face with his hands. Myrrdin waited. This was not his time to speak. This was her time. He hoped she would choose her words well. There were tears shimmering in Arthur's dark eyes.

"We saw your da, Arthur, on our way here," she said quietly. "He said to tell you that he loves you. He said to tell you that he knows you will make the choice you need to make to save our people."

In the now-silent room, her soothing voice went on, as she tried to explain—to Arthur, to Gwydion, to herself. "Choices . . . choices are hard, Arthur. Sometimes we can't choose what we want. Instead, we choose what must be. Sometimes, what must be is terrible. But we cannot turn away from it. Your father has made a choice for himself. Gwydion cannot choose for your father. No one can."

Tears spilled down Arthur's cheeks, which he clumsily tried to wipe away. Gwydion, his head still bowed, did not move.

"So he chooses to die?" Arthur whispered.

"It is a choice he must make to be true to himself. Uthyr is doing what he must do. But you mustn't think he wants to leave you. You mustn't think he doesn't care enough to stay. He said to tell you that his last thoughts will be of you."

"But, but I never. . .I never said good-bye," Arthur whispered. "I always thought, I always hoped, I would see him again."

"You can," Myrrdin said, breaking his long silence. "Look inside yourself, and you will see him. He has left that to you, now and forever. And no one can take that away. As long as you remember those you love, they can never truly die."

Caer Dathyl, Gwynedd

ARIANROD GRABBED HOLD of the sheer, rose-colored silk hangings around the four-poster bed, and yanked. The curtains tore from their moorings and floated to the polished oak floor. She trampled on them, then snatched the rose silk bedcover from the huge feather bed. She flung the spread to the floor and trampled on that, too. She glanced at the large mirror that hung over her bed and thought for a moment. No, the mirror would be less easily replaced. Best leave it alone.

Nothing had ever gone right for her. As a child, her parents had disappeared into the maw of the Coranian Empire. Aunt

Dinaswyn had looked after her out of guilt. Gwydion had used her body for years, then tired of her. Women hated her because they envied her. Men used her body because she was beautiful. She was mistrusted, misused by everyone, because they did not understand her.

And now, now that she had found a lover who actually satisfied her, she had been dragged back home by Dinaswyn, on Gwydion's orders. It wasn't fair. One minute she had been at Caer Duir enjoying herself with Aergol, Dinaswyn's son, and the next Dinaswyn herself had abruptly appeared, given Aergol a message about an important meeting, and then dragged Arianrod back to Caer Dathyl, muttering of invasion.

Worse still, when Gwydion came back to Caer Dathyl, he wouldn't be alone. That bitch, that whining, cowardly, skinny, revolting Rhiannon would be with him. She remembered her cousin Rhiannon very well from the time they had been at Y Ty Dewin together. Rhiannon had been so clever, so intelligent, sailed through all the lessons with hideous ease.

They'd be here soon. She had gone Wind-Riding just a few moments ago and had seen them riding up the mountain. Well, when they came, she'd refused to see them. She'd tell Gwydion just what she thought of him. And she'd tell Rhiannon, that fool, who had at last come out of hiding for Gwydion of all people, who had gone with him to the gods knew where . . .

Oh. Surely Rhiannon hadn't done Gwydion's bidding for that reason. Surely Rhiannon wasn't such a fool as to have fallen in love with the Dreamer. But the more she thought about it, the less far-fetched the idea seemed to be. If Rhiannon, her old enemy, thought that she could succeed with Gwydion where Arianrod had failed . . .

She whirled to her wardrobe, flinging open the doors. She donned an elegant, cream-colored undershift, then chose an elaborate, low-cut gown of amber, a color that matched her eyes to perfection. She combed out her long, honey-blond hair, weaving it through with thin, golden chains from which hung tiny amber gems. She painted her lips and eyes, and perfumed her body. Yes, very good. Now she would go to meet them.

She wafted down the halls of Caer Dathyl, out the huge doors, and down the outer steps. Dinaswyn was already there. Her aunt gave her a cool look, but said nothing.

They were coming. They crossed the stream that ran on the eastern side of the fortress, then dismounted, leading their horses up to the front steps.

"Dinaswyn," Gwydion said, nodding briefly. "Arianrod."

His voice was cool and detached, but Arianrod had seen a spark in his silvery eyes as he looked her up and down. Just as she had intended, Rhiannon ur Hefeydd's green eyes sparkled, but with an entirely different emotion. Arianrod almost smiled.

"You remember Rhiannon, don't you?" Gwydion went on.

"I do." She smiled. "My, Rhiannon, how you have changed."

"Whereas you, Arianrod, are still the same, I see," Rhiannon answered with a smile as false as Arianrod's own.

She opened her mouth to reply in kind, when movement down by the stream caught her eye. The others, following her stricken gaze, turned to the stream to look.

A woman, shrouded in black, knelt by the water. Her long, golden hair was tangled and dirty, splattered with blood and gore. On her shoulder a black raven was perched, ruffling through her bloody hair. Tears streamed down the woman's dirt-streaked face as she lifted her head to the sky and uttered a shriek of such sorrow, such misery, such utter despair that Arianrod's soul shrank back before it.

A heap of bloody garments were piled around the woman. She held up a bloodstained leather tunic with the white horse badge of Rheged sewn on its breast. The woman dipped the tunic into the stream and the water ran scarlet. She held the tunic up, the water streaming from it like bloody tears. Then she lifted another garment, this one adorned with the brown hawk of Gwynedd. She dipped it into the water, shrieking and sobbing. Garment after garment she picked up and dipped into the bloody water. They saw the black wolf of Prydyn and the white swan of Ederynion; the bull of the Druids, the nightingale of the Bards, the dragon of the Dewin. All running red with blood.

"Who is it?" Arianrod whispered, nearly paralyzed with terror. "Who is it?"

"Gwrach Y Rhibyn. The Washer-at-the-Ford," Gwydion answered, never taking his eyes from the apparition. "It is death. Coming for us all."

Rhufin, Northern Ederynion

THE MAN WALKED up the gangplank to the waiting ship bound for Andalusia. Once on the continent, it would be a fairly easy matter for him to catch another ship bound for Athelin. His master had impressed on him the need for speed, and he would obey to the best of his considerable ability. The Dreamer had told his master that the Coranians would come to Kymru soon, and the man knew he needed to get to the force before it sailed. He was under orders to go straight to Havgan, the Warleader, and offer not only the aid of his master, but also the aid of a few key disaffected lords throughout Kymru—men who thought they would rule better than those who currently had that right. With the aid of those lords and the aid of his master, the Coranians would surely triumph.

The man was dressed in a tunic and trousers of nondescript brown, for it would never do to wear his robes. Too many people might wonder what one of the Y Dawnus was doing boarding a ship. He had, of course, left his torque behind.

Just as his master, one of the Great Ones of Kymru, had ordered.

Chapter 15

Meriwdydd, Cynyddu Wythnos

He waited in the darkness, trapped, immobile, helpless, as he had done for so many years. He had lost count of those years long, long ago. The darkness was complete, but he could feel that the space was small, enclosing his prone body. He had lain there, unmoving, for so long that he was shocked to suddenly feel his arm move upward of its own volition and encounter the close-packed earth just above his head.

After all this time, the words of Bran the Dreamer still echoed in his trapped mind. The Dreamer had said to him, "You will pay for what you have done. I will make you pay. Lleu was my friend." And the Dreamer had wept. And the Dreamer had said, "Yours will be a punishment to last for hundreds of years. Your soul will not journey to Gwlad Yr Haf, to await rebirth. Your soul will be bound to the land. And when the enemy nears our shores, you will give warning. To every cantref, to every commote, to every city, to every village you will ride and warn our people of their danger. Until then, you will wait. And only when that task is complete will your soul be released."

Cautiously, he stretched forth both his arms and again encountered nothing more than dirt and rock beneath his questing fingers. He blinked again, convinced that the darkness was lifting. From somewhere a glow began to emanate. He tried to sit up, but the chamber was too small. He craned his neck to look down at his body and found that the building light was coming from himself. He was glowing.

He shifted his neck to look up, expecting to see a roof of sod. And he did, at first. But then, with a tearing, rending sound, the sod split in two, pulling up and away. Above him, he saw stars.

Slowly, strength was returning to his dead body. He sat up and pulled himself from the earth, until he stood upright beneath the starry sky. Again, he looked down at himself. He was shining brighter now with a pale, white light. He bent over his grave, reached down into it, and pulled out a silver spear. As he grasped it, the spear began to shine with the same pale light. Now he was armed and ready to ride. He heard the sound of a horse's whinny and knew that his mount had come. The horse neighed fiercely and reared up, ready for battle. Like himself and his spear, the horse glowed white in the darkness. Its eyes were blood red.

He mounted the horse and looked again up at the sky. The starry constellations told him it was springtime. And his dead soul told him it was time to ride.

Dinmael, Ederynion

OLWEN SAT UP in bed, jerked from her sleep by. . .by something. She listened, unsure what had startled her. From far off, she heard the pounding of hooves. She left the bed and went to the window, peering out into the dark night. She could see no movement, but something was coming.

Behind her, still in bed, Llwyd sat up, grumbling. "What are you doing? What's happening?"

Olwen didn't bother to answer. She flung open the door and rushed to the landing. Before she could take the stairs, her children came running from their rooms. Elen was pale and trembling. Lludd's skin was ashen, but he did not shake.

Olwen, barely pausing, pulled Elen along behind her and down the stairs, Lludd following closely. She flung open the door of the ystafell and stepped into the courtyard. It was filled with people. The sound of hooves came on, growing louder and louder. Without pausing, she ran to the closed gates of the fortress and grasped the heavy bar. Other hands helped to lift it, and she pushed at the doors. In the streets of the city, her people were pouring out of their homes, babbling questions.

And then she saw it. They all did. On the wall of the city, a horse and rider had suddenly appeared. The figure of a man stood up in the ghostly stirrups. He glowed brightly in the dark night, and lifted a glowing spear. "People of Dinmael," the phantom shouted, his voice hollow and doom-laden. "The enemy comes to our shores! Prepare yourselves to fight. The time is come!" The horse danced on the top of the wall, then leapt away, leaving only a bright afterimage before their horrified eyes.

Beside her Angharad said quietly, "My Queen. We are ready. Command us." Angharad's face was pale, her red hair in disarray. But her voice was steady.

So it had come at last. There was much to be done. "Angharad, time to tear up the docks. And ready the rowboats for the archers. Send out the contingent under Emrys to the cliffs. Have them work out the final trajectory of the catapults. Send Talhearn the Bard with them to keep the lines of communication open."

What else? There was so much to do. "Begin evacuation of the city. We won't be able hold the enemy for long. And there is a change in plan—send Lludd and Elen away with the city folk. Tell them it is their duty to lead their people to safety."

"It won't matter what I tell them. They won't go."

"Then I'll tell them."

"That won't matter, either," Angharad pointed out calmly.

"They will do as I say. Where's Llwyd Cilcoed? He goes, too."

But Llwyd could not be found.

Llwynarth, Rheged

URIEN WOKE AND leapt from his bed, his warrior instincts humming. Ellirri stirred and opened eyes heavy with sleep. They had gotten to sleep late, though they had gone to bed early. Distracted though he was, Urien had time to grin in remembrance. It had been a wonderful evening.

But now something was coming. They did not speak, but dressed hastily. So quick were they that they were ready when the door burst open and their son Elphin, the only one of their children still left in the city, ran into the room. They had already sent the others away, dispatching Owein south just a week before in the company of Trystan and sending Enid and Rhiwallon to nearby Coed Addien in the care of their steward.

Taking Ellirri's hand, Urien clattered down the stairs, Elphin following as they rushed into the crowded courtyard. Teleri, commanding in Trystan's absence, had gathered all the soldiers. She walked up to Urien calmly, and crisply reported that his warband was ready.

Before he could frame a reply, a glowing horse appeared on the top of the fortress wall. The figure of a man stood up in the stirrups. His pale face glowed, and his blood-red eyes shone brightly in the dark night. He lifted a glowing spear above his head. "People of Llwynarth," the apparition shouted. "The enemy is coming! Prepare to fight. Prepare to die!" The horse reared up and neighed fiercely. Then it sprang from the wall and was lost to their sight.

"Teleri," Urien said swiftly, "it will be as we planned. The enemy will not reach the city for another six days. Take your contingents and position yourselves just off the Sarn Ermyn road. Harass them as you can. I will gather the levies that are coming from Amgoed and Gwinionydd, and march out to meet them before they reach Llwynarth. We'll probably engage them around Peris."

A cry rose up from outside the gates. Urien bolted to the closed doors, lifted the heavy bar, and flung it aside. He pushed the doors open as a stream of people came running. They carried the body of a man and gently laid him down at Urien's feet.

The man's arm was hanging at an awkward angle. Blood poured down his face. "Fetch Bledri," Urien said to Elphin. His son took off at a dead run.

The man reached out a feeble hand and clutched his tunic. "King Urien?"

"Don't try to talk. The doctor's coming."

"No time," the man whispered.

"Da!" Elphin panted, "Mam says Bledri is gone!"

With a supreme effort, the dying man spoke again. "Morcant. Morcant Whledig. On the road. To the south."

Urien's brows raised. Morcant was the Lord of Penrhyn. Urien had already prepared for the defense of Rheged and had ordered Morcant to, when the time came, take his warriors and defend the south coast. What was he doing here near Llwynarth? He must have decided that defending the city would be more fun. Urien would have Morcant's ears for that. "Yes, he's on the road," Urien replied in a soothing tone. "He brings his men to me to fight the enemy."

"No," the man whispered. "He brings his men to fight you."

Gwent, Rheged

OWEIN'S EYES POPPED open. High above him the uncaring stars gleamed bright and cold. He frowned. Something had woken him. He sat up next to the dying campfire. All around him, men and women were stirring, coming awake. Beside him, Trystan sprang up, reaching for his sword.

Owein found himself on his feet, his spear in his hand. He looked around frantically, trying to pinpoint the source of the horse's hooves that were coming so swiftly. But it was useless. The sound seemed to be coming from everywhere.

All around him, his warriors waited, gripping their weapons tensely, peering into the dark night. Suddenly a pale horse came rushing down to them from the night sky like a falling star. The figure of a man stood up in the stirrups, raising a shining spear.

"Warriors of Rheged," it said with a huge and terrible

voice. "The enemy comes! To arms, warriors. Now is the time to fight!" Then the horse sped off into the night.

"Oh, gods, she tricked us!" Owein said.

"Who tricked us?" Trystan asked, puzzled.

"Mam," he said grimly. "She sent us away, just at the right time!"

"Our mission to supervise the defense preparations for the south coast—"

"Was a blind! It will take us at least ten days to get back to Llwynarth to help them. We'll never make it in time. Never."

"But we can try," Trystan said grimly, calling the warriors to horse.

Arberth, Prydyn

LATE AS IT WAS, Rhoram was not asleep. He sat alone at the table in his hall, sipping wine by the light of one, thin candle. A few weeks ago they had sent the noncombatants away to the hidden caves up north. Sanon and Gwen had gone reluctantly. Efa had gone willingly—the difficulty had been in making her wait for the others. But of course, he had never expected courage from her. It wasn't what he married her for, after all. Now, if he could only remember just exactly what he had married her for . . .

He must be drunker than he thought. He was hearing things now. Probably just the beginning of a hangover. It sounded like—

With a particularly vile oath, he shot from the table and ran out of the hall and into the courtyard. Achren was already there, fully dressed, her weapons at the ready. Good gods, she must sleep in them or something. Of course, that was something he had never tried to find out. He didn't fancy being disemboweled. Idly he wondered if that was how he was going to die. That was an unpleasant thought.

Achren saw him and swiftly crossed the yard to his side, followed by Geriant, who was still wearing his nightshirt, his blue eyes fuzzy from sleep. The pounding came closer.

"Open the gates," Rhoram shouted. Men and women rushed to do his bidding, and the gates swung open. The streets of the city were filled with confusion, as his people streamed forth from their houses.

A glint of golden hair crowning a slight, familiar form caught his eye. But when he looked again, it was gone. He rubbed his eyes. It couldn't have been—

A woman screamed, and pointed west to the top of the city wall. He wheeled around, and his breath caught in his throat. A pale, flickering form had materialized there. It looked like a man. But he knew that it wasn't. Not anymore.

The thing with fiery red eyes stood tall in the stirrups on his pale horse. He raised a silver spear over his head and shouted, "People of Arberth! The enemy comes! Prepare to fight for Kymru! Prepare to die!" The horse wheeled away, leaping into the darkness.

Gorwys could have put it just a trifle more diplomatically, Rhoram thought.

Someone was pushing their way through the crowd gathered around him. He blinked. It was Aidan, Achren's lieutenant. What was he doing here? Rhoram had sent him out scouting just earlier this evening. Why should he be back already?

Aidan tried to catch his breath. He looked at Rhoram and tried to speak.

"Easy, lad," Rhoram said gently. "Take your time."

"No time," Aidan gasped. "Erfin. The Queen's brother. He comes."

"Anyone's help will do, even Erfin's," he said with a grin, but with a sick feeling in the pit of his stomach.

"He comes a thousand strong. Against you."

"Well," Achren said briskly. "This changes the plan, doesn't it?"

But Rhoram did not answer. He was busy trying to convince himself that the glimpse of golden hair he had seen in the streets of what was now a doomed city hadn't belonged to his daughter, Gwenhwyfar.

Tegeingl, Gwynedd

UTHYR SAT STIFFLY in a chair by his bed watching his wife sleep. Ygraine's rich, auburn hair spread over the pillow. Her creamy skin glowed in the firelight. For the last few weeks he had done this—sat up and watched her sleep for as long as he could, memorizing every strand of hair, every breath she took, storing away in his heart every movement she made. He knew it was foolish, but he did it anyway. Because he was going to die soon. And he loved her. And he would miss her terribly.

What a fool he was.

He had sent his daughter, Morrigan, to the hiding place in the mountains, accompanied by Neuad, his young Dewin. Susanna, his Bard, and Griffi, his Druid, had flatly refused to leave. Their son, Gwrhyr, was at Neuadd Gorsedd, and when Uthyr had pointed that out, Susanna had said that she trusted her son to the Master Bard, declaring that Uthyr needed them there more than they needed to be with their son.

And Ygraine, his lovely Ygraine, had also refused to leave. He had been surprised at that. For the past year, he had felt her slipping away from him, a retreat that had begun when she miscarried. He had been sure that she would go with Morrigan, but she had refused. Unequivocally. He smiled sadly. Life with her had never been easy. But he wouldn't have traded her for the most biddable woman in the world.

He had, however, extracted a promise from his Captain, Cai, to see to it that Ygraine survived. Cai had promised, albeit reluctantly. But he would keep his word.

When he first understood what he was hearing, he realized he had been hearing it for some time. The pounding of hooves. A horse and rider were fast approaching the sleeping city. And Uthyr knew why.

Ygraine moaned in her sleep. He reached out and touched her hair. The pounding grew louder. His wife woke, her dark eyes snapping open.

"Come, *cariad*," he said gently. "We must see him."

She leapt from the bed and swiftly donned a dressing gown. Then she came to him and took his hand. "I'm ready," she said steadily.

Not hurrying, they went down the stairs and outside into the courtyard. Cai was already there, along with Susanna and Griffi. The pounding came closer. Uthyr went to the gates, Ygraine calmly walking by his side. They lifted the heavy bar, and the gates swung open. The people of the city were gathering there, anxious to see him, hoping he would allay their fears. But he could not.

Suddenly, it was there, on the top of the city wall. It glowed with a pale, white light. The horse and rider both had eyes of blood red. The rider stood in his stirrups, lifting a glowing spear. "People of Tegeingl," he bellowed. "The enemy comes! Prepare to fight. Prepare to die!" The horse danced on the top of the wall, then leapt away, leaving darkness in its place.

Behind him, Cai said quietly, "We are ready, my King."

"Very well. Ygraine, the enemy will be here in eight days. Proceed with the evacuation of the city, as agreed."

"I will, my lord," she said quietly.

"Cai, you and I march with the teulu at dawn, gathering the other levies on the way. We should confront them in Uwch Dulas as they come downriver. Remember your promise. Whatever happens, you return to the city to care for the Queen. Remember."

Uthyr opened his mouth to continue, but a gasp from Susanna stopped him. Griffi put his arm around her shoulders, supporting her.

Susanna shook her head, as if to clear it, then looked over at Uthyr, panic just behind her blue eyes. "My King, the Bard of Is Dulas says that your brother, Madoc, attacked the Gwarda there yesterday and wiped out his force. The Bard escaped and says Madoc will be here the day after tomorrow, bringing thousands of men with him."

"But what——"

"He flies his banner. And with it, the banner of the golden boar."

Ah, the banner of Corania. Gwydion had never liked Madoc. For years he had tried to persuade Uthyr to view their half-brother with suspicion. But Uthyr had always scoffed. He should have listened to Gwydion, after all.

Dinas Emrys, Gwynedd

MYRRDIN WAS TOSSING restlessly in his sleep. Suddenly, he jerked awake, uncertain of what had disturbed him. He was coated with a thin sheen of sweat. He looked over at Arthur. The boy was moaning. "No. Please. I can't. I can't."

Myrrdin rose and shook Arthur awake. "What?" Arthur blinked in confusion. "What's happening?"

They both heard it at the same time. A horse was coming, coming more swiftly than seemed possible. The hollow pounding of hooves grew louder and louder. Myrrdin jerked open the cottage door. The villagers were roused, stumbling from their houses in fear.

Arthur brushed past him, leaping out into the night. The boy peered down the mountain road, but could see nothing in the pitch black. "Where?" he cried. "Where is it coming from?"

But Myrrdin knew better than to look at the road. Instead, he scanned the dark outlines of the surrounding peaks. "There," he said, pointing upward.

A glowing white light shot across the mountains. The villagers shrieked. But the white light came on, and they could see that it was a horse and rider, with glowing eyes of ruby red. The rider carried a shining spear.

"People of Dinas Emrys," the phantom cried, then stopped abruptly. In the sudden silence, Myrrdin saw the rider staring down at young Arthur.

Arthur stared up at the rider, mesmerized. The villagers had fallen silent. Somewhere, far, far away, a hunting horn began to blow.

The phantom dismounted his ghost horse, its red eyes never wavering from the boy. And then he knelt before Arthur and bowed his glowing head. "My Lord," the phantom rasped, "My Lord, forgive me."

Arthur, his dark eyes less startled by this display than Myrrdin would have thought, slowly stretched out his hand and gently laid it on top of the phantom's bowed head. Arthur's hand took on a faint, silvery sheen as he touched the phantom. "You are forgiven, Gorwys. Fulfill your task, then go in peace."

The phantom stood. "Our enemies have come, my Lord."

Arthur straightened. "So we shall fight."

"But you shall not, for your fight is yet to come. When Cadair Idris opens to you, remember me. And pity me for a fool."

Caer Dathyl, Gwynedd

DINASWYN WAS DREAMING. She knew she was, because Awst, her sister's husband, was alive again. The sunlight shone in his glorious eyes, into eyes that were, at long last, looking at her. She smiled at him, finally showing all that was in her heart, the heart that others thought cold and dead. He was alive again, and so was she.

He reached out his hand to her. She reached out to take it, but before she could, his smile faltered. In horror, she saw a hand, a woman's hand, grasp his hair from behind and pull his head back, exposing his throat. She tried to move, tried to help him, but she could not. The knife gleamed. Sharp and deadly, it whipped across his throat, and the blood splattered onto her face, her hair, her clothes. She moaned in despair as he sank to the ground at her feet.

She woke up to the sound of her own moans. She was bathed in sweat, trembling from every limb. The fire on the hearth had died down, and the room was chilly. She got up and dressed quickly, the horror of her dream draining away from her conscious mind and back into her heart, where it always lived.

Something was coming.

Fully dressed, she ran down the hall, past the guestrooms and into Arianrod's chambers. To her surprise, Arianrod was also up and dressed for riding.

"You're awake," Dinaswyn said in surprise.

"Clever of you to notice."

Arianrod crossed to the window and opened the shutters. The night was still. Stars glittered overhead. Dinaswyn went to the window to stand next to Arianrod.

They were the only ones left in the fortress now. Two weeks ago Gwydion and Rhiannon had left on their journey to Coed Aderyn, to the old cave where Rhiannon had lived for so many years. Last week she had sent the servants to Uthyr's hiding place in the mountains for safety. Their horses had been loaded down—mostly with things Arianrod had declared she could not live without.

Dinaswyn herself had had little to add to the party's burden. Everything here in Caer Dathyl would remain unharmed. With her Shape-Moving power she had brought down the shields over the doors and windows. She and Arianrod would leave using the hidden underground exit. Then Dinaswyn would trigger a cave-in, blocking even this secret way in, leaving Caer Dathyl deserted—but impregnable. Ready for Gwydion when—and if—he returned. Dinaswyn knew, somehow, that she would not.

"Do you hear it?" she asked curiously.

Arianrod leaned out the window to scan the sky. "There."

The white light was coming at a terrific speed. Closer and

closer it came, and the pounding of hooves became louder and louder. Finally, the light resolved itself into a pale horse and a rider with a silver spear.

"Women of Caer Dathyl! The time is upon us to fight and die for Kymru! The enemy comes!" The horse wheeled away, and the light shot back into the sky.

"Yes," Arianrod said dreamily. "They are coming. I can feel it. Someone's coming for me at last."

Llyn Mwyngil, Gwytheryn

RHUFON WAS AWAKE, staring into the fire, when he heard the sound of hooves.

His son, Tybion, stumbled into the room, his face heavy with sleep. "Da?" he asked. "Now?"

"Now," Rhufon said, his silver hair shining in the light of the dying fire.

Young Lucan rushed down the stairs then stopped at the bottom, too proud to fling himself into his father's arms, his thirteen-year-old face struggling for composure.

"My son," Tybion said solemnly, his face calm, "the rider has come. Help us greet him." He put his arm around the boy's shoulders and walked outside of their snug house into the night.

Rhufon followed, feeling the weight of his years. He wondered if he would be alive when the High King returned to Cadair Idris. He would like to see it, but he knew that Tybion and, in the fullness of time, Lucan would take care of everything. Still, he would like to see it if he could.

The rider swooped down from the night sky on a pale horse. He held a shining spear above his head, and his eyes of blood were bright as he surveyed the three who stood there quietly.

"Stewards of Cadair Idris, you of the Cenedl of Caine, the enemy has come!"

"We thank you for your warning, Gorwys," Rhufon said quietly.

"You have been faithful, you sons of Caine," Gorwys said just as quietly.

"While you were faithless!" young Lucan said, his blue eyes flashing.

"So I was, young man," Gorwys said. "And this is my punishment. Long and long I have lain awake beneath the ground, waiting to ride. Think you the punishment was not enough?"

Lucan subsided, his face paling as Gorwys brandished his spear. Gorwys, seeing this, continued softly. "You will suffer no hurt from me. Guard yourselves well, for your services will be needed again. I have seen the High King himself. Be ready."

"We will," Rhufon said. "Be sure of that."

Y Ty Dewin, Gwytheryn

CYNAN AP EINON var Darun, the Eleventh Ardewin of Kymru, had indigestion. That was not, of course, unusual. But it was inconvenient. How he wished he could sleep, if only for a little while.

At least the place was quiet now, in the middle of the night. Things had been so chaotic for the last week. The library had been emptied. The surgery packed up. The herb harvest had been scant, but they had gathered all they could. He had begun, at Anieron's direction, to send small groups of Dewin to the agreed-upon refuge in southern Ystrad Marchell, on the eastern shores of Rheged. Anieron had started to do the same with his Bards. Presumably, Cathbad would refuge there with the

Druids, also. Anieron had told him in no uncertain terms that he was not to discuss any of his plans with anyone from Caer Duir. This puzzled him, but he did as Anieron bade him.

He sighed. He knew that he was no good as Ardewin. He had known that from the beginning. He wished with all his heart that they had left him alone to sing tunes in Tegeingl, deliver babies, set broken bones. Left him alone to do the little things that were so tremendously huge, the things that had made his quiet life satisfying.

He was not made for such momentous times and he knew it, though others did not think he did. There were, really, quite a few things he knew that others would be surprised to discover. For one thing, he knew that Prince Arthur of Gwynedd had been proclaimed High King the day of his birth by the Protectors. He had been there that day, and he had seen, though he had told no one, not even Gwydion, letting the Dreamer think that he lived in blissful ignorance.

Even more importantly, he knew that young Arthur was still alive. He had been Wind-Riding near Tegeingl that day when Gwydion had come to fetch the boy. He had seen. But he had said nothing when the news came that the boy had died of a fever.

He even knew that Myrrdin had disappeared, not to die, but to raise young Arthur.

He knew a great many things that he had never told anyone. He clutched at his stomach, gasping. The secrets he knew were safe and would soon be safer—for a dead man could not talk.

Then he heard it. The sound of pounding hooves. He stood up, moving slowly to the door, the pain eating away at his vitals.

Before he could reach the door, it opened, and Elstar, his

heir, rushed in, taking his arm. "Do you hear it?" she gasped.

He nodded, feeling too ill to speak. But she mustn't know. No one must know. Not yet. He made an effort and responded, "Come, let us meet him." He hurried down the stairs as best he could and out the great doors of the college. All the Dewin who remained—some twenty or so—stood on the steps, gazing tensely into the night. Llywelyn, Elstar's oldest son, joined them, putting a comforting hand on his mother's arm.

A white light rushed across the plain. The light coalesced into the forms of a horse and rider. The rider stood in the stirrups, his silver spear raised. His red eyes glowing, the words of doom came pouring out of his dead mouth. "Dewin of Y Ty Dewin, now is the time to fight! Now is the time to die for our land! The enemy comes to Kymru!" The horse shot off into the dark night.

Elstar turned to him. "Now we leave," she said.

But Cynan did not reply immediately. He was thinking of the phantom's words. *Now is the time to die for our land.* Yes. He was right. Now was the time. "Yes, Elstar," he said absently. "Tomorrow you go to Neuadd Gorsedd. Join your husband and younger son there, then go on to the caves. Take everyone with you. You'll have ten days before the Coranians get here."

"You talk as if you're not coming with us," Elstar said, forcing a laugh.

"I'm not," he answered. "I must stay."

"Cynan, no! They'll kill you!"

"I know that," he said quietly.

"Then, why? Why?"

He turned to her. For years Elstar had done her best for him. Steering him so he didn't go too far wrong, loving him through it all. And now he thought of something he could do for her.

"I'll never make it to the caves," he said gently.

Her blue eyes suddenly filled with tears as she understood at last.

Neuadd Gorsedd, Gwytheryn

SOMEONE WAS SHAKING him awake. He opened his eyes a fraction, trying to identify the fiend who was interrupting the first real sleep he had been able to get for weeks. Of course. Dudod. Who else but his brother would be so cruel?

"Anieron," Dudod said, still shaking him. "It's coming."

Anieron sighed and sat up in bed. Gods, he was tired. He'd been working too hard lately. The hideous task of clearing out Neuadd Gorsedd—of gathering books, music, instruments, and transporting them in the company of small, innocuous groups of Bards—had taken its toll. And he had been providing the same services to the Dewin. The worst part about Cynan's ineffectual leadership was that the poor man knew he was ineffectual. And if that were not enough, the task was all being accomplished in the utmost secrecy. It would never do for the traitor to find out where they were going.

The sound of hooves pounding across the plain grew louder. He made himself get up. He knew, of course, what it was coming to say. But there was no call for bad manners. He needed to be there.

The song that had been running through his mind for several days now came to him again as he and Dudod made their way down the stairs and out onto the great stone steps.

It has broken us,
It has crushed us,
It has drowned us.
O Annwyn of the star-bright kingdom;
The wind has consumed us
As twigs are consumed by
Crimson fire from your hand.

Gwenllient, his predecessor by several generations, had clearly had the war to come in mind when she composed this song. He supposed that Nudd, the Dreamer of her generation, had told her of what was to come. Broken, crushed, and drowned the Kymri would be. But they would come back from defeat. He knew it, though he did not think he would be alive to see it. Although the Dreamer had not said so, Anieron had seen that knowledge in Gwydion's eyes.

Elidyr, his heir and son-in-law, came over to him, pale, but composed. Elidyr's younger son, Cynfar, came rushing up.

"Granda!" Cynfar demanded of Anieron. "Do you see it?"

The white light that came shooting across the plain shaped itself into the figure of a horse and rider, both with eyes of blood red. The rider lifted a silver spear.

"Bards of Neuadd Gorsedd," it cried. "The enemy has come! Now must you fight and die for the land!"

"The Bards thank you for your warning," Anieron called out in return. "We will sing songs of this night, of the Ride of Gorwys."

The phantom inclined his head. Anieron could almost have sworn that the dead man grinned. And then he was gone.

Tomorrow, the remaining Dewin would arrive. Then they

would all set out on the trek to Allt Llwyd, the caves just off the sea, in the south of Ystrad Marchell.

The Druids would not be joining them, of course.

Caer Duir, Gwytheryn

CATHBAD, ARCHDRUID OF Kymru, sat by the dying hearth fire, brooding. It would be soon now. At last the Druids would once again be revered throughout the land. Just as they had been in the old days, in the lost land of Lyonesse, before the Lady Don had changed things forever by creating the Bards, the Dewin, and, most hateful of all, the Dreamers.

At last, he would come into his own. At last. It was for this that he had killed his older brother so many, many years ago, ensuring that he would become the next Archdruid. It was for this that he'd sent an assassin to Dinmael to murder Gwydion, when the Dreamer searched for Rhiannon to aid him in the quest for Caladfwlch. It was for this that he had attempted to kill Rhiannon rather than see her join forces with Gwydion to locate the sword. It was for this that he had blackmailed a band of men to attack Gwydion and his companions as they quested for the sword. It was for this that he had sent his men to the island of Afalon after the sword. Amatheon, Gwydion's younger brother, had died that day. And although Amatheon had not been the true target, Cathbad had been satisfied, for the loss of Amatheon had hurt the Dreamer deeply.

He had lost in the battle for the sword, for Caladfwlch had been found and restored to Cadair Idris. He still did not know what Gwydion's plan was for wielding that sword—for there was no High King in Kymru. He had not known where Gwydion and Rhiannon had gone until they returned with the news of the invasion. But he had turned that to his advantage, dispatching a trusted messenger to find Havgan and offer aid.

Yes, his plans were coming to fruition at last. In the past several years he had made sure that every Druid assigned to an important post had complete and total loyalty to him and him alone. Those who passed the test had been left where they were. And those who hadn't—usually the older Druids—had been quietly replaced and shipped to the most remote villages he could find. And now, everything was ready. Or almost everything.

He had been forced to go cautiously with the Druids assigned to the royal courts. Ellywen, at the court in Prydyn, had proved to be ideal for his purposes. He hadn't bothered to sound out Griffi in Tegeingl, as it would have been useless. He had high hopes for Iago in Ederynion. The man was a little too devoted to Princess Elen, but Cathbad was sure that Iago would do as he was told. Sabrina in Rheged had disappointed him, but he was sure that she, too, would come to see the light in time.

He frowned irritably. Something was up at Neuadd Gorsedd and Y Ty Dewin, and he was not precisely sure what. He knew that the colleges were being emptied, that the Dewin and Bards were disappearing with all their treasures. What he didn't know was where they were going. Apparently the Master Bard had guessed what he was up to. Anieron was very clever. More clever than Gwydion, who still seemed to be suspicious of the Master Bard. Soon the Dreamer would learn what a fool he had been. Cathbad was looking forward to that.

The pounding of hooves interrupted Cathbad's train of thought. He stood up and went to the door, stepping out into the corridor. He went swiftly down the stairs, anticipation making him feel young again. Druids streamed out of their rooms behind him, but there was no talking, no panic.

He opened the heavy doors and stepped out into the night. The sky was strewn with stars, like diamonds thrown on a silken sheet by a careless woman. Across the plain he saw the horse and rider coming, glowing as coldly as the stars.

The horse reared, pawing the air, and the rider, lifting his spear, shouted, "Druids of Caer Duir! The enemy has come! The time has come to fight! To die!"

Cathbad smiled. No doubt the people of Kymru had swallowed that, rushing to their weapons, preparing to defend the land. But not he. He was not so foolish.

The rider turned his horse, then stopped and turned back again. For a moment the rider's blood-red eyes met Cathbad's own. For a moment, the Archdruid cringed at what he saw there.

"You will not fight for Kymru," the phantom said flatly.

"How do you—"

"A traitor knows a traitor," he said. "Take warning from me and turn aside from your path. Unless you like to ride."

Coed Aderyn, Prydyn

GWYDION TOSSED AND turned, but could not sleep. He racked his brain, trying to discover if he had left anything undone. He had warned Kymru's Kings and Queens, leaving them to make their hopeless battle plans. He had warned the Bards, the Dewin, and the Druids.

He turned over to his other side, still trying to sleep. Not that he really wanted to. Of late the dream had been stalking him again. Over and over he saw the swan fall from the sky and the horses brought down in a river of blood. Over and over he saw the wolf sink beneath the onslaught and the hawk tumble end over end from the heights. Over and over he saw the nightingale torn to pieces and the dragon disemboweled. Over and over he saw the bulls attack, only to have the dream end abruptly and begin again.

He gave up trying to sleep and rose, making his cautious way to the hearth. He had to walk carefully, for the floor of the cave was rough and uneven. He glanced over at Rhiannon as she slept on the other pallet. Her long, silken hair spilled over the pillow like a shadowy flood. Her lashes formed a dark crescent above her high cheekbones. She was too thin, eating her heart out over her daughter, that ungrateful brat.

Of course, he had been eating his heart out, too. Over other things. He winced away from thoughts of Uthyr. There was no escaping it—these days it was almost as bad to be awake as it was to dream. Nightmares were everywhere before him. No escape. No matter what he did.

The faroff sound of hooves made him start. Now. Now it was coming. At last, his long nightmare of death was coming to life.

Rhiannon stirred, moaning softly. Swiftly he went to her and shook her awake. She reached out and clung to him, trembling. He held her shaking body, reveling in the feel of her, reveling in the knowledge that he was not alone, that she was by his side.

His heartbeat quickened as he looked down at her in his arms. At the same moment, she looked up. Their eyes met— glittering silver to smoldering emerald. His lips parted, to speak, or to kiss, he was not sure which he had intended, when, of their own volition it seemed, his arms dropped away from her and he stood up.

The feelings were strong. Too strong. And he was afraid. He was the Dreamer. And he must press on, unfaltering, unencumbered, to complete the tasks that the Shining Ones had given. He must not fail. And if he were bound in any way, perhaps he would. He cleared his throat. "It's starting," he said.

Rhiannon looked away, unable—or unwilling—to meet his eyes. Yet so closely was he watching her, he could see a frantic pulse beat at her slender throat. But when she spoke, her voice was cool, making him think that the uncertain light was the cause of what he had seen. "Thank the gods," she said. "The waiting was driving me mad."

She stood up, and they left the cave, passing under the waterfall and out into the dark night. Through the trees a white light was coming fast.

The horse and rider shot from the forest, coming to a stop just before them. The rider's dead eyes shone like rubies. He held a spear above his head. "Dreamer! The enemy has come! Now comes the fight for Kymru!"

"The fight began long ago, Gorwys of Penllyn," Gwydion called. "But I thank you for your warning."

The horse reared as the phantom sawed at the reins. Gwydion felt Rhiannon's hand slip into his, and he covered her hand with his own. The night fell silent. Gwydion and Rhiannon stood quietly, unmoving. The phantom sat upon his horse, so still that he seemed carved of stone. No rise and fall of his dead chest marred the stillness. This rider had breathed his last long ago.

"Gorwys of Penllyn is dead," the phantom said coldly.

"So he is," Gwydion replied. "His body is dead. His soul

has lived on to warn us. And so we thank you."

"How long—" the phantom stopped, cutting off his words in mid-sentence.

"Over two hundred and fifty years," Rhiannon said, compassion in her voice.

"Has it truly been so long?"

"Ask Bloudewedd, if you don't believe us," Gwydion said.

At the sound of that name, the phantom seemed to glow brighter. "Bloudewedd?" he said hoarsely. "She is alive?"

"In a manner of speaking," Gwydion began.

"She is Drwys Idris," Rhiannon finished.

"They put her in the Doors? O gods, they did that to her?" the phantom cried, his voice filed with horror. "Bloudewedd!" he cried out, lifting his dead face to the sky, calling to his lost love. "Bloudewedd, I am coming to you!"

And then, he was gone, shooting up into the night sky like an arrow of cold, silvery flame.

Cadair Idris, Gwytheryn

DRWYS IDRIS WAS glowing. The Doors to the deserted mountain gleamed in the dark night, bathed in light and color. Opals caught fire. Luminous pearls glimmered softly. Emeralds cast a verdant glow. Sapphires glistened with an azure light. Rubies shone like blood. Diamonds glistened. Garnets darkened almost to black. Topaz and amethysts burst into life. Onyx and bloodstone gleamed sharply.

The gods and goddesses of Kymru had clothed her in their light. It was kind of them to take the trouble, particularly for one such as her. Would he come to take farewell of his Bloudewedd, sometime High Queen of Kymru, before his soul departed?

Then she saw him. He had come back to her.

She watched him approach, a fiery white light shooting swiftly across the plain. He drew his horse to a halt at the foot of the crumbling stone steps. He gazed up at the dead mountain for a moment, remembering, perhaps, the time when it was alive with light, with laughter, with love, the way it was before they had killed it. Slowly he dismounted and ascended the broken steps.

He was not, of course, the man she remembered. The phantom before her glowed, and his red eyes shone like drops of blood. No, he was not the man he used to be. He was not a man at all.

And she? She was no longer a woman. He was gazing at the Doors that glimmered so splendidly, as though he could catch a glimpse of who she had once been within the jeweled patterns. But there was nothing for him to see of the woman he had loved. All gone, long ago.

"Bloudewedd?" he whispered, uncertainly.

"Yes, Gorwys. It is me."

"Are you—are you well?"

"I am well. And you?" she inquired politely.

He gave a sound that might have been a laugh and gestured at himself—at his deadly glow, at his blood-red eyes, at the glowing spear in his dead hands. Answer enough, she thought.

Oh, it was hard, so hard to talk. Hard, so hard to say what she really meant. So hard not to ask the same questions he was trying not to ask. Are you the one I once loved? Have you changed? Do you still love me?

At last she said, "Lleu is back."

"I know. I saw him, in a tiny village in the mountains, of

all places. I . . . I did not know that they had done this to you. I thought Bran had killed you outright."

"No. For my crime, my punishment was this."

"But why? It was I who killed Lleu Lawrient by my own hand."

She was silent for a moment. The mourning wind whipped across the plain, even now, in the dead of the night, creating swirling patterns in the wild grass. "I was his wife," she said at last. "He trusted me."

"Ah," he said, and bent his glowing head. After a moment he raised his head and spoke, his voice hoarse and shaking. "Bloudewedd, I am so sorry. So very sorry, my love."

She did not reply, and he rushed on. "Is there. . .is there anything I can do? Is there any way I can ever make up for what I have done to you?"

"What you have done to me? It would be more true to say what we have done to each other."

"Yet I persuaded you, I think, to do as we did."

"And I was willing to be persuaded."

He almost smiled. "You have changed."

"Oh, gods. I hope so," she said fervently.

"How much longer for you?" he asked gently.

"If the Dreamer succeeds, it should not be too many more years before I am released."

"If he succeeds."

"Yes."

They were silent again. The unspoken words cried out in the dead of their night.

At last, he said, "When you come to Gwlad Yr Haf, I hope I am still there. To see you once more, as you once were."

And she? What did she truly hope for? She wished she knew. But the years had made her kinder, so she simply said, "I hope so, too, Gorwys."

"I must go," he said. "My task is done. Farewell, Bloudewedd."

"Say, rather, farewell to Drwys Idris."

"No," he said, his dead mouth twisting. "To me, you will always be Bloudewedd." He turned and descended the steps. He mounted his horse and looked back at her one last time. He raised the spear, saluted her, then began to chant:

"From under earth I come

In Kymru I made my stand,

I ride on the filly that was never fowled,

And I carry the dead in my hand."

HIS FORM GLOWED, glimmered, flickered, vanished. And he was gone, leaving her alone. Again.

Chapter 16

Dinmael
Kingdom of Ederynion, Kymru
Gwernan Mis, 497

Suldydd, Disglair Wythnos—late morning

Queen Olwen sat quietly in the saddle, waiting for the sight of the Coranian fleet to stain the distant horizon. The sun had risen, turning the sandy beach into a glittering white carpet. The sea was a clear emerald green, and the waves splashed gently onto the shore. It was strange that it should be so peaceful. All too soon, the sandy shore would be drenched with blood. Some of it, she assumed, would be hers.

Her Dewin, Regan, had gone Wind-Riding this morning, reporting that the fleet would be sighted within this hour. Regan had also reported that the fleet speeding toward them consisted of thirty ships, one hundred men to a ship. Three thousand Coranian warriors were skimming across the sea to try to wrest Olwen's city from her grasp.

And they would. That much was certain. The only question was, how heavy could she and her warriors make their price? She was not so foolish as to hope for a victory. Not with only six hundred trained warriors at her disposal. The most she hoped for was a glorious death song. Her Bard, Talhearn, had promised her that.

Once again, she reviewed the defenses. Fifty men, under her son, Lludd, and her lieutenant, Emrys, were hidden with the catapults in the cliffs that overlooked the beach. Talhearn was with them to facilitate communication.

Tiny boats, only ten in all, floated just offshore to the north and south. In these boats, fifty of her best archers were stationed, with pots of burning pitch. They were to slip behind the fleet and set as many ships on fire as they could. These men and women would be lucky to get as many as three or four ships burned before they were killed.

She had left fifty more warriors on the city walls. The gates of the city behind her were firmly shut. The townsfolk who had refused to leave in the general exodus were preparing burning pitch to greet the enemy at the inevitable moment when Olwen's warriors would be forced to retreat behind the city walls.

The rest of her forces, over four hundred and fifty trained warriors, stretched to either side of her now, gathered behind the dunes, which hid them from the sight of the coming ships. To her left, her daughter, Elen, commanded one hundred and fifty. To Olwen's right, her Captain, Angharad, commanded another one hundred and fifty. Here, in the center, Olwen herself commanded another one hundred and fifty warriors.

Iago, her Druid, stood next to her right stirrup, ready to carry out her commands, watching the horizon with narrowed eyes. It would be his task, when the ships were close enough, to set as many of them on fire as he could. Iago had warned that he might have the strength to burn only one or two, but it was better than nothing. Oh, for more Druids!

She had done the best she could with the forces at her command. Six hundred against three thousand. Quite a joke, that. If only she had a sense of humor, she would have laughed. But she did not, and never had. Her dead husband, Kilwch, had considered it one of her failings. But he had been too kind to say so.

Olwen frowned. Llwyd Cilcoed, her lover, had disappeared two days ago, when the warning had come. Olwen wasn't surprised. Elen had spoken darkly of traitors, but Olwen knew better. Llwyd Cilcoed wasn't a traitor. He was merely a coward.

The sun glowed, warming the gleaming sands. Behind the dunes, hidden from the Coranians' sight, the four hundred and fifty mounted Kymric warriors sat calmly on their rock-steady horses, waiting for Olwen's signal. The sun gleamed off their bows and arrows, off their metal helmets, off their short spears, their daggers, and their round shields with the emblem of a white swan on a sea-green field. Their tunics of stiffened leather were dyed sea green, and their breeches were white. Stiff leather armor, also dyed white, covered the chests and flanks of their proud horses.

Olwen sat upon her horse like a statue. She was dressed all in white, from her leather tunic to her trousers tucked into white leather boots. Her auburn hair was braided tightly to her head and covered with a silvery metal helmet, crowned on either side with metal wings fashioned like those of a swan. The silver and pearls of the royal torque of Ederynion glistened around her slender throat.

They waited, their faces to the sea, their backs to their

proud and lovely city.

The Bard of Caereinon, standing by her left stirrup, stirred. "My Queen, Talhearn says the fleet has been sighted."

"Tell them to wait."

The Bard nodded, and his eyes took on a faraway look, as he Wind-Spoke to Talhearn on the heights.

The silence was palpable, expectant, patient. Her forces held steadily to their places. At last, the Bard said, "Talhearn says they are one league from shore."

"Release the boats."

A mirror flashed silver from the heights. Far to the north and south, out of eyeshot, the tiny boats would now be drifting behind the fleet.

"Iago," Olwen said coolly. "Mark the lead ship."

Cautiously, Iago peered over the dune. "Marked, my Queen."

She turned to the Bard. "Have Lludd begin shooting the catapults at my word. Iago, when the first ship touches shore, Fire-Weave it."

"Yes, my Queen. Almost to shore," Iago said tightly. "Almost there . . ." The sound of an explosion shook the beach. A huge spout of flame shot into the sky, and bits of wood hurled through the air, scattering burning planks onto the sand.

"Now," she said to the Bard. Almost instantly, the catapults on the cliffs began to fire. And from the tiny boats behind the fleet, flaming arrows tore through the air to catch on the sails of the ships.

Still she waited. "How many ships on fire, Iago?"

Iago craned his neck over the dune. "Four ships on fire. The men are leaping into the sea. Most of them are drowning."

Olwen's brows shot up.

"Mail shirts," Iago explained.

"Foolish."

"Catapults have taken two ships," Iago reported.

"How many men on shore?"

"Looks to be about five hundred."

Olwen turned to the Bard. "Tell Lludd to begin firing the arrows."

From the cliffs, arrows streamed into the enemy host gathering on the beach. The Coranians, armed with battle-axes, roared defiance and started north, toward the cliffs.

"Now," Olwen said, satisfied. She raised the horn to her lips and blew a long, clear note. And led the rush to death.

THAT NIGHT OLWEN stood alone on the battlements of what was still her city. She was tired, so tired that she was capable only of a weary astonishment that she still lived.

The day had been bloody—almost half of her forces had been killed. After a few hours of fighting on the beach, they had been driven back to retreat inside the city, as she had expected. During the long afternoon, as the shadows lengthened, the Coranian host had battered at the gates and walls. But the city held fast. Wave after wave of arrows had hailed down on the enemy, and burning pitch poured from the walls had helped to slake their desire to batter the walls down. For today, anyway.

She gazed eastward toward the sea, her pointed chin cupped in her hands, her elbows resting casually on the top of the wall. The torque around her neck seemed heavy, heavier than it had ever been. The full moon had risen, proudly riding the night sky, as though in honor of what Olwen's people had done that day. A beam of silver stretched across the water, shimmering and glistening distantly, like a promise made long ago.

She tore her eyes from the sea and gazed at the beach in front of the city. The sand was dotted with hundreds of small campfires of the Coranian host. A rough count of the fires had shown there were over seventeen hundred left of the enemy.

She was disappointed that, as they had fought on the beach, she had not been able to come to grips with the enemy commander. She had spotted him early on in the battle. He wore a helmet of silver, topped with the figure of a boar. He was a thin man, with dark blond hair. The shouts in battle had revealed his name. Talorcan.

To the south, two large bonfires still burned. One was fueled by the bodies of the Coranian dead, while the other burned the Kymric dead. She had watched from the walls as Talorcan had ordered that her dead warriors were to be treated as honorable enemies. This had surprised her—she had thought all Coranians were barbarians. Even more surprising, Talorcan had seen her on the walls as he gave the orders. And he had bowed to her, with the respect of one commander for another.

She stared out at the fires from her place on the walls, trying not to think of anything for the moment. Every once in a while, a catapult shot heavy rocks from the heights, straight into the Coranian camp, causing considerable confusion and an occasional casualty. Her son was working late into the night.

A weariness, a strange, fateful lassitude, overtook her as she stared at the enemy fires dotting the beach. On the brink of losing everything—including her life—she could only think of how her husband would have stood here with her. But then, in her pride, she probably would have sent him away. If only she had known then that she loved him, when he was still alive. If only she had told him so, even once. Such thoughts, buried deep within her for years, came crowding to the surface, shooting up through her weariness, to stab sharp daggers of regret and sorrow through her tired mind.

Sighing again, she got to her feet and made her way down from the battlements. Almost instantly, Angharad was by her side, materializing at the edge of the shadows.

"Where's Elen?" Olwen asked wearily.

"In Caer Dwfr, with Regan and the wounded," Angharad answered.

Olwen turned up the main street, to trudge back to the fortress, Angharad falling in beside her. The streets themselves were deserted. All the folk still left in the city were either guarding the walls or at the fortress tending the wounded. The two women passed Ty Meirw, the burial place of the rulers of Ederynion. Olwen halted for a moment, laying her hand on one of the standing stones.

"I hope," she said quietly, "they bring me back to rest here. But I doubt it."

Angharad, too loyal to pretend, merely said, "That Talorcan sounds like he might get them to do that."

"Yes."

"We gave a good account of ourselves today," Angharad said, conversationally, as they began walking again. "Four ships burned by flaming arrows, three sunk by catapult, and two burned with Druid's fire."

"A pity there hadn't been more Druids on hand today," Olwen answered.

"The forces of commote Glndyfrdwy should be here tomorrow, according to Regan. She Wind-Rode east just a while ago, and saw them."

"Another two hundred. It's not enough. I want you to leave here tonight, with Elen, join Lludd on the heights. When I am killed, take both of them to safety."

Angharad opened her mouth to argue, then apparently thought better of it. "If Elen goes, I'll go with her, at your command," she said mildly.

Yes. Angharad would let Elen do the arguing for her. She knew as well as Olwen that Elen would not leave. Olwen glanced up at the moon. Great Nantsovelta, Goddess of the Moon, Lady of the Waters, spare my children, she begged silently. Spare them from what my pride has done.

THE WOUNDED WERE laid out on the floor of the great hall. Regan passed among them, giving orders to the able-bodied to do what they could for the dying. It was little enough—change their bloody bandages, give them drugged wine to ease them out of this life, close their dead eyes. Torches flickered from the wall brackets. The banner of the swan, worked in pearls and silver on white cloth, dominated the room. The swan's proud, outstretched wings seemed to be the only thing in the city that was not bloodstained.

Olwen spied Elen, her auburn hair blood-splattered, her young face smudged with soot and blood, kneeling down beside a warrior, supporting his grizzled head as he feebly drank a cup of drugged wine. Elen looked up and saw her mother. Gently, Elen set the cup on the floor and laid the man's head back down on the pallet. She began to walk away, then returned to his side, looking closely. She knelt down again and covered the man's now-dead face with a blanket.

Elen stood up again and made her way to her mother's side. Olwen put her arm around Elen's shoulders. At her touch, Elen gave a choked sob and began to weep. Olwen led her out of the hall, Angharad following closely behind. Slowly they crossed the courtyard and entered the Queen's ystafell. Olwen sat Elen down in the canopied chair. Angharad lit some of the candles. The shadows danced across the room as Olwen poured a goblet of wine and forced Elen to drink it until her sobs tapered off.

"Better?" Olwen asked quietly.

Elen nodded and clumsily tried to wipe the tears from her face with her sleeve. Olwen took a seat on the footstool in front of the Queen's chair and grasped her daughter's hands tightly in her own.

Elen, startled to see her mother on a mere footstool, tried to rise from the canopicd chair. "Mam, this is your place."

"No, it's yours. Or will be, soon."

"Mam," Elen whispered.

"Listen to me. Tomorrow I will die."

"No!"

"Yes," she said firmly. "This was something that Gwydion ap Awst told me when he was here. He saw that I died fighting. One other thing he told me. That we would lose these battles. But that the war would go on. He said that, one day, we will have a chance to win back what we have lost."

"And you believe him?" Elen asked incredulously.

"Why not?" Olwen said simply. "He's the Dreamer. He would know."

"But you hate him!"

"True. But that doesn't mean I think he's lying—in this particular instance, anyway. Tomorrow you will be the Queen of Ederynion. And it will be your responsibility to lead our people in the battles to come, when we take back our own. For that, you must live. And to do that, you must leave. Tonight."

Elen shook her head firmly. "No."

"Think carefully, Elen," Olwen said, her voice cold. "You tell me by your too-swift response that you have not done so."

Elen was silent for a few moments. "No," she said again.

Olwen nodded. "Angharad," she said over her shoulder.

"My Queen?"

"Tomorrow, your task will be to keep my daughter alive. Understood?"

"Understood," Angharad answered briefly.

Olwen turned back to Elen. Gazing into her daughter's blue eyes, she slowly twisted the pearl ring off the fourth finger of her own right hand. She held the ring in her palm, staring down at it. Then she looked back at Elen. "The ring of Ederynion must be protected at all costs. Never, never should it fall into enemy hands."

"The ring? Why the ring?" Elen asked in surprise. "Why isn't the torque—"

"The torque is not important. The ring is. It was given to us over two hundred years ago, soon after the High King was murdered. It was brought here by Bran the Dreamer. His words were to guard the ring carefully, relinquishing it only to the Dewin who comes to claim it with these words, 'The High King commands you to surrender Bran's gift.' Have you got that?"

Elen nodded. "But there is no High King!"

"One day there will be again. Now, take the ring."

"Mam, I—"

"Take it," Olwen ordered sternly. Elen reached out a trembling hand, plucking the ring from Olwen's palm. She slipped it onto the fourth finger of her right hand.

Slowly, Olwen reached up and unclasped the royal torque from around her neck. She gestured for Elen to stand. "I do not give you this torque now. It is not fitting to do so while I still live. So I will leave it here, on the Queen's chair. Guard your life carefully, Elen. And one day, gods willing, the torque may be yours."

Olwen gently laid the torque in the now-empty chair. The room was silent as the three women looked down at the shining collar.

"Come, Elen," Olwen said, holding her cold hand out to her daughter. "Come, Angharad," she continued. "Tomorrow is my last sunrise until I am born again. I wish to spend this night under the moon with two whom I love."

Llundydd, Disglair Wythnos—early morning

OLWEN MOUNTED HER horse in the early morning light. Angharad, her green eyes underlined with the shadows of a sleepless night, yet her voice cool and calm, gave the order for the three hundred remaining teulu to mount up. Elen, her face drawn and pale, edged her horse next to Olwen's.

About twenty wounded warriors dragged themselves out of the great hall and were helped onto their horses. The rest of the wounded from yesterday were dead. Those who had not died from their wounds by this morning but were too ill to sit a horse, had chosen another way out.

Regan's light brown eyes held the sheen of tears as she emerged from the hall. Her hands and dress were blood-stained—some of the dying had needed help to hold their daggers. But they had all refused the drugged wine, saying that such an ending was not fit for warriors of Ederynion. Wearily, Regan made her way through the courtyard and came to Olwen, laying her hand on the horse's neck. She looked up at Olwen and swallowed her tears. "My Queen, Teithi ap Gwynnan brings the forces of Glndyfrdwy. They will arrive at the west gate within a few moments."

The Bard from Caereinon said, "I have Wind-Spoken with their Bard. They bring two hundred men and one Dewin."

"No Druid?" Olwen asked quickly.

"Their Druid cannot be found. None of them can."

"I see."

Suddenly Iago was at her side, his face pale, anguish in his black eyes. "My Queen, what can this mean? I don't—"

"Your Archdruid has made a deal with the enemy. Fortunately, for your sake, he did not share the details with you. You don't have to convince me of your loyalty."

"I am shamed. Shamed before you all," he whispered. His eyes flickered to Elen, then looked away.

"Never mind, Iago," Elen said gently. "It's not your fault." She reached out and patted his shoulder, as she would pat a favorite elderly horse or dog. Iago flushed.

Only the young, Olwen thought pityingly, can be that blind. She turned to the Bard. "Are they ready on the heights?"

"Talhearn says they are."

"Good. Contact Teithi's Bard. Tell them to gather on the far side of the cliffs. The plan is simple. When I sound the horn, they come in from the north. Lludd is ready with the catapults on the cliffs. We do the best we can before we are killed." She looked down at Regan. "Go to the cliffs," she said quietly. "Prepare places for the wounded there. We lose the city today."

Without waiting for Regan's reply, she turned her horse and rode down the streets of her city one last time. Behind her, three hundred warriors followed. Angharad and Elen rode to her right and left. They reached the south gate. The warrior on duty there climbed down from the wall. "The way is clear," he said quietly. "Their commander has not yet given the final battle orders."

Angharad said, "Not a trap, in my opinion. My guess is he's giving us a chance to run."

"Let's disappoint him, then, shall we?" Olwen brought the horn to her lips and sounded her last call.

OLWEN LOOKED AROUND calmly in the midst of the hopeless battle, trying to locate the Coranian commander. All around her, men and women were fighting. Killing and being killed. Dying on the bloody sands. Many of her warriors shouted her name over and over as they plunged into the melee. Almost absently, she deftly killed Coranian after Coranian, her eyes searching for Talorcan. She didn't want to die at the hands of a common warrior. She would fight their commander. Let him, then, take her life today.

Ah, there he was. She dismounted, dropping the reins where she stood. As if in a dream, she walked through the battle, feeling as though only she and this man truly existed.

He had seen her. Talorcan pulled his bloody ax from the skull of a fallen warrior and turned to face her. She threw her spear aside and pulled her dagger from her boot without breaking her stride. The commander threw away his ax and pulled his own dagger. Slowly they moved to face each other. The din of battle seemed to fade far away as she came to stand before him.

Over his blue tunic he wore a metal byrnie trimmed with silver, now blood-splattered. His helmet was of silver, with the figure of a boar at the top. His green eyes looked at her gravely. "Queen Olwen," he said respectfully. "You have lost the day. Surrender your city to me, and you will live."

"Commander, I cannot."

"In that case," he said regretfully, "I must kill you."

Olwen did not answer.

"You were prepared for us," Talorcan said. It was not a question.

"The Dreamer warned us."

"Gwydion. Yes, we know him. Havgan, our Bana, will kill him one day."

"Havgan, your Bana, will try," she corrected calmly. "Come. Let us begin."

THEY FOUGHT FOR a long time, yet the end seemed so quick. His dagger flowed smoothly into her body, parting her flesh like water. She looked up into his green eyes, which seemed to be reflecting some inner torment she did not understand. She slowly sank down to the bloody ground.

As the darkness rushed to meet her, she thought she heard Kilwch's voice, thought she heard her husband say, "I waited for you." She thought she felt a warm hand covering hers, and then the light that burst upon her was so very bright.

So she smiled. And died.

ELEN SCREAMED IN rage from across the bloody field when she saw Olwen fall. She dug her heels into her mount and struggled toward the spot, slashing those who attempted to impede her advance. Just a few feet from her mother's body, she scrambled off her horse and leapt past the enemy warrior in her way. But the man grabbed her arm as she tried to dart past him, swung her about, and lifted his battle-ax.

The ax came whistling down, aimed for her unprotected, upturned face, but it halted abruptly in midair. The warrior stiffened, the ax falling from his now-numb fingers. He sank down just as Angharad came riding up. Without a word, Angharad dismounted, then reached down and pulled her dagger from the dead man's back.

Elen stared down at the warrior who had almost killed her, and spat on him. "I think he broke my arm," Elen said faintly, through gritted teeth, indicating her left arm, which hung at an unnatural angle.

"So he did. Come," Angharad said. Swiftly she remounted her horse, then, grasping Elen's good arm, pulled her onto the animal.

"No! No! Mam's—"

"Olwen is dead, Elen. Dead."

"You don't know that," Elen screamed. "Let me go to her!"

"He killed her. And she gave me an order last night, which I intend to obey."

"No!" Elen screamed, still struggling. "I can't leave!"

"You have to, you fool. You can't fight," Angharad said calmly, deftly parrying the swing of a battle-ax with her shield, then plunging her dagger into the man's neck.

Elen stopped struggling. She realized that if she didn't, she would get them both killed. Elen bowed her head, cradling her arm against her body. Tears slowly fell from her eyes and dripped down onto her injured arm. Mam was dead. The Coranian commander had murdered her. One day she would kill him. She would.

Slowly Angharad cut her way out of the hideous melee. When they reached the fringes of the hopeless battle, Angharad rode swiftly to the cliffs. They dismounted, for the path was too narrow for a horse. With Angharad supporting her, Elen began the trek up the cliff path.

She heard footsteps rushing up behind them. Wearily she lifted her head, as Angharad grasped her dagger. The man rounded the curve of the path and halted. When Elen saw her brother, she burst into tears.

"I saw you leave the battle," Lludd said, panting. He was splattered with blood but did not appear to be wounded.

"She broke her arm," Angharad said, as she handed Elen off to Lludd.

"Mam's dead," Elen sobbed. "I saw it. The commander killed her."

Lludd turned white at the news. His brown eyes darkened, and he set his jaw. He suddenly looked much older than his seventeen years. "Take her up, Angharad."

"And where do you think you're going?" Angharad inquired acidly.

"To find that commander," Lludd answered.

"Not without me, you're not. Let's get Elen up to Regan. Then we'll both go back down." Lludd hesitated. "Do as I say," Angharad said sharply.

Reluctantly, Lludd picked Elen up, careful not to jostle her broken arm. Angharad followed as they made their way up the path to the cave. Lludd carried Elen in and set her down on an empty pallet. The cave was dim, the only illumination coming from the wide mouth of the cavern. In the dimness, Elen could just make out the bodies of a few wounded men and women. Regan came running, with Iago right behind her.

"It's just a broken arm," Elen gasped. "I'm not dying."

"Chew on this," Regan said, putting something between her jaws.

"What is it?" Elen mumbled.

"Willow bark for the pain. Go on."

When Regan straightened the arm, tears spilled from Elen's eyes. But she set her jaw and refused to scream. Swiftly, Regan bound the arm in a comfrey paste. Iago wiped her sweating brow and wrapped her up warmly. For some reason, she was very cold. Her teeth began to chatter.

"Shock," Regan said calmly. "Give her some wine, Iago."

Iago, his face pale, gently held her head and guided the cup to her lips. Elen tasted vervain within the wine. The pain began to recede a little. Someone entered the cave, and Elen looked up. "Talhearn," she said weakly, trying to smile.

The Bard knelt down by her pallet and smiled. His silver hair shone in the light from the mouth of the cave. His blue eyes were gentle.

"Talhearn, Mam's dead."

"Yes," he said gently. "I was watching from the cliffs. I saw her fall. And she gave you something before she died, I see."

Elen looked down at her good hand. The pearl ring glowed softly in the dim light. "She did. She gave me this. And said I had to live."

"My Queen," Angharad said softly. "We must go. The battle is not over."

Elen started. That was her mother's title. Queen. No, that was her title now.

"Regan," Angharad said, "you and Iago stay with Elen. Lludd and I must return to the battle."

"And I will go with you," Talhearn said.

"Ridiculous," Angharad snorted. "You're not a warrior. You're a Bard. You'll get yourself killed."

"I have my reasons for going with you," Talhearn said shortly.

Angharad shrugged. "Have it your way, old man."

"Angharad, my dear, your graciousness is beyond compare, as always."

Lludd knelt down beside Elen and kissed her brow. She frowned up at him. "Don't get killed, Lludd. I mean it."

He swallowed hard, then whispered, "As the Queen commands." He stood up quickly, then turned and left the cave.

"Angharad," she said, "look after him."

"I will," Angharad replied, briefly bowing her head, "my Queen."

"Good-bye, little girl," Talhearn said. Then he, too, was gone.

ELEN CLOSED HER eyes. The light from the mouth of the cave danced over her closed lids. Then the light abruptly cut off. Elen opened her eyes, trying to focus. Enemy warriors poured into the cavern. Before Elen could even sit up, Regan was bound tightly. Iago was struggling to release himself from the grasp of two heavily armed warriors. The other warriors rushed upon the wounded and plunged their daggers into their hearts. The hot, coppery smell of blood pervaded the cave.

The commander stood silhouetted in the light from the cave mouth. Elen tried to rise, grasping her dagger in her good hand, but he came to her swiftly and plucked the knife from her hand.

Iago had stopped struggling. He stood stiffly, trying to gather his strength. The commander calmly walked up to the Druid. "Before you do anything rash, Druid, read this." Talorcan held up a letter in front of Iago's face. The letter was sealed with the imprint of a bull's head. Elen recognized the seal of the Archdruid.

"This is a trick," Iago said thickly.

"No trick," Talorcan replied. "Open it and read it."

Slowly, Iago took the letter, broke the seal, and began to read. As he did so, Talorcan's gaze wandered over to Regan. Her arms were bound firmly behind her back. Warriors stood on either side, holding her upper arms tightly.

"My apologies, Lady Dewin," Talorcan said smoothly, "for your discomfort."

Regan glared at him, but did not answer.

Iago lifted his eyes from the letter. He was pale. "I don't understand."

Talorcan shrugged. "It's very simple. Your Archdruid and my Warleader have come to an understanding. All Druids are to cooperate with us, by orders of your leader. Something, I believe, you have already guessed."

Iago looked toward Elen, horror in his eyes. "Elen, I . . ."

"You can't do this, Iago. You can't!"

"I must," he said miserably. "It is Cathbad's command."

"And my command is that you do not cooperate! I am your

415

Queen!" Elen dragged herself unsteadily to her feet, holding on to the wall of the cave for support.

"You are more than that to me, Elen," Iago said steadily. He let the letter fall from his hand. "But the Archdruid commands me. I am a Druid, and can only obey."

One of the warriors guarding Regan asked, "Shall we take care of her now?" He gestured toward the Dewin.

Regan stiffened in their grasp, but refused to plead for her life.

"Don't be a fool," Talorcan said sharply.

"Lord," the warrior continued, "those are the orders. We are to kill the witches. She's one of them."

"She is more valuable to us alive, for I feel quite sure that the Queen would not wish any harm to come to her Dewin. Isn't this so?" Talorcan said, turning to Elen.

Elen's eyes met Regan's. The Dewin's face was calm, and her eyes told Elen to do what she must. But Elen could not do it. Regan was her friend. Elen turned toward Talorcan. "Yes, that is so. As long as she remains unharmed, I will cooperate with you."

"Elen, no!" Regan exclaimed, horrified.

"Yes," Elen said firmly.

"The wyrce-jaga won't like it," the warrior warned.

"The likes or dislikes of the wyrce-jaga are nothing to me," Talorcan said sharply. "Havgan has given me the authority to use my own discretion in such matters. Take them down to the beach. The battle is over. We will gather up Queen Olwen's body with honor and take her back to my city."

Elen stiffened. "It's not your city."

"It is now," he replied.

ANGHARAD, LLUDD, AND Talhearn began to make their way down the cliffs. Talhearn had, for some reason, insisted on taking a different way down. It was easier, he had said. Angharad couldn't see what was easier about it. About halfway down, Talhearn halted and gestured to them to peer down onto the beach.

"Look," Talhearn said quietly. "It is over."

The Bard was right. The battle was over. Enemy warriors were gathering up the bodies of the slain, creating two mounds for burning. Off to the west, Angharad caught sight of about twenty Kymric warriors, disappearing over the hill.

"Cowards," she said sternly.

"Certainly not!" Talhearn said, shocked. "Those are men led by Emrys. Didn't you see him? They are going around the cliffs to come up the other side. This battle is lost. They merely seek to gather others to fight again another day."

"And what," Lludd asked heavily, "do we do now?"

"You will meet Emrys and his men on the other side of the cliffs," Angharad ordered. "Talhearn, you go with him."

"And you?" Talhearn asked.

"I have business with the Coranian commander. I will go down."

"You fool! They'll kill you before you even get near the man."

"What if they do?" Angharad demanded. "The Queen is dead. It is not right for her Captain to still live."

"Look!" Lludd exclaimed. "It's Elen."

At the bottom of the cliffs, a procession was emerging. In front was the enemy commander, holding Elen firmly by her good arm. Elen walked stiffly, concentrating on keeping to her feet. Behind them followed Regan, her hands bound behind her. And Iago was there, too, but he was unbound. He walked with his head down, as though ashamed to meet anyone's gaze. Twenty armed warriors followed.

"We must rescue them!" Lludd exclaimed. "Quickly, before they get too far!"

Angharad jumped to her feet. Talhearn instantly pulled her down by grasping both her ankles. She crashed to the ground, Talhearn holding her down firmly.

"Let me go, old man!" Angharad said, furious.

"No! This is not your task."

"Talhearn," Lludd said furiously, reaching out to break the Bard's hold on Angharad, "what do you think you're doing?"

The old man was panting. "Trying to get the attention of you two idiots. If I may just have a few moments of your precious time . . ."

Angharad pulled free as Lludd grasped Talhearn's wrists in a grip of iron. She scrambled to the cliff edge. Looking down, she said bitterly, "It's too late. Look."

It was, indeed, too late to help Elen. The party had reached the city gates.

Angharad turned to Talhearn, who was sitting on the ground, trying to catch his breath while Lludd still grasped the Bard's arms grimly. "You traitor!" she accused. "You wanted them to be captured!"

Talhearn's fine, blue eyes turned cold. His face hardened. "You dare accuse me of that?" he said softly. "You dare? Now, listen to me. My orders from the Master Bard were to assist the Dreamer in any way possible. And I have done so. When he was here, Gwydion ap Awst left a letter with me, to be given to you and Lludd at the proper time. And this is the proper time."

"A letter from the Dreamer? What do I care about that?" Angharad exclaimed.

"Don't be stupid, Angharad," Lludd said in a withering tone. "Here, Talhearn, give me that letter."

Angharad turned to the boy in surprise. He had never talked this way to her before. Actually, he had never talked to anyone this way before. She looked at him closely. Never had she seen him look so much like his father. Maybe he wasn't a boy, anymore, after all.

Talhearn pulled the letter from his tunic and handed it to Lludd. The Prince opened it and began to read. Angharad looked on over his shoulder.

To: Lludd ap Olwen and Angharad ur Ednyved:

By now Queen Olwen is dead, the battle is lost, the city has been captured, and Elen is a prisoner. You cannot help her now. Yet know that, when the time comes, she will be freed.

My heart goes out to you in the face of so many losses. But you must not give up. A great task awaits you both. You must gather the survivors and leave the vicinity of Dinmael, finding a safe place to shelter. By stealth and by cunning you must gather a teulu that will become a thorn in the side of the enemy. From this seed will come a mighty army. For one day soon the High King will come again. And when he does, he will lead us to take back our own. I command you, in the name of the High King soon to be, that you take on this task. Though you may wish to die, you are commanded to live. This is your duty to Kymru.

Gwydion ap Awst var Celemon
Dreamer of Kymru

Angharad looked up. Talhearn was watching them steadily. She was silent, not knowing what to say. With all her heart, she wanted to disregard this letter. She wanted to die fighting, to wipe out her shame that she was still alive while her Queen lay dead. Yet Gwydion had commanded her in the name of the High King.

"How can he be sure that a High King will return to us?" Angharad demanded.

"He is the Dreamer," Lludd said absently, reading the letter again. "How could he not know?"

"He could be wrong," she insisted.

Lludd sighed. "Leave off, Angharad, will you?" Angharad fell silent. Lludd said nothing. He stood up and gazed out to the sea, refusing to look at the sight of his sister as captive. Without turning around, he said, "Where shall we go?"

"To Coed Ddu," Angharad answered promptly. She was shocked. She had no idea that she was thinking that way. But since she had started, she determined to go on. "My sister, Eiodar, rules the commote where that forest stands. It's a huge forest. I suspect that many will take refuge there."

"It would be a good base," Lludd mused, "from which to be a 'thorn in their side.' I find that I like that idea very much."

"Lludd—"

"You are the PenAethenen of Ederynion. And I am Elen's heir. For now I command, as long as Elen is a captive."

The air of authority, so new to the boy, nonetheless sat easily on his shoulders. This was something altogether new to Angharad's experience. She supposed that, since Olwen had discounted Lludd all these years, she had fallen into the same habit. It looked like that might have been a mistake, after all.

"We will do as Gwydion says," Lludd went on. "We will meet Emrys's men and take them with us."

"So we shall, my Prince," Talhearn said, rising to his feet, "if you command it. But first there is a task I must perform."

"What is that?"

"I promised to sing Queen Olwen's death song." He gestured toward the city. "And they bring her now."

Coranian warriors were carrying the body of Queen Olwen from the bloody field. Her white tunic and trousers were stained red with blood. On top of her body they laid her shield and spear. At the gates Elen's slender form stood straight and tall, Olwen's silvery helmet clutched to her side with her good arm. Iago stood off to one side with his head still bowed. Regan, now loosed from her bonds, stood next to Elen, her head lifted proudly in honor of the dead Queen.

As the procession brought the body through the gates, Elen, Regan, and the commander followed, Iago trailing behind. Then the gates closed behind them, and they were lost to sight.

Lludd's face was streaked with tears. Angharad was surprised to discover that she, too, was weeping. From behind them, Talhearn's voice sang softly.

"Was she not pre-eminent in the field of blood?
Was she not the Queen in darkness?
Oh, white swan, shining like the moon
You slowly turned red in the darkening sky.

"Is it not she who destroyed hundreds of the foe?
Is it not she who slew the raveners?
Is it not she who raised her sword with her dying strength?

My tongue will recite her death song
My eyes will burn with tears,
For our great Queen,
Has died on the field
Has died this bloody day."

Talhearn bowed his head as his tears began to fall. Angharad looked out to the sea, unable to bear the sight of her beloved city in enemy hands.

But Lludd stood stiffly, not taking his eyes from the city where he was born, from the city where his mother was being laid to rest, from the city where his sister was a prisoner. He stood there for a long time, his hands clenched on the rocks before him. At last, without a word, he turned and started down the path that led to the other side of the cliffs, to meet Emrys's men.

Talhearn, after exchanging a glance with Angharad, followed him. Angharad nerved herself to look down at the once-shining city. "Good-bye, my Queen," she whispered. Then she, too, made her way down the cliff path.

And so they began their task. "A thorn in the side of the enemy," Gwydion had written. Yes, Angharad liked the sound of that, too.

Chapter 17

Suldydd, Disglair Wythnos—early morning

King Rhoram mounted the battlements of his city. His soon-to-be-lost city, he reminded himself. He was under no illusions about that.

Achren followed behind him, close as his shadow. She carried her bow, the arrows in a quiver on her shoulder. Her black hair was bound tightly beneath her helmet. Behind Achren came Rhoram's son, Geriant; his Bard, Cian; and his Dewin, Cadell. He looked around quickly for Ellywen, his Druid, but she was not in sight. No time to wonder about her absence now.

Rapidly, he reviewed his plans—such as they were. He had a total of four hundred warriors and a city full of people that must be evacuated. And only one day to do it for once the Coranians landed tomorrow, it would be too late.

Two hundred of his warriors were mounted and ready at the southern gate, two hundred at the east gate. And the people of the city were gathered at the north gate, ready to slip out if

Rhoram could draw the enemy forces south. It was the best he could do on such short notice. For his original plans had not included the presence of the warriors now encamped outside the walls.

As he mounted the last steps, he once again tried to convince himself that he hadn't really seen his daughter among the people of the city last night. Gwenhwyfar had gone with his counselor, Dafydd Penfro, and the rest of them to Ogaf Greu, the caves far to the north, and that was that. He had been under a strain last night, what with phantoms and traitors and all manner of things demanding his immediate attention. His eyes had been playing tricks on him. He was—almost—sure of it.

He reached the top of the wall and gazed out to the eastern plain in front of the city. It was covered with over nine hundred Kymric warriors. Too bad they weren't on his side. They might have been helpful tomorrow, when the Coranians swooped down on them.

He stood there, shoulders back, head high. He wore a black leather tunic and trousers, and a cloak of forest green. His helmet was gold, with the figure of a snarling wolf's head with emerald eyes fashioned on the top of it. Around his neck he wore the emerald and gold torque of Prydyn.

A horse and rider were making their way through the crowd of warriors gathered outside the city. The sun beat down on the rider's fiery red hair. As Rhoram had good cause to know, the rider's shifty, beady, traitorous eyes were dark brown. And, no doubt, shining with glee right about now.

The rider halted before the east gate and looked up, but before he could begin his speech, Rhoram leaned over the parapet, abandoning his stern pose and waving cheerily.

"Erfin! You old dog! How wonderful to see you. I was just saying to Efa the other day—you remember Efa? My wife? Your sister? As I was saying to Efa, it's been so long since I saw poor, pock-marked, shifty-eyed Erfin. Well, she wanted to dispute the pock-marked, shifty-eyed part, but her innate honesty compelled her to admit—"

"King Rhoram!" Erfin shouted up, his face flushed as the laughter of even his own warriors sounded in his ears. "I demand that you surrender your city to me!"

"If it's all the same to you, I believe I'll keep it for a while longer," Rhoram called out. "Why don't you just trot on down the coast and hold off the Coranians who will be landing here tomorrow? That will give you something useful to do. As I was saying to Achren just the other day, it's important even for toads to feel useful. And she said—"

"Enough!" Erfin roared. "King Rhoram, you have no choice but to surrender. If you do surrender, you and your people will be spared."

Before the words were even out of Erfin's mouth, Achren had pulled an arrow from her quiver, notched it onto the bow, and let it fly. The arrow sped down to plunge into the earth between the front hooves of Erfin's horse. The horse reared, startled by the missile. Unfortunately Erfin did not fall off. He twisted at the reins, and finally succeeded in quieting the animal.

"Is that enough of an answer for you, Erfin, or do I need to make it more clear? As I have good cause to know, your grasp of subtleties is limited," Rhoram called down.

Erfin looked up at him in fury. But before his brother-in-law could formulate an answer, Rhoram mounted the wall and stood straight and proud before the traitorous Kymric warriors, his earlier, frivolous pose abandoned. He gazed down now at the over nine hundred men and women gathered to fight him. There were three hundred of Erfin's own teulu, and two hundred each belonging to the Erfin's three Gwardas. Angawdd ap Dirmyg and Eilonwy ur Gwyn looked up at Rhoram coldly. Tegid ap Trephin refused to look at him at all.

"Warriors of Prydyn!" Rhoram boomed out in a commanding tone. "Listen to me! Tomorrow morning the forces of Corania will sweep our shores. If unchecked, they will take our country. Our country! The land of Prydyn! Will you let them do this? Will you let them make slaves of the Kymri?"

There was a stirring in the ranks. Quickly, Erfin called out, "I have been promised protection for all my people! Neither they nor their families will be harmed."

"And you believe these promises?" Rhoram asked incredulously. "You are fools to do so. I call now on all who are true men and women of Prydyn to lay down your arms, taken up against your rightful King!"

Rhoram turned aside and said in a low tone, "Achren, send Geriant to head the two hundred warriors to the southern gate. I will join them there. Have my horse ready. You go with Aidan out the east gate."

"Our plans were to—"

"Look at Tegid down there, to the south. Look how he shifts on his horse."

Achren swiftly looked down at Tegid's pale face, raised her brows, then departed, taking Geriant and Aidan with her. Rhoram turned back to the traitorous warriors. "Well, men and women of Prydyn? What is your answer? Will you obey your King, or will you follow the traitor, the man who deals in secret with your worst enemy?"

"Rhoram ap Rhydderch!" Erfin shouted. "Do not think to delay the battle. It will avail you nothing. Yesterday we fell upon the Gwarda of Camian, who was preparing to march to your side! He will not come to your aid today, or any day. And I have with me Druids—one of them your own!"

From within the ranks, six Druids, dressed in the customary hooded brown robes, stepped out to stand behind Erfin. One by one, they removed their hoods. The last one was his missing Druid, Ellywen. Her cold, gray eyes gazed up at him unflinchingly.

"You cannot stand against us all, Rhoram," Erfin continued.

"Cadell," Rhoram muttered to his Dewin, "any sight of the forces of Emlyn yet?"

"Nothing yet. I'll keep Wind-Riding and tell Cian as soon as I spot them."

"Cian," Rhoram said to his Bard, "when Cadell spots them, explain the situation to their Bard. Tell them to attack the north flank."

Rhoram turned back toward Erfin, waiting down below. "Erfin, I am forced to consider your offer, for the good of my people," he said heavily. His shoulders slumped. He hoped he wasn't overdoing it. "I will give you my answer in a few moments." Swiftly, he descended the stairs and mounted his horse. Achren was there, waiting with Aidan to lead the warriors out the east gate.

"Considering surrender?" she asked, grinning in anticipation. Achren always did love a good fight.

"There's no need to be insulting." He grabbed the reins and galloped off through the city to the southern gate. Geriant was at the head of the two hundred warriors gathered there. Rhoram made his way through the ranks, until he and Geriant were side by side in front of the closed gate.

His son sat upon his horse calmly, his blue eyes clear, his face set but unafraid. Rhoram's throat tightened. He loved the boy so much. The gods grant that Geriant lived through this day. And beyond it. Far, far beyond it. He gripped Geriant's shoulder for a moment, then ordered, "You and your warriors cut east out of the gate. I'll make directly for Tegid. I think we have a good chance with him."

Geriant nodded eagerly, ready for the fight. "Yes, Da. Oh, and good luck."

The trust in the boy's eyes cut at Rhoram's heart. *O gods, O gods*, he thought frantically, *let him live. I don't care about myself. Just let my son live.*

At Rhoram's nod, the southern gate opened. At the same time, the east gate also swung back, and his warriors poured out onto the plain, four hundred against almost a thousand, in a desperate attempt to allow the people of the city a chance to get to safety.

This, Rhoram thought as he made his way straight toward Tegid, *has to be one of my more harebrained ideas.*

HE RODE FEARLESSLY through Tegid's men. Behind him he heard the din of battle as his forces clashed with Erfin's.

Tegid ap Trephin was a young man, who had succeeded his father as the Gwarda of Mallaen just last year. The young Gwarda sat indecisively on his horse. His men were waiting for orders that Tegid had not yet given.

"Tegid ap Trephin," Rhoram called out as he reined in his

horse beside the Gwarda. "Will you speak to me, man? Or will you kill me?"

Tegid paled. "I—"

"Yes, I know. Erfin is your lord. But I am your King. In the name of your oaths to me, I call on you now to fight with me, not against me. What is your answer?"

Slowly, Tegid drew his short spear and pointed it straight at Rhoram's chest.

Rhoram leaned forward slightly until the spear just pressed against his heart. "Will you fight beside me this day, Tegid ap Trephin? I can promise you nothing—no protection against the Coranians tomorrow, no assurances that either of us will live out this day. No hope of victory. Kill me or follow me. The choice is yours."

ACHREN LED HER warriors out the gate and into the fray. Calmly she leveled her spear and began to kill. But inside, she was frantic for Rhoram. If he had been mistaken about Tegid's true loyalties, he would die before the fight had even begun. She did not dare to even look toward the south where Rhoram had gone. There was no time; they were too hardly pressed. If only Tegid . . .

Then she heard it. The sound coming from two hundred throats burst into the battle, momentarily drowning out the clash of sword and spear, the groans of the dying.

"Tegid! Tegid for King Rhoram! Rhoram! Rhoram!"

He had done it. For the first time, she thought they might have a chance, after all.

HOURS LATER, RHORAM, for the hundredth time, raised his spear and killed a man he knew. He had recognized many of the men and women whom he had murdered this afternoon. The thought sickened him, but it did not stop him.

But the tide was turning in Erfin's favor, and it was the Druids who were tipping the scales. Between the six of them, they were throwing fireballs and levitating other missiles at a fairly steady rate. Fortunately, the Druids were forced to be careful not to decimate their own forces, and they had to take aim carefully.

Rhoram had countered by turning the catapults on the cliffs, set in place to maim Coranian ships, onto the battlefield. Boulders rained from the air to places where Erfin's forces were gathered thickly, but it was tricky business, trying to kill the right people.

If only they could get rid of at least one or two of those Druids. But they were so heavily guarded that he thought it unlikely. Still, he would do his best. Closing with Erfin himself would have to wait until he had taken care of this problem.

He fought his way closer to the six brown-robed figures. He knew he would never penetrate the circle of warriors guarding them. But he did hope that an arrow or two might do some good, if only he could get close enough.

A fireball, aimed right toward him, caused him to duck abruptly. The fire whizzed over his head and landed on the ground behind him, roasting two of Erfin's warriors. A bad shot for the Druid. But a good one for him.

One of the Druids—Ellywen, of course—had spotted him. She was shouting, calling out to the others that King Rhoram was within range. The six turned toward him, and he knew that his time had come. It galled him to think he would die at the hands of his own people. He had so hoped to kill some Coranians before he was killed himself.

A short spear whizzed by his shoulder and struck one of the Druids in the chest. Swiftly, Rhoram turned and saw Achren, who was now pulling out her bow to follow up on her initial attack. Quickly he knocked his own bow, but before either of them could shoot, another Druid fell, pierced with an arrow through her throat.

Rhoram's eye traced back the path of that arrow and saw a young warrior, stringing his bow for another shot. The warrior wore a voluminous cloak that foiled Rhoram's attempt to identify him. But something about the way he stood seemed familiar. Oh, no. No, absolutely not, Rhoram thought. It couldn't possibly . . .

He wrenched his attention away from that thought. No time for it now. He let loose his arrow, and it buzzed past the guarding warriors, taking another Druid in the throat. Three down, three to go. Unfortunately, Ellywen still stood. His former Druid raised her arms and prepared to burn him to a crisp.

But before she could, they both heard the sound. Ellywen and the two remaining Druids started, turning swiftly to the north. Erfin's warriors, too, halted for a moment, then turned to face the new threat.

Rhoram thought that he had never heard such a beautiful sound. Horns. Horns to the north. Thank the gods, the forces of Emlyn had come.

RHORAM SAT ALONE on the cliff edge, his legs dangling into space. He hunched forward, looking down into the black, swirling water, rushing and hissing onto the shore. Sighing, he sat back. The full moon shone overhead, brilliant and cold. He stared out to sea, drinking in the sight, knowing that this night would be his last. At least he would not have to live long with the shame of losing the country he had been born to rule.

Wearily, he ran his hands through his sweat-stained hair. They had done well today. After the forces of Emlyn had joined the battle, Erfin had been driven east. Rhoram had eventually halted the pursuit, knowing that it was a waste of precious resources. Instead, he had led his remaining army to the cliffs. The cliffs of Dayved were pockmarked with caves, which had been prepared weeks ago. Blankets, foodstuffs, weapons, and other supplies had been stored there. The horses had been picketed at the base of the cliffs, carefully guarded.

Yes, they had won the battle today. That would have been encouraging, except for the fact that it didn't really matter. Tomorrow would see an end to it all. There was no hope at all that they could hold out against both Erfin and the Coranians. It was foolish to even try, although try they would. They would not give up without a fight.

But his city had been abandoned. His beautiful city.

There had been no reason to return to it. The walls would not have kept the Coranians out for long. And all his people had escaped during the battle today. If he had brought his army back, there they would be trapped, easy prey on the morrow.

His throat tightened as he thought of his doorkeeper, Tallwch. Tallwch had died in the battle that day. Already he missed his friend.

He heard footsteps coming down the cliff path. Though it was too dark to see, he knew who it was. She stood next to him, then put a curiously gentle hand on his shoulder.

"The others await your orders for tomorrow, my King."

Still facing out to sea, he said bitterly, "You still call me that?"

"What?" she asked in surprise.

"King."

"Why ever not?"

"I've lost the city," he said, his voice toneless. "And, after tomorrow, Prydyn will be lost, too. I am not a King—I am a fool."

"You will win it back," she said calmly.

"You have great faith in my abilities, Achren. But I cannot agree with you."

"Then you are indeed a fool," she said comfortably, sitting down beside him.

"Thanks," he said dryly.

The moon illuminated her dark eyes. Her black hair, loosened from her braids, hung down past her shoulders. Her wide mouth was suspiciously close to a smile.

Taking a deep breath, he said, "Achren, I want you to—"

"Cadell has been Wind-Riding," she said in a musing tone, as though he had not spoken. "He says that he can see Erfin sitting by his campfire. He says that Erfin looks like he swallowed a handful of nettles. I wish I were a Dewin. I'd love to see that."

"Achren—"

"Cadell also says that the forces of Penfro should be here in the late morning."

Rhoram waved his hand irritably. "Two hundred. A drop in the bucket against whatever Erfin's got left and against the gods know how many Coranians. Achren, I want you to take the others and go."

"Do you?" she said coolly. "Which others?"

"Geriant, for one."

She turned to him, her dark eyes pools of shadow. "If you want Geriant out of here, tell him to go. I stay."

"Gwen is here somewhere."

"I know," she said calmly. "I recognized her this afternoon."

"We have to get her out of here!"

"Fine. If you can find her, you can take her out."

Rhoram jumped up. "How am I supposed to find her?" he demanded. "She could be in any of the caves. And how could I possibly leave?"

Achren, too, leapt to her feet. "How could I?" she demanded in her turn.

"Listen to me! It's up to you to take care of my children."

"Why don't you do it?" she snapped. "They're your children."

"Dead men are limited in that respect."

She snorted. "You're not going to die, Rhoram. Gwydion did not say so."

"He didn't have to. You heard Rhiannon. She asked Geriant to look after Gwen. Why didn't she ask me?"

"Maybe she thought you'd be too busy," she said mildly.

"Maybe she thought I'd be dead!" He turned from Achren, gazing out to sea, his shoulders slumped. Almost absently, he murmured, "And why not? Why shouldn't I die? How could I bear to live knowing that I have lost Prydyn? I have failed my people. What remains for me to stay alive for?"

She reached out and turned his face toward hers. She studied him for a moment, the palms of her callused hands resting against his checks, as though trying to measure his belief in his own words. Then her mouth hardened into an implacable line. "Coward," she said clearly, her voice bitter, her dark eyes flashing in the moonlight.

She turned away from him, but he grabbed her arm, pulling her back to him. "Coward? You dare to call me that?" he said, his voice deathly quiet.

"What else should I call you? You, who can't bear to even think of anyone but yourself. Don't you understand how much your people will need you in defeat? Of course, you do. But death is less demanding, isn't it? Always the easy way out for you!"

"You—" he said through gritted teeth. "You dare—" He pushed her from him. She almost stumbled, then caught herself against the rocks.

"When you feel up to acting like a man, the others are waiting for you," she spat. Then she was gone.

COWARD, SHE HAD said. She had called him a coward. Somewhere deep inside, coming from a place he had thought emptied by despair, a red rage began to grow.

Red-hot, the rage washed through him. Rage against Erfin, his worthless brother-in-law, who had dared to take up arms against him. Against Efa, his own wife, who had failed him for so many years. Against Ellywen, his Druid, who had chosen loyalty to Cathbad over loyalty to her King. Against himself for so many things.

And lastly, a rage against the Coranians, who would dare to invade his country, who would dare to come against him and his.

And as the rage grew inside him, he straightened his shoulders. He raised his head. He clenched his hands into fists and smote the rock before him. He lifted his face to the sky and hurled his war cry to the stars. All across the cliffs, warriors popped their heads from their caves at his cry. As one, they echoed him, shouting their challenge to the night.

As he strode up the path, his despair forgotten, the cries of defiance still ringing in his ears, the thought came to him that Achren had known exactly what she was doing when she dared to speak to him that way.

AS HE ENTERED the cave, they all looked up at him. Something in his face made them rise instantly to their feet. Achren was there, of course, and Geriant. Aidan, his lieutenant, stood next to his brother, Idwal, the Gwarda of Emlyn, whose forces had saved the day today. Cadell, his Dewin, and Cian, his Bard, stood with the Dewin and Bard the Gwarda had brought with him. Tegid was not there. He had died today.

For a moment, they stared at Rhoram. Then Geriant, his blue eyes wide, came to him. "Da?" he asked, his voice uncertain.

"Cadell," Rhoram said crisply, ignoring his son for the moment, "I want you to tell me Erfin's exact location. I want to know the number of warriors he has left, the layout of his camp, how many horses he has, everything. Most particularly I want to know where the horses are being kept. And what tent the Druids are in." Cadell and the other Dewin nodded. Without a word, they both sat down crosslegged on the floor of the cave, their eyes taking on an abstracted look.

"Achren," he went on, his voice cool. "How many warriors are left?"

"Three hundred and fifty," Achren replied, her tone like ice. "And one hundred people from the city who refuse to leave the area."

"I want the city people left here in the cliffs, armed with bows, rags, and pitch. I wish to arrange a proper greeting for the Coranians."

"As you command, my King," Achren replied, her mouth twitching.

"So I am," he agreed gravely. "Aidan, you will be in charge of the initial defense against the Coranians. Catapults and one hundred bowmen are all I can offer you. Do the best you can with what you have."

The two Dewin stirred. Cadell raised his head. "It is done."

Rhoram handed him a piece of parchment and charcoal. "Show me," he said.

A FEW HOURS later, Rhoram rose. He stretched, trying to work the stiffness out of his legs. Sitting crosslegged on the floor of a cave was a job for a younger man. "That's it, then. Ready, Achren?"

"Ready when you are," she replied crisply.

"The rest of you have a few hours before you begin. Sleep if you can. Give me a few moments, Achren. Geriant, come with me." Rhoram led the way out of the cave. He put an arm around his son's shoulders, and the two walked together down the path.

"Da," Geriant began. "Why can't I go with you and Achren? I—"

"Because I have something else for you to do." Rhoram gestured toward a rock jutting out from the cliff face. "Sit with me here, and I'll explain."

Geriant sat crosslegged on the rock, and Rhoram took a place beside him. Without further preamble, Rhoram said, "Gwenhwyfar's here. I saw her in the battle this afternoon. She saved my life by killing one of the Druids."

"I can't believe it! She's supposed to be with Sanon and the others at the caves—leagues and leagues away from here!"

"Believe it," Rhoram said grimly. "That's why I can't take you to Erfin's camp tonight. You have another task. Find her, see to it that she comes to no harm. You promised Rhiannon that you would. Tomorrow, when we are overrun by the Coranians—and we will be overrun—you are to take her and go north to the caves."

"But, Da—"

"This is a direct order from your King, not your father. Your life is not your own to throw away. You must live, and you must see to it that Gwen lives also."

Miserably, Geriant nodded, then looked away.

Rhoram's gaze softened. "I have not forbidden you to fight tomorrow. I forbid you only to fight to the death. You may be part of our battle with Erfin. But when the Coranians land, you must go. And you have yet another task to fulfill." Slowly, Rhoram twisted the emerald ring from his finger. "Your task is to guard this ring."

"The ring? I don't understand."

"This ring was given to us many, many years ago by Bran the Dreamer. It has been passed on from ruler to ruler, generation by generation. It is never to fall into the hands of anyone outside our house. One day, this ring will be asked for. Listen carefully to Bran's exact words. 'The ring is to be given up only to one of the House of PenBlaid who asks for it using these words: "In the name of the High King to come, surrender your ring to me."' These words exactly will be used, and no others."

"But, Da, why give it to me now? You are still King. Gwydion did not say you would die. He—"

"Ah, Geriant. Geriant. Never mind that now. Take the ring."

Very, very slowly, Geriant reached out to take the ring. He set it on his finger, his face bowed. Gently, Rhoram touched his son's golden hair. Geriant's face came up, streaked with tears. Rhoram reached out and held his son close to his chest, letting Geriant's scalding tears spill over his heart.

To say that Erfin was surprised when his guards were murdered, his horses were stolen in the middle of the night, and two of his Druids (who had emerged from their tent to see what was happening) were shot full of arrows, would have been a serious understatement.

Rhoram, who was able to catch sight of Erfin in the confusion as his brother-in-law stamped and swore at the sight of his horses disappearing beyond the hill, was highly gratified. Which was another understatement.

His only regret was that Ellywen had not died. She had been too canny to come out of her tent. Rhoram shrugged. He'd have another chance a few hours from now, when he brought his army back with him to finish the job.

Rhoram nodded to Achren, and the two faded silently away from Erfin's camp into the night, their work done. For now.

Llundydd, Disglair Wythnos—morning

A PALE PINK blush was just staining the sky when Rhoram and Achren returned to spy on Erfin's camp. Erfin had chosen to camp in a slight valley, fringed with low, grassy hills. Incredibly, he had not replaced the watch that Rhoram and Achren had murdered just a few hours ago. Even more amazing, Erfin's troops were not yet ready for battle. Morning campfires still blazed, and warriors were just emerging from their tents and bedrolls. He was counting, apparently, on the scheduled arrival of the Coranians to deter Rhoram from making another attack.

"By the gods," Rhoram murmured in Achren's ear. "That's insulting."

"You will teach him today to take you more seriously," Achren replied. "Let us hope he won't live long enough to profit from the lesson."

"He won't," Rhoram said shortly.

Achren lightly touched Rhoram's arm and jerked her head. She was right. Time to go back to the horses and begin the attack.

They crept away from the crown of the hill, then separated, she to lead her quarter of their remaining army, he to lead his. On the other side of the hills that ringed the camp, Geriant held their forces in readiness.

On the ride from the cliffs, Rhoram had noticed a tiny warrior riding behind Geriant's horse, the warrior's hooded cloak pulled up securely. Rhoram had caught Geriant's eye and the boy had nodded slightly. Silently Rhoram had petitioned the gods to allow his children to live through this day. Then he had put the thought of their danger from him, locking his fears securely in his heart. He could do nothing more.

Reaching the base of the hill, Rhoram mounted his horse. Stretching in a solid ring around the hills, his army waited for his signal. He lifted his arm, made a fist, then pumped it twice. His warriors urged their horses up the hill, silent as ghosts.

To Erfin's forces in the valley, Rhoram's army seemed to rise straight up from the ground. One man, standing by his campfire, chanced to look up, and shouted.

Rhoram's army poured down the slope, straight into the

confused camp, and the slaughter began.

CADELL TURNED TO Aidan, the warrior in command of the defense against the Coranians. Cadell's eyes were still slightly glazed from Wind-Riding, but his voice was firm as he said, "They're coming."

Aidan nodded and signaled the men and women at the catapults to begin loading. In shallow caves across the cliffs, both men and women readied their bows. They wrapped their arrows in rags soaked in pitch, torches at the ready.

Aidan stared out to sea, waiting calmly for the sight of the enemy ships to stain the horizon.

RHORAM GRIMLY FOUGHT one warrior after another, killing with calm efficiency. His one goal, his only conscious thought, was to cut his way through the press to Erfin—wherever he was. He would not be satisfied until the blood of his treacherous brother-in-law stained his blade.

"My King!" a voice shouted from behind him. Turning swiftly, Rhoram confronted Cian, his Bard.

"The Bard from Emlyn has just relayed to me that the Coranians are landing," Cian panted. "The catapults and arrows have managed to destroy five ships. But over two thousand men are now on shore. Cadell says that a contingent of Coranians are coming this way to rescue Erfin!"

"How many?"

"Five hundred."

"Is that all?" Rhoram grinned. "Another insult."

"Half of them are occupying the city. The others are flushing us out of the cliffs. Cadell and Aidan are retreating with the people they have left."

"Tell the Bard to have them swing around and come in from the north. Has Cadell seen anything of the forces from Penfro?"

"They are on their way. They'll be here within the half hour."

"All right. We pull out from here and make for the north. We'll use the cover from the vineyards. We'll harass that Coranian contingent, but we won't meet them head on. There aren't enough of us for that." He raised his fist in the gesture for withdrawal.

Rhoram's army fought their way out of the camp and up to the crown of the hill. What was left of Erfin's army preferred to nurse their wounds, and did not pursue.

Rhoram reached the top of the hill, and, turning west, saw the sun glinting off the armor of the approaching Coranian contingent. To his vast relief, he saw Geriant, bloodied but apparently unhurt, with a small warrior riding closely behind him.

Achren rode up beside Rhoram. She, too, was blood-stained, but unhurt. "All out. Time to go," she said, nodding toward the sight of the advancing army.

Rhoram surveyed the men and women who were left. There were only one hundred and fifty of them, but they were not done yet. He could see it in their fiery, determined eyes, all fixed on him.

"Well, my friends, shall we show a proper Prydyn welcome to these Coranians?"

"Rhoram! Rhoram!" they shouted, their voices clear and determined.

"Come, my children of the sword," he called. "Let's teach them the way we do things in Prydyn!"

They followed him, galloping north away from the plain

and into the cover of the vineyards. He stopped, turning back to the south, surveying the plain before the valley. Quickly, his warriors dismounted, taking cover at the edge of the vineyards, readying their bows and arrows.

A warrior hailed him as they waited. "My King! Aidan and his folk are here!"

"I have lost the cliffs," Aidan said as he arrived, his blood- and soot-streaked face drawn.

"I never thought you could hold them. You know that." He clapped Aidan on the back. "Come, man. It's what we expected after all. Done in yet?"

"Never," Aidan said fiercely.

"Good. There's work left to do."

He glanced again out at the plain, judging the approach of the contingent to the valley. Something caught his eye as the sun glinted off the fiery red hair of a man running across the plain, heading straight toward the advancing army. All else was forgotten in that sight. "Achren, take command," he ordered, as he leapt onto his horse.

"What are you doing?" Achren called after him. "You can't—"

"Oh, yes, I can!"

"ERFIN!" RHORAM CALLED out fiercely. Erfin turned his head to see Rhoram's horse bearing down on him. He tried to run faster, but Rhoram thundered down, grasping Erfin by the back of his tunic and dragging him along. Then he let go, reined in his horse, and vaulted from the saddle. As Erfin tried to rise, Rhoram sailed into him, knocking him flat.

"You!" Rhoram panted, getting to his feet and allowing Erfin to rise. "You lily-livered dog! I'll see you dead today!"

Swiftly, Erfin reached into his boot and drew his dagger. He crouched. "I'll see you dead," he raged.

"You'll try," Rhoram said contemptuously. "Where were you when your warriors were fighting? Hiding? Afraid to face me?"

"I'll face you now," Erfin growled. The two men circled each other. Rhoram feinted to the right, and as Erfin jumped left, Rhoram's dagger sliced against his arm.

"You'll never make it out of here alive, Rhoram," Erfin panted. "My friends are on the way."

"I don't mean to make it out of here alive," Rhoram answered, crouched and ready. "I never did. But I won't die at your hands, traitor."

ACHREN WATCHED RHORAM ride off. "Stupid, stupid man," she raged. Geriant leapt to his horse and started after his father. With a mighty leap, Achren grasped the horse's bridle, dug in her heels, and pulled. The horse reared, and Geriant came tumbling down to the ground. As he lay there, trying to get his breath back, Achren came up to stand over him. "Not you, idiot. You've got other things to do."

She mounted her horse. Her dark eyes pinned Aidan to the spot. "Distract the Coranians. Keep them away from Rhoram and Erfin until it's settled."

"What about you?" he asked.

"I'm going to make sure no one interrupts that fight."

As THE CORANIAN contingent came over the hill, Penda stopped in astonishment. In the middle of the plain, two men were fighting. To the east, warriors, struggling out of a shallow valley, sat down to watch the contest.

Penda squinted, then recognized the man with the red hair. It was their erstwhile ally, Erfin. Penda knew him by description. The other man, with golden hair, had also been carefully described. It could be no other than King Rhoram himself.

He supposed he should interfere in the fight, save Erfin's life, and kill King Rhoram, but, in truth, he was not much inclined to do so. Rhoram deserved his chance to kill the man who had betrayed him. Yet he had his orders, orders that had already made him do so many things he did not wish to do. This would be just one more of those things.

From the north, a woman came riding out of the vineyards, galloping straight toward the fighting pair. She reined in her horse between the fighters and Penda's forces, sitting defiantly in the saddle.

This was too much. Did she think to prevent them from stopping that fight? One lone woman against five hundred warriors? He had been told that the Kymri were crazy, but he had never really appreciated that fact before this. He sighed, then led the charge.

A hail of arrows from the vineyards to the north broke into his ranks before he had even gone a few feet. Penda gave some hasty orders and sent his troops streaming toward the vineyards. But he himself did not go. They could handle this without him. He wanted to see more of this fight.

Penda neared the two men. The woman on the horse urged her mount closer to him, barring his way. "You are forbidden to interfere, Coranian," the woman spat.

"I am Penda, son of Peada, the Eorl of Lindisfarne, from the country of Mierce, in the Coranian Empire. I greet you in the name of our Bana, Havgan, son of Hengist, who has come to take this land for his own."

"I am Achren ur Canhustyr, the PenCollen of Prydyn, Captain to King Rhoram. I greet you in his name and bid you to leave this land."

"Ah. I regret that I am unable to comply with the wishes of so fair a lady."

"Your men fight our warriors. Shouldn't you join them?"

"I think not. Erfin is a friend of ours, and it looks like he could use some help. If you will not stand aside, then I must kill you."

Achren laughed and dismounted. "Come then, son of Peada. Try."

OUT OF THE corner of his eye, Rhoram saw Achren begin to battle the Coranian leader. Good gods, that woman would never do as she was told. But then, what woman did? Rhoram quickly wiped away the sweat that was running into his eyes, took a fresh hold of his dagger, and leapt at Erfin.

His dagger sliced across Erfin's cheek, laying open the man's face. Erfin screamed. He would, Rhoram thought contemptuously. Erfin fell to his knees, one hand covering his face, blood seeping through his fingers.

But as Rhoram stepped forward, his dagger held high to administer the final blow, Erfin, moving swiftly as a snake, grabbed a second dagger from his boot and sprang up. His dagger slid smoothly into Rhoram's ribs.

As Rhoram sank to the ground, he could only think that he had been taken in by one of the oldest tricks in the world. Achren would be furious.

Then the hungry darkness washed over him, and he knew

nothing more.

AS ACHREN SAW Rhoram go down, she screamed in rage. All thoughts of Penda deserted her. Turning away from his ax, she leapt toward Erfin, who was raising his dagger for another blow.

She knocked Erfin to the ground and wrestled the knife from his hand. She drew it back for a killing blow, but her hand was caught in a vise grip, and she dropped the knife. She whirled around, whipping her arm from Penda's grasp.

Slowly, almost hesitantly, Penda raised his ax. She faced him unflinchingly, her dark eyes unafraid. But before the ax had begun to swing down, the sound of horns rang out from the north. Penda lowered his ax. Enough of this fight. From the sound of the horns, he had a bigger battle on his hands. He was needed elsewhere. He would let her live, for now. Her courage deserved some sort of reward.

Grinning, he saluted Achren, then left them to it.

ERFIN'S SURVIVING WARRIORS, who had been watching the fight, surrounded Erfin, Achren, and Rhoram's still body. Two men lifted Erfin and helped him back into the valley. Achren, kneeling down by Rhoram's body, looked up at the circle of hard, set faces.

"He's dead," Achren said to them bitterly. "Isn't that what you wanted?"

A warrior bent over Rhoram's still body, placing a hand against the King's throat. Two more warriors grasped Achren's arms and lifted her to her feet.

"I ask that you kill me now. I have no wish to be taken to Erfin."

No one answered her, and after a few more silent moments, the man bending over Rhoram straightened.

"Achren ur Canhustyr," the warrior said quietly, "King Rhoram is dying. But not yet dead." The man hesitated, scanning the faces around him. Four warriors came forward, gently lifting Rhoram. Another came up, leading Achren's horse.

"Take him," he said. "Take him and go. If you hurry, he may live."

Stunned, Achren mounted her horse. They lifted Rhoram gently, then placed him across the saddle in front of her. "I will not forget this," Achren said. "The King will not forget this, if he lives."

The warrior smiled ruefully. "Erfin will not forget, either."

"Come with me. All of you," she urged.

"No. If we see you again, we will kill you. You understand."

Achren nodded. She did understand.

"Go," they said.

ACHREN RODE AWAY swiftly, knowing that time was of the essence. They were right—Rhoram was still alive. But for how long?

She reached the dubious cover of the vineyard. She could see fighting not far to the west. As she rode carefully through the trailing vines, Geriant came riding up. His face was pale. Carefully, they helped Rhoram down from the horse. A tiny warrior ran up and knelt by Rhoram's body.

"Gwen," Achren said sternly. "Fetch some water. And leave your cloak here. I need cloth for bandages."

Gwen shed her voluminous cloak and took off her helmet. At a dead run, she made for a nearby stream and filled her helmet with water. When she returned, her face was wet with tears. But she knelt down quietly by her father's body. Geriant had removed Rhoram's leather tunic, laying bare the bloody, gaping wound.

"Find Cadell," Achren said, tearing the cloak into strips. "Rhoram needs a doctor."

"I'll get him," Geriant leapt onto his horse, riding back toward the fray.

"He's dying," Gwen said, her voice muffled with tears.

"Yes, he is," Achren answered shortly, pressing a pad of cloth to the wound. The green cloth, instantly soaked in Rhoram's blood, turned black.

Geriant returned with Cadell following. The men dismounted, Cadell grabbing his saddlebags. Swiftly Cadell laid his hands on Rhoram's wound, his eyes closed in concentration as he Life-Read. Abruptly he opened his eyes and looked over at Achren.

"Well?" she asked with her heart in her throat.

"There is life in him yet, if we work quickly," Cadell replied. From a large pouch, he took some crushed leaves and packed the wound, then wrapped it tightly. "That's all I can do here," he said. "We've got to get him to a quiet place where I can stitch him up. We need a litter of some kind. And we can't go far."

"Do you think we can get him as far as the next hill? There's an underground cave that might do for a day or so," Achren suggested.

"Good. We need a few more horses."

Cian and Aidan came riding up. Cian flung himself from his horse. "The forces of Penfro are drawing them off, farther west."

Achren looked up. "Aidan, keep them busy until nightfall.

Then pull out with anyone who is left. Make for the caves up north. The rest of us will join you there later with Rhoram."

"If he lives," Aidan said, swallowing hard.

"He'll live," Achren said grimly.

Between Cian, Cadell, Geriant, Gwen, and Achren, they got Rhoram to the underground cave still alive. As they laid him down, his eyes opened. He took them in one by one, his eyes resting longest on Gwen's tear-stained face. He tried to speak.

"Shh," Cadell said gently. "Drink this." He held a cup to Rhoram's lips, but Rhoram feebly batted it away.

"Let him speak," Achren said quietly.

Rhoram's tortured whisper resounded in the cave. "Go," he rasped. "Leave me."

"Fool," Achren snorted. "Drink and pass out if that's all you have to say."

"Don't . . . want . . . to live . . . defeated. Leave me."

Slowly, Cian withdrew a piece of parchment from his tunic. The Bard hesitantly cleared his throat. "I have a letter here. From Gwydion ap Awst. He left it in my care when he came here last. He said that I would know the time to give it to you all."

"Gwydion?" Rhoram whispered. "Read . . . it."

Cian broke the seal and read aloud, his words echoing strangely in the cave.

To: Rhoram ap Rhydderch, Achren ur Canhastyr, Geriant ap Rhoram, Gwenhwyfar ur Rhoram:

By now the battle is lost, the city overrun, and Rhoram is gravely wounded. Yet know that I believe he will not die, if he does not choose to. You must not give up. A great task awaits all of you. Gather the survivors, and make for the caves. By stealth and by cunning you must gather a teulu that will become a thorn in the side of the enemy. From this seed will come a mighty army. For one day soon the High King will come again. And when he does, he will lead us to take back our own. I command, in the name of the High King soon to be, that you take on this task. Though you may wish to die, you are commanded to live. This is your duty to Kymru.

Gwydion ap Awst var Celemon
Dreamer of Kymru

RHORAM'S TORTURED BLUE eyes began to soften.

"Well, Rhoram ap Rhydderch?" Achren said sharply. "Will you deign to live?"

"A . . . thorn . . . in their side," he whispered. "I like the sound of that." He drank the drugged wine and fell back into unconsciousness, a smile on his ashen lips.

A thorn in their side, Achren thought. She liked the sound of that, too.

Chapter 18

Suldydd, Disglair Wythnos—early morning

Urien ap Ethyllt, King of Rheged, took another hearty swallow of ale, wiped his mouth with the back of his sleeve, and belched hugely.

"Excuse me, *cariad*," he said apologetically, though absently.

"Of course," Ellirri replied cordially. After over twenty years of marriage, she was used to Urien's table manners. And she had many more important things to worry about. At this moment Morcant Whledig, Lord of Penrhyn, was camped to the plain just south of the city with seven hundred warriors at his back, his purpose to be the new King of Rheged.

Even worse, the Coranians had now landed and were marching toward Llwynarth. Urien said they had five days until the Coranians came over the horizon to finish the job that Morcant would begin today.

Urien was counting heavily on the forces of Amgoed, and the teulu of Hetwin Silver-Brow, Lord of Gwinionydd, to come to their aid within the next few days, as had been agreed upon months ago. But Ellirri was not so sure. It was obvious that Morcant had laid his plans with the Coranians long ago. Surely he would have taken the possibility of aid to the city into account and come up with a plan to prevent it.

She thought of her children, as she often did these days. Elphin was with them here in the city, waiting in the courtyard now for his orders. She hoped with all her heart that he would survive, but she didn't expect it. She had sent her two youngest children, Rhiwallon and Enid, to the forest of Coed Addien, under the protection of her steward. It was true that Isgowen was Morcant's sister, but Ellirri did not fear for the safety of her two youngest. Isgowen would be shamed when she found out what Morcant had done.

Her thoughts turned to Owein, her troubled, troublesome son. She had sent him south weeks ago, in the company of Trystan, Captain of Urien's teulu. By now he would be on his way back to Llwynarth, having guessed that she had sent him on his errand to keep him away. They could not possibly arrive before it was all over—for good or for ill. She expected that things would be very ill, indeed. But at least Owein would still be alive.

She had not even attempted to fool herself. The knowledge that they would die in the invasion had been in Gwydion's eyes the night he had come to them. Since that night, neither she nor Urien had spoken of it, for there was nothing that could be said. What would be, would be. They would face death together, as they had faced life.

Her eyes roved around the huge, comfortable room. Here, on the thick carpet just before the hearth, all her children had taken their first, tiny steps. Across the room, in the huge canopied bed, she had slept night after night in Urien's strong arms, reveled in the feel of his hands on her body, wept on his strong shoulder, lay dreaming, safely cradled in his unchanging love.

Urien took another swallow of ale and belched again. He looked curiously at the mug. "You know," he said, "I truly believe this to be a very poor grade. I understand Morcant sent this batch to us a few months ago. He must have kept the best for himself. But that's Morcant all over, isn't it?"

"Yes, *cariad*," she replied absently, still checking the arrows in her quiver, one by one. "Perhaps we should speak to him about that before we kill him."

"Oh, I think we should," Urien said earnestly. "After all, Rheged has a reputation to maintain." He tested the edge of his spear with his thumb, nodded, and laid down the whetstone. "Almost ready?" he inquired.

"Just about." Carefully, she strung her bow and tested the string. Satisfied, she stood, slinging the quiver over her shoulder.

Urien rose also, picking up his helmet of gold fashioned like a horse's head, studded with opals. The badge of the white horse, rearing proudly in defiance, shown white against his red tunic. His cloak was red, worked with gold thread. The gold and opal torque of Rheged hung about his neck like a river of flame.

"Shouldn't you leave that here?" she asked, nodding at the torque.

"No, no," he said, shaking his shaggy head. "I want Morcant to try and take it."

"Ah. Of course." She, too, wore all red. Her red-gold hair was tightly braided against her scalp. Carefully she settled her own helmet over her head.

Urien's brown eyes lit up, and he grinned down at her. "You look very nice." He held out his arm to escort her from their chambers. Ellirri came to him, taking his arm.

As they walked from the chamber, she held her head high and did not weep. Everything she had ever wanted out of life, this man had given her. He had given her children, warmth, and a secure place in his unchangeable heart. And she had made a vow that she would keep, no matter what. They would die together.

And with this, she was content.

Gwaithdydd, Disglair Wythnos—early evening
THREE DAYS LATER, Urien stood on the battlements, looking down at Morcant's camp. Hundreds of tiny campfires dotted the plain. Urien's decimated forces were still holding the city. They still stood alone, for no help had come from Amgoed, or from Hetwin Silver-Brow. Esyllt's call had gone unanswered. Urien knew now that they would never arrive.

Three desperate battles had been fought, and each time Urien's warriors had beaten Morcant back from the city walls. But Morcant's forces now numbered four hundred, and Urien had only two hundred warriors left. Even at odds of two to one, he would be inclined to pit his forces directly against the enemy—if it wasn't for the Druids. Morcant had three Druids in his army, and the havoc they caused was unbelievable. Balls of fire and huge boulders had rained from the sky. His Druid, Sabrina, had done her best against them from the city walls, but it was not enough.

And he was running out of time. The Coranians should arrive at the city in two more days, and that would be the end of it.

He gritted his teeth, his hands clenched firmly on the stone wall. What he wouldn't give to feel Morcant's scrawny neck beneath his callused palms. With any luck, Morcant would come back to this world as a chicken and have his neck wrung. Better still, Urien would come back as the farmer who would wring it. Now that was a satisfying thought.

Tired of staring at the enemy fires, he looked up. Absently, his eyes picked out the five bright stars of the constellation of Beli. Beli had been the husband of the Lady Don in the far off days of Lyonesse, before that land had sunk beneath the sea. The Druids had killed Beli, burning him to a crisp, and seized his lands. The Lady Don had fled, and then worked in secret for many years to get her revenge. Poor Beli. Someone should burn the Druids to a crisp. See how they liked it. Someone should . . .

And that was when he got an idea.

"A MIDNIGHT STRIKE," he said with satisfaction. "Right in the heart of Morcant's camp. They won't expect it. We hit the Druids' tent, and that is that."

His son, Elphin, grinned, his brown eyes alight. Teleri, his lieutenant, smiled wickedly. Esyllt, his Bard, frowned, and March, her husband, frowned also. The reaction seemed fairly mixed. Urien turned to Ellirri. Hers would be the deciding vote.

She smiled. "An excellent idea, *cariad*," she said calmly.

"It will be done, my King," Teleri said eagerly. "I will do it."

"No—let me," Elphin put in quickly.

"No! I will do it." Sabrina, her face pale, her slender figure stiff and unmoving, stood at the chamber door. Her tangled black hair spilled down her back. Her brown Druid's robe was torn and bloodstained. Her blue eyes were cold. "I will do it," Sabrina continued, "to make up for my shame."

Esyllt jumped to her feet, her face flushed with anger. "How dare you! The King will not consider it!"

"And why not?" Sabrina snapped.

"Because you can't be trusted, why do you think?" raged Esyllt. "You're a Druid. A traitor. How do we know you won't betray—"

"Enough." Ellirri's cold voice stopped Esyllt in mid-rant. The Bard opened her mouth to protest further, but the Queen's glance stopped her. Esyllt abruptly sat down, her head bowed. "Urien, may I speak to you for a moment?" Ellirri asked.

Urien nodded. The two walked out of their chamber and down the hallway. "What's Esyllt's problem?" he asked curiously.

"Lower your voice, *cariad*," Ellirri begged.

"Sorry."

"Esyllt is jealous of Sabrina. I told you that once. Remember?"

Oh, yes, he remembered now. Both women were after Trystan, or something like that. It was most confusing. One of those female things he could never understand.

"Well, I don't care about all that," he said dismissively. "I need to decide who's to go. I think myself, Teleri, and Sabrina can handle it."

"I agree. With one change. You stay here. Someone else can go in your place."

"Why?" he asked. "Why not me?"

"I think someone quieter would be better."

"Why, I can be quiet. Are you suggesting—" Quite suddenly, Ellirri's blue eyes filled with tears. Shocked, Urien pulled her to him, cradling her in his strong arms. "*Cariad, cariad,* what have I said? Why are you crying?"

For a moment, her shoulders shook, then she took a deep breath and raised her head, looking up into his eyes. "Urien," she whispered. "Don't go. I want to face death by your side. If you go without me, you may not come back. Please, *cariad*. Please. Stay here. Do this for me."

"Of course, Ellirri. I will send Elphin in my place. All right?"

She nodded and wiped her eyes. He kissed her, then drew her back down the hallway and into their chamber, his arm around her slender shoulders.

"We have decided," he announced. "Teleri, Sabrina, and Elphin. You three will go. At midnight. Be ready."

Elphin leapt up, his brown eyes shining. "I will. Thank you, Da!"

Sabrina bowed, her face tight and pale. "Thank you. I will not fail you."

Abruptly, Esyllt stood and left the chamber, followed by her husband. Sabrina and Ellirri exchanged a look. Urien sighed. One of those female things. He'd never understand.

URIEN AND ELLIRRI watched Morcant's camp from the battlements. It was almost midnight. The campfires had died down, glowing wanly in the still night. Suddenly, fire blossomed and flared in the middle of the camp.

"Sabrina's quite good," Urien said proudly.

They watched for a few moments longer. Warriors poured out of their tents, scurrying like ants as they searched for the source of the attack. Some arrows were shot into the night, and there was a great deal of shouting and screaming.

Suddenly, Ellirri shivered, clutching at her heart. Blindly, she turned to Urien. But before she could speak, he cried, "Come, *cariad*, they'll be returning soon. Let's meet them." He leapt down the stairs, Ellirri following much more slowly. A great weight had fallen on her heart, though it was obvious that the foray had been successful.

As she came to the gate, she saw Sabrina and Teleri standing awkwardly, tears streaming down their faces, the blood of her eldest boy staining their hands. Urien sat on the ground, cradling his son's dying body in his arms.

Elphin's breathing was ragged. A spreading pool of blood spilled through the fingers clutched around his belly. "We did it, Da," Elphin whispered, looking up at his father and trying to smile. "Killed all Morcant's Druids."

Urien tried to smile back. "Of course, you did it, my son. I knew you would."

As if in a dream, Ellirri went to them, kneeling by her son, laying her cool hand against the cheek of her dying boy. "Do not go far, little one, without us," she whispered gently. "Your father and I will soon follow." She kissed his forehead tenderly and smiled a last smile for him as he looked up at her. And even as she gazed down on him, the darkness gathered up the light in his eyes and took him far, far away.

Meirgdydd, Disglair Wythnos—morning
THE NEXT MORNING they laid Elphin to rest in the barrow of Crug Mawr. In the early morning hours, Urien and Ellirri had prepared the body of their son for burial, washing the blood away, dressing him in his finest clothes, combing out his tangled, brown hair. Then, when all was done that could be done, they had sat next to his body, each holding one of his cold hands,

looking down upon their son and remembering.

In those hours, once and once only had Ellirri spoken. She had said in a distant, puzzled tone: "All those months he grew in my body. All those hours I labored to bring him into the world. It is strange."

"How is it strange?" he had asked.

"That it took so long to give him life, but it took only a moment for him to die."

When dawn at last broke over the stricken city, Urien, his huntsman, March, his doorkeeper, Cynlas, and Dynfwael, his chief counselor, picked up the pallet on which Elphin lay and bore him out of Caer Erias to the barrow. Ellirri, Sabrina, Teleri, and Esyllt followed behind, each carrying a flaming torch. Urien's warriors, mounted on rock-steady horses, lined the street leading to the barrow, their swords drawn, their faces like stone, meditating upon their revenge for the death of their Prince.

The stone was rolled back from the doorway, and they carried Elphin into the cool depths of the resting-place of the dead. Gently, they laid the pallet within one of the niches carved into the stone wall. The men stood back as Ellirri stepped forward and placed Elphin's quiver and arrows at his feet. "Use these with honor, in the world to which you have gone," she said, her voice clear and firm.

Urien stepped forward and laid Elphin's spear and shield on the brier. "Use these with honor, in the world to which you have gone." He hesitated for a moment, then added, "Good-bye, my son."

Ellirri then laid her hands on either side of Elphin's still, white face. She kissed his forehead and whispered, "Sleep well, *cariad*."

One by one, the others left the barrow, until only Ellirri and Urien were left. They gazed down at the body for a moment. The torches burned in the wall sockets, illuminating the still, white features of their boy. Then Urien placed his arm around Ellirri's shoulders and gently began to pull her from the barrow.

They reached the doorway, then looked back at their son one last time.

"I'm glad he knew that we loved him," Ellirri said quietly.

Slowly, the stone was rolled back into place. The finality of that sound tore into Urien's heart. Inside him, a rage began. He was tired of skulking behind these city walls. He longed to see blood shed today, in payment for the life of his son, his bright, beautiful, beloved son, cut down before he had even truly begun to live.

It was not to be borne. Not to be borne without a fight.

Urien turned to his warriors. A scant two hundred left, but they were the best. They gazed back at him, their faces stern, their eyes eager, their spears ready.

"We hide no more behind city walls!" Urien suddenly bellowed. "Today we march from the city and cut them down!"

As one, his warriors raised a cry, "Urien! Urien! Urien!"

Dynfwal was suddenly by his side, holding Urien's spear and shield ready. Reins were thrust into his hands. He mounted his horse and took up his weapons. Beside him, he saw Ellirri do the same, taking her weapons from Sabrina's hands. Side by side, they rode to the city gates, their warriors following.

Just before the gates were opened, Urien turned to his wife. Her face was calm, her hands steady, her heart was in her beautiful, blue eyes. "Ready, *cariad*?" he asked.

"Always," she said.

His warriors poured from the gate, aimed at Morcant's still scattered forces like a gleaming arrow. With a resounding crash, the two armies came to grips with each other. Blood began to soak the plain, pouring from the bodies of the dead and dying.

But though Urien's fighters were brave and steadfast, they were outnumbered two to one, and slowly, slowly, they were pushed back, giving ground inexorably as they fell.

Urien, leading charge after charge, saw Morcant in the distance, hiding behind his warriors like the coward he was, always too far away to be reached. Urien was losing this battle, and he knew it. It would all be for nothing if he could not face Morcant himself.

And he could not. The odds were too great. They would have to pull back. In shame and anger, he raised the horn to his lips to sound the retreat.

But just before his horn could sound, he heard other horns. Horns, blowing the charge as six hundred Kymric warriors of Amgoed poured down onto the plain.

It was over. Surely these forces had come to Morcant's aid, not to his.

So it was with unparalleled astonishment that he saw this new force plunge straight into the heart of Morcant's army and begin to kill.

Gwyntdydd, Disglair Wythnos—morning

URIEN SAT UPON his horse patiently at the open east gate, waiting for the enemy to come within sight. Not long to wait now.

In truth, patience was not his strong suit. But each moment when he could turn to his wife, as he did now, and see the sun flashing off her red-gold hair, as he did now, and see the love and trust in her eyes, as he did now—well, those were moments not to be tossed away lightly.

She smiled at him and, as she had done often in the past hour, laid her slender hand on his arm, as though to assure herself that he was still real, that he was not yet dead.

Ah, well, he and Ellirri had lived a good life together. And eventually they all had to move on to the next world, to wait in Gwlad Yr Haf, the Summer Land, for their turn to be born again.

He was sure that whoever he came back as, wherever he came back, Ellirri would be near him. He was equally sure he would recognize her, as he had, no doubt, for countless lifetimes. His life with her would not end. No matter what happened today.

He let his thoughts drift back to the battle yesterday and grinned with pleasure. How Morcant's forces had run! Morcant had run faster than any. And so he still lived today. Morcant had last been seen going east. Urien knew he was meeting his Coranian allies and would return today, bringing their deaths with him.

Thank the gods his Gwardas of Amgoed had finally come yesterday. Urien had given them up for good, thinking them traitors. But that was not so. After the battle, they had met with him, telling him that their Dewin had received Wind-Ridden messages from Bledri, Urien's Dewin, stating that the plans had changed and commanding them to stay put and defend their own lands.

It was not until refugees from Llwynarth reached west Amgoed that the Gwardas had begun to think that they had been tricked and banded together to ride to Urien's aid.

If he could only get his hands on Bledri, but his Dewin was long gone, no doubt joining his true masters by now.

If only Hetwin Silver-Brow would come from the south! But that seemed unlikely. It was obvious that Hetwin, too, had received similar messages. And, since Esyllt's Wind-Speech had raised no answer, he would still not know of the need.

Nonetheless, he had sent Esyllt south yesterday, to bring word to Hetwin of their peril. He had given his opal ring to her, along with the words that Bran the Dreamer had spoken so long ago. Esyllt would see to it that Owein received the ring.

Urien had thought to send Sabrina away, too, but she had refused, saying that she had not yet paid for her shame and thus could not retreat. Teleri, too, had refused to leave. Her place, she had said firmly, was leading his teulu. Well, he couldn't argue with that. But he was able to extract a promise from her—and hard work that had been, too. She had finally agreed that, should she find herself alive after today's battle, she would find Owein. He had given her the torque of Rheged to clasp around Owein's neck. He also charged her with delivering the helm of Rheged to his son. Though Urien wore the helm now, he knew Teleri would be able to retrieve it before they laid him in his grave. A clever, reliable woman, Teleri. She would survive. He felt sure of it.

Unlike himself. And his wife.

Once again, he turned to Ellirri, drinking in the sight of her. And once again, she lightly touched his arm, smiling that special smile that she reserved only for him.

Ah, he was a lucky, lucky man.

There it was, movement to the east. A cloud of dust had

risen. The earth rumbled slightly. Urien glanced behind him to see the set, grim faces of the men and women who would fight—and likely die—today. Proud he was to lead them in this final, hopeless stand. The Bards would sing of this battle. Of that he was sure.

One last look at Ellirri before the end. Gently, she reached out and touched his cheeks, framing his face with her hands. He laid his palms over her slender fingers, then kissed her passionately. Their last kiss for this lifetime.

And it was sweet. So sweet.

Then Urien gave the order. And he led the charge to death.

And, in a way, that was sweet, too.

ELLIRRI RODE FEARLESSLY by Urien's side through the press, her blue eyes focused on the distant figure of Morcant, who was standing at the top of the hill next to a Coranian warrior. The warrior was wearing a silver helmet, shaped in the fashion of a boar. Surely this was the leader of the Coranian army. Mechanically she cut down the Coranian warriors in her way. She had spent her arrows long ago and now worked with spear, shield, and daggers.

As they neared the crest of the hill where Morcant stood, Urien began to shout. "Morcant!" he bellowed. "Come and fight, coward! Come and fight!"

The Coranian commander said something to Morcant. Then the commander barked orders in a language Ellirri did not understand, and suddenly their way was clear, the warriors pulling back to give them a straight path toward their goal. Urien leapt from his horse and rushed up the hill toward Morcant, a gleaming dagger in each hand.

At the sight of Urien coming for him, Morcant tried to turn and run, but the Coranian commander grasped Morcant's shoulder, forcing him to stand. With a roar of rage, Urien confronted Morcant. And now the traitor, unable to run, drew his own daggers and faced the King he had betrayed.

Ellirri jumped from her horse and ran up the hill, closing in on the commander, who was watching the contest with a sneer. After a few moments, it was obvious that Morcant would sooner or later die at Urien's hands. The commander, deciding to interfere, drew his ax and started toward the two men.

Ellirri hoped that the man understood at least a little Kymri. "Coranian dog!" she shouted. The commander stopped and turned to her, his ax at the ready.

Insolently, he looked her up and down. He was stocky with light brown hair and dark brown eyes. "And who might you be?" he asked, in perfect Kymri.

"I am Queen Ellirri PenMarch," she said clearly.

"I am Baldred, son of Baldaeg, the Eorl of Tarbin, of the country of Dere, in the Coranian Empire. My Bana has come to take this land. There is no escape from him."

"We do not seek to escape," Ellirri said contemptuously. "Tell me, Baldred, son of Baldaeg, do you know how to fight? Or do you only know how to talk?" Morcant was still desperately trying to defend himself against Urien's furious blows. She wanted Baldred to be distracted from that fight. This was her job.

So she raised her daggers and waded in.

URIEN RAINED BLOW after blow upon Morcant with the flat of his blades. A quick death was too good for the bastard who had killed his son, who had consorted with Kymru's bitterest enemy, who thought he should be King of Rheged. King! Ha!

Out of the corner of his eye, he saw his wife engaging the enemy commander. Perhaps it would be best if he made a quicker end to Morcant, for the commander fought well with his ax, and Ellirri was tired.

He had raised his daggers for the killing blow when the low groan of his wife distracted him. His eyes flickered toward her, and he saw with horror that her daggers had gone spinning out of her hands as she fell to the ground from the force of the commander's blow. The commander raised his ax high. The sun flashed off the killing blade as it began its deadly descent toward his wife's beloved face.

With a shout, he leapt toward the commander in a desperate attempt to knock the ax from the man's hands. But just at that moment, he felt a huge burning, a rending, a tearing in his heart. He looked down in astonishment at the sight of Morcant's dagger protruding from his chest. Blood spurted from him in a wave, and all his strength drained from him. Slowly, as though in a dream, he fell, and watched helplessly as the Coranian commander ruthlessly buried the ax into Ellirri's breast.

With his last strength, he reached out for his wife. The darkness was coming for him, but he would not yield to it. Not until he felt her touch for one last time.

ELLIRRI KNEW THAT she was dying. The sounds of battle faded away. The colors of the morning had gone dim. A mist had fallen over her eyes.

She was puzzled that she was not yet dead. Why? What was keeping her here? There was something she had to do, but she was too tired to remember what it was.

And then it came to her. Her husband needed her. He was by her side, wounded to the death, his hand reaching for her own.

She tried to stretch out her hand. But she was weak, so weak. And tired. So very tired. Yet her Urien needed her. From somewhere deep within, from a place no death-blow could ever touch, she found the strength she needed, and stretched out her hand for that final measure.

Their hands clasped tightly for a moment. Then slowly, ever so slowly, their grip slackened. And they were gone. Together.

Meriwdydd, Disglair Wythnos—late afternoon

OWEIN AP URIEN var Ellirri urged his horse on to greater speed. Weary, but eager to please him, his horse galloped faster through the hilly, woody country of Gwinionydd. The late afternoon sun warmed the green land, and the springtime air was light and crisp. But Owein did not, could not, feel the beauty of the day. All his awareness was focused on the still faroff city of Llwynarth, the place where he longed with all his soul to be. Two more days still before they knew if the city still stood. Two more days before he knew if his mother and father yet lived.

Behind him, Trystan and his band of twenty warriors followed closely. Only twenty were left of the one hundred with which he had set out a week ago, for the Coranians had taken a toll. For the last seven days, they had been encountering small bands of Coranian warriors. But Owein and his men had merely fought their way through, then fled, for he would not be waylaid on his journey to Llwynarth.

A shout just a few paces to his left made Owein rein in his horse abruptly. A strange Kymric warrior stood at the base of a hill, gesturing for them to come to him. Owein glanced back at

Trystan. They had heard rumors that some of his countrymen were in league with the Coranians.

"He's wearing Hetwin's badge," Trystan said quietly.

"What do you think?" Owein asked.

"I'm not sure. Let's talk to him for a moment."

Trystan gestured for their warriors to draw in closer. The warriors fanned out in a circle, letting the stranger through and then closing up the path behind him.

"Owein ap Urien?" the man asked. "Is it really you?"

"Cadar?" Owein asked uncertainly. Cadar was the Captain of Hetwin's warband.

"Yes, it's me," Cadar replied. "Hetwin saw you coming. He wants to talk."

Owein glanced around. "Saw me coming? Where is he?"

Cadar pointed to a tiny forest less than a league to the north. "Our base is there, for now. We had to abandon Neigwl."

"Your city is lost?"

"Man, all the cities are lost."

"But Hetwin is here? Didn't he go to Llwynarth? That was my father's plan."

"But Urien changed his plan! Hetwin got a message from Bledri."

"Impossible," Owein said flatly.

"I tell you, he did." Cadar frowned. "You'd best come with me and talk to him. I fear some mischief is afoot."

"Some mischief, indeed, if all the cities of Rheged have fallen."

"They have, Owein. They have."

OWEIN, TRYSTAN AND their warriors made their way through the trees to the tiny clearing where Hetwin Silver-Brow now

469

stood. Hetwin was a huge man, who had served Urien devotedly for years. His large hands were nicked and callused with the scars of war. His silver hair fell over his broad shoulders.

"Owein ap Urien," Hetwin bowed. "What news from Llwynarth?"

"What news?" Owein repeated blankly. "I do not know."

"You don't come from there?"

Owein shook his head. "We come from the south. I am on my way to Llwynarth now. I know nothing. Why are you not there?"

It was Hetwin's turn to look blank. "Urien changed his plans. My Dewin received a Wind-Ride from Beldri."

"So you have no news of what is happening in the capital? No news of my family?"

Hetwin shook his grizzled head. "Nothing. But do you think—" Hetwin broke off with a puzzled frown.

"I don't know what to think," Owein replied slowly.

"Hetwin," Trystan broke in. "We have traveled far and fast. Is what Cadar says true? All the cities have fallen?"

"I do not know if all of them have. But word has it that all the cantrefs on the coast have fallen to the enemy. I know this only by the word of the city folk who escaped. And pitiful few that is, too. And you know about the Druids."

"What about the Druids?" Owein asked.

"Why, they are in league with the Coranians. My own Druid disappeared a week ago. They fight with the enemy."

"All of them?" Trystan gasped.

"Most. Perhaps only a handful of them are faithful. I do not know."

A rustle in the trees made them all stop talking. They tensed, laying their hands to their weapons. Then came a muffled hail and Hetwin relaxed. "A scout. He must have news," Hetwin said.

And so he did. He had Esyllt with him. She was white and drawn. Her eyes were shadowed, and her tunic was torn. Her hair was tangled and dusty. But her weary face lit up when she saw Trystan. Trystan took a step toward her.

But before she could even greet her lover, Owein leapt at her, grasping her by the arms. "Esyllt! What news? Tell me!" Owein demanded.

"Let her sit down, Owein," Trystan broke in. "And give her something to drink."

"Tell me now, Esyllt!" Owein persisted, not letting go of Esyllt's arms.

"Morcant Whledig attacked the city," she said tonelessly. "Neither the Gwardas of Amgoed nor Hetwin Silver-Brow came to our aid."

"But—the message!" Hetwin gasped.

"False. Put out by Bledri, in league with Morcant."

Hetwin paled. "I . . ." he began in a strangled voice.

"Never mind that now, Hetwin. Go on, Esyllt," Owein urged.

"Four days we fought without aid. On the fourth day, Amgoed came and relieved us. But the Coranians were only one day away. That was two days ago. I don't know what happened after that. Urien sent me to bring Hetwin's men when his Bard would not answer me."

"He was killed three days ago," Hetwin said heavily, anguish in his old eyes.

"We thought you did not come because you had betrayed us."

"You know something else," Owein said, his eyes narrowing. "Tell me!"

"Owein," Trystan said gently, "let her sit down, at least."

"Tell me now!" Owein demanded.

Esyllt looked up into Owein's face and sighed. "Elphin is dead. Your brother died on the third day."

Owein abruptly let her go and stepped back. Trystan put his arm around Esyllt's shoulders and gently lowered her to one of the fallen logs scattered about the clearing. He then sat down beside her and cradled her as she began to sob.

Owein stood unmoving. Elphin dead. The thing that he had half-wished for, the thing he was ashamed to have ever hoped for, had happened. He had loved Elphin—and envied him for his future as King of Rheged, for his betrothal to Sanon of Prydyn. And now Elphin was dead. Owein felt no elation, no joy. Only shame. Only sorrow. He was lost and alone, and if he could have had one wish, it would have been to see Elphin standing before him now, alive and whole.

He remembered that night many months ago when he had stood with Gwydion and Rhiannon, when the Protectors had come with their Wild Hunt. The words that Cerrunnos had spoken to him, words that he had not understood at the time, came back to him now, and they were bitter: "Be careful of what you wish for, boy. For you shall surely get it."

Esyllt, her face streaked with tears, pulled herself from Trystan's embrace and rose to stand before Owein. "Your father gave me something to give to you." From a small pouch at her waist, she pulled the opal ring of Rheged and held it out to him.

"These words King Urien bade me say to you," Esyllt went on, her voice trembling. "These are the instructions of Bran the Dreamer, given years ago when he gave this ring to the House of PenMarch. Guard this ring carefully. One day it is to be surrendered to the Dreamer who asks for it. And the Dreamer will ask for it with these exact words: 'The High King commands you to surrender Bran's gift.' To the Dreamer who speaks these words, and none other, is the ring to be given."

Before Owein could reply, before he could even begin to speak around the tightness in his throat, another shout from the woods reached them.

One of Hetwin's warriors was leading someone to the clearing. It was Teleri, Urien's lieutenant. Her tunic was bloodstained. Her right arm was wrapped with a field dressing, the bandage dirty and bloody. Lines of pain were etched across her drawn face. Her gray-green eyes were bloodshot. Her steps dragged with weariness, and she clutched a cloth-wrapped bundle to her breast.

As she saw him, some of the tension left her face. She stumbled to him and clutched at his arm. "Owein ap Urien var Ellirri. I have found you. I have fulfilled my task." She opened her mouth to say more, but her knees buckled and Owein caught her before she fell. He sank to the ground with her slight form in his arms. Hetwin handed Owein a brimming mug of ale, and Owein brought it to Teleri's lips and forced her to drink.

When she was done, Owein said, "Tell me."

"Llwynarth has fallen," she croaked. "Before the battle, Urien gave me a task. If I lived, I was to find you. And so I have. I have come to offer my service to my King."

"King!" Owein said, startled. "I am not—" He broke off, silenced by the look in her gray-green eyes. "My father . . ."

"Dead. I saw him fall."

"My mother . . ."

"Dead. They fell together."

No one moved in the now-quiet glade. Old Hetwin's face twisted with grief. Trystan's jaw clenched tight. Esyllt's eyes filled with tears. But no one spoke.

At last, Teleri broke the silence, "Urien gave me this to give to you." She reached into the sack and pulled out the opal torque of Rheged.

Owein stared at the torque. The sun, peering through the trees, flashed fire, setting the opals shimmering. To his suddenly tear-blinded eyes Teleri seemed to hold a river of gold and flame, cascading in a flood from her hands.

Teleri reached up and clasped the torque around Owein's neck. "He gave me words to say to you," she said. "He said to say: 'Owein, my beloved son——'"

"Stop. Oh, stop for a moment," Owein begged. It was too much to bear. Beloved son. Beloved son of a father he would never see again.

Again, Teleri reached into the sack and this time she pulled out Urien's helmet. Sunlight danced on the golden helm and the opals in the horse's fierce head glittered. "I took this the night of the battle as his body was waiting to be buried. He wanted you to have this, too. Against the day you would return to Llwynarth to take back that which is yours. He said: 'To you I give all that I have, for your brother is dead. Hail to Owein, King of Rheged.'"

King of Rheged. But there was no Rheged. Rheged was gone, crushed under the heel of the enemy. But Morcant still lived. Ah, but there was a remedy for that. Owein stood and turned to leave the clearing. Trystan's sudden grip on his arm stopped him.

"Where are you going?" Trystan demanded.

"To Llwynarth."

"Llwynarth is lost, Owein."

"Morcant's in Llwynarth."

"And?"

"And I'm going to kill him," Owein said impatiently. "What do you think?"

"And how do you plan to kill him? Do you think you can just walk up to him and put a dagger in his ribs? Do you think the Coranians will just part the way for you and cheer you on?"

Owein wrenched his arm from Trystan's grasp. "Let me go!"

Then Esyllt was in front of him, blocking his way.

"Get out of my way, Esyllt. Don't make me hurt you," Owein warned through gritted teeth.

But Esyllt did not answer. Instead, she pulled a letter from her tunic and held it in front of his eyes. He jerked his head back. "What is this?"

"Word from the Dreamer. He left it with me months ago. He said I would know when to give it to you. And so I do. Read it."

Owein raised his arm to sweep her from his path. He didn't want to read it. Didn't want to do anything but kill the man who had done this to him and his.

"Your father would have read it," Esyllt said.

Owein froze. Very well. He would read it and then be on his way. He didn't care what Gwydion said. Nothing, nothing was going to stop him from what he chose to do now. He snatched the letter from her hands. And read aloud, in a toneless voice.

To: Owein ap Urien and Trystan ap Naf:

By now Elphin, Urien, and Ellirri are dead, and your country is in the hands of the Coranians.

My heart goes out to you in the face of so many losses. But you must not give up. A great task awaits all of you. Gather the survivors, and find a safe place to shelter. By stealth and by cunning you must gather a teulu that will become a thorn in the side of the enemy. From this seed will come a mighty army. For one day soon the High King will come again. And when he does, he will lead us to take back our own. I command you, in the name of the High King soon to be, that you take on this task. Though you may wish to die, you are commanded to live. This is your duty to Kymru.

Gwydion ap Awst var Celemon

Dreamer of Kymru

Very well, he had read it. Now on to Morcant. Owein thrust the letter into Trystan's hands. Again he turned to go.

"Leave the torque and the helm with me if you are going, Owein," Teleri said clearly. "I must give them to Rhiwallon."

Owein stopped and turned back to Teleri. "To Rhiwallon?"

"To Rhiwallon, your brother. He will be King, if you will not."

"King?" Owein laughed harshly. "King of what? King of nothing! There is nothing left of Rheged to be King of!"

"You understand nothing. The Dreamer himself tells you that the High King will come again and lead us out of bondage. He tells you that you have a duty to live. But you won't even bother to hear it. Go and be killed by Morcant, then. I intend to do my duty to Kymru, as the Dreamer commands." Teleri's gray-green eyes flashed with contempt as she held out her hands for Urien's gifts.

Owein was silent. His duty. He could not do just as he wished. And the knowledge was bitter. All that he had ever wanted had come to him, and the weight of it crushed him. He thought of the horrible choices to be made for the rest of his life, of the choice between duty and longing, between what he must do and what he wished to do.

And he knew then what he would do, bitter as it was. He would do his duty.

But he could say none of those things. He was young and did not know how. And so, instead, he turned to Esyllt. "Their song. Their death song. Do you have it?"

Esyllt nodded. "It is done."

"Then sing it. Sing it now for us."

Esyllt had no harp, no drum. But that did not matter. Her voice rose in song, clear and sweet, as she gave the Bard's farewell to her King and Queen.

"Before Urien,
I saw white horses jaded and gory,
And after the shout, a terrible resistance.

"Before Ellirri,
I saw horses white with foam,
And after the shout, a terrible torrent.

"In Llwynarth I saw the rage of slaughter,
And biers beyond all number,
And red-stained warriors.

"In Llwynarth I saw the edges of blades in contact,
Men in terror, and blood on the breast
Of Urien, great son of Rheged.

"In Llwynarth I saw the weapons
Of men, and blood fast dropping,
And Ellirri raise her spear.

"In Llwynarth they were slain,
And before they were overpowered,
they committed great slaughter.

"Brave they were before the foe.
Urien and Ellirri.
Brave before the foe."

Owein listened to the song, unmoving. As the last note died away, he listened to his heart. He listened to that part deep with him where Urien and Ellirri lived on still. And always would.

A thorn in the side of the enemy. He liked the sound of that.

Chapter 19

Llundydd, Disglair Wythnos—morning

King Uthyr gazed down from his place at the top of the city walls into the grinning, gleeful face of his traitorous half-brother, Madoc.

Uthyr's face was stern and set, showing none of the pain and bitterness he felt at his betrayal. His hawk-shaped helmet, fashioned of silver and studded with sapphires, glistened in the morning light. His dark blue cloak, fastened onto his broad shoulders with sapphire brooches, stirred slightly in the fitful breeze. Around his neck hung the silver and sapphire torque of Gwynedd, glittering on his breast in the morning light.

His wife, Ygraine, stood by his side, her auburn hair braided tightly to her proud head, her slender body clothed in a plain tunic of blue and brown. Behind the couple, Cai, the Captain of Uthyr's warband, stood armed and ready with spear and shield. Beside Cai stood his nephew, Bedwyr, lieutenant of Uthyr's forces.

On Uthyr's other side stood Griffi, his Druid, on whose pale face freckles stood out in bold relief. His usual infectious grin was absent as he surveyed the army drawn up before the gates of the city. Next to Griffi stood Susanna, Uthyr's Bard and Griffi's lover. Her red-gold hair shone in the sun, and her blue eyes were cold.

"What do you do here, brother?" Uthyr called down, as though the seven hundred warriors at Madoc's back did not exist, as though his half-brother did not fly the banner of the golden boar, the symbol of the Warleader of Corania.

The sun turned Madoc's bright hair to spun gold, and his blue eyes were fastened hungrily on the torque around Uthyr's neck. "All Kymru is under attack by the Coranians, brother," Madoc replied. "The Kymri have no chance against them. Their Warleader will crush us beneath his heel, unless we co-operate with them. Gwynedd needs a new King, one who can bring our kingdom safely through these perilous times."

"Ah. And you are that man?" Uthyr asked.

"I am. I have come to take the torque of Gwynedd for my own. Submit to me, and you will be unharmed."

All these years, Uthyr mused, he had ignored warnings about Madoc. Instead, he had given Madoc control of one of the kingdom's richest cantrefs. He had given his half-brother gifts of horses, fine clothes, bright weapons. He had given his trust. And for all that, he had been betrayed. The betrayal left a bitter, bitter taste in his mouth. And there was only one way to rid himself of that.

So he spat, and the bile arced through the air to land squarely on Madoc's upturned, triumphant face. Madoc's expression darkened, suffused with rage as he hastily wiped the spittle from his check.

"Your life is measured in hours, Uthyr!" Madoc raged. "I have seven hundred warriors, and you have only four hundred. We have already killed the Gwarda of Is Dulas. Reinforcements cannot come to your aid in time. Your city will be mine!"

"Pit your seven hundred against my warriors, brother! And you shall see how true warriors of Gwynedd fight! Come against me, then. We are ready for you!"

Madoc grinned fiercely. "I have more than warriors, brother. I have five Druids to do my bidding!"

Griffi stiffened from his place next to Uthyr. The red-haired Druid furiously shouted, "What Druid dares to betray their King? Come forth, traitors, and receive your punishment!"

"Druid of Uthyr," Madoc replied, "you do not understand. The Druids act on the will of the Archdruid himself."

"You lie!" Griffi shot back.

Madoc gestured, and five Druids cowled in brown robes trimmed with green stepped up from the ranks of the army to stand before him. One Druid handed Madoc a scroll, tied off with ribbons of brown and green.

"I have a message for you from your Archdruid," Madoc called, holding up the scroll. "Read it."

Contemptuously, Griffi gestured, and the scroll flew out of Madoc's grasp, arced up high in the air, and came to Griffi's waiting hands. As Griffi read, all color drained from his freckled face. At last, he raised his head and looked at Uthyr.

"My King," he rasped. "The Archdruid has bound all Druids to the Coranian Warleader. We are ordered to support those acting on this Warleader's behalf."

Griffi and Uthyr, Druid and King, stared at each other. "What will you do, Griffi ap Iaen?" Uthyr asked softly. "If you wish, I will give you safe passage out of the city. I owe you that much for the many years of loyal service you have given me and mine."

In a choked voice, Griffi answered, "How can you ask me such a thing? Do you not know me?"

Slowly, Uthyr smiled. He reached out his hand for the Archdruid's letter, and Griffi handed it to him without demur. Uthyr crumpled the letter into a ball and tossed it high in the air. When the paper reached its apex and began to descend, Griffi gestured, and it burst into flame. Ashes drifted down onto Madoc's upturned face.

Enraged, one of Madoc's Druids stepped forward and, with a wave of his hand, sent a ball of fire whistling through the sky, heading straight toward Griffi. But at Griffi's gesture, a wheel of flame shot forth from the walls. High in the air, the ball of fire was met by the wheel of flame. The wheel consumed the enemy Druid's fire, then sped on through the sky to land in the middle of Madoc's army. Men and horses scattered. Some were not fast enough, and they screamed as they burned.

Quickly, Uthyr turned to Ygraine, who still stood unflinching by his side. "Better organize a fire brigade," he said. "Looks like things are going to get hot in the city."

"Certainly," she replied crisply.

"Cai, Bedwyr," Uthyr called, turning to his Captain and lieutenant. "Now is a good time, while they are still scattered. Let's go." Uthyr swiftly kissed his wife. To Griffi he said, "Stay here with Ygraine. Fight those fires."

The three men raced down the stairs and mounted their horses. Without further pause, Uthyr gave the order, and four hundred men and women of Tegeingl poured out of the city to face seven hundred warriors. And the killing began.

U<small>THYR SAT ALONE</small> in the eastern watchtower in the city he still held. Night had fallen, masking the field where the armies had fought that day. He was grateful that the dark spared him the sight of the bloody ground. He did not want to look at the meadow where so many of his people had died. For they had all been his people—even those who had fought for Madoc.

As dusk fell, Uthyr's warriors had gathered the bodies of their comrades, intermingling peacefully with Madoc's warriors who had come to the field to claim the bodies of their own dead. At the edge of the field, a huge bonfire rose into the night, set to burn the bodies of the enemy dead. The dead of Uthyr's warband were to be burned in the marketplace at the center of the city. In a few moments he must leave the tower and lead the ceremony in their honor.

The glow of the fire mesmerized him. Madoc had lost half his force today, and the fire was tremendous. It blossomed in the night like an evil flower, fed by the power of Madoc's three remaining Druids.

Over and over in the battle today, Uthyr had come close to Madoc, only to be turned from his prey by the vagaries of battle. It was the dearest wish of his heart to come to grips with his brother, to make him pay for what he had done.

He sighed. He was fated to die. But, please the gods, not at Madoc's hands. He raised his eyes to the starry sky. Let someone else kill me, he begged silently to whatever Shining Ones might be listening. Do not let it be Madoc.

He closed his eyes, remembering the last sight of his beloved thirteen-year-old daughter, Morrigan. Her dark eyes, so like her mother's, had been misted with the sheen of tears that she had struggled to prevent from falling. She had tried to smile bravely at him as he said farewell. He had known he would never see her again. And she had guessed that truth somehow, as well. He had seen the knowledge in her tear-filled eyes.

He had taken the ring from his finger, put it into her slender hands, and solemnly spoke the words handed down to the rulers of his house for the last two hundred years, words he himself had last heard from the lips of his dying mother.

"This ring," he had whispered, his throat tight, "is never to fall into the hands of any but those of our house, the house of PenHebog. Surrender this ring only to one who speaks these words, words first given to us by Bran the Dreamer: 'In the name of the High King to be, surrender Bran's gift to me.' Give the ring to one who speaks those words and no other. Do you understand?"

Morrigan had nodded her head and repeated the words perfectly. Then he had held her in his strong arms and kissed her good-bye, giving her into the keeping of Neuad, his Dewin. Neuad would escort Morrigan to the mountains, to a hiding place already prepared against this day. As she rode away, Morrigan had sat straight on her pony, her thin shoulders unbowed. And so she was gone.

Arthur was safe in Dinas Emrys. Now Morrigan was safe in Mynydd Tawel. His children would live. And, with the help of Gwydion, they would drive off the enemy and take their rightful places in Kymru. Morrigan would be Queen of Gwynedd. And Arthur would be High King of Kymru itself.

He heard light footsteps ascending the tower stairs. He knew that rhythm as he knew the beat of his own heart. At last she had come to him. He felt her cool hand smooth his hair back from his forehead, then she settled on the floor next to him. She did not speak, and he, too, kept silent.

At last she turned her head to look at him, and he forced himself to meet her gaze. Her tunic and trousers were blood-stained. Her auburn hair was not yet loosened from its tight braids. Weariness lined her proud face. But her dark eyes were clear and bright, undimmed by tears.

"Husband," she said at last, "you are late. They wait for you to begin the burning."

He rose to his feet, helping her to stand also.

"I have heavy news, Uthyr. Arday cannot be found."

"Arday?"

"Our steward," she said crisply.

"Yes. Thank you. I know who she is. I just don't—"

"Our steward, who is also the sister of Menwaed, the Lord of Arllechwedd."

"You think her brother is planning something? In league with Madoc?"

Ygraine shrugged. "She is gone. I fear that she slipped out of the city because she knew that her brother was to join Madoc in battle against us."

"Well, why not?" he said bitterly. "What's one more trai-tor? All in a day's work here in Gwynedd."

She ignored his bitter tone. "Arllechwedd is to the far north. I fear that his task is to keep the forces of northern Rhos from coming to our aid. And if northern Rhos does not come to our aid, we are lost."

"Ah, Ygraine," Uthyr said, "we are lost anyway."

"Perhaps," she said coolly. "Perhaps not. We are not done

trying yet."

He looked into her dark eyes, pools of shadow in the fading light. For the first time in many years, he saw something in them he had thought gone forever. Something that had fled from her eyes long ago.

"I want you to leave tonight," he said abruptly, forcing the words past his aching throat. "We lack the power now to even wage war beyond the city gates. You must go. Morrigan will need you. One day she will be Queen of Gwynedd. And you have sworn to stay alive for her."

She stood silently for a time, her head bowed. At last she whispered, in a broken voice that Uthyr had never heard from her before, "But, *cariad*, life without you means nothing to me."

Uthyr was shocked. For years now he had thought her love for him was dead. For years he had given her every shred of himself that he had to give, in hopes that she would turn back to him. And now, now that it was too late. . .

She raised her head, and tears were in her eyes. Through the years, he could count on one hand the times he had seen her cry. She studied his face, as though storing up memories of him for long, cold nights when he would be gone from her side. "Ah, Uthyr," she whispered, "did you really not know? Had I not said? You are my life. You are my heart. Without you, I have neither, and life holds nothing for me."

He reached out and touched her face, her tears washing over his hand. "Would that I had known that years ago, my love. Much loneliness you might have saved me."

"Would that I had known, too. And now it is too late. There is so little time left to us. Oh, Uthyr, do not send me from you. Let me die here with you. Please."

"Ygraine, you cannot stay. Morrigan needs you. You have promised. I know you too well. You keep your promises."

She pulled away from him and stood at the tower's edge, staring out at the fire in the meadow. At last, she turned to him. "I remember saying I would choose my time to leave your side. And that time is not yet."

"Then when?"

"Soon. Why, do you tire of my presence?"

For an answer he grabbed her and pulled her to him, his mouth crushing hers in a passionate kiss, a kiss she returned so enthusiastically he was left weak at the knees. Her dark eyes were full of promise, and a hint of desperation, as she reached out to him at last, now in the shadow of death, finally understanding all she would lose when he was gone.

KING AND QUEEN approached the market square hand in hand, their heads high, as they came to honor the dead. Men and women who had fought to the death that day lay in long rows, pale and cold on the cobblestones. Surviving friends and family had done the best for their fallen, washing away the blood, straightening mangled limbs, placing weapons into dead hands.

Around the square the people stood silently. Uthyr saw Nest, Cai's wife, standing next to her husband, holding his hand. Cai's other hand rested on the shoulder of his twelve-year old son, Garanwyn.

Griffi, his brown robe an inky shadow at the edge of the torchlight, stepped out from the fringes of the crowd and stood before Uthyr and Ygraine. His freckled face was sooty, and his robes were torn. But his dark brown eyes were steady.

"All is in readiness, my King," he said, gesturing toward the fallen warriors. "I await your command."

Susanna bowed low, her harp clutched between her hands. At Uthyr's gesture, she raised her clear voice in the traditional song of farewell to departing souls.

"In Gwlad Yr Haf, in the Land of Summer,
Still they live, still they live.
They shall not be killed, shall not be wounded.
No fire, no sun, no moon shall burn them.
No lake, no water, no sea shall drown them.
They lie in peace, and laugh and sing.
The dead are gone, yet still they live."

As the last note faded away, Uthyr stepped forth with Ygraine at his side. The King and Queen of the dying kingdom stood proudly and saluted the dead. "Farewell, brave men and women," Uthyr called up to the sky. "Fare you well until we meet again!"

"Go now, good souls, and await rebirth," Griffi intoned. "Go now and know you live on in our hearts. Go now to meadows sweet in the Land of Summer. Soon we shall meet again!" So saying Griffi raised his hands. Fire sprung from his fingertips. He gestured toward the bodies, and the flames shot forth, hungrily consuming the bodies.

Griffi lowered his hands and bowed his head in grief and loss. Susanna clasped his hand, her eyes brimming as she stared at the flames. Suddenly, her head snapped up, her eyes opened wide.

"Susanna!" Ygraine exclaimed, grabbing the Bard's arm.

Susanna turned to Uthyr, her blue eyes alight. "It is the Bards of northern Rhos! They speak to me! The Gwardas of Crueddyn and Uwch Dulas are leading them to our aid. They are over four hundred strong, and will be at our city gates by morning!"

Uthyr gestured for Cai and Bedwyr to attend him. "With these four hundred I will see Madoc driven from the field. Come, all of you, we have plans to make."

"Wait," Griffi cried. "Susanna, are there any Druids in their train?"

Her face clouded. "None," she said gently. "Their Druids have gone."

Griffi's shoulders slumped, and he turned toward the fire, not daring to look at anyone. Uthyr put his hand on the Druid's shoulder. "We knew this," Uthyr said. "There could have been no other answer."

"No one," Griffi said dully. "No one has defied the Archdruid."

"What is that to you?" Ygraine asked sharply.

Griffi's head snapped up, his eyes wide and hurt. "What is that to me? It is my honor at stake!"

"No," Ygraine said coldly. "It is not your honor. You alone hold that. You answer only for the honor of Griffi the Druid. And your honor remains. Unbroken. So you will stand, even to the last."

For a moment Griffi was silent, his head bowed. Then he slowly raised his face to the challenge in Ygraine's eyes. "Yes, my Queen. So I will stand. Even to the last."

Meirgdydd, Disglair Wythnos—late morning

TWO DAYS LATER, Uthyr led four hundred warriors out of Tegeingl, with the intent of finishing off Madoc's depleted forces.

In the battle yesterday, Madoc's army had been trapped

by Uthyr's remaining one hundred and fifty warriors and the fresh forces of northern Rhos. The two forces had closed in on Madoc like a hammer and anvil. But to Uthyr's disappointment, Madoc had not fought to the finish, but had gathered his weakened army and retreated south.

Uthyr, determined not to wait for his brother to find reinforcements, now led his warriors to finish off what yesterday had started. Cai was on his left and Bedwyr on his right as they rode through the countryside to come to grips with Madoc.

He turned to one of the Bards of northern Rhos who had come with him on this errand. Uthyr had left his own Bard, Susanna, back at the city to aid Ygraine, whose task it was to hold the walls. Not that Uthyr expected the city to see any action today. Their speculation on the movements of Menwaed of Arllechwedd was just that—speculation. As a precaution, Uthyr had left one of the Dewin from Rhos in the city with orders to scout the countryside for trouble. The other Dewin he had with him now, scouting for the whereabouts of Madoc's army.

Uthyr's warriors moved swiftly on their horses in the bright morning. They had come a good four leagues or so in the last few hours. The Dewin halted his horse and signaled to Uthyr. He pointed to the fringe of the great forest of Coed Dulas. "Here is where they shifted into the forest early this morning, as I saw in my Wind-Ride," the Dewin reported.

"Where are they now?"

The Dewin shook his head. "I'm not sure. I have been checking through the forest, but can see no sign of them."

Suddenly, the Bard stiffened in his saddle. Uthyr, his heart pounding, waited for him to speak. Blinking rapidly, the Bard fixed his gaze on Uthyr. "Susanna calls me. The Dewin has spotted the forces of Arllechwedd coming downriver from the north."

"What banner?" he asked urgently. "What banner do they fly?"

"They fly the banner of the golden boar. The banner of the Coranian Warleader."

"How many?"

"Over five hundred. And they are only an hour away by river. My King, they will reach the city before we do!"

"King Uthyr!" the Dewin shouted. "Madoc's army, I have spotted them! They doubled back toward the city, to join with Arllechwedd and attack!"

"Then we ride," Uthyr said, the grimness of his tone masking his terror. "We ride back to Tegeingl as though the hounds of Cerronnos himself are at our heels."

ALL THROUGH THAT terrible ride, the Dewin and the Bard rode next to Uthyr, each reporting what they were seeing and hearing from the city. The forces of Arllechwedd had attacked, but the city still held. The west gate had nearly been breached. Griffi's fire had so far been able to keep the back the enemy, but the other Druids were seeking to batter the gate with tremendous boulders. The city was moments away from destruction, but Ygraine still held on. Uthyr gritted his teeth and rode.

At last the sights and sounds of battle reached them. Quickly, Uthyr arrayed his army. No time for fine points now. They must break the battle at the west gate immediately. But as he rode down to the gates, his army shouting defiance behind him, he saw he was already too late. The gate had been burned to the ground, and the combined forces of Madoc and Menwaed were streaming into the city.

A shout of pure rage was torn from his throat as he hurled his horse into the beleaguered city. Behind him his warriors followed and began to do battle. With Cai on one side and Bedwyr on the other, Uthyr descended upon the enemy like a whirlwind. The three men hurled their spears, then, as one, drew their swords and began to kill.

Out of the corner of his eye, Uthyr saw Ygraine near the gate, calmly ordering the noncombatants to drench the flames. A group of warriors guarded the townsfolk as they fought the fire. If the fire gained a greater foothold into the city, it would all burn.

With a shout, Uthyr battled toward her, followed by Cai and Bedwyr. But the line of warriors surrounding the fire fighters was breached. Enemy warriors began to slaughter the towns-folk, their aim to let the fire rage.

Beside him, Cai gasped, then shouted "Nest!" He called out his wife's name, and she turned her head from fighting the fire just long enough to see the sword of the enemy warrior glitter before her eyes in the afternoon light. Just long enough to reach out a hand toward her husband as the blade buried itself in her chest. The enemy warrior wrenched the sword from her body and raised his blade for another blow when Garanwyn, Cai's son, leapt up and grabbed the warrior's wrist. Swift as lightning, the warrior pulled a short knife from his belt and stabbed the boy through the heart.

"No!" Cai's cry of despair and rage tore through the battle. "No!" He leapt from his horse, and before the enemy warrior could even turn, he grabbed the man from behind, snaked an arm across his windpipe, and in one abrupt motion broke the man's neck.

Sobbing, Cai knelt on the ground, cradling the bloody body of his wife in his arms, rocking and moaning, begging her not to leave him. With his other hand, he reached for his son, laying still on the ground in a pool of blood.

Uthyr tried to go to Cai, but both he and Bedwyr were too hardly pressed. If Cai didn't get to his feet and back to the fight soon, he would die.

But then Ygraine was there, pulling Nest from his arms, pushing Cai to his feet, back toward the battle. "They're dead, Cai! You can't help them!" she shouted. "Your place is with my husband! Kill them, Cai! Kill them all!"

Cai's face changed. The pain flooded away and a terrible need took its place. A need to see the blood of others run into the ground as the blood of his family had. A need to deal out death as mercilessly as it had been dealt out to his wife and son.

All this Uthyr saw in the face of his Captain, as Cai changed into someone Uthyr had never seen before, changed into someone that Uthyr could never know.

All through that terrible day, as Uthyr's warriors slowly reclaimed their city, Cai killed and killed, and killed again. But it was not enough. It would never be enough.

Addiendydd, Disglair Wythnos—afternoon

TWO DAYS LATER, Uthyr paced the north watchtower, straining his eyes for signs of his scouts returning. He had not wanted to send Cai and Bedwyr north to spy on the enemy army. But both Dewin had been killed in the battle a few days before, and there was no one left to Wind-Ride. So, Uthyr had to rely on more mundane methods to find out the strength of the enemy.

For two days they had battled the combined forces of Madoc

and Menwaed. Finally, what was left of the enemy had again retreated—but they had gone north this time. North for what? That was the question that bothered him. And he was afraid that he knew the answer. The Coranians were coming from the north.

This morning he had called the remaining warriors together. Three hundred men and women had gathered to hear his orders. He had given them a choice. They could quit the city today, with honor, and escort the remaining townsfolk to safety. Or they could stay with him and face the Coranian forces he knew were coming. Though each warrior knew that this last battle was hopeless, they had all elected to stay. He wished he could give them something better than death. But he had nothing else to give.

Movement in the fading afternoon light caught his eye. Two warriors rode swiftly from the north. Uthyr gave a shout, alerting the guards to open the gate. He hastily descended from the tower and rushed to the north gate. Even as he got there, Cai and Bedwyr rode in, their horses lathered and trembling with fatigue. As the two men dismounted, Ygraine, Susanna, and Griffi came running up.

Uthyr picked up a water bucket and handed the brimming dipper to Cai. The Captain drank noisily, while Griffi picked up another bucket and helped Bedwyr to drink.

At last catching his breath, Cai panted, "They come. Over one thousand strong. Along with what is left of Madoc's and Menwaed's forces. In ships from the north."

"When will they be here?" Uthyr asked quietly.

"Tomorrow," Bedwyr rasped. "Morning."

"Ah," Uthyr said. It was no more than he had expected.

He turned to Ygraine. In a tone that would brook no argument, he said, "You leave now."

"Husband—"

"Now!" he shouted. "This moment. No more arguments. No more!"

Ygraine said nothing. She bowed her head. Uthyr went to her, put his hand beneath her chin, and raised her head. The sheen of tears made her dark eyes sparkle. But she was too proud to let the tears fall.

"Morrigan," Uthyr said, naming their daughter.

"Morrigan," she whispered.

"Yours to protect, yours to see Queen of Gwynedd. I leave her in your hands."

She swallowed hard, her dark eyes searching his face. She straightened her slim shoulders. "I will not fail you," she said clearly.

"No. I know you will not." He grasped her hand, then turned to Cai. "Honor your promise to me. See her safely to the mountains."

"My King, I cannot go."

"Yes," Uthyr went on implacably. "You have given me your oath."

Cai drew himself up. "You shame me, Uthyr. I, the Captain of your warriors, the PenGwernan of Gwynedd, to be sent from your side."

"You are my daughter's Captain now. I give to you the lives of my wife and my daughter. Remember your oath to me and have done with this argument. Bedwyr, you go with your uncle and the Queen."

"My King—"

"Do it," he said shortly. "Your role in this life is not over. Go with them."

"Susanna," Uthyr said to his Bard. She stood stiffly by Griffi's side, her hands gripping her lover's arm. "You go with them."

"No."

"Yes. Come here."

Slowly she approached Uthyr and Ygraine. Speaking softly, he said, "Years ago you tested my son. You are one of the few who know what he is."

"Please—" she began.

"No. You have a task to finish. Your life is to be given to seeing my son reign in Cadair Idris. You will give Gwydion all the help you can, in my name."

For a long time she was silent. Then she said softly, "Very well, my King. It shall be as you say. But Griffi will give you trouble. He won't want to go."

"Then he will not."

"What?" she said, shocked, her voice rising. "You would have me leave him?"

Swiftly Griffi crossed to Uthyr's side. "You will let me stay?" he asked eagerly.

"You may stay, if you wish," Uthyr said. "But you, Susanna, must go."

"Never. Not without Griffi. I won't—"

"For the reason I have just given you, you will. You know what that reason is. Is it not enough for you, this reason?" Uthyr asked quietly.

Susanna opened her mouth, then shut it. She bowed her head, and her tears dropped to the ground.

"Go now," Uthyr said, his eyes traveling from Ygraine's

pale face, to Cai, to Bedwyr, to Susanna, then back again to his wife. "Griffi and I will fight a last battle of which the Bards will sing."

Susanna raised her tear-streaked face, her eyes fastened on the face of her lover. Slowly, she nodded. "Yes," she whispered. "The Bards will sing of it."

Uthyr called for the fresh horses he had ordered. He had already seen to it that their belongings were packed and ready. He helped his wife to mount her horse. Then he took the torque of Gwynedd from his neck and pressed it into her cold hands.

"For Morrigan," he said softly.

"Yes," she whispered. "For her."

Uthyr removed his helmet and held it out to her. The hawk's sapphire eyes sparkled. "This, too, for her. She will need it on the day she returns to take back what I will lose today."

"I love you, Uthyr ap Rathteyn," Ygraine said fiercely. "I will love only you until the day I die."

"May that day be far, far off, my lady. Yet on that day, I will be waiting in Gwlad Yr Haf to greet you. You will see me again. I swear it."

"I will hold you to that promise," she whispered. Gently she bent down and touched his face with her hand. And then she rode away. She did not look back.

Meirgdydd, Disglair Wythnos—morning

UTHYR AND GRIFFI sat calmly on their horses just outside the open north gate of the city. They watched without comment as the dust from over a thousand tramping feet rose over the horizon, signaling that the Coranian forces were nearing Tegeingl.

The morning dawned bright and clear. A slight breeze

stirred through the unmoving ranks of Uthyr's warriors. Three hundred men and women sat upon their horses proudly. Their spears and shields shone bright and deadly. And in their grim, set faces was the knowledge that they would die, and the determination to sell their lives at the greatest possible cost.

A glimmer to the north winked in the distance. At last the enemy army itself could be seen. On foot they poured over the blameless green hills. There were over a thousand soldiers. They carried shields and huge battle-axes. Daggers were tucked into the tops of black leather boots. They wore byrnies to their knees and heavy iron helmets.

"Formidable," Griffi said quietly.

"They'll move slower in battle. Heavy helmets, and those byrnies. And they do not ride. We should be able to do some damage before it's over."

"Good enough," Griffi said. "But don't you think it would be best to fight them from behind the city walls? Instead of out here in the open?"

"No," Uthyr said absently, still scanning the distant army. "I don't want them damaging the city too much. It will be Morrigan's, one day."

"Ah, yes. Of course. Look, there's Madoc."

Madoc was striding at the forefront of the mighty army. Next to him was a Coranian. The man wore a metal byrnie, trimmed in silver, and green trousers tucked into black boots. A huge battle-ax was in his hands. He wore a helmet of silver, with the figure of a boar fashioned at the top of it. Blond hair flowed from beneath the helmet. His handsome features were arrogant. The commander, without a doubt.

Uthyr's eyes were drawn back toward Madoc, back to the

brother who had betrayed him.

"Foolish of Madoc to stand in the forefront, don't you think?" Griffi said, reading Uthyr's mind.

Uthyr grinned a wolfish grin. "Very foolish." He raised the horn of Gwynedd to his lips and blew the challenge. His horse leapt forward, Griffi's horse keeping pace with his. Behind them, the rest of the warriors gave a mighty shout and began their last ride.

MADOC GASPED AS Uthyr rode straight toward him, his warriors following behind. "Uthyr's crazy," he said in disbelief.

"Looks like he's coming straight for you," Catha smiled unpleasantly.

"Well, hold him off. Do something! By the gods, there are over a thousand warriors here. Kill him!"

"Oh, I think not," Catha said lazily. "It looks like he wants to talk to you. Let's give him a chance, shall we?"

At Catha's signal, the Coranian forces broke and ran across the field to close with the Kymric warriors, and the slaughter began. But the warriors left Uthyr alone. Catha would let the King approach. And see what the man would do.

UTHYR RODE THROUGH the ranks of the Coranian warriors, who seemed to melt from his path. Griffi still kept pace with him. He could see Madoc standing as though frozen at the top of a low hill.

With a shout, Griffi rose in his stirrups and began to gesture toward the Coranian commander. But the commander must have understood what was coming, for before the shout had died from Griffi's lips, the commander had thrown his ax.

Griffi froze on his horse, astonishment spread across his freckled face as he looked down to see the ax buried in his chest. Blood bubbled from his mouth, and his lips moved. "Susanna," he whispered, then toppled from his horse.

Catha calmly bent over the dead Druid, wrenching his ax from Griffi's chest. He turned toward Uthyr, arresting the King's movement toward his friend's still body.

"I am Catha, brother of Ceadda, the Eorl of Pecsaetan, in the country of Mierce, in the Coranian Empire. My Bana has come to take this land. Surrender to me now."

Uthyr laughed. He leapt from his horse, then grasped the dagger from his boot. "I am Uthyr ap Rathtyen var Awst, King of Gwynedd. And neither myself nor my people will surrender to you."

"Your warriors are even now being slaughtered," Catha said, gesturing toward the bloody meadow.

"But they sell their lives dearly. So shall we all."

"You will all be defeated."

"For a time, Catha, brother of Ceadda. For a time."

Catha's brow rose. "And then?"

"And then death will come to you all. At that moment, remember me. Don't move, Madoc," Uthyr hissed.

Madoc, who had been slowly backing away, halted. Uthyr turned back to Catha. "This," he said, gesturing contemptuously at Madoc, "is my brother. My half-brother. I have better ones than this, of course."

"Of course. I have met Gwydion ap Awst. In Corania."

Uthyr nodded. "He will bring you all down, one day."

Catha grinned unpleasantly. "Words, King Uthyr. Just words."

"You will see. For now, my other brother and I have unfinished business."

"Go to it, then," Catha said.

"You will not interfere?" Uthyr asked.

"I will not interfere. For the moment."

"Catha!" Madoc gasped.

"Are you a man?" Catha asked, contempt in his blue eyes. "Fight your brother, Madoc, you who think you should be King."

Without another word, Uthyr closed in on Madoc. Back and forth they fought, daggers in hand, twisting and slashing. Then Madoc stumbled. Uthyr grinned. He had known Madoc would be no match for him.

But as he raised his dagger to strike, a huge, burning pain slashed across his back. Falling to the ground, he felt another wrench as something was pulled from his body. A foot planted itself on his shoulder, then turned him over so that he was lying on his back. He tried to get up, but could not move. Blinking sweat from his eyes, he looked up into the face of the Coranian commander.

Sighing, Catha said, "You are the better man, King Uthyr. But I could not let you kill such a fine tool."

The morning light wavered in front of Uthyr's eyes, the colors bleeding from his sight. He blinked again, for everything had become suddenly bright. Catha's face, Madoc's face, faded from his sight as a white light built before his eyes.

He whispered the names of his wife and daughter, and held up his son's image before his eyes, for, even in death, he would not speak Arthur's name to the enemy.

He thought of his brother, Gwydion, whom he loved so. He would leave his family in Gwydion's capable, faithful hands.

And that thought comforted him.

A sigh escaped him as blood bubbled from his lips. He was ready now. And as the Shining Ones came to take him away, he whispered his dying thanks that his prayer had been answered.

He had not died at Madoc's hands. And it was enough.

WHEN EVENING FELL, their party was just at the fringes of the huge forest of Coed Dulas. Tomorrow they would venture across the border into the cantref of Rosyr and follow the tiny secondary roads that wound through the mountains.

Ygraine knew that Uthyr was dead. Sometime that morning, as they rode silently through the forest, she had felt a wrench inside. This world no longer contained the living soul of her husband. She rode numbly, barely seeing the forest around her. She was not even aware that night had fallen until Cai called for a halt.

Wearily, she dismounted at the edge of the clearing, tying her horse to a nearby bush. Bedwyr was already digging a shallow hole.

"We risk a fire?" she heard Susanna ask Cai.

"Not much of a risk. The enemy is busy elsewhere. And it will be a small fire," Cai had answered.

Morrigan, Ygraine thought desperately. She forcibly turned her thoughts to her daughter, to the only reason why she had not died with her husband today. And now, now that she knew she was truly alone in this world, now that there was no one who would ever again try to reach behind her icy walls, she knew that her reason to live had not been enough. The world would never again hold anything for her.

Involuntarily, she glanced up and caught Cai's face as he

stared into the fire. It was the face of a dying man, the face of a man who had nothing left to care for. Susanna sat down with a tired sigh. Her blue eyes were sad and dull.

For a time no one spoke. Ygraine knew that they were each holding the dead in their thoughts. At last Cai said, "I will see you all safely to Mynydd Tawel. Then I will go. Bedwyr, you will be Morrigan's Captain."

"Where will you go?" Bedwyr asked, startled.

"Back to Tegeingl. To kill Madoc if Uthyr has not done so."

Ygraine nodded. "Fine. I go with you."

"No," Cai's eyes flashed. "Uthyr gave me a last command. To see you safely to the mountains. And I will. After that, my life is my own."

"After that, your life can be measured in minutes!" Susanna exclaimed. "Don't be a fool."

"A fool? Only a fool would outlive his King."

"Uthyr ordered you—" Bedwyr began.

"To see the Queen to safety. And I will."

"But you can't keep me there," Ygraine pointed out. "I will return with you. As you say, only a fool would outlive their King."

"Uthyr told you to look after Morrigan," Susanna said quietly. "You promised."

"Uthyr's gone. My promise to a dead man does not hold."

Susanna reached for her harp case. She opened the leather bag and pulled out a crumpled parchment. "I have a letter here. From the Dreamer."

A letter from the Dreamer, from the man who had broken Ygraine's heart by taking her son away? What did she care for Gwydion's words?

"He gave it to Uthyr, who gave it to me when he was last here. He said that I would know when to open it. And I do," Susanna went on.

"The Dreamer has nothing to say to me," Ygraine spat.

"Nor to me," Cai said abruptly. "I tell you, I am going back there."

Without another word, Susanna opened the parchment and began to read aloud.

To: Ygraine ur Custennin and Cai ap Cynyr,

By now Uthyr and Griffi are dead. Cai's family has perished. Tegeingl and Gwynedd are lost.

My heart goes out to you in the face of so many losses. But you must not give up. A great task awaits all of you. Gather the survivors, and make for the hiding place that Uthyr prepared for you. By stealth and by cunning you must gather a teulu that will become a thorn in the side of the enemy. From this seed will come a mighty army. For one day soon the High King will come again. And when he does, he will lead us to take back our own. I command you, in the name of the High King soon to be, that you take on this task. Though you may wish to die, you are commanded to live. This is your duty to Kymru.

Gwydion ap Awst var Celemon
Dreamer of Kymru

Cai bowed his head. Bedwyr walked over to his uncle, knelt down next to him, and put a hand on his shoulder. After a few moments, Cai reached up and laid his hand on top of his nephew's.

And Ygraine knew Cai would not go back to Tegeingl. He

would do as Gwydion had commanded. In the name of the High King to be, Gwydion had written. The High King to be. Her own son. She remembered her promises. With a voice she could scarcely recognize as her own, she turned to Susanna. "His death song. Do you have it?"

Susanna nodded, her eyes bright with unshed tears.

"Sing it, then," Ygraine whispered. "Sing."

And in the dark forest, by the fitful light of the dying fire, Susanna sang.

"A billow of death over the land,
A wave in which the brave
Fell among his companions.
Preeminent is Uthyr
even before the grave.

"There is blood in the ground,
the fields run red.
Before the supremacy of terrors,
he was fierce, dauntless, irresistible.

"Long is the sun's course
Longer still our memories for
Uthyr of the bright heart.
Truly valiant was he
All the days of his life."

Somewhere far away, a wolf howled in loss.

"A thorn in the side of the enemy," Cai said softly. He raised his head and looked at Ygraine. "I like the sound of that."

Slowly, she nodded. She liked the sound of that, too.

Chapter 20

Gwytheryn, Kymru
Gwernan Mis, 497

Meirgdydd, Lleihau Wythnos—morning

When Havgan first caught sight of Y Ty Dewin, gleaming in the morning light like precious ivory from Carthage, he felt as though he had come home.

It was a feeling he rejected the moment he felt it. He had come to Kymru to conquer the witches, to kill them as his God had commanded. Not to become one with them. Not to feel anything for them but loathing and hatred and contempt. Not ever.

Y Ty Dewin, the college where the Dewin, the clairvoyant physicians, learned their skills, was a pentagonal-shaped building built of white stone. To the east of the building, a grove of ash trees stood, surrounding a stream of sparkling water that flowed in a five-sided shape around a central pool. It was early spring, and the trees had not yet put forth their leaves. Long, purple flowers hung in clusters from the branches. Many petals had already dropped from the trees, covering the ground like a violet carpet.

To the north, huge gardens were laid out where the Dewin had grown medicinal herbs for healing balms and concoctions. The gardens had been stripped. Bare branches of chamomile, of comfrey and fennel, of horehound, pennyroyal, and rosemary, drooped dispiritedly above the unwatered ground.

Behind him, his army spilled over the plain. The clear morning light gleamed off of the helmets, shields, and byrnies of his warriors; glistened off their spears and battle-axes; sparkled off the bright yellow robes of the preosts of Lytir; even set the black robes of the wyrce-jaga to shimmering darkly.

Havgan himself was a figure of shining gold. His metal byrnie was chased with gold. Beneath it he wore a golden tunic, and gold trousers were tucked into black boots. His honey-blond hair was covered with the golden helm of the Warleader. On top of the helm, the figure of a boar with ivory tusks and ruby eyes glowered. At his waist hung the Bana's sword, with its hilt of gold and rubies.

At last, the Golden Man had come to Kymru.

After landing eleven days ago off the coast of Ystrad Marchell, Havgan had led his three thousand men directly to Gwytheryn by way of Sarn Ermyn, the great east/west road that bisected the island. And for the last eleven days, Kymru had slowly curled up and died. The invasion was almost complete.

Everything had gone as planned—in spite of the fact that Gwydion had obviously seen Havgan's secret plans. That bit of spying had done the Dreamer no good, because Gwydion hadn't known of the traitors within Kymru, whose actions had tipped the balance. At the time Gwydion had seen the plans, even Havgan hadn't known of these traitors. It wasn't until a man claiming to be from Kymru had come to him that

Havgan knew anything about those who were willing to betray their country. That the chief of them had been the Archdruid himself had been quite a surprise, but one Havgan had instantly understood was to his advantage. He had taken the Archdruid's offer.

For now.

In Ederynion, Queen Olwen had been killed on the second day of the invasion. Her daughter, Elen, had been captured. It would be easy to rule Ederynion through the captured princess. Prince Lludd, Olwen's son, had somehow escaped the carnage, but the boy would be hunted down and killed soon enough.

In Prydyn, Penda's forces had aided Erfin, King Rhoram's brother-in-law, in taking Arberth. Erfin had sworn that he had killed the King, though Rhoram's body had disappeared. Rhoram's heir, Prince Geriant, had also escaped. Still, these were minor matters. All of Prydyn was now Havgan's, and he would rule that land through Erfin.

In Rheged the final battle had been fought on the fifth day of the invasion. Baldred reported that King Urien, Queen Ellirri, and their heir, Prince Elphin, had all been killed. As ordered, Baldred had then set up that fool, Morcant Whledig, as the new King of Rheged. Havgan had agreed to let Bledri, the traitorous Dewin, live and share in Morcant's newfound power. Through these two, Havgan would rule Rheged. Yet there were three children of the dead King and Queen still unaccounted for.

He had received word just this morning that, four days ago, King Uthyr had been killed by Catha. Now Gwynedd was in his hands, too. And Madoc was King of Gwynedd, as planned. Uthyr's Queen had managed to escape the city. His heir, Princess Morrigan, had also not been found. But they would be.

Now there were only a few more places yet to subdue. Y Ty Dewin and Neuadd Gorsedd, the colleges of the Dewin and Bards, would be taken. The witches there would be killed, and their great colleges given to Havgan's own preosts and his witch hunters. Then on to Caer Duir, to meet with his new ally, Cathbad the Archdruid.

Then, and only then, would he journey to Cadair Idris. He would enter Cadair Idris in the name of his God and become the High King of all Kymru. Then the land would be truly his. In spite of Gwydion, Havgan's false, traitorous friend, the man whom he had called brother, the man whom he had loved and whom he now hated in full measure. Gwydion, his enemy.

He would find the Dreamer. Find him and kill him.

But all that would be later. Today, they would deal with the Dewin.

The gleaming building was quiet. The great, silvery doors were firmly shut. The tinkling of the stream was the only sound about the place. He had hoped to spit the Dewin on spears before the doors. But it was not to be. They had all run. Not one had been left to face him.

But in that he was wrong.

As Havgan mounted the steps with Sigerric, now Over-General of Kymru, with Sledda, now the Arch-wyrce-jaga of this land, and with Eadwig, the new Archbyshop of Kymru, close behind, the doors opened.

From a pool of shadow between the doors, a man stepped out. He wore a formal robe of rich sea green trimmed with silver. The man's gray hair gleamed. His eyes gazed gravely at Havgan and his army. The man's face was lined with pain, and a faint sheen of sweat beaded his brow. But he stood proudly, as though he, not Havgan, was the one with an army at his back.

"Who are you?" Sledda inquired in his harsh voice.

But the man ignored the wyrce-jaga. Instead, his gaze was fastened on Havgan, and something within the stranger's gray eyes flickered with recognition. "You are the Warleader?" the man asked, astonishment written over the lines of pain on his face.

"I am Havgan, son of Hengist, Bana of the Coranian Empire. I demand that you surrender this place to me."

The man shrugged, still not taking his eyes from Havgan. "You may have it, for now. There is nothing here for you. All my people have gone to safety."

"Where?" Sledda asked eagerly.

The man shrugged again. "Elsewhere."

"You will tell us where the witches are hiding if you want to save your life, old man," Sledda hissed.

"I have a sickness in my body that is killing me even as we stand here," the man said, quite calmly. "I will be dead soon and beyond your threats. I am Cynan ap Einon var Darun, the Ardewin of Kymru, and I have chosen to stay here to warn you."

Havgan's brows raised. His amber eyes glinted. "Warn us? You will warn us? Kymru is mine, Ardewin. Mine. My generals have taken each of your kingdoms. And I have come to take Cadair Idris."

"You cannot," Cynan said calmly. "The Doors will not let you in."

"You think any doors can hold against me and my army?" Havgan asked contemptuously.

"These will hold. You cannot get into that mountain, Warleader. You are foolish to try. Listen now to my warning.

You must leave Kymru. And maybe you will live."

Havgan's amber eyes narrowed dangerously. "You dare to threaten me?" he inquired softly.

"You do not believe me," Cynan went on calmly. "I did not expect that you would. Yet when I saw you, I knew I owed it to those I had loved long ago to try."

Eadwig, the Archbyshop, asked curiously, "What do you mean?"

And then Cynan opened his mouth to tell them. Quicker than thought, Havgan buried the blade of his dagger deep into the man's chest. Blood spilled over his hand as he twisted the blade, seeking to ensure that Cynan did not speak, though he did not know what it was he feared to hear.

Cynan's dying gray eyes caught and held Havgan's amber ones. With his last breath, Cynan mouthed a word that only Havgan heard—a word that would haunt his dreams, the only place where he would allow the memory to come to him. A word he would hide from himself, even as he heard it, from that moment until the day he died.

Nephew, the dying man had whispered. *Nephew.*

Gwyntdydd, Lleihau Wythnos—late afternoon
THE SILENCE HUNG heavily over Neuadd Gorsedd, the college of the Bards. Just to the east of the building a grove of birch trees stood. The white trunks and drooping branches, covered with tiny, yellow flowers, sagged heavily in the stillness.

The huge, triangular-shaped building of shadowy blue stone loomed above them as Havgan, trailed by Sigerric and Sledda, slowly mounted the stone steps. He was half expecting a Bard to come out of the doors to greet them.

But there was no one. The Bards were gone. They had not even bothered to bar the doors, which opened smoothly at Havgan's touch. His eyes, momentarily blinded by the morning sun, could make out only a shadowy corridor.

"Be careful," Sledda warned, nervously licking his lips as his beady eyes darted over the corridor. "There may be traps."

"I doubt it," Sigerric replied contemptuously.

"It's possible," the wyrce-jaga flared. "Else why would they desert the place?"

"Maybe they just didn't feel like being killed today," Sigerric answered dryly.

Havgan did not even bother to comment. He walked down the corridor to another closed door and opened it. The great hall of the Bards of Kymru was filled with silent shadows. The two-storied chamber echoed hollowly with the sound of their footsteps. Rows of empty wooden benches lined the hall. On the far wall Havgan could just make out a huge banner of blue and white. He came closer and saw the outstretched wings of a nightingale with sapphire eyes, so lifelike that, for a moment, he wondered that it was not singing.

"They have gone," Sledda said in disappointment. "There are no witches here."

"And no traps," Sigerric said, cocking a sardonic brow at the witch hunter.

"They had their escape planned, long before our arrival," Havgan said.

"Gwydion," Sigerric said.

"Yes. Gwydion's warning has cheated us of getting our hands on these witches."

"Yet Cathbad might know where they are," Sledda volunteered.

"The Archdruid had better," Havgan said grimly. He turned to Sledda. "Since I have given Y Ty Dewin to the preosts of Lytir for their headquarters, you and your wyrce-jaga may have Neuadd Gorsedd for your own."

Sledda smiled and bowed slightly, satisfaction in every line of his thin body.

"Of course," Havgan went on smoothly, "you will have many tasks to perform, so you won't be here that often."

Sigerric grinned as Sledda's smile faded. "Won't be here often?" Sledda faltered.

"Your job is to hunt witches, isn't it?" Havgan said impatiently. "And this land is full of them. The Bards and the Dewin. They went somewhere. And you will find them."

He strode from the room, through the shadowy, empty corridors and back out to the stone steps. No witches here. No witches at all. For a moment it seemed to him as though all Gwytheryn was empty, mocking him.

Where had they gone? Where had the Dewin and the Bards run to?

ANIERON, MASTER BARD of Kymru, sat on a convenient log and took off his boot with a sigh. He upended it, and a stone fell out onto the forest floor.

"I told you," Anieron said to his brother. "And you said it was because I was old."

"You are old," Dudod replied equably.

"You are only two years younger than me," Anieron pointed out. "If I am old, what does that make you?"

"Younger," Dudod said with a grin, his green eyes laughing. "As always."

Cariadas turned her head to hide a smile, but it died almost before it had begun.

"Leave my da alone, Dudod," Elstar said as she tethered her horse to a tree at the edge of the clearing. "Here, gather firewood. Make yourself useful."

Dudod, still grinning, made his way back into the forest.

"Da," Elstar went on, "those horses could use some looking after. And then why don't you scrounge around in the packs, see what we've got for dinner?"

Anieron cocked a brow at the daughter who was so carelessly ordering him about. But perhaps something he saw in Elstar's face set him limping off to the horses without another word. He began to murmur softly to the tired horses as he unloaded their saddlebags.

"Come here, Cariadas," Elstar said gently, taking Anieron's place on the log.

Obediently, Cariadas came to sit next to the Ardewin's heir. "Where did Elidyr go?" Cariadas asked.

"My husband is Wind-Riding, gathering news." Gently, the woman put her arms around the girl's taut shoulders. "What's wrong?"

Cariadas sat quietly, fighting to hold back a rush of tears. Finally, she whispered, "Da. I'm scared something has happened to him."

"Believe me, child," Elstar said in an acerbic tone, "if there is anyone who can look out for himself, it's Gwydion ap Awst."

"But no one even knows where he is. There's been no word at all."

"He's in hiding. The Warleader and his Coranian generals know him by sight."

"And will kill him," Cariadas whispered.

"If they can," Elstar agreed. "But your Da is clever. And Rhiannon is with him. She can be trusted to keep him from doing anything too crazy."

"No one can stop Da from doing anything he wants to do," Cariadas said with an odd sort of pride.

"I think Rhiannon might very well be up to that job," Elstar retorted crisply.

At that moment Dudod returned to the clearing, holding armfuls of dead wood. Dudod spotted Anieron rummaging through the packs. "You're not cooking, are you?" Dudod asked nervously.

"What if I am?" Anieron demanded.

"Then I'll eat bark tonight. It's better than anything you can put together."

Young as she was, Cariadas understood that the two men were trying to distract them from the cares and grief that weighed upon them in the twelfth day of their desperate flight through war-torn Rheged to reach the caves of Allt Llwyd.

Theirs had been the last group of Dewin and Bards to leave Gwytheryn—a group the Coranians would love to get their hands on: Anieron, the Master Bard, and his brother, Dudod; Elstar, Anieron's daughter and the Ardewin's heir; Elstar's husband, Elidyr, Dudod's son and heir to the Master Bard; and Cariadas herself, heir to the Dreamer.

Elidyr came back to the clearing. Elstar looked up from the tiny fire she was kindling. Her face tightened at the look in her husband's eyes. "The children?"

"They are well. Their band is still four days ahead of us." Very gently, he went on, "I have news of Cynan."

"He's dead, isn't he?" Elstar asked quietly. "The illness?"

"No. The Warleader," Elidyr said, his voice clipped.

"The Ardewin dead. Oh, poor Cynan," Elstar said, her voice full of tears.

Anieron pulled something from his tunic. He came to Elstar and held out a shimmering torque of silver and pearls. Without a word, he clasped the torque around his daughter's neck. Elstar, her head still bowed, laid her hand hesitantly against her throat, fingering the necklace.

"You are Ardewin, now, daughter," Anieron said. "There is no sacred grove of ash trees where The Lady of the Waters can come to you. But she is here nonetheless. Tonight you must go into the woods and hear her words to you."

Dudod made a swift gesture of negation, then just as swiftly suppressed it as Anieron caught Dudod's eye. "It would be best, brother, if you gathered more firewood," Anieron said firmly.

"Ah, yes. Good idea."

Before Cariadas could even gather her wits to ask what was going on, Dudod vanished into the forest. Both Elstar and Elidyr were frowning in puzzlement at Anieron.

Say nothing, Anieron spoke to their minds. *Act naturally.*

"What did you find for dinner?" Elstar asked her father.

"Cheese and bread. How about that?" Anieron replied casually.

"Lazy," Elidyr grinned. "Let's take a look at those packs. I think a nice stew would go down very smoothly. Stew is my specialty."

A rustling in the bushes made them all jump. Anieron, moving very swiftly for an old man, darted toward the sound and was lost to sight. "What's he doing?" Cariadas asked of no one in particular. "I don't—"

And then, as Dudod and Anieron between them led a small figure into the clearing, she did understand. The girl was disheveled and dirty as though she had been sleeping on the ground for many nights. Her reddish brown hair was dusty and tangled. Her gray eyes were red-rimmed as though she had been weeping continuously.

"Sinend?" Cariadas asked, in confusion. "What are you doing here?"

"Now that's a good question," Anieron said smoothly. "Just what is the daughter of the Archdruid's heir doing here? You've been following us since we left Gwytheryn."

"Were you spying on us? For the Archdruid?" Elidyr asked roughly. Sinend's head shot up. She shook her head, but did not reply.

"Does he know where you are?" Elstar asked.

"No," Sinend replied, speaking for the first time. "Oh, no."

"You found out, didn't you?" Cariadas guessed. "You found out what Cathbad and your Da were doing. You didn't know before."

Sinend's shoulders began to shake. Cariadas went to her friend and put her arms around her. "She didn't know," Cariadas said pleadingly, looking up at Anieron and Dudod. The two men said nothing but exchanged a look that spoke volumes.

"Why don't we let Sinend speak for herself?" Elstar suggested coldly.

Sinend fought for control. Slowly the tremors died down. Grief and shame were written in the tired lines of her face. At last, she whispered, "I heard them talking. They didn't know I was there."

"I knew Cathbad was planning something with the enemy, and that Aergol was fully aware of it," Anieron said coolly. "But I don't understand what they get by supporting the Warleader. The Coranians think that the Druids, like the Bards and the Dewin, are witches. How does Cathbad get protection for the Druids? What does he hope to gain?"

"Cathbad wants the old days of Lyonesse back," Sinend said tonelessly, "when the Druids were the only power. When there were no Bards, no Dewin. No Dreamers."

"So Cathbad wants to rid Kymru of all but his Druids. And the Warleader will gladly kill any witches he can get his hands on. But what does the warleader get for sparing the Druids after they have helped him win his battles?"

"Kymric priests of the Coranian god."

"What?" Cariadas exclaimed.

"The Druids will give their allegiance to Lytir, the Warleader's god. They will help to convert all of Kymru. That's what the Warleader wants."

"The Warleader wants to convert Kymru?" Anieron asked incredulously.

Sinend nodded. Anieron and Dudod looked blankly at each other for a moment. Then Dudod began to grin. And Anieron grinned back. And then the two men were laughing in genuine delight.

"Convert the Kymri," Anieron managed to say through his laughter.

Dudod sputtered. "Oh, this is really something. I can't believe it."

"Cathbad's mad," Elstar said wonderingly. "Quite mad."

"They all are," Sinend said quietly.

THE MAN STOOD silently in front of the doors of Caer Duir, the college of the Druids. The golden doors glimmered in the torchlight. The emeralds that marked out the runes for Modron, the Great Mother, winked balefully.

The steps to the great, round building of black stone were lined with Druids in their cowled brown robes, silently watching Havgan and Sigerric mount the steps. To the west of the main structure, a slim tower rose up, piercing the night sky. Havgan had been told that this was the observation tower, which the Druids used to study the stars. To the east a grove of oak trees stood dark and silent.

The man at the top of the steps bowed. "I am Aergol, heir to the Archdruid," he said. His smooth saturnine features gave nothing away. His dark eyes were opaque as he glanced at Havgan's army settling down to camp for the night in front of the college.

"And the Archdruid? Where is he?" Sigerric asked.

"He waits to greet you in his quarters. Please follow me."

Torches burned at regular intervals throughout the corridors. The stairs were worn smooth with generations of scurrying feet. The Druid led them down another corridor, then opened a plain door of sturdy oak.

The room was bright with the light of hundreds of candles. A fire burned in the massive hearth. The floor was covered with fine, intricately woven carpets of green and brown. Tapestries covered the walls, worked in black and silver, each showing a different segment of the night sky. Massive tables of oak were covered with papers and books and strange instruments, the purpose of which Havgan did not know. Jeweled vessels of gold were strewn carelessly about the room, goblets and chalices chased with emeralds, platters and plates rimmed with precious stones.

Before the hearth a gray-haired man sat in a massive chair of oak. He wore a fine robe of green, trimmed with bands of brown. A torque with two circles of gold-studded emeralds glittered around his thin neck. His eyes were dark and—this was something Havgan had already been prepared for—quite mad.

Cathbad rose and lifted a thin hand, gesturing for Havgan to sit in the other chair in front of the fire. Havgan sat while Sigerric stood behind Havgan's chair, and Aergol took up a similar position behind Cathbad's.

The Archdruid silently poured wine into a golden goblet and handed it to Havgan. "My lord Havgan, Bana of the Coranian Empire, I am Cathbad ap Goreu var Efa. I trust your journey was pleasant?"

"The Dewin and the Bards have gone," Havgan said abruptly. "Where?"

Cathbad's face hardened. "Anieron, the Master Bard. That fox. He found out. He must have, else he would have included the Druids in his plans for escape."

"You were clumsy."

"I was not clumsy," Cathbad said sharply. "Anieron is wily. And clever. There is nothing that man cannot discover."

"Then you do not know where they have gone," Havgan said flatly. "I am displeased." The understatement was palpable. Cathbad stiffened.

"I have done as we agreed. I have given you the support of my Druids in your battles. I have given you their services for your God. And you will rid Kymru of the Dewin and the Bards. And the Dreamer. That was our agreement."

"We of the Coranian Empire call Druids witches, too," Sigerric said softly.

"You would be unwise to turn on me now. There is far too much to be gained by working together. Now, to business," Cathbad went on briskly, anxious to turn the conversation. "Aergol here is my heir. His daughter, Sinend, will be Archdruid after him. Aergol, fetch Sinend so that she may greet the Warleader."

But Aergol did not move. Instead, he gazed into the fire as though he had never seen one before. "I cannot," Aergol said softly. "She is gone."

"Gone! When? Where?" Cathbad asked in a shrill voice.

Aergol shrugged. "I am not sure. It has been some days since she has been seen."

"You saw her go," Havgan accused.

"She is my daughter," Aergol said defiantly. "If I let her go, it is no business of yours, Warleader."

"So, your daughter did not agree to your plans. How many more Druids will feel that way when you make them fully known?"

"None," Cathbad said sharply. "I have made sure of that."

"As sure as you were about Sinend?"

"She is young. And idealistic. The rest of my Druids are not."

"Where is Gwydion ap Awst?" Havgan asked suddenly. "I want that Dreamer."

Cathbad's face was filmed over by a look of stony hatred. "I do not know."

"He told you about the invasion, I know. Did he say anything else?"

"Nothing." Cathbad's eyes flickered. "Just that you were coming."

"You lie. I can see it." Havgan reached forth and grasped the Archdruid by the neck of his robe. Swiftly he pulled the old man toward him. "Tell me. Now. Or I will snap your neck in two."

Aergol took a step forward, but Sigerric was there, his dagger pressed against the man's neck.

"Do not think to try your witch's tricks on me," Havgan said softly. "You will be dead before you do."

Cathbad swallowed hard. "He spoke of. . .of a High King. One who waits to take back Kymru from you."

Contemptuously, Havgan released the Archdruid. Cathbad subsided back into his chair, his dark eyes wide. Havgan sat back, reaching for his goblet of wine. He sipped, never taking his amber eyes from Cathbad's face.

"Who?"

Cathbad shook his head. "He would not say. And I do not know."

"There is much you do not know," Havgan cut in.

"I know enough to give you Kymru on a platter," Cathbad said quickly. "Enough to turn this country over to your God."

"So you do," Havgan said, smiling coldly. "I suggest that you pray to my God that this will be enough to keep you alive for a while yet."

Meriwdydd, Lleihau Wythnos—night

THE NEXT NIGHT Havgan and his army were camped around Cadair Idris, the hall of the High King. The mountain stood like a silent, unmoving sentinel under the waning midnight moon, waiting.

It was not him that the mountain waited for, Havgan thought.

No, he would not think that. He would enter here, at tomorrow's first light. This place would be his. He would be High King of Kymru.

In the moonlight he could just make out the outline of what they called Drwys Idris, the Doors. The jewels flashed gray and black under the silvery light. By day they would flash all colors of the rainbow. By day the Doors would shine and beckon him in.

The mountain did wait for him. It did.

A stirring by his side did not even make him jump. He knew who it was.

"I've been around and around that mountain," Sigerric said quietly, settling down on the lowest step next to Havgan. "It's not made of anything I can understand."

"It's rock. It's stone."

"It's something else. Something, I think, that will withstand you tomorrow."

"I'll get in."

"The old man, that Ardewin, said that you would not. Give it up, Havgan. Please. Like the old man said."

"Sigerric," he sighed, "what is it that makes you try my patience at every turn?"

"Do rescue attempts try the patience of a drowning man?"

"If I am ever in danger of drowning, you have my permission to try my patience as much as you please. But for now—"

"You are drowning. Can't you see that?"

Havgan turned to the man who had been his only friend

when he was a boy, to the man who perhaps was still the only friend he had ever had, or would have. Havgan's amber eyes gleamed in the moonlight. The rest of his face was in the shadow cast by the mountain that was not a mountain. "At last my dreams are coming true. And you say that I am drowning?"

"Your dreams. Your diseased dreams," Sigerric said bitterly. "You came all the way across the sea to find the Woman on the Rocks, the woman from your dreams. And when you do, what will happen? Will you kill her like all the others?"

"Not like all the others. I have not harmed Aelfwyn," Havgan reminded him.

"Not killed her, you mean. As for harm . . ."

Havgan shrugged. "When her father is dead and I am Emperor, when she bears me a son who I am sure is mine, then— and only then—you may have her."

Sigerric's face became very still. But Havgan had known his friend for a long time. "Sigerric, I know you love her. And you can have her when I am done, for all that I care. But I tell you that she is poison. She'll dine on your heart if it suits her, and wash it down with my blood. That's the way she is. Twisted."

"Twisted? Coming from the man who strangles whores to see the look in their dying eyes, that's laughable!"

Swift as a snake, Havgan reached out and grasped Sigerric's tunic. But Sigerric looked at him steadily, unafraid. Slowly, Havgan released his friend. "If you are so sure I am doomed, why do you try to save me?"

"I hardly know anymore. Habit, I suppose," Sigerric shrugged. "Like going to the graveyard to leave offerings for the dead. You know they can't hear or see you, but you do it just the same."

Calan Llachar—early morning

ONE, TWO . . . HE counted silently to himself as he began to mount the eight once-white and shining steps to the High King's hall.

Three, four. Red rockrose trailed the broken stairs like beads of blood.

Five, six. White alyssum twisted over the cracked stones like skeletal fingers.

Seven, eight.

He was here. Now would the doors open to him. Now.

But Drwys Idris remained closed.

Yet something was happening. A humming sound came from the air around him, building in intensity. The jewels on the door began to glow. In the center, Arderydd, the High Eagle, came to life. The symbol of the High King shimmered and beckoned and glowed in the eerie light.

The wind moaned softly. The Coranian soldiers surrounding the mountain tensed and gripped their weapons tighter. Sigerric, close to Havgan's back, stiffened. Sledda, at the base of the mountain, heading a full contingent of black-robed wyrce-jaga began a chant designed to break this evil power of the witches of Kymru. Eadwig, the Archbyshop, led his yellow-robed cadre of Lytir's preosts in prayers for the protection of the Warleader. Cathbad, standing next to Sigerric, smiled mockingly at the chants and prayers of the Coranians.

And Havgan, glimmering like the jewels in the morning sun, golden from head to toe, stood unflinching. Now was his moment. Now would the mountain open to him.

Then a voice spoke, light and musical, coming from nowhere,

from everywhere, "Who comes here to Drwys Idris? Who demands entry to Cadair Idris, the hall of the High King?"

"It is I, Havgan, son of Hengist. I demand that you open to me."

"The halls are silent. The throne is empty. We await the coming of the High King. He shall be proven by the signs he brings," the voice went on. "Have you Y Pair, the Cauldron of Earth, Buarth Y Greu, the Circle of Blood?"

"I am the Bana. The Slayer. None can withstand me."

"Have you Y Llech, the Stone of Water, Gwyr Yr Brenin, Seeker of the King?"

"I demand—"

"Have you Y Cleddyf, the Sword of Air, Meirig Yr Llech, Guardian of the Stone?"

"—that you—"

"Have you Y Honneit, the Spear of Fire, Erias Yr Gwydd, Blaze of Knowledge?"

"—open to me!"

"You have not the signs. You may not enter here. Still must I wait in silence and sorrow for the coming of the King."

"I will be your King!" Havgan shouted. "I am here. Open to me!"

But there was only implacable silence from the mountain.

Without even turning his gaze from the jeweled doors, Havgan snarled to Sigerric, "Batter them down."

"Havgan, it won't—"

"Do it!" he screamed. He must get in, he must! "Do it!"

Sigerric leapt down the steps and gave the necessary orders to the waiting army. The wyrce-jaga chanted louder, as though to be sure that the gods and goddesses of Kymru could hear their threats. The preosts of Lytir raised their voices in prayer, to ensure that Lytir himself would turn to them and see their plight.

Cathbad stepped up next to Havgan. "Let me try."

At Havgan's furious gesture to proceed, the Archdruid called, "Bloudewedd! It is Cathbad ap Goreu. I have brought you the High King! Open to him."

"He has not the signs. He may not enter."

"Bloudewedd—"

"I am not Bloudewedd. I am Drwys Idris, Archdruid. Call me that, traitor to Kymru. I hear you not."

"You will let me in," Havgan broke in, his voice trembling with rage. "You will let me in, or I will break you. You will die."

"I am already dead. And you cannot break me," the voice said in a tone of infinite calm.

"We shall see," Havgan threatened. He turned and marched down the steps, Cathbad scurrying after. The ram was ready, so huge it took more than twenty men to lift it, banded with iron and covered with pitch. The head was carved in the shape of a boar with mad, red eyes. Goltre-Bana, they called it. Boar-Slayer.

And then, at Havgan's signal, the ram began to pound the doors.

LESS THAN TWENTY leagues away to the west, on the other side of the lake of Llyn Mwyngil, Gwydion and Rhiannon lay still in the patchy shelter of the reeds that surrounded the lake.

They faced the east, though Havgan's army was too far to be seen with the naked eye. They could just make out the point of Cadair Idris piercing the horizon. They could just make out a rhythmic booming, carried on the wind like a faint rumor of thunder.

"It's time," Gwydion said, reaching for Rhiannon's hand.

She put her hand in his as they both closed their eyes and Rode the Wind.

THE RAM WAS having no effect on the doors. None at all. Even the jewels remained whole and shining. The unscarred surface of the doors mocked him. Eluded him. Refused to acknowledge his might, his power.

He would not be defeated. He would not. Again, he gave the signal. Again, Boar-Slayer hammered on the doors of the mountain.

And then he saw a glimmer. No, two glimmers, one on either side of the doors. Two glowing fragments of light took shape. One was a swirl of black and red. The other a weave of green and silver. The shapes elongated, hemmed in, solidified.

And they were there, standing before him, yet beyond his reach still.

Gwydion was clothed in a formal black robe lined with red. Around his neck he wore a torque of gold, opals studding the dangling two interlocking circles. Rhiannon wore a robe of sparkling sea green, trimmed with silver. Around her neck she wore a slender torque of silver with a single pearl dangling from a pentagon.

The warriors bearing the ram leapt back. The ram slipped through their now-uncertain hold and clattered down the broken stairs. As one, the warriors drew their axes.

Sledda came panting up the stairs, the Archbyshop just behind him, to join Havgan, Sigerric, and Cathbad.

"Kill them!" Sledda shouted to the warriors. "Kill the witches!"

The warriors gave a cry, then leapt forward, their axes raised for the kill. But the axes bit deep into the two figures, passed through the flickering shapes, and rang against the mountainside. And still the figures stood, unflinching.

"It is called Wind-Riding," Cathbad murmured. "They project a picture of themselves to this place. But their bodies could be leagues and leagues away."

"How many?" Sigerric said sharply.

"Up to thirty leagues."

Sigerric signaled to the warriors, giving them the task of finding those living bodies. Soon the entire army would be beating the plain, moving west, east, north, and south. Havgan did not countermand Sigerric's orders, though he knew it was useless. They would be gone long before his warriors could find their bodies.

Havgan stepped forward until he could almost touch the figures of the man and woman in front of the doors. Without turning away from them, Havgan asked over his shoulder, "Can they hear me? Will I be able to hear them?"

"They are both telepathic. They will be able to project their thoughts to us in such a way that they will seem to be speaking," Cathbad replied.

For a moment, no one spoke. Havgan stared at the man who had betrayed him, at the man he had sworn to kill. "I loved you as a brother," Havgan whispered. "And you betrayed me."

"No. I was never your brother," Gwydion replied, his voice clear and cold. "I was your enemy. From the beginning."

"Yet you saved my life. Twice. Why did you do that?" It was a question that Havgan had wanted to ask for a very long time.

"I . . . I no longer remember."

"Then perhaps Rhiannon does. Well, Rhiannon? Do you remember?"

"He saved you because he loved you," Rhiannon replied gently. "He felt a kinship with you. A bond that, for a moment in time, was stronger than his resolve."

"And that moment is over."

"No. That moment lasts forever," Gwydion rasped. "But the resolve will never falter again. I have come to tell you to leave Kymru. Cadair Idris will never let you in."

"Unless I bear the signs. The Treasures."

Gwydion shot a look at Cathbad that actually made the Archdruid momentarily cringe. "You have been well schooled, I see. But that is of no matter. You will never find the Treasures. You do not know how to seek them."

"Nor do you, or they would be in your hands by now," Cathbad spat.

"I do not have them because it is not time. When the time comes, I will."

"Words, Gwydion. Only words," Havgan spoke. "I will find those Treasures. And I will seek you out, both of you, and kill you. I will find that High King of yours. And kill him, too. Kymru is mine. I have taken your land."

"Kymru is not yours. She will never be yours," Rhiannon replied. "Never. As long as this mountain is closed to you. As long as the Dewin and the Bards live. As long as there is one man or woman of Kymru with breath in their body, this land is not yours."

Havgan laughed. "Your rulers are dead. Their kingdoms belong to me. King Urien and his wife and son, Queen Olwen, King Rhoram—they are dead."

"I would not count someone as dead unless I saw their body, Havgan," Gwydion said, a note of amusement in his voice.

So, King Rhoram did live, after all. Well, that would soon be remedied. "And King Uthyr, your beloved brother, Dreamer, lies cold and lifeless in Tegeingl." Havgan smiled. "Catha, cut him down."

"And Catha will die for it," Gwydion said steadily, but the agony in his silver eyes flared and burned.

"Just a few days ago," Havgan went on in silken tones, "I killed your Ardewin."

"But another has already taken his place," Rhiannon said coldly. "Kymru is not without an Ardewin. You cannot take us, Havgan. Go back to your Empire."

"Do you remember what you wrote of me once, Gwydion? The song you wrote for my triumph as the tournament? I remember very well.

> *"From poet's breast   These words took wing*
> *Which all the rest   Must learn to sing."*

"I remember," Gwydion said tonelessly.

"You will sing my tune," Havgan promised. "All of Kymru will do my bidding. I rule here now."

"You do not. Kymru slips through your fingers even as you grasp to hold it. Even as you reach for it, it disappears."

"No! No, and no! It is mine! MINE!"

"Even now the High King lives and thrives in secret. Even now he waits for his time! Even now he prepares!" Gwydion proclaimed in ringing tones. "Look!"

Havgan followed Gwydion's pointing hand and looked up. An eagle, its proud wings spanning the sky in solitary splendor, was circling the mountain. "It is Arderydd. The sign of the High King! Come to take your challenge!" Gwydion cried.

"Witch!" Sledda screamed up into sky. "You cannot withstand the power of our God! Go from this place before he destroys you utterly!"

The eagle shrieked, then plummeted. With a rustling of mighty wings, the proud bird swooped among them. And with a swipe of its claws, Sledda's face was torn and bloodied. The eagle ascended, clutching something in its talons.

Sledda was screaming, his hands covering his face. Sigerric pulled the wyrce-jaga's hands away, trying to determine the extent of the damage. "By the God!" Sigerric whispered in horror. "His eye. It took his eye."

Still shrieking, the eagle soared upward and again orbited the mountain, Sledda's eye held firmly in its grasp. The shrieks of the eagle mingled with the screams of pain from Sledda, sounding hugely in the shocked silence.

Then, from the west, a fierce wind gusted across the plain, flattening the grass in wild patterns. Coranian warriors struggled to keep to their feet in the face of the sudden gale. Havgan's banner of the golden boar snapped from its moorings and was flung, spinning, into the sky. The wind carried with it the faint sound of exultant hunting horns, the exuberant baying of dogs, the pounding of sure-footed hooves, and an echo of the triumphant cries hunters sing when they have sighted their prey.

The eagle screamed triumphantly in answer to the wind. It circled the mountain once, twice, three times, then shot to the west, its huge wings beating, leaving behind a mocking cry.

"Arderydd, the High Eagle, flies to join the Wild Hunt!" Gwydion cried. "Cerridwen, Queen of the Wood, and Cerrunnos, Master of the Hunt, call to him! The Protectors have come to challenge you! They will hunt you all, and harry you to your deaths. Sledda is the first of you to suffer their revenge. Who will be the next?"

"You will be the next, Dreamer! You! You are a dead man!" Havgan cried.

"You threaten much for one who is left standing on the mountain's doorstep like a beggar," Gwydion said softly. "For the love I have for you, in spite of myself, I do not demand that you leave Kymru. I beg you."

"I will see you beg," Havgan cried, freshly enraged by the pity in Gwydion's eyes. "I will find the Treasures, and the mountain will open to me. I will find your High King and kill him. I will crush you all beneath my heel."

"And so become a man of worth," Rhiannon said softly. "If you wish to be a man, Warleader, look to the inner, and not the outer world. Look to yourself, not to Kymru."

Havgan's amber eyes burned in his white face as he turned to face Rhiannon. "You will die for that. I promise you."

"Go from this land, Havgan, son of Hengist," Gwydion said again. "Go from here before Kymru swallows you utterly."

"So speaks the brother of my heart," Havgan replied bitterly. "My friend."

"Yes. So speaks your brother and friend," Gwydion agreed with a sigh.

"And my enemy."

"Yes, and your enemy. I am all those things. And always will be."

Before Havgan could say another word, the figures of Gwydion and Rhiannon were gone. He stared at the now-empty place where they had stood, where they had defied him, thwarted his will, betrayed him yet again, and had dared—had dared—to pity him. He stared at the still-closed Doors, the Doors that glowed with the light of the shining jewels, the Doors that could not be broken, the Doors that he could not open.

And then Havgan, glowing golden in the light of the morning sun, threw his head back, and cried out in rage to the uncaring sky.

Go, they had told him. Go.

But he would not. He could not.

He would build a fortress here, facing the mountain that had defeated him. He would find and kill the witches of Kymru. He would find the Treasures and kill the High King in waiting. Then he would enter the mountain in triumph.

And maybe, just maybe, if he did all these things, he would find peace, the peace that had eluded him all his life.

And maybe, just maybe, the Woman on the Rocks from his dream would come to him. Maybe it would be here that he would find her, and she would turn to him, and he would at last see her face and know her.

She would be his.

All of it would be his.

Epilogue

Kymru

Celynnen Mis, 497

Coed Ddu, kingdom of Ederynion

Angharad, Captain of Ederynion, sat crosslegged on the forest floor, still as a statue. The fading afternoon sunlight filtered through the trees, splashing on her unbound hair, making her red tresses glow like fiery embers.

She closed her green eyes and breathed deeply, groping for the peaceful center she needed, the center that had continued to elude her ever since Olwen had died, since Elen had been taken prisoner, since the Coranians had come just a month ago. Her sorrow stabbed her, the way Amatheon's death had done two years before. Though her heart still ached for her dead lover, the searing pain was gone. So she knew that this pain would also pass.

Two weeks ago, Angharad and her lieutenant, Emrys, along with Prince Lludd, Talhearn, and twenty warriors had arrived in the dark forest of Coed Ddu after their escape from the fallen city of Dinmael. And here they had found others who had survived the first slaughter, a handful of lords and Gwardas who had brought with them their surviving warriors. But they were few, pitifully few. How they could ever become the seed of a mighty army, as Gwydion had written, she did not know.

And if she had ever believed it might be so, now she no longer did.

How strange it was to be alive when her Queen was dead. How strange to break her oath to her ruler and live beyond the last beat of her Queen's heart. She wondered again, as she always did, if she had done right to run from the fallen city, done right to believe in the Dreamer's words. Maybe she hadn't. Maybe . . .

A sound from the trees startled her, and she opened her eyes, leapt to her feet, and drew her dagger in one smooth motion. A flicker of movement, more sensed than seen, caused her to glance up.

There, perched toward the end of a branch, sat the most enormous eagle she had ever seen. The eagle's fierce, gray eyes transfixed her. And then, her heart in her throat, she realized what this was.

Arderydd, the High Eagle. Sign of the High King.

The eagle cawed once, the fierceness of the sound making her jump. Then it took to the sky, making its way upward effortlessly through the dense trees.

It was gone. But she had understood its message. No more regrets. No more questions. The High King would come again, as the Dreamer had said.

And when he did, Angharad and the warriors of Ederynion would be ready.

Ogaf Greu, kingdom of Prydyn

ACHREN SHOOK HER black hair from its braid and idly combed out the snarls with her long, slim fingers. Her black eyes narrowed as the afternoon light bounded off the surface of the sea, flashing brilliant sparks across the water.

They had reached the caves of Ogaf Greu, hidden within the cliffs off the coast of Aeron, less than two weeks ago. Over and over during that desperate journey from Arberth, she had feared that Rhoram would not survive his wound. But day after day and night after night as they struggled to get him to the caves, he had continued to breathe.

At last, just a few moments ago, after weeks of anxiety, Cadell said that the King had turned the corner. He would live. They had gone wild with joy.

It seemed that only Queen Efa was not pleased at the news. Achren did not think that Efa had any use for a husband who had lost his country. At first they had suspected Efa of being in league with her traitorous brother, Erfin. But the Queen had been just as shocked, just as angry as the rest of them. And Achren understood what Efa was truly angry about—that her brother had dared to displace her, for she was now no longer the Queen of Prydyn. In a way, it was funny.

What wasn't funny was the way that Rhoram's daughter, Sanon, drifted about the caves like a ghost. Word had reached them just a few days ago that her betrothed, Elphin of Rheged, was dead. When she heard this, something in Sanon had died also. For Achren, the paleness of Sanon's face, the listlessness in her movements, the pain in her dark eyes, were all reason enough to destroy the Coranians. If it could be done.

And suddenly, so suddenly it almost took her breath away,

her buoyancy was gone, her hopes shriveled in the light of the enormity of the task. There were barely a handful of warriors left alive. How, in the name of all the gods, could they do anything against the might of the Empire? Kymru was crushed and bleeding, never to rise again.

Above her, she heard the rustle of wings. A seagull, she thought. But she looked up anyway and was startled to see the largest eagle she had ever seen. It hovered over the cliffs, not even beating its wings, riding the drafts of the wind, wild and free. She heard the bird's proud cry. A cry not of sorrow or despair or loss, but a cry of courage in the face of them.

She knew what it was. Arderydd, the High Eagle. Sign of the High King.

As Gwydion had foretold, the High King would come again.

And when he did, Achren and the warriors of Prydyn would be ready.

Coed Addien, kingdom of Rheged

TRYSTAN, CAPTAIN OF the once mighty warband of King Urien, made his way through the forest. His green eyes glinted like emeralds in the fitful light that sifted through the trees.

He found a tiny clearing and sank down onto the forest floor, his legs tucked beneath him. He wiped the sheen of sweat from his brow and drew his dagger.

If only Queen Ellirri had not sent him away with Prince Owein, he would have been in Llwynarth, would have defended his King and Queen with his last breath, would have died with them. And though he knew Ellirri had done it so that he would live and aid her son, it no longer mattered. Nothing mattered, except that, in just a few moments, he could join his King and

Queen in Gwlad Yr Haf and be done with his shame.

OWEIN DIDN'T MATTER. The boy was strong; he would find another Captain to help him take back Rheged—if it could be done. Even Esyllt, his beloved, didn't matter. She had never really loved him. Always she had clung to her mockery of a marriage and refused to end it, while enticing Trystan with her fine, blue eyes, her lovely, throaty voice, her beautiful smile, her eager, white body, giving him everything but her elusive heart.

Trystan, along with Owein, Teleri, and Esyllt had come to the forest of Coed Addien just two weeks ago. Here they had found Enid and Rhiwallon, Owein's younger sister and brother, under the watchful care of Isgowen Whledig, King Urien's steward. Isgowen had been horrified to discover the part her brother had played in betraying Rheged. She had even begged Owein to kill her, to spill out her blood in payment.

But Owein had refused. He had taken Isgowen's hand and made her rise. And he had said that there was one way only to expiate her shame. That way was to live and to serve his family, to do what she could to further the task of taking Rheged back.

Oh, no. No. He didn't want to remember Owein's words now. They stung him. Made him hesitate. Made him unsure. He gripped the knife and slowly brought it up to his throat. Let it all end. A Captain should not outlive his King.

A rustle in the branches above him made him look up. The largest eagle he had ever seen perched in the boughs above him. And he knew what he was seeing.

Arderydd, the High Eagle. Sign of the High King.

The proud bird fixed him with its eyes, and Trystan could not look away. Then the eagle cawed fiercely and launched itself from the tree, flying off through the forest.

Had it been contempt that he had seen in the creature's eyes? Slowly, and with shaking hands, he sheathed his dagger.

He knew, he knew, now, that the Dreamer had written truly. The High King would come again.

And when he did, Trystan and the warriors of Rheged would be ready.

Allt Llwyd, kingdom of Rheged

ANIERON MADE HIS way cautiously to the mouth of the cave. Cautious, not because he expected danger, but because his joints ached in the damp, sea air, and a fall on the spray-slicked rocks wouldn't help his old bones any. He wished he had thought of this before he had picked the caves as the best hideout for the Bards and the Dewin.

He and his party had arrived here only two weeks ago, on the day he had heard of the confrontation with Havgan at Cadair Idris. Gwydion and Rhiannon had challenged the Warleader, and that vile wyrce-jaga, Sledda, had lost an eye. He smiled, remembering the fierce joy he had felt when he heard that. Remembering, too, how relieved he had been to know that Gwydion and Rhiannon were alive and well. He had taken great pleasure in informing Cariadas of that fact.

That news even seemed to relieve poor Sinend. The young Druid was still too pale, too listless, too shamed. But Anieron thought that she would perk up after a while. She was a fetching little thing, and the monstrous plots of her father and the Archdruid should not be held against her. Would not be, as long as he had any say in it.

As he neared the cave entrance, the brilliant light from the cave mouth caused him to narrow his shrewd, green eyes. Flashes of light played off the cool, green sea. Waves washed onto the shore, leaving swirls and indentations in the sand, patterns that Anieron knew he did not have the means to understand.

How long? How long until Kymru became theirs again? Idly he wondered if he would be alive to see that day, and thought it unlikely.

The rustle of wings above drifted down to him. An enormous eagle landed just outside the mouth of the cave and pinned him with its clear, gray eyes. Ah, of course.

Arderydd, the High Eagle. Sign of the High King.

Gravely, Anieron bowed to the bird. The eagle dipped its head in return and flashed away, riding the sky, proud and free. Free.

Oh, yes. The High King would come again.

And when he did, the Dewin and the Bards of Kymru would be ready.

Mynydd Tawel, kingdom of Gwynedd

CAI, ONCE-CAPTAIN of King Uthyr's teulu, made his way up the mountain easily. He went rapidly up the rocky slopes because he didn't care one way or another if he fell. There was nothing here in this world to keep him, except for a promise he had made to his now-dead King.

A promise that he regretted, passionately, now that so many of those whom he loved were dead. His wife and son had died in Tegeingl. He had received word a few weeks ago that his father had died in the fighting in Eyri. And his King was dead. Uthyr was dead, yet Cai still lived. And the taste of that truth was bitter. Very bitter, indeed.

Cai, along with Ygraine, Susanna, and Bedwyr had made it

to the hidden slopes of Mynydd Tawel in the mountains of Eyri just a week ago. Neuad, Uthyr's Dewin, had been here already with young Morrigan. And Dinaswyn, the former Dreamer, along with her niece, Arianrod, had also been here.

Another careless handhold, another careless step, and he was atop Mynydd Tawel, the tallest peak in the mountain range of Gwynedd. The air was crisp and thin, barely filling his laboring lungs and cutting through his leather tunic. Wind whistled in his ears with a mournful sound. Below him the jagged tips of the mountain range gleamed black onyx. The mountain slopes were emerald green, broken here and there with the silvery ribbons of mountain streams.

He wondered if it would be so bad to break his promise to Uthyr. He wondered if it would not be better to dive off the mountain, to break his body against the rocky slopes, to be free of this world and to come to Gwlad Yr Haf, where his wife, his son, his father, and his King waited for him.

A rustle of wings brushed past him, startling him so that he almost did plunge straight down the mountain. He pulled his dagger, whirling to meet—

The most enormous eagle he had ever seen.

The eagle settled on the rocks and then began to ruffle through its feathers. And at that moment, Cai knew what it was.

Arderydd, the High Eagle. Sign of the High King.

The bird settled its feathers and fixed Cai with an unblinking stare. Then the eagle pulled itself fully upright and shrieked in defiance, taking to the air with a speed that left Cai gasping. It flew over the peaks, still shrieking, until it was gone.

Cai understood. The High King would return. And when he did, Cai and the warriors of Gwynedd would be ready.

Dinas Emrys, kingdom of Gwynedd

ARTHUR WIPED THE sweat from his brow, anxiously surveying the mountain slope. One, two . . . eleven, twelve . . . twenty-one. Yes, the sheep were all there. He had never seen them run so, and all from a bird, too. He thought it very strange. He himself had not seen the bird clearly. He had been too anxious that he would lose the sheep.

Arthur settled down on the slope, reaching for the pouch that contained his afternoon meal of bread and cheese. Slowly he ate, not really hungry but knowing that he should try to eat, swallowing hard when tears threatened to block his throat.

Only one week ago he had heard that his father was dead. Uncle Myrrdin had given Arthur that news, with pain in his wise, dark eyes. And Arthur's dreams had died then, too. Dreams that his father would come for him. Dreams that they would at last be together. Dreams now shattered beyond repair. They would never come true, now.

Myrrdin had also told Arthur of the confrontation at Cadair Idris. The Doors of the mountain had stayed closed against the Warleader. And Arthur knew what had been in Myrrdin's mind, then. That one day, the Doors would open for Arthur. If he had the Treasures. If he had the will to be High King.

But Arthur didn't want to be High King. All he had wanted was to be with his father. But Gwydion had taken him away long ago and had never given him back. One day Gwydion would come to Dinas Emrys, wanting to take Arthur to find the Treasures. And on that day, the boy had vowed, he would not go. No matter what. Let Uncle Gwydion find another pawn for his games.

A rustle of wings, the whoosh of something flying past him, a momentary pain in his cheek, yanked Arthur from his thoughts. He leapt up, gazing wildly about him. And there, just a few feet away, perched the most enormous eagle he had ever seen.

He put a hand to his cheek and pulled it away, bloody. The bird gazed at him calmly, as though the wound was only his due. And when he realized what this was, he thought that maybe the wound was what he deserved.

For this was Arderydd, the High Eagle. The sign of the High King.

For a moment, he considered explaining to this creature that King Uthyr was dead. That Gwydion's plans for him should be thwarted at all costs, so that the Dreamer would feel at least some of the pain the he had given out so freely.

But he knew that the eagle would care for none of this. He stared at the bird, thinking how the eagle's gray eyes looked so much like the Dreamer's. Cold, calculating, prideful. And then the eagle gave a cry so fierce that the sheep were set once again to running. But Arthur stood transfixed by the eagle's eyes.

And then the boy nodded, once, reluctantly. The eagle darted into the sky. Arthur watched it until it was nothing more than a speck in the distance.

And wondered if he would be ready.

Coed Aderyn, kingdom of Prydyn
GWYDION STRETCHED A little, then settled down again at the edge of the pool. The somnolent sound of the waterfall splashing over the rocks soothed him, taking away the rough edges leftover from the argument this morning. It seemed that he and Rhian-

non were always arguing now. It was times like this he cursed the dream that had told him she was the key to going to Corania.

Yet, even as he thought this, he knew he did not mean it. He knew they only argued because of the tension that came off of him in waves. The tension that pulled at him to trust her, touch her, give himself to her. The tension that pushed at him to stand apart, unfettered, alone, trusting no one.

At least he was sleeping better. The old nightmare had finally left him, its purpose accomplished. He no longer dreamt of the death of those whom he loved, for it had all come true. And yet there had been a change. In his dream, the Master Bard had been killed. But Anieron was still alive. Perhaps, he thought tentatively, not even liking to contemplate it, this was something that would happen at a later time.

And Cathbad was revealed as a traitor. Gwydion gritted his teeth, for he now knew who had been behind Amatheon's murder. Cathbad would pay, in full measure, for that.

He thought of his daughter, for she was with Anieron in the caves of Allt Llwyd. His heart failed him at the thought of Cariadas being captured or killed. He wished he could see her, but it was too dangerous. He must remain hidden until the time came for him to lead the search for the Treasures.

He dipped his hand in the silvery pool. In spite of everything, he liked it here, deep in the woods of Coed Aderyn. It was a good hiding place, close enough to Cadair Idris so that they could Wind-Ride whenever they needed to, keeping a close watch on Havgan.

And the caves that fanned out beneath the earth from Rhiannon's home! Since they had come back here months ago, they had explored the caves and found that one branch took them as far as Llyn Mwyngil, the lake to the west of Cadair Idris.

That would come in very handy when the day came to return to Cadair Idris with the Treasures in hand.

He wondered yet again how long until he had the dream the Protectors had promised, the dream to tell him it was time to begin the Quest for the Treasures.

While far above him, unseen, an eagle glided, flying on the wings of the wind.

Gwydion closed his eyes, and waited for the dream.

Glossary (Kymri)

Addiendydd: sixth day of the week

aderyn: birds

aethnen: aspen tree; sacred to Ederynion

alarch: swan; the symbol of the royal house of Ederynion

alban: light; any one of the four solar festivals

Alban Awyr: festival honoring Taran; Spring Equinox

Alban Haf: festival honoring Modron; Summer Solstice

Alban Nerth: festival honoring Agrona and Camulos; Autumnal Equinox

Alban Nos: festival honoring Sirona and Grannos; the Winter Solstice

ap: son of

ar: high

Archdruid: leader of the Druids, must be a descendent of Llyr

Arderydd: high eagle; symbol of the High kings

Ardewin: leader of the Dewin, must be a descendent of Llyr

arymes: prophecy

Awenyddion: dreamer (see Dreamer)

awyr: air

bach: boy

bachen: little boy

Bard: a telepath; they are musicians, poets, and arbiters of the law in matters of inheritance, marriage, and divorce; Bards can Far-Sense and Wind-Speak; they revere the god Taran, King of the Winds

bedwen: birch tree; sacred to the Bards

Bedwen Mis: birch month; roughly corresponds to March

blaid: wolf; the symbol of the royal house of Prydyn

bran: raven; the symbol of the Dreamers

Brenin: high or noble one; the High King; acts as an amplifier for the Y Dawnus

buarth: circle

cad: battle

cadair: chair (of state)

caer: fortress

calan: first day; any one of the four fire festivals

Calan Gaef: festival honoring Annwyn and Aertan

Calan Llachar: festival honoring Cerridwen and Cerrunnos

Calan Morynion: festival honoring Nantsovelta

Calan Olau: festival honoring Mabon

cantref: a large division of land for administrative purposes; two to three commotes make up a cantref; a cantref is ruled by a Lord or Lady

canu: song

cariad: beloved

celynnen: holly

Celynnen Mis: holly month; roughly corresponds to late May/early June

cenedl: clan

cerdinen: rowan tree; sacred to the Dreamers

Cerdinen Mis: rowan month; roughly corresponds to July

cleddyf: sword

collen: hazel tree; sacred to Prydyn

Collen Mis: hazel month; roughly corresponds to October

commote: a small division of land for administrative purposes; two or three commotes make up a cantref; a commote is ruled by a Gwarda

coed: forest, wood

cynyddu: increase; the time when the moon is waxing

da: father

dan: fire

derwen: oak tree; sacred to the Druids

Derwen Mis: oak month; roughly corresponds to December

Dewin: a clairvoyant; they are physicians; they can Life-Read and Wind-Ride; they revere the goddess Nantsovelta, Lady of the Moon

disglair: bright; the time when the moon is full

draig: dragon; the symbol of the Dewin

draenenwen: hawthorn tree; sacred to Rheged

Draenenwen Mis: hawthorn month; roughly corresponds to late June/early July

Dreamer: a descendent of Llyr who has precognitive abilities; the Dreamer can Dream-Speak and Time-Walk; the Dreamer also has the other three gifts—telepathy, clairvoyance, and psychokinesis; there is only one Dreamer in a generation; they revere the god Mabon, King of Fire

Dream-Speaking: precognitive dreams; one of the Dreamer's gifts

Druid: a psychokinetic; they are astronomers, scientists, and lead all festivals; they can Shape-Move, Fire-Weave, and, in partnership with the High King, Storm-Bring; they revere the goddess Modron, the Great Mother of All

drwys: doors

dwfr: water

dwyvach-breichled: goddess-bracelet; bracelet made of oak used by Druids

eiddew: ivy

Eiddew Mis: ivy month; roughly corresponds to April

enaid-dal: soul-catcher; lead collars that prevent Y Dawnus from using their gifts

eos: nightingale; the symbol of the Bards

erias: fire

erydd: eagle

Far-Sensing: the telepathic ability to communicate with animals

ffynidwydden: fir tree; sacred to the High kings

Fire-Weaving: the psychokinetic ability to light fires

gaef: winter

galanas: blood price

galor: mourning, sorrow

goddeau: trees

gorsedd: a gathering (of Bards)

greu: blood

Gwaithdydd: third day of the week

gwarchan: incantation

Gwarda: ruler of a commote

gwernan: alder tree; sacred to Gwynedd

Gwernan Mis: alder month; roughly corresponds to late April/early May

gwinydden: vine

Gwinydden: vine month; roughly corresponds to August

Gwlad Yr Haf: the Land of Summer; the Otherworld

gwydd: knowledge

gwyn: white

gwynt: wind

Gwyntdydd: fifth day of the week

gwyr: seeker

haf: summer

hebog: hawk; the symbol of the royal house of Gwynedd

helygen: willow

Helygen Mis: willow month; roughly corresponds to January

honneit: spear

Life-Reading: the clairvoyant ability to lay hands on a patient and determine the nature of their ailment

llachar: bright

llech: stone

lleihau: to diminish; the time when the moon is waning

lleu: lion

Llundydd: second day of the week

llyfr: book

llyn: lake

llys: court

Lord/Lady: ruler of a cantref

mam: mother

march: horse; the symbol of the royal house of Rheged

Master Bard: leader of the Bards, must be a descendent of Llyr

Meirgdydd: fourth day of the week

meirig: guardian

Meriwdydd: seventh day of the week

mis: month

morynion: maiden

mwg-breudduyd: smoke-dream; a method Dreamers can use to induce dreams

mynydd: mountain

mynyddoedd: mountains

naid: leap

nemed: shrine, a sacred grove

nerth: strength

neuadd: hall

niam-lann: a jeweled metallic headpiece, worn by ladies of rank

nos: night

ogaf: cave

olau: fair

onnen: ash tree; sacred to the Dewin

Onnen Mis: ash month; roughly corresponds to February

pair: cauldron

pen: head of

Plentyn Prawf: child test; the testing of children, performed by the Bards, to determine if they are Y Dawnus

rhyfelwr: warrior

sarn: road

Shape-Moving: the psychokinetic ability to move objects

Storm-Bringing: the psychokinetic ability to control certain weather conditions; only effective in partnership with the High King

Suldydd: first day of the week

tarbell: a board game, similar to chess

tarw: bull; the symbol of the Druids

tarw-casgliad: the ceremony where Druids invite a dream from Modron

telyn: harp

teulu: warband

Time-Walking: the ability to see events in the past; one of the Dreamer's gifts

tir: earth

triskele: the crystal medallion used by Dewin

ty: house

tynge tynghed: the swearing of a destiny

Tynged Mawr: great fate; the test to determine a High King

tywyllu: dark; the time when the moon is new

ur: daughter of

var: out of

Wind-Riding: the clairvoyant ability of astral projection

Wind-Speaking: the telepathic ability to communicate with other humans

wythnos: week

yned: justice

Y Dawnus: the gifted; a Druid, Bard, Dewin, or Dreamer

ysgawen: elder

Ysgawen Mis: elder month; roughly corresponds to September

ystafell: the Ruler's chambers

ywen: yew

Ywen Mis: yew month; roughly corresponds to November

Glossary (Corania)

Afliae: the most powerful of the old gods and goddesses

ansuz: the rune for divinity

asbru: rainbow

blot: sacrifice

byrne: mail coat worn by soldiers

byrnwiga: warrior

Byrnwiga Necht: Old Religion ceremony honoring Tiw, God of War; Autumn Equinox

chalk: the dead man's rune

churl: peasant

cynerice: kingdom

cyst: best

daeg: day

Dagmonath: the fifth month of the year, roughly corresponds to May

deore: beloved

Deore Necht: Old Religion ceremony honoring Fro and Freya, God of Peace and Goddess

of Fertility; Summer Solstice

Dis: the old gods

Disir: the old goddesses

dol: foolish

Dol Daeg: festival commemorating the day Lytir first preached to the multitude; corresponds to the Old Religion festival of Molnir Necht

Dondaeg: fifth day of the week

dyrne: secret

Dyrne-Hwata: a board with letters used to discern messages from the spirit world

ealh: temple

eho: the rune for change

Ermonath: the fourth month of the year; roughly corresponds to April

faeder: father

Faeder Necht: Old Religion ceremony honoring Narve, God of Death

Falmonath: the sixth month of the year, roughly correspond to June/July

Fredaeg: sixth day of the week

galdra: magic

Galdra Necht: Old Religion ceremony honoring Wuotan, God of Magic; Spring Equinox

gar: the rune for power

gesith: warband

Gewinnan Daeg: festival commemorating Lytir's tournaments; corresponds to the Old Religion festival of Byrnwiga Necht; Autumn Equinox

Godia: a priestess of the Old Religion

goltre: boar

gulden: golden

Heofan: Heaven

Heiden: hidden; a worshipper of the old gods

Hod: the sacrificer, the male assistant to a priestess

Holdmonath: second month of the year, roughly corresponds to February *hul*: hall

hwata: divination

hwitel: knife; the sacrificial knife used in religious ceremonies

jaga: hunter

kranzlein: a string of beads, used to say prayers in the New Religion

Logmonath: the tenth month of the year, roughly corresponds to November

maeder: mother

Maeder-godia: the high priestesses of the Old Religion

Mandaeg: second day of the week

Modcearu: the six weeks between Dol Daeg and Sar Daeg; commemorates the imprisonment of Lytir

modra: variant of mother

Modra Necht: ceremony honoring Nerthus, Goddess of Earth; Winter Solstice

molnir: hammer

Molnir Necht: ceremony honoring Donar, God of Storms

monath: month

Nardaeg: seventh day of the week

necht: night

Nemonath: the third month of the year, roughly corresponds to March

Natmonath: the ninth month of the year, roughly corresponds to October

needen: the rune for necessity

Ostmonath: the eighth month of the year, roughly corresponds to September

preost: priest

sar: pain

Sar Daeg: commemoration of the day Lytir was sacrificed to Donar; Winter Solstice

Saxmonath: the first month of the year, roughly corresponds to December/January

scima: light

Scima Daeg: the festival commemorating the arrival of Lytir; corresponds to the Old Religion festival of Modra Necht

seid: a reading of the runes by a valla

seidr: the rues, used for telling fortunes

Sifmonath: the seventh month of the year, roughly corresponds to August

Soldaeg: first day of the week

sweltan: die

Sweltan Daeg: the festival commemorating Lytir's departure; corresponds to the Old Religion festival of Faeder Necht

thorn: the rune for dark force

Tiwdaeg: third day of the week

undeadlic: immortal

Undeadlic Daeg: festival commemorating the resurrection of Lytir; corresponds to the Old Religion festival of Galdra Necht; Spring Equinox

valla: a seeress

Walcyries: the warrior women who collect the souls of dead heroes

Wiccan: those that possess the psychic gifts of telepathy, clairvoyance or psychokenesis

Witan: the Emperor's council

Wodaeg: fourth day of the week

wynlic: joyful

Wynlic Daeg: festival commemorating the time when Lytir ruled Ivelas; corresponds to the Old Religion festival of Deore Necht; Summer Solstice

wyrce: witch

Wyrce-jaga: the arm of the church tasked with rooting out The Heiden

Wyrd: the three goddesses of fate

wyrd-galdra: fate-magic; cards used for telling fortunes

For more information
about other great titles from
Medallion Press, visit
www.medallionpress.com